S

THE HORNS OF CAPRICORN

The Horns of Capricorn

by

HELEN TOPPING MILLER

APPLETON-CENTURY-CROFTS, INC.

New York

THE HORNS OF CAPRICORN

1

Taffy Keeling walked into the house ahead of her mother and sister, pirouetted before the tall mirror in the hall, and tossed her black hat on a table, letting her red hair tumble about her cheeks.

"How are you, Miss Keeling?" She bowed to her reflection. "An heiress, I believe?"

"Taffy," reproved her mother, unpinning her bonnet. "That's no way to behave, coming straight from a funeral."

Lydia Keeling's faded gray eyes were puffy and dim from weeping. She had not seen her brother, Daniel Neary, for twenty years. In all those years her feeling toward Daniel and his wife had been one of vague and bewildered resentment, but his death and burial had affected her as any emotional event was prone to do. She had enjoyed an orgy of tears.

"I'm not thinking about the funeral, Mama," declared Taffy. "I'm gloating over the will."

"She was furious." Lydia folded her black gloves neatly, laying the fingers precisely together. "I could feel her eyes simply boring into me, and she was gnawing her lips she was so mad. But after all, it was only fair and just. That was my father's home. It's only right and proper that it should stay in the family as long as Daniel had no children. She wouldn't have any. He did the decent thing, at least, willing the property to you girls."

Frances, the older Keeling daughter, pulled off a black straw hat that smelled faintly of the shoe polish that had been used to refurbish it, sniffed disdainfully at it and tossed in on a chair.

"I certainly felt foolish," she said, "wearing mourning for a man I never saw in my life! Mama, it wasn't the house Uncle Daniel's wife was so indignant about. It was because when she

1

dies Uncle Daniel's share of Grandfather Taft's brass foundry goes to you."

"I might not outlive her," sighed Lydia. "She's hardy, although she *is* past seventy, but it will be a nice inheritance for you girls when I'm gone. It's a judgment on her, anyway. She always ignored all of Daniel's family and scrounged every penny out of him that she could for her own nephews and nieces. Taffy, put the kettle on. I'm simply limp. I need a cup of tea."

"You'll own two-thirds interest in the brass business if you do outlive her, Mama," Frances said. "It will make a nice income for you when you're old. I know it's taken about all you've had lately to pay for the doctors and nurses for Papa. I know you've had a hard time. I'll be glad to see you with a little money to spend on yourself again."

"Daniel was the oldest," Lydia said. "He was twenty-five when I was born. I was a little afterthought in our family. Mother'd lost four children after Daniel, so I was always close to her. Daniel married when I was small, and after that he never came home except when my father was killed. That was when my mother gave him the place on Pamlico. She didn't want to stay there any more on account of the Cavitts."

Frances brought a taper from the closet and lighted the gas overhead. All the shabbiness of the narrow brick house sprang out of the shadows: the hatrack that needed varnish, the tan wallpaper with brown figures like centipedes crawling to the ceiling, the worn rugs.

"I wish I could have seen more of Washington," she remarked, "but I knew you didn't want to linger in Uncle Daniel's house. He never went to live down on Pamlico, did he, after your father died? We have to realize, Mama, that the place may be a ruin now. There may have been a kind of irony in his willing it to Taffy and me."

"It was a well-built house. Grandfather Neary built it and he always had to have the best. It was my home!" Her mother sighed. "All these years I've thought about that river. In Grandpa Taft's gloomy old house and then after I married your papa and lived in rented places like this—" she looked sadly about the dreary, worn rooms, the cracking plaster, the scarred floors, "all the time I was remembering that river—and the lilacs! They were so sweet in the spring after a rain. I had a little room under the roof and mockingbirds used to sing in the trees outside my window."

"Mama, you mean you'd like to go back there? To live?" asked Frances, with a slight sharpening of incredulous consternation in her voice.

"It was home!" repeated Lydia. "There's the land, too. There used to be more than a hundred acres. Papa always kept horses and a cow. Anyway, it would belong to us, and I've never lived in a house that belonged to me since I left there, in all my life!"

Frances stood still, a little stunned at the idea of being uprooted from the prosy sort of life they had lived for all of her twenty years. She seemed to see her mother, suddenly, as a person, as someone with dreams and desires; a thought that had never come to the girl before. Mama had always submerged herself in her family. Frances knew, with the clarity of youth, that her father had been a good, gentle, but ineffectual man. Always he had worked in Grandfather Taft's brass foundry because the job had been given him there when he married Lydia. Then for years he had lain ill, coughing and growing thin and yellow, while Lydia's little income went to purchase what comforts could be had for him. And now Mama was renting her room to schoolteachers and sleeping on a cot in the dining room.

"Could we afford it, Mama?" she asked.

"I don't know." Lydia dropped into a chair. "It's just an idea I had. Maybe it isn't practical. You know I've never been very practical, Francie. I was never taught to be practical. I've just had to live a day at a time."

"Tea, ladies," interrupted Taffy, bringing in a tray. "We'll have it in the parlor, as becomes heiresses. Could we get any money out of that old ruin down there in North Carolina, Mama? Enough so that maybe I could go to college?"

"Mama wants to live there," Frances said deliberately, clearing a place for the tray. "Sit over here, Mama. Taffy's even made sandwiches."

Taffy put the tray down slowly, as though it were very heavy.

"Live there?" she exclaimed. "But—it's miles from nothing! You always said you went there by boat, Mama."

"It's quicker to go by boat and we always had boats, but there's a good road. It's two miles from the little town. We always had a carriage and a team. It was a pretty place, Taffy, on the bluff by the river. We could see the boats going by."

Frances spooned sugar into her mother's cup as the silence stretched a little. Then she pulled up a chair for herself. The narrow parlor was always dim, with only two small windows facing the street.

"Light the gas in here, Taffy," she said. "Is that China tea? It smells wonderful."

Taffy squared herself. "No evasions, if you please!" she snapped, her chin up and her brown eyes narrowed. "You've been plotting while I was working. Do you mean to tell me you actually want to go down there into a wilderness—to live?"

"It was never a wilderness," protested her mother. "When I was small it was supposed to be a beautiful estate. The house has about ten rooms, and then there's a kitchen—it was built outside with a passageway. We had servants, of course; old Amanda and her daughters. We'd have no rent to pay, Taffy."

"No roomers, either." Frances heard the hard tap of heels on the floor above them.

"Good heavens, you mean you want to go too, France?" demanded Taffy.

"At least," Frances argued, "it wouldn't hurt to see the place. We own it, and it was Mama's home."

"Forty years ago!" retorted Taffy scornfully.

"Not forty—let's see." Lydia counted on her fingers. "Papa was killed when I was thirteen, and we came away that fall. Thirty years since I've seen it, Taffy."

"You mean you're only forty-three now, Mama?" Taffy looked incredulous. The naïveté of youth, that stamps all adults as senescent, was stark on her face.

"For goodness sake, sit down, Taffy, and stop yelling!" scolded Frances. "Of course Mama's only forty-three. Papa was only forty-six when he died, and Mama isn't old. Drink your tea and calm down. We can talk this over reasonably. Probably we couldn't sell the property as long as we're neither of us of legal age yet, and it might not bring much money anyway."

"I always wanted a home," persisted Lydia. "Your papa always planned to build a house for us, but his salary was never large. Grandpa Taft didn't believe in paying his men any more than he could help, and then after Papa's health failed and we had to get along on my little income there was just never any chance to do better."

"I think we should go down there," announced Frances flatly. "We can see whether the place looks promising or not. How do you get there, Mama? By boat or train?"

"We came on a boat from Norfolk, as I remember, and smaller boats go up the Sound. My father had a boat—the *Mary Conner*. He was killed on that boat. The Cavitts had boats too."

"Do we have enough money for a trip like that?" Frances asked.

"My foundry check always comes on the tenth—that's Tuesday. And Miss Baker pays for her month this week. Why don't you go down alone, Francie? Then you could decide if there's any use trying to live there or not."

"No, you should go too, Mama. Taffy can go along if she wants to."

Taffy had perched rigidly on the edge of a chair all through the conversation, her mouth jerked in at one corner.

"I think it's perfectly crazy!" she cried. "Going off and leaving all our friends! I'm supposed to play with the mandolin club on the thirtieth. And how about Cliff Houchins, France?"

"We can wait till after your mandolin affair," Frances said. "As for Cliff—" She did not finish. Cliff Houchins was still a question mark in her mind. She had thought herself in love with him once or twice, but he was still a medical student at Johns Hopkins, and he had a dependent and possessive mother whom he had to placate anxiously if he so much as went walking with a girl.

"Cliff Houchins couldn't support a wife if his mother would let him marry one—which she won't," stated Lydia firmly. "Not for years."

"Well, if you ask me, I think this Carolina business is fantastic!" Taffy spun to her feet and gave her bright hair a savage fling. "We've always lived in Baltimore; now you want to go away off somewhere in the woods where we'd never see anybody or meet any boys or anything."

Frances walked to the window. She was tall and slender and when she put on a grave face, as she did now, her dark eyes were large and thoughtful against the pale ivory of her skin. She had a firm mouth, but gentleness softened it when she smiled. She was not smiling now, however. She parted the curtains and looked out. The house was a "row" house flanked on either side with identical brick walls, identical stone doorsteps that were scrubbed clean every day. On the rutted cobbles of the street, horses clinked iron shoes and wagon tires rattled and now and then a rubber-tired buggy rolled by with less commotion.

"Look out here, Taffy," she said quietly. "It isn't terribly pretty, is it? Remember how many years Mama has had nothing to look at but this street and the inside of these walls. How long since you had a new dress, Mama—really new?"

"Why—why—this one isn't so terribly old. I just made it over this spring. I don't go places where I really need nice clothes. If you don't want to go, Taffy,—" She stammered, distressed that she was being considered, thought about, that there was conflict between her daughters. "If you don't want to go I wouldn't want you to—not if you'd be unhappy down there. Not on my account."

Frances turned, her face grim. "I think it's time something was done on your account, Mama," she said. "If your old home is fit to live in and you want to live there, I think Taffy and I would be a pair of beasts not to let you live in it."

"Suppose the roof is falling in? Suppose it's just a horrible old wreck of a place that needs thousands of dollars spent on it?" stormed Taffy. "Meanwhile we'd have spent all the money we could have had for spring clothes on a perfectly useless trip."

"Taffy, Mama hasn't been anywhere since we were born, you know that! Unless you count running down to Washington to a dismal funeral a trip. If you act mean now about going to see this old house, you should be ashamed!"

Taffy blinked. "I wasn't trying to be mean. Good gracious,

you don't have to put an ugly motive into everything I do! I was trying to be practical. Mama always says she's not practical, and I certainly don't think you're taking a practical attitude toward this shambly old house, France. Mama admits this place is miles from anywhere. Suppose she got sick? It was bad enough here with Papa, when all we had to do was run three or four blocks to get the doctor. Why can't you write to somebody down there, a minister or a lawyer or somebody, and find out about the place? We ought to have a lawyer anyway if we're property owners."

"I guess Uncle Horace could find out for us," faltered Lydia. "He has always managed my business at the foundry."

"Uncle Horace would pooh-pooh the whole thing," declared Frances. "You know that. He never approved of Mama marrying Papa, and he's implied that she's slightly weak-minded ever since. What money Mama has is hers and it's none of Uncle Horace's business how she spends it, though he does try to boss every move she makes. Mama and I are going, Taffy, and if you'd rather stay here and practice mandolin duets with that pimply little Chapman boy, I'm sure Miss Baker will be glad to chaperone you."

"Oh, no you don't! You aren't going to dump me on Miss Baker! I've heard enough about how stupid the school board is and what awful brats the kids are in the third grade. If you're determined to be so foolish, I'm going along. Anyway, I've never been on a boat," Taffy argued. "Talk about Mama being frustrated! Here I am, seventeen years old, and what have I ever had, France Keeling, but your old dresses made over and secondhand algebra books? I don't suppose I can even wangle fifteen cents for a new E-string."

"Why, Taffy," Lydia protested, "you know you can have fifteen cents! Just because I said I thought we could clean your old leghorn hat with lemon juice and touch up the flowers a little—"

"And dye France's old slippers and put some new lace on my old organdy—" Taffy's eyes brimmed. "All right, all right!" She grew shrill. "I'll shut up. If I ever have another practical thought I'll swallow it."

Lydia began to cry. "I never thought I was making so much

trouble," she whimpered, "just because I get homesick sometimes for green trees and the river and Mama's tulip bed and everything!"

Frances patted her arm. "You stop blaming yourself, Mama. You deserve a little consideration and you're going to have it. Taffy can do as she pleases, but half that place is mine and it won't be sold or disposed of in any way till I've had a look at it. I'll go downtown in the morning and inquire about transportation."

The girls' little room was under a flat roof over the kitchen. It was cold in winter; tolerable in spring, except that sometimes the smell of garbage came in from the alley when the windows were open; but in summer it was a stifling box with scrim curtains hanging limply at the windows and mosquitoes continually oozing through the hole in the screen that Lydia had patched ineffectually with a sewed-on piece of black silk.

Frances sat on the edge of the bed unbuttoning her shoes, flicking the dust from the ruffle on her long petticoat with quick, white fingers, rolling off her cotton stockings.

"I feel a little excited about that old place, Taffy." She ignored Taffy's hostile back. "We could be going into some kind of adventure."

Taffy, patting buttermilk into her spring crop of freckles, hunched a shoulder, made a wry mouth into the mirror.

"Pirates, I suppose," she said dryly. "Papa always teased Mama about her great-grandfather being a pirate. I suppose you hope you'll meet somebody dark and dashing with a knife between his teeth."

"Great-grandfather Neary was a blockade-runner in the Civil War." Frances wriggled out of the stiff whalebones of her corset gratefully. "Anybody who owned a boat tried to help the South by bringing in food and guns and things past the Yankee blockade. That wasn't piracy."

"If he'd been caught he'd have probably been hung."

"He wasn't hung. He lived to be an old man and left a very comfortable fortune to Mama's father."

"Which vanished, apparently, except the little that Uncle Daniel got hold of and held on to after Grandfather Neary was killed when that boat blew up. We've heard that story a hundred times, more or less."

"Listen, Taffy, Mama isn't to blame for her limited viewpoint. Nothing has ever happened to her except trouble."

"Did I say anything disrespectful? You know we've heard about that silly boat race and Grandpa Neary being blown to pieces when his old boiler blew up, a hundred times. France, I thought you might be going to get engaged to Cliff. I'm rather glad you're not, for nobody could ever live with that awful mother of his—and Cliff hasn't got a shred of gumption, you know that."

"Maybe I want too much, Taffy," Frances said, as she turned back the thin cover on the bed. "Maybe I want the moon with a diamond ring around it. But everything we've ever had has had to be so—utilitarian. I don't want love to be that way, if it ever comes my way—not added up in columns and inches and hours. I want it to be—glorious, and full of thrills and little shivers up my backbone! Does that sound silly to you?"

Taffy drew a long breath. "I think it sounds wonderful," she sighed, diving headfirst into her cotton nightgown. "France —one thing let's agree on. Let's not marry anybody till we find someone horribly rich. You could do it. You've got that kind of elegant look and nice eyes—if you'd just let yourself go a little and not be quite so—regal!"

Frances laughed. "I don't feel regal a bit, honey. I feel more like the beggar maid."

"Well, anyway, I hope there's some decent furniture in that house," Taffy said, giving the bed a poke. "Beds without lumps in them. At least there'd be no Miss Baker!"

"Be careful; she keeps her ear glued to the wall. She'll have to get some other teacher to stay with her while we're gone. Of course, we may be awfully disappointed in the place."

"Maybe we can sell the land for something anyway."

"I just have a nasty feeling that Uncle Daniel wouldn't have left it to us if it was worth anything, though goodness knows he didn't need the money. That house must have cost thousands, and those horses and a colored man to drive."

"I'm not going to let myself think that. I'm going to think kindly of him, if I can."

"All right, you be the holy one and I'll be the nasty Keeling. That way we'll keep the family in balance, because you know Mama—she's a sweet little old echo; she sides with whoever spoke last."

Even after Taffy had been long asleep, curled in a knot on her side of the bed, Frances could not sleep. She was thinking about life reaching out before her. So much of it! Years and years. With new places, new faces—and not one face looked the least bit like Cliff Houchins. Eagerly, in the dark, she reached out for life, tingling a little, every nerve alive as though body and soul surged to meet it.

2

The hired horse limped on one front foot. This made him lurch a little with every step so that the reins jerked in Frances' hands and made a red mark on her palms. With every lurch the buggy moved forward a little on the sandy road and Lydia's hat lurched sideways so that she was continually clutching at it.

Taffy sat bolt upright in the middle of the back seat, a waiting and judicial look on her face. She was still in a pessimistic mood and waiting to be shown, and she regarded the narrow North Carolina road, twisting past marshes and through ragged-looking woods, with no enthusiasm.

"If you'll take my advice, Francie, you'll turn straight around and go back to that stable," Mrs. Keeling said, clutching her purse in her free hand. "The idea! Charging us a dollar and a half for a crippled horse! The poor thing's in pain."

"Probably a nail in its foot," suggested Taffy, slapping at the gnats that whirled up in the low places.

"I don't see any place to turn around," worried Frances, clucking at the animal in a tone intended to be comforting. "This road is so narrow and no lanes turning off anywhere. It shouldn't be much farther, Mama. You said two miles."

"Everything has grown up so—it's all changed," sighed Lydia, looking at the small enameled watch pinned on her bosom. "We've been almost an hour already. Wait, Francie" —she edged forward eagerly—"I remember—this is where we turn! There's the big gum tree and the creek."

"Here?" Frances regarded dubiously the thin, overgrown track that turned abruptly into a thicket. Grass grew high between the wheel marks, bushes hung low on either side. "Are you sure, Mama? This looks like a cow path to me."

"Of course I'm sure." Lydia was almost bouncing now with excitement. "There used to be brick gateposts—look, there's

11

one fallen there in the grass! And farther on there's a little bridge."

"We hope there's a bridge." Frances coaxed the reluctant animal into the grassy trail. "How far now, Mama?"

"Just a little way. Papa always kept this wood cleared out like a little park. There used to be a statue—there it is!" she cried, pointing to a mildewed, leaning marble figure almost lost in a tangle of briars. "Grandpa brought that home from Spain with him once when he was a sea captain. It's supposed to be an angel, or something."

"The angel needs a bath," observed Taffy brutally.

"There's the house!" exclaimed the mother. "Oh, Francie—" Her voice broke and tears brimmed in her eyes. "It looks just the same! It looks like home. I was afraid I might not remember, but I do."

Frances reached to pat her mother's knee gently, then snatched the reins tight as the horse stumbled and went almost to his knees. Behind her she heard Taffy's flat voice saying, "They certainly haven't wasted any paint on it, have they?"

Frances said impatiently, "Those are weathered shingles. It would be a shame to put paint on them. From here it looks lovely, Mama."

It was a long low-roofed house standing on a grassy rise with great trees on both sides. Tiny dormers projected like quizzical eyebrows from the silvery roof, and huge chimneys flanked it on either end.

"Where," Taffy pursued, "is this much-advertised river?"

"Oh, it's beyond the house, down the bluff. This is the back, you see," Lydia explained. "The house fronts on the river and that little brick building was the kitchen. Francie, you gave me that key Uncle Daniel's wife gave you—where in the world did I put it?" She began fumbling anxiously in her purse. "It had a tag tied on it—oh, here—no, that's the key to the basement back home."

A wooden fence, sagging in places, confronted them and the horse stopped with a kind of collapsing relief, his head over the top board. Taffy was out swiftly.

"Gate's padlocked. What do we do—climb over?"

"There's a little gate. Oh, here's the key—it must be the

one, with this red tag tied on. You'd better tie him up, Francie —not that he's likely to run away, but it's safer."

"Wait, Mama, I'll help you down. Don't tear your dress on the step. Goodness, Taffy went over that fence like a rabbit. I could see her stockings clear to her knees."

"I hope the little gate isn't locked, I never was much good at climbing—no, it isn't. My, this grass is long for so early in the spring!" Lydia puffed a little as they mounted the rise of ground.

The windows of the house reflected the spring sunlight flatly. Frances noticed the latticed well house, where a rusty pump stood on a platform of mossy bricks; the apple trees were already beaded with tiny hard fruit.

Taffy was yelling from the back porch. "Never mind the key. This window is open."

Lydia hurried behind Frances, breathing in small gusty sobs, murmuring to herself.

"Mother's rose bed! And there are the lilac bushes. My father always kept this walk covered with shell."

The long back porch was still firm underfoot, although the railings were decayed and leaned outward. The back door opened on a wide, dim hall that went all the way through the house. Taffy's footprints were plain on the dusty floor. Dark wood paneled the walls and Lydia laid a loving hand on the doorframe.

"The best wood! The best of everything went into this house. The Nearys were like that."

A staircase curved up at one side, unsupported, and on the steps rectangles of faded red carpet clung to rusting nails. Taffy had run up the stairs and kept calling from above, but Lydia moved about dreamily, opening doors and muttering to herself.

"Grandma's old sofa! Mama had it covered with that blue plush. And the secretary, too! I'm surprised nobody has carried off this furniture, the house standing open and so lonely. There used to be a secret drawer in here—I knew how to open it once, I must have forgotten. Look—old letters here yet! Look at the postmark—1865!"

A round marble-topped table leaned a bit perilously on one

leg; a cane-seated rocker had a broken arm. Frances bent and picked up a sheet of dusty music from the parlor floor. "Boulanger's March" read the title page. The great fireplace was heaped with rubbish, and the hearth had sunk below the level of the floor. The whole house smelled of wood smoke, of mice and soot.

Taffy came pounding down the stairs, her skirt dusty at the hem. "Four rooms," she announced. "They could be kind of cute if they were cleaned up. And there are two beds, but no mattresses—just rusty springs."

"We always had ticks and feather beds," Lydia said. "Mama had the ticks filled with new straw every summer."

"No closets. They hung their clothes on nails on the backs of doors." Taffy flung open the door on the right, at the front of the hall. "This was the dining room. Look—the river! And that old sideboard—priceless! But they've put hot dishes down on it. Isn't it a wonder Uncle Daniel's greedy wife didn't sell all this old stuff? This table must be mahogany, France."

"I doubt if she ever came here," her mother said. "Anyway, I don't believe Daniel would have let her sell old things that had been in our family. He had tenants in here for awhile, she said—but there's even Grandmother's little sewing stand still here—and a thimble!"

"I should have thought your mother would have moved everything to Baltimore when she went," Frances said. "I would have hated to leave these old pieces here."

"We couldn't take much, there wasn't room in Grandpa Taft's house—and of course Mama thought that Daniel would come here to live."

Frances explored the rear of the house. The kitchen, down three steps, was brick-floored, huge and dark, with cupboards painted dirty brown and a cistern pump in a rusted iron sink. Taffy came down presently and began jerking open drawers and doors.

"Rats," she said, sniffing. "And would you look at that monstrous stove?"

"No doubt old Amanda cooked marvelous meals on it," Frances remarked. "And probably Mama sat in that corner with a kitten on her lap and listened to Amanda's tales of pirates and ghosts."

She went back after a little to join her mother, who stood dreamily at the front door.

"What do you think, Mama?" she asked. "Would you be happy here? It would be a frightful job to clean up the place and make it livable, but perhaps we could do it."

"I don't know, Frances. I'm just so broken up at seeing it all again—you might be lonely here. I wouldn't want to be the one to decide. After all, it belongs to you—you and Taffy."

"There's cute paper in one room upstairs," announced Taffy, appearing abruptly. "Ladies with parasols, and fountains, and elegant gentlemen on horseback with plumes on their hats. I'm going down to look at the river."

"Let's walk along, Mama," urged Frances. "We have plenty of time to make up our minds. Of course, it would take money."

"I know—and we wouldn't have so very much." Lydia stopped suddenly, staring at a dead, blackened chimney half-hidden under some tall ragged bushes. "Amanda's cabin! It burned. But look at the fig trees! My mother planted those cuttings when I was a little girl. Sometimes the frost turned all the leaves black in spring."

A brick-edged path overgrown with moss ran toward the river. Taffy had flown down that way, but at the edge of the bluff Lydia stopped and her face changed and stiffened.

"The Cavitt place! It's still there. Someone lives there, too; there's a Negro man trimming the hedge. I do hope they've sold it to somebody else."

"The Cavitts," Frances recalled. "It was a Captain Cavitt, wasn't it—his boat?"

"It was Bascom Cavitt who killed my father just as surely as though he had held a pistol at his head," stated Lydia grimly. "They both ran boats on the Sound. Papa had the *Mary Conner* and Bascom Cavitt built the *Agnes J.* He had the keel laid in Philadelphia and sailed her down here when I was about eleven years old. Papa had the best of the shipping business then, but this new boat of Cavitt's had stern propellers and it was faster, and the Cavitts began cutting in on my father. Bascom Cavitt was some kind of foreigner, my mother always said—Papa thought he was Portuguese—and they told all along this coast that the first Cavitt was a pirate. You know there are caves all along up this coast, and they did find chests and skeletons and things hidden in them."

"Let's walk back, Mama. You don't need to look at that house over there, ever, you know, if it depresses you." Frances turned Lydia about and urged her gently toward the house.

"I can't help remembering that awful day," Lydia said plaintively. "Let me sit down on the steps, Francie. This is virgin's-bower, this vine. It always smells so sweet at night. The way it was, Captain Cavitt kept taunting my father and blowing his whistle at him scornfully, and out in deep water he'd swing his boat in too near and the wash would make the *Mary Conner* roll and frighten the passengers and make the cargo break loose in the hold. Then he challenged Papa to a race. I remember how Mama cried and begged him not to be so foolish, but he was hot-blooded, and hardheaded too. Eleven people were killed when the *Mary Conner's* boiler blew up; they saved a lot more from drowning. Papa was killed instantly, they said, and Bascom Cavitt had the gall to send a wreath to his funeral."

"And your mother took it down and threw it in the river, I remember you told us."

"She waited till Amanda's children came running to tell us that Captain Cavitt had come in off his boat and was sitting on the porch and then she marched down to the river with all the little Negroes trailing after and flung that wreath out into the river. Captain Cavitt couldn't help seeing, but he never moved. At least he didn't have the effrontery to come to the funeral."

"Would the Cavitts spoil the house for you, Mama?"

Lydia's round jaw set. "I never wanted to leave in the first place. I didn't want the Cavitts to think they could drive us away, and I wouldn't let a Cavitt keep me away now. My mother was a helpless woman, though. She had never had any responsibility and she didn't know how to manage without a man to advise her, so she decided to go back to her father, Grandpa Taft, and I had to go with her. But I was never happy there, nor was she."

"All right, Mama, we'll come back." Frances sat down beside her mother on the stone step worn to a hollow by many feet, and looked out upon the green stillness of the quiet country, so isolated except for the silver highway of the Pamlico River below the bluff, so old!

Adventurers had explored those tidal waters in past centuries, buccaneers had pre-empted its secret inlets, navies had fought, and early Americans had built proud houses along its shores. Now commerce had moved inward, northward, southward, dreading the stormy waters off Hatteras; industry had moved on to the Piedmont, leaving the coastal country to its quietude, the silence of its old graveyards walled, lichened, moss-hung—old, so very old!

All so old. That little town they had left. Old and still—and she, Frances Keeling, was still young. What could life offer them—Taffy, so ebullient, so eager for gaiety, here where everything wore the aspect of having already met death and been contented with it when it came? She looked down at her mother, who sat with her hands lying calmly in her lap, a dreaming sort of nostalgia in her faded eyes. There was so little that Lydia had ever had, so little that they could give her now, except contentment.

"We'll come back, Mama," Frances said again firmly, the firmness directed at her own misgivings. "I'd better find Taffy now. It will take hours to get back to town with that horse."

Lydia shrilled after her, "Don't you hush me now, Francie, for I'm certainly going to give that man a piece of my mind—renting us a lame horse!"

Halfway down the path Frances saw Taffy coming up the bluff, a young man walking beside her. He was very dark and tall, with short curling black hair and straight, almost fierce eyebrows. He wore white trousers and a soft shirt and a white cap pushed far back on his head.

Taffy called, "Francie, this gentleman was out in a boat and he says he knows about horses. He says he'll have a look at that limping beast."

The dark young man touched his cap. "I'm one of your neighbors. I'll have a look at this lame horse if you'll allow me."

"Thank you. That will be wonderful," Frances said. "He's tied down there."

She walked beside the stranger through the little gate to where the horse stood with sagging head and slumped shoulders. Taffy untied the hitch rope and the young man backed the horse away a few paces.

"Hired him from Marsh Goodwin, didn't you? Hold still, old boy, till I have a look at this foot." He picked up the hoof skillfully and examined it.

"You know how to handle horses, don't you?" Taffy said admiringly.

"I rode with Roosevelt in Cuba," he answered. "Bad shoeing job, here. Nail pressing on the frog. Pains him just as a nail would in your own shoe. I'll have to pull that shoe. Better tie him up again till I fetch a tool from my boat."

He went up the path at a trot, and Taffy held the rope, patting the animal's nose and talking baby talk.

"Who is he, Taffy? Did he tell you his name?" Frances asked.

"No, he didn't introduce himself. He was sailing up the river in a boat and he came in close to our landing and asked me if I was looking at the old Neary place, so I said we owned it now. We got to talking about how sad it was the place had been so neglected. Then I happened to mention that we had to get back to town because our horse was lame, so he said would I like to have him look at it, as he knew about horses? Then he just tied up the boat and came along with me. He's romantic-looking, isn't he? Maybe it won't be so bad down here after all, Francie."

"You watch the horse, Taffy, and I'll help Mama lock the house. Remember to be dignified. After all, the man is a perfect stranger."

"Oh, for heaven's sake, you sound like Miss Baker! Head off Mama, she'll be bound to ask him a thousand questions. Bring my purse, France; I left it in the kitchen."

The strange young man had already removed the offending horseshoe and was tossing it into the carriage when Frances and her mother closed the little gate. He straightened and wiped his hands, and touched his cap to Lydia.

"He'll travel better now I think," he said. "That foot may be a trifle tender still, but it will pass."

"We're so grateful to you," Frances began, but the stranger, nodding briefly, was already over the fence in a bound.

"A very precipitate person, I'd say," remarked Lydia. "Did you ask him his name?"

"I did," said Taffy, in an odd voice. "I asked him whom I was to thank. He said his name was Foxworth Cavitt."

"Cavitt?" repeated Lydia, "I should have known. He looked like that breed. He must be old Bascom's son. Bascom married a young woman just before we left here, somebody from upstate. Goldsboro, I think. He was a middle-aged man then."

"Mama, get in," urged Taffy. "I don't want to hold this brute all night, and it's getting late. Anyway, even if he was a Cavitt, he was a gentleman and handsome as anything."

Lydia sat glumly all the way back to town. She even forgot to berate the livery stable owner in her heavy preoccupation. Back in the room they had at a little inn, she faced her daughters uncertainly.

"I've been wondering if it would be wise for us to come back here," she began. "After all, we're used to Baltimore and all your friends are there—"

Taffy set her chin in impish stubbornness.

"Just because a decent-looking man shows up! Now you change your mind! No dice, Mrs. Keeling. France and I own that house and we're going to live there. Feuds don't have to endure to the third and fourth generation. Of course, Mama, if you'd rather stick in Baltimore and live with Miss Baker, we can't prevent you."

"That's enough, Taffy." Was she going to have to keep on forever intervening between the two of them? Frances wondered. "You changed your mind rather suddenly yourself, so don't talk to Mama like that."

Taffy giggled and hugged her mother swiftly. "Mama isn't mad. You thought he was exciting, yourself, didn't you, Mama? He should have had a knife between his teeth though; it would have suited him exactly. Or some horns. Cute little goat horns sticking up out of that black hair. Mama thinks all Cavitts have horns, anyway." She danced across the room, her coppery hair tossing and shining. "Let's move as soon as we can. I can't wait to encounter our handsome enemy. I wonder how many sons old Captain Cavitt has? I'm putting you both on notice right now that I want the little room upstairs that looks out across the river."

3

But June was half gone when they finally returned, and Frances was the last to leave Baltimore. Lydia and Taffy went ahead to be on hand when their household goods arrived, and Frances was delegated to remain until all Lydia's affairs were arranged to suit the change of residence.

"You tend to it, Francie," Lydia begged. "Lawyers and Mr. Bennet at the foundry always get me so rattled I forget to read things before I sign them, and I never do put my name on the right line. And Uncle Horace scares me to death, even if he *is* my own great-uncle. But you can talk straight to him. I want the foundry money sent every month from now on instead of by the quarter. And you tell him that there certainly should be more income for me now that everybody is buying these new brass beds!"

Taffy wailed at having to take care of Mama, who got so seasick on boats that she insisted on going by train. This meant a long ride at the end in a jolting, horse-drawn hack, but Lydia was firm. So Frances was left with power of attorney arranged by Uncle Horace, and the prospect of a solitary trip on a coast steamer.

"At least I can rest and be quiet. I won't have to talk to a soul," she comforted herself.

In a little locked valise she was carrying all Mama's bonds and a hundred dollars in cash from Uncle Horace, and she kept this constantly in her hand. Uncle Horace had argued that the bonds should be left in the bank, but Lydia had wanted everything she owned where she could put her hands on it, and she was sweetly obstinate when she set her mind to anything. So Frances spent three days guarding the locked satchel, putting it beside her at meals and pushing it to the back of her bed at night.

At the terminus of the coastal trip there was a wait for the boat across the Sound. Frances found herself standing on a wharf in the hot noon sun, clutching the valise, her bags at her feet, and watching along with a dozen other passengers, all vague and impersonal to her mind, for the plume of smoke on the horizon.

Negro boys trundled up a dozen heavy barrels, each exuding a sticky fragrance, and boxes redolent of spices.

"Ole Man Matson got a heap of 'lasses goin' up to sweeten his chawin' terbaccer," they shouted at each other, white teeth flashing. "Got likrish and stuff in them boxes, too. 'Lasses come all the way from N'Awleens, I reckon."

A tall, very broad-shouldered young man with bright yellow hair under a flat straw hat, moved out toward the barrels.

"Take it easy with Pap's molasses, boys," Frances heard him say. "If anybody busts one of these barrels you'll hear him holler clear to Savannah, Georgia."

Frances caught this stranger's eyes upon her curiously.

"Is that the ferry?" she asked, indicating the growing feather of smoke.

"That's the old *Agnes*. Tide's against her right now, so she's a little late. Are you going up the Sound? I'm traveling that way, too. I'm Wylie Matson. Are you visiting someone up Pamlico way?"

"I live there," she answered. "I'm Frances Keeling. Is that the old *Agnes J.*—the Cavitt boat?"

"That's the *Agnes*. She creaks and she wallows, but she's sound and fast and Fox knows how to run her. So you're a Keeling? That means that your mother was a Neary and you're moving back to the old Neary place."

"You knew my mother?"

"I suppose my family did. Everybody on Pamlico knows all about everybody else, as you'll discover if you settle down here. I'm glad you're doing something with that old house. It's been a ghost castle along this shore for a long time. A good solid house too. Do you think you'll like living down here with us Tarheels?"

"It was my mother's old home. I hope she'll be happy in it. Do you live up there too?"

"We live in town. My father's in the tobacco business.

Matson's Golden Twist. You'll see the sign on his new factory this side of the landing. I'm in law myself. Just came down from Washington where I've been doing some lobbying on a harbor bill. Is all this baggage yours?"

"Those two bags. I'll carry the small one." She gripped the handle tight. Wylie Matson had very blue eyes and a generous mouth that quirked easily into a smile and undoubtedly he was all right, but Mama had always warned the girls to be on their guard with strangers.

"Family jewels, no doubt?" He laughed. "You'd better stand back a little, Miss Keeling. They'll load the freight first, and these boys work fast and don't always look where they're going."

The *Agnes J.* swung slowly up to the landing now, and Frances moved back and stood rigidly as the heavy ropes were hurled to the planking and snatched swiftly around bollards by black hands. Smoke rolled from the stack and twisted over their heads and Frances anxiously brushed flakes of soot from her crisp shirtwaist and gray wool skirt.

Then she saw Foxworth Cavitt. He did not wait for the gangplank to be lowered but leaped over the rail, his white nautical cap cocked to one side, a board with papers clipped to it in his hand.

"Snap it aboard, boys!" he shouted. "Tide's against us." He turned then and his face lighted. "Hello, Wylie. Going aboard?"

"Please—" Frances stepped forward. "I should like a ticket to Sandersonville."

"You don't buy a ticket, Miss Keeling," Wylie Matson told her. "You give Fox a dollar and if his old tub sinks under you, you make him give the dollar back."

Frances put her satchel down and searched her purse nervously, aware that Fox Cavitt was watching her. A man's eyes upon her levelly always made her feel untidy and inadequate. So few men except Cliff had ever looked at her long, and she was innocently unaware that her skin was flower-fair and her mouth sweet, for all its strength, and that there was an unconscious reserve about her that could be a challenge to the masculine mind.

She swallowed hard as she handed him a crumpled bill.

"Do I go on board at once?" she asked.

"I'll see you aboard, Miss Keeling." Wylie Matson picked up her two bags. "Watch your dress. Some of these boxes have nails in them."

"Cabin's 'midships—second door," Fox Cavitt yelled after her, then turned back to his freight handling.

The deck was scrubbed clean, piled with barrels and boxes, and wagon wheels fastened together with rope and coils of wire. Frances made her way through the jumble, trying to keep up with Wylie. She opened one door and then closed it swiftly, her face burning red. The door gave on a ladder that dropped abruptly into a steaming pit full of shining wheels and reeking with the smell of hot oil.

"Engine room," Wylie Matson called back, smiling at her embarrassment. "Don't break your neck getting through this stuff. Fox never bothers to lower his freight below on the up trip. Makes her top-heavy, but she won't roll on this tide."

He opened a second door and followed Frances into a glass-enclosed space furnished with varnished benches that had leather cushions, several brass cuspidors, an axe and saw painted red under glass, and a festooning of gray, mildewed-looking life preservers hanging overhead. The cabin was hot and empty, and Wylie went about flinging up the glass windows, evicting a few bumbling flies with his hat.

"How far is it?" Frances asked, making sure that the precious small valise was safe on the seat beside her.

"Get there about suppertime. No land wind today to speak of." He looked at her with sudden sharpness. "Look here—you missed your dinner, didn't you? So did I. Hey, Fox—" he rushed out shouting, "hold her a minute. This young lady hasn't had anything to eat."

"Oh, no—please!" Frances called after him, but he had run off down the gangway and she saw him presently sprinting across the sandy square of the little port town.

The cabin door swung back with a bang then and Fox Cavitt came in, with his board and papers and pencil.

"I need your name and address for our manifest, please," he said, poising the pencil.

"My name is Frances Keeling, and I don't know my address except that I live directly across the river from you," she told him.

His face seemed to change and tighten a little, and his eyes took on a blank evasiveness. He nodded briefly and scribbled on the pad.

"How do you spell that first name? With an E or an I?" he asked curtly.

"With an E. The I is masculine," she said as curtly.

"I should have known that. Thank you." He went out without looking at her.

Frances frowned at his vanishing back. He might be handsome, but he was the rudest person she had ever known, she told herself. Yet he had been easy and friendly with Taffy when he had helped them with the lame horse. Apparently the old feud was still alive and the Cavitts had decided to breathe vitality into it, now that descendants of the hated Neary family had returned. The idea presented a kind of challenge and Frances found herself responding to it with a grim quickening of her pulses. She leaned from an open window and watched Fox Cavitt climb the iron ladder to the high wheelhouse. Almost immediately the whistle shook the air with two impatient blasts, barking back from the buildings on shore. She saw Wylie Matson running toward the boat, saw him plunge up the gangplank as the Negro hands waited to raise it.

"Made it!" He came laughing breathlessly into the cabin. "There wasn't much to choose from." He handed her a paper sack.

"You must let me pay for it," Frances insisted, getting out a half dollar. "I can't accept it, really, unless you let me pay."

"Split it then. I only spent sixty cents and I intend to eat half of it. Those crackers may be a little stale, but the cheese looked fresh. I was dubious about the cakes but I bought two. If they're dry we'll feed them to the gulls when we pass the fish dock."

"The captain was slightly irritated at the delay, I think," Frances said. "His whistle sounded definitely angry."

"Who—Fox?" He divided the contents of the paper bag,

got out his knife, wiped it on a very clean handkerchief and began slicing cheese into thin wafers. "Fox wouldn't leave me on shore. This is going to be dry going, I'm afraid. I'll get some water. It will be lukewarm, but at least it will be wet. I've been telling Fox he ought to have a galley on this boat. On long hauls, at least, the passengers could have a cup of coffee."

He went out and came back presently with two tin cups of water.

"Wash it down, anyway," he said.

The engines were throbbing now below and Frances saw that the shore was drawing away, flattening oddly so that buildings and trees and the people watching from the wharf became suddenly a picture of two dimensions, foreshortened curiously, seen whole and different from the distance. A dirty wave rolled up against the land, curling back, bringing with it bits of paper, cigar butts, a flotsam of trash.

"We're off." Wylie helped a cracker down with a gulp of water. "You were talking about Fox Cavitt. That's just his manner. Though I suspect that there may be a touch of frustration at the bottom of it. Fox quit college in the middle of the second year when the war with Spain came along, and when he got back after the war, Zach—he's the older brother— had pulled out and left the old Captain alone with the *Agnes*. So Fox was stuck with this ferry business. He tried to talk the old man into building a new boat, but the Captain's more or less senile and this old tub is his whole life. Try a cake, Miss Keeling. They're not too bad. I looked for some bananas but no fruit has come in lately."

"So there is more than one Cavitt son?"

"Fox and Zachary. Zach turned into a rover. Never has stuck long in any one place or at any thing. He's back now, I hear. Brought a French wife, or anyway he married her in France. If Zach would stay at home, Fox might have a chance to get away and get himself educated for something. He's a deep thinker. I was at the university with him and he was always surprising the professors."

"I had to give up my education, too," Frances said. "My

father was sick for years and my sister and I were lucky to finish high school."

"You're young yet. Fox is about twenty-seven, I think. We're near the same age. Would you like to go outside? It's cooler out there and there's more to see."

"Is it permitted?" She looked up at a faded sign that stated that passengers would please remain in the cabin.

"That's old stuff. Nobody pays any attention to it. It does relieve the owner of responsibility if you should happen to ruin your clothes on deck or fool around and get yourself washed overboard. We'll go up in the bow. There'll be a breeze there."

"Thank you, I'd like to go." She picked up the little satchel.

"You can leave everything. Nobody will bother it. No incentive to steal anything when you can't walk ashore with it."

"This is my mother's property. I had orders not to let it out of my sight," she insisted.

"Let me carry it for you then."

"Thank you, no. It isn't heavy."

"You don't trust anybody, do you, young lady?" he laughed, holding the door open for her.

"Not when I'm following orders. Is this the old *Agnes J?*" she asked as they passed the wheelhouse where Fox Cavitt perched on a stool. "I mean was there another boat of the same name before this one?"

"Not within my memory. This old craft has been sloshing up and down the Sound ever since I was born, but she's well built and the old Captain has her kept in first-class condition. I told you there would be a breeze up here. Maybe I can find you a camp stool."

"Don't bother. I like leaning on the rail." But even as she gripped the steel barrier Frances felt a queer kind of guilt. This was the same boat with which old Bascom Cavitt had challenged her grandfather to that fatal race. She drew her hands back a little, as though even in accepting the support of this bit of metal she was somehow betraying her family.

Low before her a blue wave was turning back, sculptured in aquamarine beauty, flung in lovely perfection on either side of the cleaving bow. The shore was far and vague, but she noted that the *Agnes* was turning inshore a little, toward the bank where a small, spidery dock pushed out. On the end of that landing a group of people stood waving.

"Ha!" said Wylie Matson abruptly. "Those are some of my Pap's folks. I reckon I'll have to attend to this business for him."

"What is it?" she inquired.

"Those Negroes there on that landing have gathered up a lot of deertongue. It's a plant that grows all along this coast in the marshes—a kind of wild vanilla. They use it to flavor tobacco. Just wait here, Miss Keeling. I'll be back."

The *Agnes* did not approach the landing. Instead it stopped, and Frances saw an old rowboat being pushed off by two Negroes and rowed toward the ferry. The stern of the little boat was piled high with greenish-brown bundles wrapped crudely in ragged sacking. As it came close to the side of the *Agnes* a net on a rope was let down and the bundles hauled up to the deck.

"A hundred and four pounds," Wylie Matson announced when he returned. "It's cheaper than tonka beans, and gathering it gives these swamp Negroes a little income when there's no cotton to pick or other jobs. Tonka beans have to be shipped in from South America and cost a lot, besides the duty and shipping expense."

"I didn't know they had to flavor tobacco," Frances remarked. "Papa smoked a pipe when I was small, but he gave it up when his cough got so bad."

"They treat tobacco with a lot of different things. Sugar and honey, licorice and anise. My father sticks to molasses and deertongue. That's why he's able to make a good profit."

The *Agnes J.* was under way again, and for an hour the green shores slid by, shadowy and mysterious. Now an expanse of lime-colored marsh moving like another sea in the slow wind, with black birds perched on tall reeds and white birds winging out of dark-green groves to cut silvery sickles in the air above the boat.

Wylie Matson talked of many things—of the pirate caves that were still to be found in the high bluffs, of wrecks that had been towed in for salvage in the old days, of the blockade-runners that had kept the Sound open for a long time during the Civil War.

"My great-grandfather was one of them," Frances said.

Then a clutter of buildings appeared on the south shore, and the *Agnes* turned that way, slowing, the engines bumbling softly.

"Fish dock," stated Wylie. "Fox always stops here. Loads their fish in the morning going out and picks up ice to take home coming back. They make their own ice in that little brick building. New method. Used to be that the only ice we ever saw was shipped all the way down here from Maine, packed in sawdust."

"We had manufactured ice," Frances said, "in Baltimore, I mean. We may miss it here, though the house has a cool cellar."

"Commercial fishers in that place. Ship a lot of fish to New York and Philadelphia."

"Don't like it!" croaked a voice suddenly behind them. "Stinks up the boat. Don't like it."

Frances turned, startled. Half hidden behind a pile of dusty sacks a very old man sat hunched down in a huge chair. A nautical cap was pulled low over his eyes, which were small and dark and very piercing. His face was shriveled as a walnut, a stiff gray mustache hiding his sunken mouth. His body had a fleshless, collapsed look under a wool robe that he clutched to his chin with dry, yellow hands.

Wylie shouted amiably, "Howdy, Captain, didn't see you."

"Nobody sees me," grumbled the old man. "Nobody pays me any mind. Cold out here, ain't it?"

"Sun's warm, but the wind is cool for June. You ought to sit inside, Captain." Wylie raised his voice.

"Inside?" the Captain bellowed. "When they shove me inside they can just shove me overboard. Never was one of these cabin sailors. Always been a man on deck. Where you travelin', Wylie? Heading someplace to sue somebody for bitin' your hound dog?"

"Going home now, Captain. Been up in Washington trying to get your ports dredged out for you."

The old man mumbled something profane, but Frances did

not heed it. She was gripping the rail with rigid fingers, feeling a queer sort of excitement.

"Is that Captain Bascom Cavitt?" she asked in a whisper.

"That's the old Captain himself and you needn't whisper. He can't hear you unless you yell your head off."

"He's awfully old, isn't he?" She glanced back, her eyes carefully indifferent, and caught the old man peering at her from under the beak of his dragged-down cap.

"Who you got with you, Wylie?" he shrilled. "Likely-looking piece of a gal. You been goin' courtin'? All the young sparks got to court in the spring. Deer, they rut, and fish spawn, and young fellers pick something pretty to hang on their elbow. What's your name, young woman?"

"This is Miss Keeling," Wylie shouted while Frances tugged warningly at his sleeve.

"Don't tell him who I am," she urged. "There is bad feeling between the two families."

But her warning was useless. The old man spat, dabbing his mustache with the back of his hand.

"Keeling," he repeated. "One of John Keeling's girls. Mother was a Neary. I knew your father. He ran old man Henry Taft's foundry. 'Brass' Keeling all the shipping men called him. Bought many a piece of brass from Keeling. I'm Bascom Cavitt. Reckon your mammy's told you about me; I'm the man the Nearys hate. Was you your own grandma you'd cut my throat."

"That's all bygone, Captain," Wylie argued. "That's all past history."

"It ain't so bygone," declared the Captain, "Look at her face. Scared to death of me, ain't you, gal? Waiting for me to pull out a knife from my belt, or lookin' to see if I've got horns and a tail. Come here, young woman!"

"Oh, no!" gasped Frances, but Wylie gave her a gentle push.

"He's just an old man, he won't hurt you," he urged.

Frances took two reluctant steps nearer the chair. Captain Cavitt let the robe fall, held out a long, fleshless hand. Frances laid her own hand in the horny palm.

"Now," he chuckled, "a Neary has shook hands with a Cavitt. That's a piece for the log, Wylie. You're a right pretty gal, Miss Keeling. You've got nice eyes. You didn't get those eyes from any Neary. All the Nearys have got little gray eyes cold as a fish's belly. Reckon you look like your father. Got a compass and binnacle up in the house yonder right now, come from Keeling's place."

He seemed to forget them entirely, as the *Agnes J.* slid into the fish landing. He half lifted himself from the chair and glared at a Negro boy who had come forward and stood ready with a line.

"Now look at you!" the old man roared at him. "Foul that line in spite of thunder. Get your feet out of the bight! Miss the bollard three times, 'y granny! Always miss it three times! Heave her straight now! Widen your bight! Hell's afire!"

"Let's go," whispered Frances.

They walked down the deck, keeping out of the way of the business of mooring the boat. Two clean boxes had been lashed down near the stern and Frances sat down on one of them. For no reason at all her right hand still tingled and her face was flushed and hot.

"Great character, the Captain." Wylie dropped on the other box. "Every time this boat shoves off he has to be on board. He held to the wheel till he got so blind he ran her aground down off Swan Quarter, ripped her bottom open and ruined a good screw. Almost killed him when he had to let Fox take over. I reckon Fox is stuck here on this boat as long as the Captain lives or she holds together."

"I don't think the young Mr. Cavitt would be very easy to know," Frances observed. "His eyes are so disillusioned, as though he'd been cheated some time and never expected to believe in anything again."

"You're a shrewd observer of people, aren't you? You're right. No one ever has known Fox Cavitt intimately. I doubt if his own family does. I'd never thought about it especially till you put it into words, but even as a boy Fox was a self-sufficient fellow—didn't hold himself aloof exactly, but he was never part of the gang. Nobody was ever quite sure what he was thinking or how he was going to react to any situation. When we all went to Chapel Hill together, it was the same. Fox was the lone wolf, even up there. Then the war came along and he went off without telling anybody he intended to enlist.

Since he's come back he's just Fox—and nobody's bothered to analyze him. People don't go in for analysis much in little communities, they just accept you with all your oddities and quirks, or you're an outsider and your ways are your own business. We just know Fox, the way he is, and let it go."

"He's lonely," Frances said. She knew about loneliness, she was certain. But now she wondered if being lonely was strength or if it was merely being weak, being too submissive, too inclined to take the easy way, spare other people's feelings and avoid conflict? Had she been weak in agreeing to move down here to this remote place? Had that been another piece of her expedient acceptance of the inevitable?

She would not let herself think that a touch of excitement at having a young man with dark, guarded, enigmatic eyes look at her might have any part in the decision. Taffy had been intrigued by Fox Cavitt, but Frances was certain that she was entirely uninterested in him except as a study in personalities. What lay behind the insolent and secret stillness in his face could be a challenge to a woman, but she was confident that she was not the type to accept challenges. She was so certain of this that she walked off the boat with her chin very high, when the *Agnes* docked at Sandersonville at twilight.

Taffy was waiting there, in a red-wheeled buggy drawn by a very fat brown mare.

"Our new carriage and four," Taffy announced. "Mama traded four acres of pasture for this rig, and now she has to get herself appointed guardian over us so she can sign the deed. You might as well make up your mind to it, France, for we certainly can't get along without some kind of transportation. Oh, how do you do?" she bowed politely as Frances introduced Wylie Matson, who had brought her bags.

"This is my sister Henrietta," Frances said. "And thank you, Mr. Matson, for making my trip so pleasant."

"I'll bet it was pleasant!" jeered Taffy, when they drove away. "Trust you to pick up a good-looking man with shoulders like a fullback! Is that why you're all starry-eyed and excited?"

"I'm not excited. I'm just thankful to be here, and getting Mama's bonds delivered safely."

"No," declared Taffy, "you evade cleverly, but it's a man. If it isn't the blond behemoth, who is it?"

"Mr. Matson is a lawyer. I wasn't terribly impressed with him, though he was nice and friendly. There isn't any man."

Taffy flicked the new buggy whip over the mare's fat rump.

"You certainly make mighty little of your opportunities," she grumbled. "Here I've been stuck for two weeks, scrubbing woodwork and wiping off wallpaper, while you gallivanted around the country all alone! Such a waste. Did you see our handsome friend, Foxworth Cavitt? He runs that boat, doesn't he?"

"Yes, I saw him. Also his dreadful old father! He's horrible —and pitiful, too, Taffy. No one should hate him any more."

"So you weren't impressed with Fox Cavitt, either. I give you up, France. You're as bloodless as a turnip and as sexless as bread dough! If you aren't lying—which I halfway suspect that you are!"

"I'm not lying. I'm not man-struck, I'm glad to get home. This is supposed to be home now, isn't it? I hope I've got a bed to sleep in. Three nights on that cast-iron bunk thing have put kinks in my spine."

But even though her bed was ready, a bed she would have to herself in a room that would be all her own, she did not sleep.

The moon was high and hot and white, and under it the river lay like a still road of silver, an open road with no secrets hidden from the moon. But across the river she could see one small, hot light burning in the old Cavitt house.

Was he there? Was he reading some deep book perhaps? What was he thinking?

4

Tulia Cavitt wore her dark hair sleekly brushed back and coiled in a neat and involved figure on the back of her head. Her long gold earrings swung lightly against a neck as white as milk, her gray eyes were cool and half hidden by lashes, thick and alluring under perfectly arched black brows. Her nose was a trifle thin and high, with patrician nostrils that had an impatient flicker at times.

The lure of her lashes kept men from observing that her lips were thin and might seem inclined to cruelty when she forgot to wear her careful smile. At times she deliberately forebore wearing it and jerked her mouth into bitter lines, as now. She stood before the old mirror, patting her nose with a wad of pink lamb's wool. A hard line was slashed between her brows as she glared into the glass.

The room was comfortable enough, with a heavy old cherry bed set against the opposite wall and covered with a spotless white counterpane. Starched pillow shams leaned against the headboard, ruffled and prim, though one was crushed and indented now by the black head of Tulia's husband Zachary, the elder son of old Captain Cavitt.

Zachary's long legs were flung out on the spread, one foot hanging down. One arm lay loosely behind his head, the other was poised in mid-air, the hand holding a strong, black cigar. It was Zachary at whom Tulia glared in the mirror, Zachary flicking cigar ashes on the braided rug, Zachary with his big body relaxed and his face lazily amiable, his mouth under a small, black mustache drawn into a mocking grin.

"You make me sick!" snapped Tulia. "You disgust me beyond words!"

She stuffed the powder puff into a glass receptacle and snapped the lid down with a vicious clink.

"Never beyond words, my pet," drawled Zachary. "In your

geography no such point exists. And don't mention being sick downstairs or you'll get a dose of my mother's boneset tea."

"Smoking that stinking thing in the bedroom!" she fumed. "The air will be foul in here all night. You can't smoke downstairs for fear your mother's precious curtains might be contaminated, but if your wife is asphyxiated it's of no consequence at all."

He sat up, jabbing a rumpling elbow into the virginal pillow sham. "Asphyxiation is an easy death, I've heard, but slow. The quick way would be a short rope's end around your beautiful throat. No blood, no mess, just your eyes bulging and your tongue sticking out, then a brief gurgle and gasp—and a lot of silence."

"Don't bother," Tulia said coldly. "I have no thought of being laid out with a royal-purple face and my tongue hanging out. When the time comes and I can't stand it any more, I'll take a nice dose of Paris green."

"Tastes nasty," he teased. "There's a lot of river out there, good and deep. Goes down to the Sound and the nice, cool ocean. Think of all the cute little fishes swishing their blue and green tails through your trailing hair."

She shrugged a shoulder, disdaining to look at him, and moved to the window that looked out on the river.

"They're tearing down part of that old house over there— the little brick part at the back. There's a man on the roof, too, nailing on shingles. When I think what we could have done with that place—"

Zachary lounged to his feet, tossing the cigar into the flowered slop jar where it smoldered odorously and hissed out.

"If I've told you once I've told you a thousand times that that Neary place wasn't for sale," he shouted.

"Anything can be had, for a price. The woman's a widow with only a small income, so I've heard. What does she want with a house like that?"

"From all indications she wants to live in it. Even if she could be tempted with money she wouldn't sell to us at any price. She'd never sell to a Cavitt. They've hated us for thirty odd years. Even," he added, "if we had that kind of money, which we haven't as you know mighty doggone well!"

"Your father has it. You know he has it, even though they do drive that ratty old buggy and hoard every egg and every drop of cream. Your mother likes living like a peasant, onions hung up in the kitchen, never enough food left over to keep a mouse from starving."

"My mother was born thrifty. It can be a virtue, my love, though neither you nor I will ever learn that, I suspect. I don't know how much money my father has, or even if he has any. The old boat makes a living, but eventually railroads and roads are bound to come into this coastal country and when that happens the ferry business will dwindle and he knows it. It's already happening in the North, the decline of water transportation. What the Captain has he'll need. My mother's not an old woman." He buttoned his shirt in leisurely fashion, took his tie from the bedpost and knotted it with deliberation.

"You said she wouldn't sell to a Cavitt. Why not? What have the Cavitts ever done to her? I saw her out there yesterday, a dumpy, frumpy little creature in absolutely shapeless clothes."

"It's a story." Zachary put on his coat. "Get the Captain to tell it to you sometime. It will take him hours and he'll enjoy it. That woman over there believes that the Captain was responsible for her father's death. She wouldn't sell to us for a million dollars—if we had a million dollars."

"You can tell me the story yourself, if a time comes when I'm ever interested. I'd go mad trying to scream at your father to make him understand and then he'd go mumbling on for hours, saying the same thing over and over. Oh, Zach, can't you see that I can't bear living here? What is there for us here? Why we ever came back is a puzzle to me."

"We came back because we had no other place to go," he said, with a slow bitterness in his voice. "Because we'd run through every cent I'd been able to raise, and were in debt besides."

"And because we had to leave Cuba suddenly so you wouldn't be flung into a Cuban jail to rot for ages!" she answered just as bitterly.

Something dangerous came into his eyes. "My loyal wife!" he sneered. "Much you'd care if they threw me into every jail in creation!"

"You had no business getting into that mess with Gonzalez in the first place! Cleverer men than you were in on the army deal to begin with, men who had the inside track like Alger. Then that stupid business of buying up all that Argentine beef! You were going to make a fortune, exporting it to France!"

"Could we help it if the ship got caught in a hurricane?" he barked. "Could we help it if the war with Spain ended before we got our operations under way?"

"You could help it that you didn't have proper insurance. You could help it that the whole business was dishonest to start with. You were an American and Gonzalez was an enemy of Spain, yet you know you intended that beef to get to Spain eventually!"

He took a menacing step toward her, but she curled her long fingers into claws and he jerked back, swearing.

"You would have sold me out!" he said savagely. "I suspected it all the time. Didn't we offer the beef to the United States Army? We had a fortune invested in it; we had to get it out."

"*You* had nothing invested in it, you know that! Nothing but your glib tongue and your arrogant manner. So we had to leave Cuba in a stinking little boat in the night, with nothing but our clothes and the few dollars I had been shrewd enough to hide!"

"How could we know Dewey was going to be so damned lucky at Manila? I suppose if you hadn't married me you would have gotten rich painting little pictures in Paris? You were hungry enough when I met you, walking wet streets with holes in the bottoms of your shoes!"

"My mother would have helped me then. She won't do it now."

"No, she won't do it now because she married again and the fellow will keep a tight fist on her money. You could be in Paris now, walking the streets—and the competition was pretty fierce in that profession from my observation. Anyway, I've got plans."

"Plans," she jeered, "always plans! More tricky schemes to fall to pieces and leave us ruined worse than we are now, I suppose?"

He pulled a small box from his pocket and opened it, tossed some white cylinders on the bed.

"See these?"

"Turkish cigarettes!" She wrinkled her nose. "Are you going to start smoking those foul things again?"

He gathered them up and put them back in his pocket. "No, I'm not smoking them. I'm going to make them. Here—on Pamlico."

"And compete with people like Duke, I suppose, who can spend millions on machinery and advertising!"

"No, not with Duke. With those people in Richmond who still make fine handmade cigarettes. There's always a market for an exclusive, better-quality product."

She twitched a shoulder. "Arrogant, as always!" she snapped. "Who's going to do the handwork? Am I to be stuck into a tobacco factory? Thank you, no! Just where are you going to get the money to launch this fantastic enterprise?"

She caught his eyes sharply upon her then, and swiftly turned a square yellow diamond on her finger inward to her palm. She had clung to that diamond with savage tenacity. It had come to her from her father, who had been a gambler famous on three continents.

"With brains I won't need money," Zachary drawled.

"While you're hatching this scheme, what am I supposed to do?" she demanded. "Sit on the porch listening to the maundering of those old people downstairs, till your fine plans go to pieces under you again and we have to move on between dark and daylight?"

"You can keep on riding up and down Pamlico on the *Agnes*." Zachary's voice held something a little deadly. "You and Fox seem to get on very well."

"What else is there to do?" she parried. "At least I can sit in the bow of the boat and let the wind blow on my face and pretend that I'm actually going somewhere, not just coasting along mudbanks from one silly landing to another! Fox sits up at the wheel and never speaks a word except to yell at the deck hands. I doubt if he even knows that I exist. All he's interested in is seeing that those stupid ropes get thrown over the right posts."

"My dear, if you're going to be nautical at least say lines and bollards. Go ahead and go to sea in the old tub if you get any pleasure out of it; but you could give the Captain a kind word now and then. He's a lonely old man." Zachary turned at the door, his hat in his hands.

"He always pretends he can't hear me, and he chews tobacco and that sickens me. Where are you going?"

"Out. To see a man. Maybe to see two men. To get drunk, perhaps. How do I know? Your so charming company now and then ceases to charm. Also I have things to do."

"More schemes!" She was scornful. "You don't mind at all leaving me marooned in this place. If there's cold rice and cornbread again for supper I'll throw my plate on the floor. I swear I will!"

His eyes seared her, hot and black. "You will behave yourself before my mother like the lady I told her you were!" he barked.

She looked him slowly up and down, with a blanched and bitter face, her brows springing to arcs of pure contempt.

"The proud Cavitts! Black pride and cold rice. And men who smell like goats!"

He moved his hand swiftly but she was quicker. The curved fingers reached for his face and he jerked back cursing and slammed the door in her face. She heard his heels, iron hard, pounding down the stairs.

She sat at the window till she saw him drive away, driving the slow old horse that pulled his mother to church on Sundays. She heard Mrs. Cavitt shrilling some admonition after him from the back porch, and noted Zachary's ignoring back. *She* was the one who must be courteous to Zachary's mother! To Tulia, her mother-in-law was stupid and tiresome almost past enduring.

"She married the Captain for his money," Tulia told herself. "She was a young woman, and no young woman would marry a middle-aged man for love!"

No woman with any hope at all would shut herself up in a dreary old house like this. Not that the house could not be made attractive and livable—even flinging open a few doors and windows and letting out the decayed, aging air that reeked of cooking, carpets and cats would help.

When Zachary was out of sight Tulia kicked off her thin slippers and pulled on some walking shoes, picked from a row set along the wall. That was another irritation, no closets in this house, so that the few decent clothes she owned had to be kept crumpled in her trunk or dangling from hooks on the wall.

Walking lightly on her toes, she went down the stairs and let herself quietly out the front door, always kept closed against the wind that moved on the river. The path went down to the river from the lawn and was overgrown with long grass that switched at her ankles and scattered seeds on her skirt. There was a dock at the end of the path, well built of stout planks. Fox kept his sailboat tied there, and often when he came in off the ferry run he took the sailboat out into the Sound and stayed there alone for hours.

Tulia walked down the landing and got into the moored boat, slipping under the swinging boom. The air that stirred with the current cooled the burning, angry flush on her face as she leaned her elbows on her knees and gazed across the stream to where the old Neary house stood aloof, half hidden by tall trees.

The smoke of a bonfire drifted there. She saw a girl moving about the fire, obviously a very young girl with a bright drift of hair carelessly caught up on her head. She was piling trash on the flames and poking at it with a rake. Presently another young woman came out with an armful of old bandboxes which she tossed into the fire, and the two stood watching them burn, backing away when the smoke wavered too near.

"Women!" muttered Tulia. "No doubt Zach has already seen them over there and that's why he's so set on staying here!"

The girls returned to the house, but Tulia still sat, occasionally dipping a hand idly into the water, letting it trickle over her fingers. The sun was low. In an hour the *Agnes J.* would dock. If Fox took his little boat out tonight there was a slender chance that he might ask her to go with him. A very slender chance, she knew. Till now Fox had been coolly polite, evasive and, she felt, on guard against her. But in every man,

she knew shrewdly, there was a breaking point. She had won
Zachary by appealing to his protective instinct, by being frightened and helpless in a foreign city; perhaps Fox would take
pity on her if she were lonely enough and desolate enough.
She formed her face into a tragic mask, then lifted her head
sharply as she heard the dip of oars close by.

A little skiff was being rowed downstream by a slight, sun-
browned young man in a sleeveless undershirt and soiled white
trousers. He stood erect when he saw her and brought the skiff
around till it floated close to the landing.

"Hello," he said. "You're Zach Cavitt's wife, aren't you?"

Tulia pushed back her hair. "I'm Tulia Cavitt," she said
coolly. "Do I know you?"

He gripped the gunwale of the sailboat, holding his craft
steady against the turn of the current.

"No, you don't know me. I know Zach. I heard he'd come
home from Cuba. I'm Ren Matson."

"I seem to remember that name. Matson— I remember now.
I saw it on a roof."

He grinned. " 'Matson's Golden Twist. Smoke and Chew
the Best.' That's our place. Pap always did make chewing
tobacco, but he's trying smoking now—going after old Bull
Durham's hide!"

"Loathly stuff!" remarked Tulia. "I suppose there must be
money in it."

"We're not doing so badly." His eyes, she saw, were very
blue. "We started in our shed a few years ago, all handwork.
Now we hire twenty-one people, just bought us a new Pease
cutter and we've got four women sewing on the outside making
tobacco bags." He shipped his oars and gripped the sailboat
more firmly. "Going to stay here awhile?"

Tulia shrugged. "I sincerely hope not."

"Why? Don't you like us? We're pretty good folks on
Pamlico. We have a good time. Everybody knows everybody
and we have square dances in winter. Good fiddling, too. Like
to dance?"

"I used to dance—in Paris. And in New York before that,"
she said sadly. "I've almost forgotten how."

"Oh, yes, Paris—that's in France, isn't it. You lived there, didn't you?"

"I studied there before I was married. My father lived there for a number of years."

He shifted his gaze across the river. "New girls over there," he remarked. "Not bad-looking, I've heard."

"Aren't they?" she replied acidly.

"Not jealous, are you?" he bantered.

"You're being impertinent, don't you think? I don't even know you."

"Give me time," he argued. "How about a little boat ride? She rides smooth if I keep her in the river."

"Thank you, no. I don't care for boats."

"Don't like boats? You have to like boats if you're going to be a Cavitt."

"I'm not a boat Cavitt."

"It's Fox you like then, huh? I've seen you, riding around all day on the old *Agnes*. Can't blame you a bit. Fox always was the best-looking Cavitt. Always could charm the girls and never tried a mite. Zach was the friendly one, though. Zach liked the girls and Fox didn't give a hang—funny that way."

Tulia sprang back to the landing with one lithe fling of her slender body.

"I don't think I care to continue this conversation. Good evening, Mr. Matson," she said icily.

He shoved his boat off, unperturbed, turning to wave a mocking hand at her. Her eyes blazed at him. Then she ran up the slope and back to her room where she banged the door hard and stood taut in the middle of the floor, breathing gustily.

This vile, snoopy, foul-minded little town! These people who had filthy minds and insatiable curiosity concerning a stranger! That creature in the boat would repeat his low innuendoes for the sake of excitement, and what if Zachary heard them? What if Foxworth heard them?

Fox, she suspected, would only be amused. She would see it in his sardonic eyes, hear it in the ironic slowness of his voice. But Zachary's quick, unpredictable temper would be an ugly thing to deal with.

There had been a little homesick, youthful attaché in Cuba, just a boy who wanted to talk about home. She had worn the blue marks of Zachary's fingers on her arm for days after that silly incident. As though she cared a whit about Fox Cavitt!

She sank on her bed, pressing her hot face into her palms, and a slow, mounting misery troubled her. The truth haunted her, that it was because of Fox Cavitt that she was able to endure this place, that what little peace she had was when she sat in the bow of the ferry, knowing Fox was there, high on his stool, remote from her—but there. Was that the reason days like this dragged out interminably till the *Agnes* was moored and Fox came home?

"I won't have it like that!" she said aloud, twisting her hands into fists. "I hate them all!"

She sat there, knowing all the while that she was powerless to change what was so ruthlessly true, and that now life would be a nightmare of being afraid: afraid of Zachary, afraid of the searching of Foxworth's slow, amused eyes, afraid most of all of herself.

5

Taffy Keeling was painting the porch floor when the bright-wheeled buggy stopped at the gate and she saw two people, a man and a girl, coming up the slope toward the house.

"Merciful fathers!" she muttered, scrambling up and pushing a lock of hair out of her eyes, leaving a smudge of brown paint across her nose and a swipe at one corner of her eye. Skirting the wet paint she ran to an open window and called a warning through the screen. "Get beautiful, quick, you gals! Company coming!"

Frances, perched on a stepladder with a half dozen nails between her teeth, was trying to anchor a bracket to hold a wooden curtain pole. She had on a faded calico dress, her head was tied in a towel turban, her black stockings were plainly visible beneath the too-short skirt.

"Oh, golly!" she cried in consternation. "Head them off, Taffy. I'm a sight."

"What do you think I am?" wailed Taffy. "France, it's that Matson man that you met on the boat and there's a girl with him. I'm going to run."

"Don't you dare!" Frances scrambled off the ladder. "Do something! Give me time to wash my face at least."

"How about my face?" moaned Taffy. Then Frances heard her company voice lifted in polite greeting. "Oh, how do you do? Sorry I can't ask you in this way. I've painted in front of the door. If you'll just go around to the river side—that's the front door really—"

Frances snatched off the towel, gave her hair a frantic dab and poked the pins in tighter. She shrugged her belt into place, tucked in a wild lock, looked despairingly at her grimy hands and went through the hall. At the opposite door she stopped and put her head in at the paneled room that had been her grandfather's library.

44

"Some people are here, Mama," she whispered. "I'll go—and give you time to change."

Lydia, on her knees polishing andirons, looked up in dismay.

"Why in the world don't people give us time to get settled before they come calling!" she complained. "I can't get dressed up now, Francie, I simply can't. Everything is wrinkled and I haven't time to press anything—"

"Hurry!" Frances ignored her protests. "They're coming in the front door now."

She heard a girl's voice lilting brightly in the parlor. "Oh, how lovely! I always did want to see the inside of this house."

Taffy was doing the honors with a face like a clown and a glare of fury in her eyes when Frances came in.

"My sister Frances. You've met Mr. Matson, France. Now if you'll excuse me—we're in an awful mess and so little help—"

Taffy fled, and Wylie Matson, very natty in a light-gray suit and holding a straw hat in his hand, shook hands with Frances.

"Glad to see you again, Miss Keeling. This is my sister Bliss."

The girl was very young and fluffy, in a frock of blue with a wide blue hat with huge pompons of maline upon it and a bow of maline under her chin. She had the cleanest, most beautiful yellow hair Frances had ever seen; her white shoes were snowy and she wore white gloves.

"I won't shake hands." Frances managed a rueful laugh. "I'm much too dirty, but the chairs are clean. Will you sit down? My mother will be here presently."

"I was just admiring everything," Bliss Matson babbled. "This house is so much nicer inside than I had ever imagined. We used to think it was haunted when we were all growing up."

"It was," Frances agreed; "by cobwebs and mice and bushels of ancient dust. Of course everything we brought with us was packed in straw or nailed up in boxes. Getting things in order has been a slow business."

"You seem to have succeeded mighty well," Wylie approved the room.

Thank goodness, at least this room was finished, Frances was thinking. The carpet was down and the old gold-medallioned wallpaper wiped off carefully with wads of stale bread. Mama's plush curtains had been too short, but by skillful draping they had been made to look right; and Grandmother's blue plush sofa was brushed and the old secretary polished to a gleam.

"Such lovely old things!" Bliss Matson studied the gilt-framed mirror and Grandfather Taft's portrait in its massive gold frame. "And look, Wylie, you can see the river!"

"We especially enjoy looking at the river." Frances tucked a smudge on her dress under a fold and out of sight. "The view is best from the dining room. We're turning that room into a kitchen, however, and it's full of barrels of china and things we haven't found a home for yet."

"But isn't it fun!" Bliss exclaimed. "I do wish we could have fixed up an old house. Papa built a new brick one though, and he's awfully proud of it. Of course we like it, too—"

"We lived twenty-five years in an old house," her brother reminded her. "You didn't like it very well then, Sis."

"A horrible, shabby old place! You've no idea! Walls sealed up with wood and cracks in the floors and the wind simply shrieked through the place when it stormed and sometimes snow drifted in under the windows."

"Do you have bad storms here?" Frances asked. "My mother is timid in storms."

"Hatteras, as you may have heard, Miss Keeling," Wylie said a trifle pompously, "is the old home of half the storms in the world. Your great-grandfather made a fortune salvaging wrecks that were blown into the Sound, in the old days."

"I wish he'd kept a little more of it," laughed Frances.

"Bliss, the Keelings are busy," Wylie went on, still in his courtroom manner. "Hadn't you better deliver your message and we'll be on our way?"

"Oh, yes. I was so excited over seeing your house that I almost forgot what I came for." Bliss got to her feet, her eyes shining. "We're having a party on Friday night. We want you to come, you and your sister—she didn't tell us her name—"

"Her name is Henrietta, but she's always been called Taffy."

"Taffy—how terribly cunning! It suits her, doesn't it, with that hair? You will come, won't you? It's at eight and we're asking all the young people so you can meet everybody and make friends."

"I'll speak to my mother," Frances hesitated. "We haven't

been out at night yet. We have to drive and the road's quite lonely."

"Oh, but Wylie will come for you, won't you, Wylie? And he'll see that you get home safely, too. You must come, we'll be fearfully disappointed if you don't. Everyone is so excited at having some new girls in town. Then when you're really settled you must give a party, too! This house was just made for parties, though my father says he never remembers any being given here. You could have colored lanterns out there—they'd be reflected in the river—"

"I'll be delighted to see that you arrive and get home safely, Miss Keeling," Wylie interrupted his sister's expostulations. "Bliss has her heart set on your coming. Come along, Bliss, we must go now."

"Won't you wait and see my mother? She should be down in a few minutes."

"Some other time." He bowed a bit elaborately. "We were inconsiderate, dropping in like this without notice. Then, unless I hear from you to the contrary, Miss Keeling, I'll call for you on Friday a little before seven?"

"But I don't know how we would get word to you. We might not be going into town, and we don't know where you live."

"It's the big brick house where this road turns off, just by the cemetery," Bliss said. "You can't miss it; it's the only new house in town. And oh, I'll tell you! I'll send Ren—that's our brother Renwick. I'll send him up here on Thursday. He's always going up and down the river in that silly old boat of his and he can stop and bring us word—but do please come! We do want you, really!"

"I hope we may. We'll try to arrange it. Good-by—and thank you for the invitation."

When they were gone Taffy popped out of the dining room, still in her disheveled state.

"A gushy gal, if I ever saw one!" she said with young scorn. "That was a cute hat though. Maybe I could fix up my leghorn with some fluffy stuff like that—if I had some fluffy stuff!"

"That's not your type, Taffy. With your high color and your cute little nose you'd be extinguished if you turned fluffy. You'll always have to be smart and wear rather severe, extreme clothes and hats. A sailor tilted insolently over one eye would suit you better."

"How do *you* know about types? She was quite naïve though, wasn't she? Baby-blue eyes and a brain to match. Lord knows I'd welcome a chance to be chic and arrogant, but how can I do it with your old organdy shortened and patched up and that hat. And we won't dare spend any money for ages, you know that."

"I don't know how we ought to look, Taffy. Heaven knows I've never had much chance to learn whether I was right or not, but it's just a feeling I have. We're invited to a party Friday night. Wylie Matson says he'll come for us and bring us home."

"A party? Do you suppose Mama will let us go? She won't. She'd be afraid we might look at a Cavitt. And what would we wear?"

"We can talk to Mama—after all, we are going to live here and we can't go around all the rest of our lives elaborately avoiding the Cavitts. Probably they'll take care of that by avoiding us, anyway. We'll have to contrive some clothes. If you'll help me get the sewing machine uncrated maybe we can remodel something for you. Taffy, you look horrible! Go and wash your face before we talk to Mama."

"What's the use? I'm going to finish the porch. France, that blond behemoth was taken with you. You weren't exactly a thing of beauty either, but I could see him beam. Mama scooted upstairs a little while ago. I think she's up there hiding."

They found Lydia sitting on the edge of her bed in her high boned corset, her ruffled drawers drawn up over her knees, a stocking stretched over one hand. Her face was hot, seamy and unhappy.

"I started to change," she sighed, "then I happened to look out the window and saw them leaving. Who were they? They were awfully dressed up. There's a little hole in this heel— I've got to darn it before it gets any bigger—"

"They were Matsons," Taffy said. "Mr. Wylie Matson and his sister Bliss. The name suits her. She has tapioca for brains and she burbles. They came to invite us to a party."

"Matsons?" Lydia almost squeaked. "When I lived here the

Matsons were nobody at all. Croff Matson was a big good-for-nothing boy. He must have been about twenty then, but all he did was hang around the wharf and work on tobacco barges. Their father kept a saloon and they had a daughter about my age who was the tackiest girl in school."

"From being nobody they have obviously become somebody," Frances remarked. "They have the only new house in town and Wylie's a lawyer who makes trips to Washington. I met him on the boat. They own that tobacco place with the big sign on top. Wylie offered to come for us and fetch us home. I think we should go, Mama."

"But nobody ever knew the Matsons," insisted Lydia. "They were not accepted anywhere. If any Matson had ever come to this house Amanda would have sent him around to the back door. That girl—Cleo, her name was—ran off with somebody. She couldn't have been more than sixteen. She had yellow hair, too—and she could have been kind of pretty in a common way, but she never took any pains with herself."

"Times change in thirty years, Mama," Taffy reminded her. "We weren't terribly important in Baltimore, you may remember. Probably our Taft relatives were a little ashamed of us. Anyway Uncle Horace's wife never came to call and only sent us stingy little notes at Christmas."

"Your father," said Lydia severely, "never had the position in Grandpa's establishment that his rearing and intelligence deserved. He was never a forceful man, but of course his bad health was to blame for that. But down here we're Nearys—and the Nearys were always people of consequence."

Frances dropped into the little maple rocker that for as long as she could remember had always stood beside her mother's bed.

"It occurs to me, Mama, that it's a trifle silly to be proud of your ancestors. I'd rather let my ancestors be proud of me. If the Matsons have made themselves people who are respected from such a dreary beginning, that's to their credit, don't you think?"

"Mama always said it was very unkind to encourage climbers," stated Lydia smugly. "She believed in blood and that people are born to their proper station."

"All of which failed to work in our case," Taffy argued. "We may have been born to a proud station but we haven't stuck there. The idea is undemocratic anyway and I don't like it much. I think I want to go to the Matsons' party, if I can cobble up any clothes that won't disgrace the elegance of my ancestors."

"I intend to go," announced Frances with a firmness that surprised her self more than anyone.

Lydia drew her mouth in at the corners, obviously offended. "Of course I can't forbid you, Frances. You're of age. But I shan't allow Henrietta to go and mingle with people whom I feel are entirely unsuitable!"

"Oh, Mama, don't be such a stuffy prig!" stormed Taffy. "You talk as though we were rich as Jay Gould, and queens to boot! It's my opinion we should be pleased to have anybody down here notice us. If France goes to this party, I'm going too. If it hurts your feelings I'm sorry, but personally I think you're being obstinate and silly."

"Taffy, please let me discuss this calmly with Mama," begged Frances as Lydia's eyes began to brim and her chin to quiver.

"Don't bother," she cried, "don't bother about me at all just because I'm your mother. I'm old-fashioned and stupid and a prig because I want you to know the sort of people your background entitles you to know." Lydia gulped on a sob and gathered up a corner of the counterpane to wipe her eyes. "Oh, go away!" she wailed as Frances essayed to comfort her. "Leave me alone! Nobody cares what I think."

"Oh, Mama," Frances moved away stiffly, "don't make us believe you're like that! Taffy lost her temper, but of course you'll let her go to the party. After all, we're your daughters. We should have enough discernment to know whether people are worth knowing or not. You worried so much for fear we'd be lonely here and now when we do have a chance to meet people you raise unfounded objections."

"I know the Matsons. What do you know about them? Except that from somewhere they've been able to get money enough to buy some fancy clothes?"

"I know that Wylie went to the University, so they certainly must have improved their way of life if they can send their children to college."

"Anybody can go to college—anybody with money."

Frances shrugged wearily. "Let's end this useless argument and go down and have supper. Taffy, you could shorten my old yellow dress and take it in at the waist and it would do for you. Maybe Mama would lend you her topaz pendant."

"I could take out the yoke. That would make it look more like an evening dress." Taffy recovered with alacrity. "Mama, I'm sorry I was mean. Dry your eyes now and help me plan how to be beautiful so we can knock all the other gals dead."

Lydia scrubbed her nose with the grimy handkerchief Taffy offered, and then looked down at herself aghast.

"My goodness—me sitting here all undressed! Hand me my petticoat, Taffy, and my shoes. How can you go to a party with no good white slippers, either of you? I don't suppose you could buy a pair in this town. There's only that little general store—"

Frances said, "I'll put the kettle on," thinking that her mother was an adorable child, variable, notionable, easily influenced. "I wish you were going to the party, Mama," she added impulsively.

Lydia sniffed audibly. "I don't think I could bring myself to be polite to the Matsons."

Taffy shrieked with laughter. "Mama, you're precious! You should have seen that big blond, Wylie. He was all shaven and shorn and smelled up with bay rum, and his eyes simply ate Francie up!"

"The Matsons I remember weren't so elegant," declared Lydia. "I remember that Cleo—her hair was never washed and it was a clear yellow. They must have had some Norwegian blood somewhere—"

"This girl, Bliss, had hair like butter. Why did I have to have this carroty mop, so curly I can't make it part anywhere? Why couldn't I have been born soft and cute, or else tall and stately like France?"

"My heavens, am I stately? You flatter me, Taffy."

"Well, you can be kind of handsome when you fix yourself

up. Right now, even, with your placket more or less perilously fastened, you look impressive."

Frances made a swift, dismayed snatch rearward. "I hope it didn't gap when they were here. But don't get any silly ideas about Wylie Matson, either of you. He may be very fine-looking, but he doesn't impress me at all."

"You like 'em dark and mysterious, don't you, Francie?" teased Taffy. "All right, all right, go and cook supper. I'm going to paint as long as I can see."

Frances went out quickly, wondering if that had been a look of suspicion that she had caught in her mother's following eyes. Whatever Lydia was thinking was always reflected instantly in her good, plump face, her small and rather shallow eyes. Her moods were as fluid and changeable as the water that gulped into the kettle whenever the pump handle went down.

Frances wondered if her own rather lax complacency about life was the result of the ease with which she and Taffy had always been able to manage their mother? If ever she encountered a strong character, she wondered, would she be mistress of the situation? Too well she knew that whatever metal she might have in her had never been tried. She had been able to keep Cliff Houchins tractable, but that had not been a test. Cliff had been a little in love with her, but there had been no fire or passion in the affair, and on her part she knew now that there had been little besides a thin feeling of satisfaction that she had been able to interest a man in herself, and a liking that she had never been able to warm into real affection.

Except for Cliff and her gentle father she had known few men, and no red-blooded ones at all. A little twinge of trepidation went over her, and she let the kettle run over and splash on her wrists before she stopped pumping. She bumped the kettle down in the improvised kitchen, and then remembering that she could be stately, went about mending the fire with graceful, studied gestures. For no reason at all the air of the kitchen was suddenly tinctured with something high and heady that defeated the musty atmosphere of the old house. There was impending drama in it, and a faint touch of panic.

What would she do with life when she met it?

Regal—that was Taffy's word. To be regal was to be in command.

She looked out across the river, suddenly, and saw a white sail moving there slowly, like a wedge of silver in the setting sun.

"Someday you will look at me, Mr. Foxworth Cavitt!" she said aloud. "Someday you will really see me!"

6

Dobbs, Amanda's shambling, middle-aged son, had attached himself to the Keelings. He appeared one morning, shuffling in from the road, asked for a scythe and a rake and when tools could not be found rummaged a dusty clutter in the barn till he located what he wanted.

"Knowed them things was there all the time," he muttered, as he set about clearing the thorny thicket that submerged the marble angel. "Mis' Em'ly, she wouldn't like it, all this yere trash growed up around this yere stone woman," he explained when at noon he came back and accepted the plate of food Frances offered him. "Mis' Em'ly, she wanted everything kep' good and pretty. I got to stay 'round here till I git Mis' Em'ly's place fixed up."

Touched by his devotion to his Mis' Em'ly, who had been her own mother, Lydia had let him stay on, though he was obviously weak-witted and slightly palsied, dragging one foot and lurching as he moved. She gave him a blanket to make himself a pallet in the barn and a dollar now and then, both of which Dobbs received with effusive gratitude.

"I knowed Mis' Em'ly's chillun ain't goin' to let ole Dobbs starve," he declared often.

"Do you think it's safe, Mama, letting him sleep out there?" Frances worried. "He isn't quite right in his head. Suppose he stole the horse or something."

"Dobbs? Good gracious, he grew up on this place! He was always underfoot in the kitchen and my mother made him tend her flowers and wash off the porches. He's just my age and he was never very bright, but he wouldn't harm a hair of our heads or take anything that belonged on the place."

Dobbs tended the fat mare and polished the buggy with loving care, and on Thursday he harnessed the mare for Taffy, who was being sent to town to try to find white shoes for the party.

As she invariably did, when it was obvious she could not prevail, Lydia had done an enthusiastic about-face concerning the Matson party. She had sewed all one day, remodeling a yellow dress for Taffy, and she had even agreed that Taffy should go to town alone if she would promise to whip the mare if she met any strangers.

"You let me go alone to meet the boat," Taffy argued. "As though whipping would do that creature any good! She just wiggles her ears and I think she grins. Now write down everything you want, Mama, for heaven's sake, so you won't have to chase me all the way to the gate and holler."

"Well, if you should meet a man you hold to that whip, Taffy," insisted Lydia, who had always been too inhibited to disclose to her daughters that they were female, and could not put into words the dangers that she imagined might befall them.

"They're our woods. If I meet anybody trespassing I'll wrap the lash around their necks."

"Don't forget to bring back a bottle of bluing. I want to stretch the dining-room curtains tomorrow. I declare, I don't know if I'll ever get this house the way I want it to be!"

Taffy drove away, her mother's voice trailing after her like pale, anxious smoke. The mare had been in the barn for a week and she was restive and eager. She trotted lightly down the rutty road to the gate, the buggy bouncing and Taffy sitting stiffly on the edge of the seat, gripping the reins in what she was sure was the best horse-show manner, hoping her hat would stick on and the hair that anchored it would not go sliding down her back.

She did not see the man who sat under the big gum tree a little way along the road till the mare stopped abruptly, shied a little, shivered and stood still while the man got to his feet. Taffy slashed with the whip but the animal did not move. The stranger bowed and smiled amiably. He had a vaguely familiar look, but Taffy was certain she had never seen him before.

"No use beating her," he remonstrated, "she knows me. I raised her." He patted the mare's neck and she twitched her ears in a sort of coquettish ecstasy, turning her lips to nuzzle his hand. "Hello, Chloe, how are you?" He pulled one ear down and blew into it gently. "You remember me, don't you?"

"Her name is Daisy," Taffy said coldly. "Will you get away and let me go, please? I have errands to do in town."

"Her name is Chloe," he insisted, ignoring the icy fury faintly tinged with panic in her voice. "She used to follow me everywhere. Look—I'll show you. Come along, Chloe."

He walked a few paces down the road and the mare followed, biting playfully at his arm and shoulder, stopping when he stopped. Taffy had gotten over her first sharp fright but she was still angry. After all, the man was good-looking and his clothes were not those of a vagabond or highwayman.

"Thank you, that was very interesting," she remarked when the mare stopped again. "Now if you will go about your own affairs, please, I should like to go to town." She gave the reins a jerk. "Get up, Daisy!"

"Call her Chloe and she'll travel." He came near to the buggy and there was nothing evil or terrifying in his face, only a lazy good humor. "No self-respecting horse could possibly like being called anything so infantile and idiotic as Daisy! You're one of the Keelings, I suppose? You wouldn't let me drive her to town for you, of course?"

"I certainly wouldn't! I don't talk to strangers and I'm in a hurry. Will you stand aside, or must I get nasty about it?"

"I'll be delighted." He moved a little but still kept one hand on the wheel. "Since you won't be neighborly enough to give a very tired man a lift to town, there's nothing else for me to do. It would be entirely possible for me to stop being a stranger, you know. I'm Zachary Cavitt and I'm very safely married. I have no designs on thee, you peppery, red-headed damsel. My only thought at the moment is that I have two very weary, aching feet. I've walked a long way and the day is warm, as you may have noticed." There was a gay sort of mockery in his voice and Taffy felt her fingers tingle with an odd excitement.

"So you're a Cavitt?" she said dryly. "I might have known."

He was darker than the Cavitt who had helped them with

the horse. He was obviously as arrogant, but he was more amiable and relaxed about it.

"I'm a Cavitt," he repeated. "You said that exactly as you might have said 'So you're the devil?'—which shows that you have been reared on suspicion from the cradle. Who told you all Cavitts wear horns?"

"My mother," answered Taffy frankly. "She'd have a fit if I let a Cavitt ride with me but—all right, all right, you can ride but you're not going to drive. And I'm not a child, Mr. Cavitt. I'm grown and I can take adequate care of myself." She moved over a little on the seat, feeling out her powers, hoping she could think of clever, scornful things to say and think of them right away, not after she got home.

"I thank you very much, Miss Keeling." He walked around the buggy gravely and got in, sitting as far away from her as possible.

"Get up, Daisy!" Taffy flicked the whip. The mare wiggled an ear questioningly.

"Down the road, Chloe!" ordered Zachary Cavitt.

Instantly the animal swung into motion, so abruptly that Taffy almost lost her hat.

"Now you've ruined her!" she stormed. "She won't mind me at all."

"Oh, yes she will, if you call her by her name. And don't feed her so much. She's far too fat for an elderly lady."

"The man Mama got her from said she was six years old."

"When I was ten she was three years old. My father bought her for me then. Now I'm thirty-one. Figure it out for yourself." He did not look at her. He had a little scrap of white paper in his fingers, and from his pocket he took a bit of wood with a groove in it. He laid the paper in the groove, shook a bit of tobacco into it from a sack, sat looking at it and turning it in his fingers. "Stop her a minute," he said bluntly.

"I will not! What for?" demanded Taffy.

But Chloe-Daisy had heard the word "stop." She stopped of her own accord, sagging on one hip.

"Look." He held up the wood and paper. "If you were going to roll this into a small, perfect cylinder which way would you move your hand? See, you're going to do it with your flat palm, the fingers turned a little back, like this—"

"I wouldn't roll it at all," balked Taffy. "That's tobacco, isn't it? I wouldn't touch it for anything."

"But, without contaminating your maiden soul, you could indicate to me just how you'd go about pushing this paper into a roll, if you were going to roll it, couldn't you? This is business. This is important."

"There wouldn't be any earthly reason why I'd ever be going to roll it! If I did roll it, it would turn out to be a cigarette, and every one of them is a nail in somebody's coffin!" said Taffy piously.

"Pretend for a minute that you're black as the ace of spades, you've got three kids at home—and your home is a leaning plank cabin with no glass windows and a leaky roof. There's nothing to eat in your house except one rancid meat rind and a spoonful of meal and your kids are hungry. If you roll these things all day you can make enough money to buy a poke of grits and a little bit of lard, and then if you're lucky enough to snag a fish after you get through work you can eat and the kids can eat. That is, if it's a big enough fish. Do you have any imagination at all?"

She had too much, Taffy was certain. The trouble was that Mama hadn't any at all, and little sense of humor. She was the most literal person in the known world, and she wouldn't like any of this. Nevertheless Taffy laid her hand flat on the white paper, and tried to coax it to roll with no success.

"It can't be done with the palm of your hand. You'd have to use your fingers," she stated. "Get up, Chloe! Get up, this minute!"

Chloe resumed her sluggish trot. Sand spun from the wheels and rattled like rain on the leather mudguards of the buggy. The woods smelled rich and deep and moist, and lusciously of something blooming. Zachary Cavitt tossed the paper into the road, put the wooden cylinder again into his pocket.

"I've walked miles, turning this idea over in my head," he said. "We have to get away from fingers. They moisten them in their mouths, and that would be unsanitary. Yet I wouldn't consider making a machine-made cigarette; any more than I'd consider turning out a product like Mr. Crofford Matson's Golden Twist chewing tobacco. My idea is a high-quality, more expensive product for a limited and exclusive clientele, with discreet and dignified advertising only in the high-class publications."

"And what do you have besides an idea?" asked practical Taffy. "Not that the whole business isn't repulsive to me. I can't think of anything more revolting to talk about than tobacco, on a nice June day."

"So far I've nothing but the idea, but I'll have more. I'm working on it. Just as soon as I can make Mr. Matson see the light, I'll be ready to develop my plans. And in the form of money, tobacco isn't so revolting. There's going to be big money made in the cigarette business soon. Big money. Already it's underway up there in Durham and Winston, and Richmond has sixty-odd factories right now. Or rather I should say the state of Virginia, though Richmond has the bulk of the business."

"There's money in running a saloon, too," declared Taffy, "and in robbing banks or being a pirate. Tell me something, and don't think I'm impertinent in asking—I'm just intrigued by rumor. Was your great-grandfather a pirate?"

He laughed aloud, good naturedly. "I'd never think you impertinent, Miss Red-Top," he said. "You're as refreshing a person as I've met in many a dull day. Unfortunately, for all the local legend, my poor great-grandfather was only a sea captain and a rover. But great-great-grandfather—now there was a swashbuckler for you! He was a freebooter and a privateer, he owned four big sailing craft and he gave the British a lively time of it in 1813. Of course he might have knocked off a Spanish vessel or two occasionally just to keep his boys happy, but he never got on the wrong side of the law in this country that I ever heard of."

"Did he bury his loot in caves?" Taffy inquired naïvely.

"I wish he had, if he'd left his descendants a map. I could use a well-stocked pirate cave right now, for it's going to take money to get my ideas going."

"Listen," said Taffy abruptly, "the next corner is the cemetery and I don't think I ought to be seen driving into town with you. You'd better walk the rest of the way. How are you going to get home anyway, across the river?"

"I'll catch Fox and go up in his small boat. Not for all the tea in China would I compromise so spirited a young lady as you, Miss Keeling. Whoa, Chloe! This is where old friends part." He sprang over the wheel lightly, landing on the balls of his feet, his white teeth showing in an audacious grin. "Good-by, old sweetheart!" He patted the mare's nose. "Take my young enemy home safely and don't forget me, and if they call you Daisy any more kick the whiffle tree to pieces, Chloe; very small pieces!"

"Get up, Daisy!" ordered Taffy, her chin up.

"Go 'long, Chloe." Zachary spanked the mare's fat rump. "I'll see you again. Thanks for the lift, my dear."

"I'm not your dear, and personally I think you're the most arrogant human being I ever met," Taffy said bluntly as the buggy rolled away.

He tipped his hat and grinned at her, standing back on the sandy path to let her pass. The mare moved on reluctantly, turning her head twice to look back.

"So he thinks he's irresistible to ladies, even lady horses!" sniffed Taffy to herself. But somehow her anger would not return. She felt instead a half-guilty, exhilarating excitement. No man had ever talked to her before as though she were grown up and had brains. The men of her mother's family always brushed her off gently as though she were about ten years old, and the adolescent friends she had left behind in Baltimore dimmed to pimply insignificance when she compared them with Zachary Cavitt. The fact of his being married added some piquancy to the adventure, and she wondered what sort of woman his wife was. A ninny probably. Interesting men with a vague aura of danger about them were always married to ninnies in the books she had read.

It was late afternoon when she got home again and not a hair of the mare's hide was sweated.

"She poked all the way," Taffy grumbled, carefully avoiding any hint of her afternoon experience, "and the only shoes they have are horrible old black things with pointed toes."

"So we go to the party in our old shoes," Frances remarked.

"Well, at least we can clean them up and put new ribbons on the toes."

"Oh, yes," remembered Taffy suddenly at the supper table, "I met the man who raised Daisy. He says she is more than twenty years old and her name was Chloe. She likes that name better, I discovered."

"Then I was cheated!" Lydia exclaimed indignantly. "Four acres of good grassland for a horse more than twenty years old! That man will certainly hear about it from me."

"As soon as I'm of age," Taffy said, "I'm going to sell some of my share of this vast estate and buy me a boat. One with an engine in it. I could have gone down the river and back in an hour. I want a little boat like that one the Cavitts use to go down to the wharf and back every day."

"You couldn't run an engine, and when you got anywhere you'd be all over grease and bilge," remarked Lydia. "I remember what an awful time Amanda used to have with my father's white trousers in summer. There were always awful spots that had to be bleached out with soft soap and turpentine."

"But you said you always went back and forth by boat, Mama," argued Taffy. "Women aren't helpless now as they were when you were young. Well, I'd better have a look at your old slippers, if I have to wear them, France. Maybe I can put whiting on them. I'm not likely to sit on anybody's lap and wipe white streaks on his pant legs."

"Taffy, don't be vulgar!" protested her mother.

"Well, I remember how Papa used to fuss about our white shoes when we were little. He was always going around grumbling and swiping at himself with a whisk broom."

"I'll wash up these dishes," volunteered Lydia. "You see about the shoes, Francie."

"France," Taffy began when they were upstairs, "have you looked across the river? Have you ever seen any women over there?"

"I haven't had time, Taffy. I did glance over one evening but only the old captain was there, sitting on the porch. He was looking at this house through a spyglass, so I got away as fast as I could." Frances was on her knees, rummaging in a trunk, and she looked up with sudden sharpness over her shoulder. "Why? Have you been listening to gossip about the Cavitts?"

"I met the married one—he was walking and he was tired and I gave him a ride. I just wondered what his wife looked like."

"I knew you'd been up to something! You had a glint in your eye. I knew you couldn't possibly have spent all that time driving four miles. Were you out of your mind to do such an indiscreet thing? Girls have had ugly stories started about them for much less. Mama will never let you go to town alone again if she hears about it."

"Mama won't hear about it unless you tattle. Anyway I let him out on the fringes of the metropolis," stated Taffy blithely. "If you are so unwise as to blab, Missy, I might drop a few sidelong remarks about the way you wander to the river window every time that little Cavitt boat comes up from the ferry dock."

"I do not. I look out at the river at all hours of the day because I like looking at it."

"Hm! I'm not blaming you at all. I thought he was fascinating when he pulled the shoe off that horse. The married one is really exciting. He has beautiful manners. Their grandfather wasn't a pirate at all. They did have an ancestor who was a privateer; he fought against the British."

"There's practically no difference. A privateer is licensed by the government to prey on the enemy, but most of them turn pirate anyway. As for Fox Cavitt, Miss Snoopy, his brother may have manners but he hasn't any. He's as agreeable as a glacier," Frances said emphatically, hoping no silly red was running up the back of her neck while her face was hidden by the lid of the trunk. "Do you want bows on the toes of these slippers?" she asked abruptly.

"Lord, no! It would be tacky as anything. I've had to fight with Mama every inch to keep her from sticking something frilly and fussy on my dress. The other Cavitt is dark, too. His hair grows down in front of his ears a little and he has a cute, devilish little mustache. All he talked about was the mare—and going into the tobacco business. He raised the mare. She knew him and she wouldn't move till he got into the buggy, that's why I had to let him ride," Taffy explained a trifle lamely.

"Suppose one of us is driving into town someday with Mama and Daisy sees him again. That would certainly be embarrassing."

"I'm going to call her Chloe. Maybe she hates Daisy as much as I hate Henrietta. If one of us had to be named after sour old Grandpa Taft, why couldn't it have been you?"

"Because I had to be named after Grandpa's wife," Frances said. "Look, Taffy—there comes a boy up from the river."

Taffy flew to the window. "Nobody I ever saw before. Skinny and small and blond. Oh, it must be that Matson brother who was coming today to find out if we could go to the party. I'll run down and head off Mama."

Renwick Matson, Taffy decided a half hour later, showed promise of turning into a nuisance. He was eager, he was impressed, he wanted a promise of half her dances at the Matson party. He was slightly bucktoothed and not at all attractive like his brother Wylie. Also his fingers were stained dark to the palms, the nails almost entirely black.

"Tobacco," he said when he saw her looking at them. "I work with my father in the factory."

He was grateful that his feet were well covered, knowing that they were dyed black, too. On shorthanded days often he had to get into the sweetening vats with the Negro boys and trample the sticky mixture of molasses, licorice and deertongue into the shredded tobacco that would later be pressed into black, sweet plugs. His father was always talking about buying an Adams machine, but he'd never gotten around to it, Renwick knew, because of Croff Matson's dislike of using borrowed money.

"You weren't very nice to that young man, Taffy," Lydia remarked when Renwick had gone back to his boat. "Not that I care much for Matsons, but a lady is always polite to her inferiors."

"He smelled sweet and nasty," Taffy sniffed. "He works in that tobacco place of his father's. There is money in tobacco though, they say. Didn't your family ever grow any, Mama?"

Lydia snorted elegantly. "Goodness no! Tobacco has always been a poor-folksy business in North Carolina. Negroes worked in it and some white people, but never anyone who was at all genteel."

"I'd grow anything that would bring in some money. I'd even grow opium," declared Taffy, "or anything that would make enough money so I could go to a city and buy a whole trunkful of gorgeous clothes!"

She wondered if Mrs. Zachary Cavitt would appear at the Matson party? Mrs. Cavitt would have on something limp and pink and sappy, Taffy was willing to predict. She'd sit around looking adoringly at Zachary, no doubt, and never know— poor thing—that what he really admired was a spirited woman.

7

Tulia Cavitt duly appeared at the Matson party, but there was nothing limp or naïve about her.

Taffy, putting on city airs and a bright pose of sophistication slightly tinged with condescension, had been enjoying herself, even though the made-over dress did bunch a little exasperatingly in the back. She had danced two waltzes with the Matson brothers and done a rollicking square dance with their father, bluff, sandy Croff Matson, whom Taffy liked immediately.

Croff jigged and pounded his heels and swung Taffy off her feet until his wife, a lean, colorless woman protested that the new acetylene chandeliers were swaying perilously. Taffy was getting her breath in a small chair against the parlor wall, surveying the ruin of her carefully whitened slippers, when a sort of hush fell over the roomful of perspiring, fanning, laughing young people. Tulia Cavitt was making an entrance.

She stood on the threshold, smiling mechanically, looking as exotic and strange as a crested macaw in an assembly of sleek young pullets. Her dress was bright green satin cut with a daring line, tight over her slim body as the calyx of a flower, flaring slightly at the hem to reveal gold slippers with rhinestone buckles. Her black hair was brushed back smoothly, revealing her small ears where great hoops of rhinestones hung. She wore five bracelets and instantly every girl who had been proud of her one gold circlet looked down at it in betrayed dismay.

Zachary followed his wife, the white linen suit he wore making his darkness even darker. He looked like an East Indian prince, Taffy thought; he looked wonderful and wicked and handsome as everything! When little Mrs. Matson bustled up he bowed over her hand gallantly, but Taffy saw the amused line of mockery around his mouth, the impish quirk of his brow as he grinned across the room at her. As soon as the round of introductions had ended he brought a chair boldly and dropped down beside Taffy, lighting a cigarette, ignoring Mrs. Matson's shocked expression.

"Well, Red-Top," he said, "are you enjoying yourself among us yokels?"

"I was till now," retorted Taffy pertly. "You've been away a long time, haven't you? You've forgotten that gentlemen never smoke in parlors."

"How lucky for me that I'm not a gentleman," he drawled. "What do you think of my gal Tulia?"

"She's very—handsome." Taffy had almost said "showy" but caught herself in time. Tulia was dancing with Wylie, her litheness a foil for his big bulk. Wylie was light on his feet as so many heavy men are, and people drew back, one couple after another, to give the pair the floor. "Why aren't you dancing with her yourself?" asked Taffy.

"The host has the prior claim. Anyway I'm not very good at that jiggy kind of thing." He looked around for a place to deposit the half-smoked cigarette, found none and tossed it into the fireplace that had been decorated with a tall jug of fern. "Waltzes are more my style. Slow enough for an old man. Will you waltz with me if they play one presently?"

"I think not," said Taffy. "After all, you are a married man."

"A stickler, eh? A little prude, out here in the bushes! Your eyes don't have that look at all."

"What look do they have?" Taffy was intrigued, though she was trying to remember that Mama expected her to be a lady.

"The rebel look. Hat-over-the-windmill sort of thing. As though you'd throw away the book if it interfered with having fun."

"I'm new here," she reminded him. "I don't think I should make myself conspicuous."

"Am I conspicuous?"

"Aren't you?" She got up and moved away, going into the dining room where Frances was drinking punch with a group of girls. The dining room was very modern, as Bliss Matson was assuring them. Everything was in the new mission style, the walls paneled with burlap stained a dark green, the furniture all square-cut and stained green too, with dark leather and copper nails on the seats. An ornate plate rack just above their heads held a half dozen plates painted with fish, fruit and flowers, and two beer steins stamped as souvenirs of the Chicago World's Fair.

Her mother, Bliss was explaining, was distressed by the steins, but Pa was awfully proud of them because he'd won them in a shooting gallery. The other girls listened absently, their eyes straying to the other room.

"Who's she dancing with now?" one whispered.

"Still with Wylie. Why on earth doesn't Ernestine stop playing that silly tune? Everybody's sick of watching her perform."

"Oh, Wylie's showing off," remarked Bliss. "He always does. Every time he comes back from Washington he's insufferable for weeks."

"That dress may be smart and expensive," mused a thin girl, dipping another cup of punch, "but it makes her look fast just the same."

"The Paris look, my dear!"

"Did she buy it in Paris?" Taffy inquired innocently.

"Zach married her over there, hadn't you heard? He went over on a cattle boat or something and she was studying art. They say her father and mother are divorced and in my opinion she's *years* older than Zach."

"Wrong guess, sister," drawled a slow voice behind them.

The group all jumped and squealed. "Fox Cavitt! You sneaky thing! Creeping around listening at keyholes!"

"No keyholes." He walked past them without looking back and Frances felt an odd tingle in her skin and prayed that no hot blush was running over her face. Like his brother, Fox wore a white suit and a bright blue tie pinned with a pair of gold cavalry sabers. He moved up to the punch table. "That stuff wet?" he asked.

Frances dipped a cup quickly and handed it to him. He drank it in two gulps, muttered thanks, walked away. Taffy gave Frances' arm a pinch.

"If he asks you to dance, grab him," she whispered.

"I will not! Anyway he won't ask me."

"He might. Don't be an idiot, just for some old family row that happened years before we were born. He's grand-looking, isn't he? I'm going to dance with him if I can possibly fix it," Taffy declared. "Oh, here comes that sticky Matson boy! Steer him away from me, Francie, please!"

But there was no diverting Renwick Matson. He had Taffy's arm before she could slip away and Frances saw her put on her bright social face, though her mouth was a trifle set. New sets for a square dance were being formed in both rooms, and the dark, older Cavitt son came heading in Frances' direction. She had not been introduced, but he held out a hand to her boldly.

"I'm Zach Cavitt. Would you care to romp through one of these frolics with me, Miss Keeling?"

"Thank you—" Frances faltered uncertainly—"I think I promised someone—oh, yes—excuse me." She darted quickly through a side door and found herself on an unlighted porch where couples sat whispering in the swing or on cushions on the steps. She walked past them quickly, murmuring apologies, and out to the open lawn. An ornate iron bench between two tall shrubs was unoccupied and she sat down on it, pressing her hot cheeks with cold palms.

Why was she so provincial, so inhibited? She told herself that she was being loyal to Mama, that it would be a concession, a surrender of family pride to dance with a Cavitt, but she knew in her honest heart that she had not really enjoyed dancing with anyone. Some flinching, maiden thing in her had winced away from the clasp of a man's arm around her waist, the touch of warm hands even in the impersonal attitude of the waltz. Wylie Matson's hands had been hot and possessive, his breath on her hair had made a curious unease run over her, the nearness of his big lusty body had been as disturbing as a violation.

Was this stupid diffidence going to cramp her forever, doom her to frigid loneliness and the unfulfilled emptiness of spinsterhood? Lydia, as fearful of realities and plain speech as a nun, oppressed by the certainty that sex must never be discussed except in vague hints and inferences, had done little to prepare her daughters for living. All men, possibly excepting

Papa and Uncle Horace, in Lydia's mind were potential seducers, deceivers and adventurers. Frances had been reared on warnings, never quite clear and therefore twice as ominous. What she knew she had learned from other girls, from books read in secret, and from Taffy's crowd who, though only a few years younger, were ten times more worldly-wise and informed than she.

Taffy would dance with the Cavitts unabashed, if opportunity came, and brag about it. Taffy could parry bright conversation with any man and hold her own with a young, gay, inoffensive impudence. None of the young men at this party were especially attractive or exciting, yet Frances had seen already how their eyes followed Taffy. Taffy would have a dozen beaux before the summer ended, she would care little for any of them but she would enjoy herself.

Why am I such a silly fool, Frances pondered? She must overcome this supersensitiveness herself, and the thing to do at this moment was to go straight back into that house and begin. She had to learn to achieve ease of manner with men, something she'd never been able to do, not even with Cliff Houchins. Always there had been the intruding rigidity, the unconscious shrinking. She tried to get herself off the bench, with its uncomfortable iron curlicues prodding her spine, but before she could move a white shape came out of the shadows and dropped down beside her.

"Don't get up and run," said Fox Cavitt brusquely. "You're hiding out here and so am I."

"I'm not hiding," declared Frances, edging away a few inches. "It was very hot in there. I came out to get cool."

"The first time I saw you," he remarked in the same remote tone, "I knew you were like me."

"How am I like you?" she demanded, startled out of her stiffness.

"Lonely. And you don't like to be touched. You don't want people intruding into your little private world."

"You know a great deal about me, don't you?" she asked hoarsely, furious because her heart was scudding.

"I know that you're afraid of Cavitts," he answered.

"And why should I be afraid of the Cavitts?"

He did not move. He made no presumptuous gestures. He merely sat still, looking off into the dark sky, his attitude indicating that whether she ran away or stayed to listen was a matter of no concern.

"You answer that," he said. "Even the poor old Captain. That day on my boat you looked as though Wylie was trying to feed you to a crocodile."

"But—my grandfather—he was the one—your father I mean," she floundered in confusion, feeling that she was trying to justify something profoundly silly, glad that he could not see her face.

He let the silence stretch a little. "I know. I was raised on that funny story too," he said at last.

"It wasn't funny!" she flared. "People were killed. Numbers of people. My grandfather was blown up and his body wasn't found for days and then no one could look at it."

"A couple of hotheaded old boys decided to show off." He dismissed the legendary tragedy. "What has that got to do with our generation?"

"They belonged to us. They were our family!"

"You don't pick your family. You put up with what you get. Would you have picked out old Captain Neary for a grandfather if you'd been consulted?"

"How do I know whether I would or not? He died years before I was born."

"You can bury your dead. You don't have to let them mix up your life for you."

"I'm not letting anyone mix up my life."

He leaned back and folded his arms. "Why don't we sit out here in the dark and tell each other the truth?" he asked abruptly.

"I'm sure I don't know what you mean by the truth," argued Frances, still a bit hoarsely because her throat kept cramping. "I don't know you very well, and I don't know why I sit here at all and let you talk to me like this."

"The truth," he went on obliviously, "is that neither of us likes people very well. So we sit out here and make weighty speeches while other people are having fun."

"I haven't heard any weighty speeches yet."

"Have I wasted all my ponderous words of wisdom? There are two friendly things in this world, did you know that? The sky and the water. They're considerate, too. They respect your mood and never intrude with a lot of annoying conversation."

"Why don't you go inside and have fun?" Frances inquired. "I'm sure I'm not detaining you."

"You *are* detaining me. You're a puzzle of a girl and puzzles intrigue me. You have possibilities, and I like to probe those too. You have spirit and I like spirit. I'm a Cavitt, but I'm not a fighting Cavitt."

"You went to war," Frances reminded him, letting herself soften a little. This had been the vague, stifled dream that had lingered with her these last days, that someday he would seek her out, that she would learn what lay behind the still, guarded darkness of his eyes. She had nòt let herself grow maudlin over the dream, but it had persisted, locked deep in her mind; an unrest, a question, an unvoiced wish. Now it had happened, and still her silly shyness made her prickly. She battled it valiantly, tightening her fingers into fists, swallowing the lump in her throat.

"That was a dare," he said. "I dared myself to have enough gumption to go out and fight. Anyway, I learned to ride a horse."

"What was it like in Cuba? Was it interesting?"

"Interesting if you call flies interesting. And heat and bad smells and sleeping on a thin blanket on hard ground. Also being shot at. At least I found out I wasn't afraid. That was something I had to find out. But now I don't seem to be able to fight any more. I'm letting life go by because I can't fight for what I want."

He has never talked like this before, Frances was telling herself with a little thrill of exultation. He's talking to me and saying things he's never said to anyone.

"What do you want?" she prompted gently.

He leaned forward, his elbows on his knees. There was a boyishness, an engaging youngness about him as he sat there; it stirred the maternal in her and made her eyelids sting.

"I'll tell you what I want," he said harshly. "I want to scuttle that old ferryboat and sink her in the deepest hole in Pamlico

Sound. Then I want to go out and see what men are doing—big things, new things—in chemistry, in electricity, in internal-combustion engines! Automobiles. They're going to change the world."

"They haven't been very successful as yet," she remarked. "There are a few in Baltimore. They're always breaking down and being pulled in by horses."

"They will be successful. A whole new world is opening up and I'm stuck up in the wheelhouse of a rotting old boat—because I'm not a fighting Cavitt."

"What you mean is that you can't fight your old father," Frances remarked. "But don't you see that you're fighting yourself, what you want—doing a thing you hate because it's the decent thing to do?"

He drew a long breath. "Is that the way you see it?" he asked, an odd sort of relief in his voice.

"Why—that's the way it is!" she insisted. "If you ran away you wouldn't be fighting, you'd be evading, wouldn't you?"

He reached a hand suddenly and laid it on her own. Her heart gave a wild flutter and there was a singing in her ears. Here it was—the sweet danger, the thing all the songs were about! Here it was, and she was not afraid, nor cold nor hesitant.

He said gravely, "I knew you were like me. Let's walk around, shall we? Let's walk over to the cemetery and bury your Grandfather Neary again."

Without protest she rose and went with him. He did not touch her, he kept his hands in his pockets and did not move to help her officiously over every little rise of ground, as Wylie Matson would have done, pressing her arm and walking too near. They crossed the sandy street and rounded the corner of the lichened brick wall that enclosed the old, old churchyard. Ilex trees grew tall and close in the enclosure, there was no grass underfoot, only the soft whisper of sand, and in places the reaching tendrils of myrtle that caught at their heels.

There was a fragrance of something in bloom, and the smell of age and quietness and deep, warm peace. A little way off stood the small brick church, with its square tower and wooden doors from which all the paint had long since blistered away.

Frances picked her way between the gravestones uncertainly, following the white shadow of his tallness.

"I don't know where the grave is," she said anxiously. "Mama wouldn't come here. Cemeteries make her nervous."

"I know where it is." He put out a hand then to lead her between leaning marble walls overgrown with some scrambling vine. "There's a very vindictive inscription on the stone—or maybe you know that. I used to come here and spit on it when I was a kid."

"I've never seen it. I don't know what's there." She caught up with him and they stood close together above a line of flat stones that reflected the thin light of the sky dimly. "Is this the Neary plot?"

"Here lie the Nearys. About a dozen of them, I think. Here's your grandfather."

"Grandma wasn't buried here. Her father had her buried in the Taft lot in Baltimore. My own father is there too."

He lit a match and held it low over the mossy slab of stone. "Can you read it?"

Three matches had flickered out before she spoke again. "It says 'Slain by a rival, in the destruction of the boat *Mary Conner*. August 2nd, 1872,'" she said unhappily. "But that makes it sound as though he were murdered!"

"Your grandma was a ruthless little soul apparently. She wanted the last word with the Cavitts and she got it, carved in stone!" he said.

"But—if it had been my husband, if I had loved him, I'd have felt vindictive too," she argued. "Any woman would. It's because we're so defenseless, I guess. We haven't any weapons but words!"

"If you loved a man you'd fight for him fiercely, wouldn't you?"

"Why—of course! Wouldn't you? If you loved a woman, I mean?"

"It would depend a lot on the woman." He touched her then, turning her away from the quiet rank of sleeping Nearys. "Yes, I think it would depend a lot on the woman. She'd have to be loyal—she'd have to be mighty loyal, she'd have to believe in me, no matter what happened, no matter what people said."

"But that's what love is about, isn't it?" she asked. "Being loyal, believing—no matter what happens?"

"I've never known," he said soberly. "I'd like to find out."

They crossed the street again and at the Matson gate Taffy came whirling out, followed by the Matson sons.

"Where on earth were you, France?" demanded Taffy shrilly. "It's almost midnight. We'll have to go. Mama will have a fit. Wylie brought the buggy around a half hour ago."

Frances looked at them all vaguely. Her heart had been pumping so swiftly for a long time that it caught at her breath and made her voice hoarse once more. She felt confused and lightheaded, as though she were breathing rarified air.

"Oh—of course. I'm ready—we have to say good-by," she stammered, avoiding Wylie's detaining hand. At the door she looked about anxiously. Foxworth Cavitt was nowhere to be seen. He had vanished into the darkness, as silently as he had appeared there on the lawn.

She made her farewells politely, saw the shrewd appraising eyes of some of the girls move down to the sandy hem of her skirt, her dusty shoes. At the gate an argument was going on between Renwick Matson and his brother.

"Why can't I go along too?" Ren demanded. "Why can't I take the Keelings home by myself?"

"I promised to take them home and I don't need any help doing it," Wylie snapped. "May I help you in, Miss Keeling?" His voice was a little frosty, his manner stiffly formal. Frances drew back and maneuvered Taffy into the middle, certain that Wylie would drive with one hand and lay his other arm familiarly along the back of the seat as he had done earlier.

Taffy was obviously stimulated by an inward, triumphant glee. She tipped her head back and sang loudly, replying to all of Wylie's remarks with pert, saucy brightness. Frances sat in silence, her mind in a tumult of delirious uncertainty. Was this being in love? It must be, for nothing like this had ever happened to her before. But being in love with an enigma, with a mystery unspoken, inarticulate—being in love and *not knowing*—that could be torment! And with a Cavitt! Taffy's smug and mischievous air told her what would lie ahead without the addition of Wylie Matson's offended attitude and the sly looks that had met her in the Matson house.

What if there were gossip, what if Mama heard it? She had been on guard against Fox Cavitt ever since the incident of the lame horse. Almost she had refused to return to North Carolina on his account, Frances knew. I must have gone a little crazy, she told herself dismally. She hardly knew when the buggy turned in past the stone angel, till the horse came to a halt at the gate. Then she got down quickly, giving Wylie no chance to put his hands upon her. Taffy landed in his arms with a jump and a squeal.

"Let's walk down to the river and make faces at old Captain Cavitt!" she proposed. Wylie threw back his head and laughed loudly.

"Let's do no such thing!" snapped Frances. "It's late and we're keeping Mama up. Good night, Mr. Matson. Thank you so much. It was a lovely party."

But he would not let her go so easily. He had her arm, helping her up the path that Dobbs had lately raked and tended.

"Listen, I know some places I want you to see," he was saying eagerly. "How about Sunday? Will you be at home Sunday —say about three o'clock?"

"She's always at home Sunday," put in Taffy before Frances could answer. "I'm always at home, too."

"I'll—I'll let you know. Thanks so much—and good night." Frances pulled herself away from those hot hands.

Mama was coming, thank goodness! She was coming down the hall carrying a lighted lamp. Mama unlocked the door, spoke a cool greeting to Wylie, dismissing him as firmly as though he had been an errand boy, and ushered her daughters inside.

"It's time you were in bed, Henrietta Keeling," Mama said primly when the door had closed on Wylie. "'Way past midnight!"

"Don't blame me. Blame France. She was the one who was enjoying herself," Taffy said with spirit. "I waited for her for an hour!"

At her own door, when they had gone upstairs, Taffy waited till Mama was out of hearing. Then she flashed into Frances' room and stood, head tilted, eyes dancing.

"You should have seen the Lady Tulia!" she said, low. "She was furious! She was on the porch when you came walking back with Fox Cavitt, and there was a dagger in her eyes that would have cut your throat!"

"But—but she's a married woman!" protested Frances. "He wanted to talk, Taffy. He's awfully lonely—"

"Don't make a lot of stupid explanations," snapped Taffy. "Nobody asked you to explain. Wylie Matson was boiling mad, and so was she. Personally, I think it's wonderful! But for a quiet person, France, who's always been scared to death of men, you certainly have stirred up a hornets' nest."

"If you dare to tattle to Mama—if you get her all worried—" Frances cried desperately.

"I'm not saying a word." Taffy pursed her mouth. "Not a word!"

8

I f Taffy meant to keep silent on the events of the Matson party, it was swiftly obvious to Frances that Taffy meant to capitalize on that silence.

She began her campaign of sweet blackmail by dawdling in bed until almost noon on Saturday, drifting down in a limp wrapper, barefooted, to yawn and heat up the coffeepot, ignoring Frances' flushed face and grimy hands and the piles of dishes spread around the room that was to be the kitchen.

"A girl has to have her beauty sleep," Taffy headed off any reproaches. "I should think you'd be exhausted too, France, after such an exciting evening."

"It wasn't particularly exciting and I knew all these dishes had to be washed and unpacked. Now you can have the job of arranging them in the cupboards," Frances stated coldly.

"I don't see why you had to wash them all anyway," argued Taffy. "Why didn't you just dust them off and we could have washed them as we needed them? I see that you put the table where you could keep your eyes out the window."

"There's nothing out the window except the river, and that's the logical place for a table, where we can get the light."

"Don't be so prickly. I've no objection to your looking out the window! Anyway the ferry doesn't dock till five o'clock. Did he kiss you in that cemetery by any chance? It's supposed to be the famous village kissing place."

"He did not!" flared her sister. "Do you have to be coarse as well as silly?"

"Kissing isn't coarse, not when it's done expertly and with co-operation. You're never going to get anywhere if you culti-vate that stiff, spinster attitude. I'll bet even Mama let herself go now and then—she must have had a few moments or you and I wouldn't be here! Imagine Mama and Papa in an amo-rous pose! Baffles you, doesn't it? Papa was more of an old maid

77

than Mama, too. Maybe she had to do all the love-making."

"You're disgusting," Frances said, "and you have very little to say about talking to the Cavitts."

"Have I said anything about the Cavitts? It must be a tender spot, if you turn brick red and fly at me. I think the Cavitts are intriguing, both of them. I like men with a touch of the devil down under a suave exterior. Anyway, they're good-looking and dashing and they make all the other men around here look like sides of beef or worms or something loathly. That Wylie! I could wind him around my little finger, and he practically swoons at your feet, France; but who wants him, the big ox?"

"Certainly I don't want him," Frances remarked. "You'd better put some clothes on and get at those dishes. Mama wants the house to be in order for Sunday."

Taffy put her cup down and pulled the wrapper tightly around her slim hips. Her bright hair was a tumbled mop, her even teeth showed in a calculated smile. "Somebody," she stated coolly, "has to go to town and buy the week's groceries. I think that somebody will be little Henrietta. I'll tell Mama and you tell Dobbs to get the buggy ready."

"I will not. You're not going to shirk all the work, Miss Henrietta!"

"Oh, dear, then I'll have to go out and tell him myself! Probably the poor old fellow will be shocked by my dishabille. If I have to go tell him myself, I'll ask Mama to go into town with me. She might enjoy the trip and there might be a few spicy bits of village gossip she'd get a thrill out of hearing."

"You callous thing!" snapped Frances. "I never knew anyone so completely selfish. Very well, then, I'll be stupid and tell Dobbs. I could also tell Mama that you pick up strange men on the road."

"That's an idea," agreed Taffy. "Let's have a family confessional. Mama would be so pleased to know that we've made friends with her ancient enemies, the Cavitts."

"I'm not trying to deceive Mama, I'm simply protecting her from worrying over things that are unimportant and have no evil in them whatever. And you're taking advantage of me in an abominable way."

"That's because I'm clever and you're not, Francie. Also I'm ruthless. I mean to keep on being ruthless, but you'll never learn because you have a conscience. I never intend to have a conscience. I'd feel as though I were haunted. You'd better write out a list for me. I may have to shop around to find what we need."

"It should be a very prolonged search—since there are only two grocery stores."

Taffy gathered up her wrapper and made a regal exit, poking her head back through the door to remark with studied sweetness, "If everyone is nice to everyone else in this house from now on, life will be lovely for all of us. Besides, being nasty has a way of putting lines in your face, and you surely don't want to look any older than you are already."

Frances bit her thumb hard to keep her tongue and restrain the impulse to throw something, then resignedly she hung up the tea towel and went out to the yard where Lydia was sitting in a kitchen chair, her plump face flushed, an old straw hat on her mousy hair, her cotton stockings sadly wrinkled over her button shoes, while she directed a perspiring Dobbs at pruning the shrubbery.

"I suppose Taffy might as well go," Lydia agreed. "She seems to know how to manage that horse. In my day it wasn't proper for a young lady to go driving in a buggy without an escort, but everything is so changed now. Dust off the buggy cushions, Dobbs, and be sure the harness is all in good order."

When Dobbs had shuffled off, Frances sat down on the grass beside her mother.

"Mama," she began abruptly, "were you in love with Papa?"

Lydia's round face puckered as it always did when she was confused and startled. "What a ridiculous question! Would I have married him if I hadn't been in love with him? Didn't I take care of him till his last breath and pay all the expenses when he got too sick to work any more? Whatever put such an idea into your head, Francie?"

"I just wondered," Frances evaded. She sat in silence, pulling a blade of grass, winding it around her finger, remembering her father—the tall, grave, subdued man who had, it appeared, taken whatever life had to offer without comment or protest;

poor fortune, broken health, pain and obscurity and death. Her imagination struggled to clothe that long, gentle figure with youth, with passion, with romance. He had been considerate, self-effacing, patient. He had, she was certain, been much put upon and frustrated by grim Grandfather Taft, but if there was any spirit or resentment in his nature his daughter could recall no sign of it.

"Did Papa tell you that he loved you," she went on presently, "or was it just one of those affairs people drift into because their families expect it or it's business or something?"

Lydia bridled. "I hope you don't think that I asked him? Of course he loved me. And my family weren't too pleased about it, either. He was just a clerk then in Grandpa's factory, and Grandpa and Uncle Horace were both convinced he'd never amount to anything. But I married him anyway."

"And you were never sorry—even if it did upset your family?"

"For goodness' sake! When you marry a man that's the end of it. Families get reconciled—there's nothing else for them to do. I wasn't pleased because your papa was never given the opportunities he deserved and it made it worse that it was my own family that stood in his way and held him back. Before he got sick he was practically running that foundry, but he never did have the authority he should have had, nor the money, either. Whatever started you off on this subject anyway, Francie? Have you got some man on your mind?" Lydia asked sharply. "Not that big, beefy Matson man, I hope?"

"Oh, no—there's nobody. But I'm twenty years old, Mama, and naturally I wonder what's going to happen and how I'll meet it when it comes; how people fall in love—if it's all chancey and haphazard or if there's any fate or order about it."

"Well, it's chancey but then so is living. Falling in love is about the chanciest thing there is, but you can guard against a bad chance if you keep your head. You're the one I worry about, Francie. Taffy takes after the Nearys—they were all calculating people, though I didn't inherit their hard, practical minds. I take after my mother and she was a woman with a temper but not much backbone or independence. You're like your papa. You'd better go and fetch my purse. Taffy will need about four dollars and I'd better give Dobbs another dollar today. He'll likely wander down to the wharf and gamble it all away, but I have to encourage him—he's faithful."

So I am like Papa, who never fought for anything in his life, Frances thought drearily as she went back to the house. Taffy was already dressed, pinning on a floppy hat at the mirror. She had scooped it into a jaunty shape and pinned a bright velvet bow at the collar of her old brown dress that gave it an air of maturity and sophistication, and she had borrowed her mother's topaz jewelry.

"Those earrings are too old for you," commented Frances, on the stairs.

"I think they give me quite an air." Taffy tilted her chin. "Especially with my hair up like this."

"You've put red on your cheeks. You'd better not let Mama see you, going off looking like a street girl."

"Crepe paper," stated Taffy coolly. "You wet it and then put powder over it and the effect is very natural. If only I didn't have these darned freckles!" She sighed. "When I see the kind of skin you have and what I could do with it—not that you haven't sort of caught up with your opportunities of late! I didn't know you had it in you. Why don't you fix yourself up, France, and come into town with me?"

"I don't want to go to town. At any rate I'm not going to fix myself up so that loafers will whisper behind my back," scorned Frances, running up the stairs. "Here's four dollars and the list," she said when she came back, "and please remember that you're supposed to be a lady."

"As though I'd ever be allowed to forget it in this family! You'd think this was a nunnery. All we need are some iron doors and a statue in the hall. Trailing black and a coif would suit you, though, France. Crossed hands and a sweetly resigned expression. Or would they, I wonder? I've wondered quite a lot about you lately."

Somehow, she was determined, as she sent fat Chloe trotting down the lane, she was going to have to jolt Francie out of her repressed and timorous attitude. Timidity and ladylike reserve had gone out with fainting, crinolines and abysmal female ignorance. Some girls Taffy knew were even refusing to wear corsets now, and walking skirts showed a bold three inches of ankle, which certainly saved a lot of brushing and sewing new braid on at the bottom. She had even seen nightgowns without sleeves in a shop in Baltimore.

Women everywhere were shrugging off the cocoonlike shell of prudery that had set in some time back when Mama was young, and were wondering how they had got shut up in the Victorian thing in the first place. Emancipation was the new word and Taffy liked the sound of it. Not that she could ever go as far as the French women she read about in library books who even drank liqueurs and smoked Turkish cigarettes—the demimondes of course, and she knew what that word meant too. But freedom could be intoxicating and poor Francie was afraid of it. Or were there secret, unplumbed depths in Francie's nature that she carefully guarded behind that pose of rigid modesty?

By the time she reached the big gum tree Taffy was convinced that Francie might be sly as well as quiet, and that she would bear watching. Fox Cavitt, of all people! Every girl Taffy had talked to at the party had explained that Fox was odd and unsociable, that he avoided girls, and that it was rumored that Zach's wife was after him but that Fox was too self-centered to care. He was certainly good-looking, with that aloof, skeptical air he had, and the grudging, half-mocking way he had of talking when he talked at all.

At the gum tree Chloe slowed and Taffy tightened the reins and frowned.

"How did you know I'd be coming along this road today?" she demanded as Zachary Cavitt got up from the big bent root of the tree.

"This is Saturday," he remarked, moving up to pat the quivering mare on the nose and send her into twitching ecstasy. "Country gals always go to town on Saturday."

"Suppose Mama had come along with me? Do you haunt this road, or have you moved into that tree?"

"If Mama had come along I'd have bowed curtly and observed all the protocol of a feudist. This is my beat." He got into the buggy without waiting for an invitation. "I walk up the river on the Cavitt side. At old Dave Fisher's fish camp I hire Dave to row me across, and take a log road that runs down the bank on this side. Beyond the marsh I cut across the sacred Neary fields, hit this highway and presently I meet you. Down the road, Chloe! She's entirely too fat. You should feed her less and drive her more."

"More often past this gum tree, I suppose?"

"I do not continually haunt this tree. Sometimes I inhabit the upper reaches of this little road, where there stands a decrepit old mill."

"I don't care for decrepit mills. There are always snakes hanging around places like that."

"No snakes in my mill. At this particular moment my mill is occupied by a dozen big tuns, all packed with the prettiest bright-leaf tobacco I've been able to talk their owners into gambling on."

"Cigarettes, I suppose?"

"Beautiful cigarettes! Each in a delicate white garment of pure rice paper imported from China with a dry, sanitary tip made—not from expensive cork, my dear—but from plebian Carolina rice straw. I've finished some samples. Have a look at this one." He took a little packet wrapped in silver paper from his pocket. "Imagine these—wearing the gold monogram and royal crown of Edward the Seventh, the new king of England, or of William McKinley, president of the United States. Or of Lillian Russell or Adelina Patti."

"They wouldn't smoke them. No lady would."

"On that I would like to make you a small wager," he said complacently; "say a nickel or maybe a dime. However, I yield the point. We'll eliminate Lillian, though Jimmy Duke does put her picture in the packs of Cameos and Sovereigns he peddles. And Marion Crawford puts smoking ladies in his novels. But we'll agree to keep the fair sex dainty and delicate and engrave only the monograms of dissolute males on our product—males with plenty of money and a yearn for exclusiveness. You'd be surprised how many there are in this country."

"You made those by hand—and stuck that stuff on and everything?"

"Everything. Shows it can be done. Design a clever package, secure the right advertising in the right places, and except for a few struggling little concerns we have no competition in the

United States. In five years you and I will be wearing diamonds and driving our own horseless carriages."

"I? I have nothing to do with this business. Get up, Chloe."

"You have a very important part to play in the project. For your faith and encouragement you will be voted a block of stock by the directors. You could do a small job of promotion that would facilitate matters, however. You could charm and influence the very susceptible Mr. Renwick Matson."

"That awful lump! Anybody could charm Ren Matson, anybody who wanted to be bored to death. Thank you very much. Convey to your directors the information that I'm not interested. What do you want Ren Matson charmed for?"

"Because I need the Matson factory. And because old Croff is a hardheaded reactionary who sees only catastrophe in change and progress. I haven't approached the old man yet. I want some groundwork done before I begin. I've already mailed packets of these cigarettes to important people in New York and Washington with a letter asking for comments and suggestions. I may be able to persuade my wife to put the monograms on with gold paint; if not I'll devise some way to have them stamped. If I get some letters and have a little groundwork done, I'll be able to approach Croff Matson with some convincing arguments. Money interests him. If he can see money in a proposition he'll weaken. Wylie's already interested but he isn't employed in the plant, and he's agreed to handle any legal angles for us. Ren's the boy we need. How about doing a little fascinating in that direction? You're wonderfully equipped for it, as you know."

In spite of herself Taffy found herself melting slightly under the suave flattery of his eyes, at being treated like an intelligent equal by a worldly man like Zach Cavitt. But the idea of Ren Matson was still repugnant.

"Ren seems like a very insignificant person to me," she protested. "I doubt if he'd have much influence with his father. Anyway, Mama would never let me get mixed up in the tobacco business—she hates it."

"I don't think Ren Matson is so insignificant," he argued. "His father depends on him. As chairman of the board of directors of the Pamlico Tobacco Company, I'd consider voting you a nice little block of stock—say ten shares, which should be worth about a thousand dollars to begin with. Exciting things are happening to tobacco stocks. You can learn all that by reading the New York papers. However, I never try to persuade a lady against her will, especially when she shows no interest in diamonds or gasoline buggies. The red-wheeled ones with big brass lamps are cute, Taffy. Well, here's my corner. I'd better leave you here so that your young reputation will remain unsullied. I'll meet the ferry and take my wife home. She's been riding around on the old *Agnes* all day. The sea air is obviously beneficial to the complexion."

He stopped the mare with a low command, got down and slapped her affectionately on the flank, bowed to Taffy, showing his white teeth in an affable smile, and walked quickly into the cemetery. Chloe tossed her head impatiently but was finally persuaded to move when Taffy gave her an irritated flick of the whip.

"Someday you'll learn who you belong to, you stubborn thing!" she stormed. "Of all the impudence! Ren Matson! That sickly fawning creature. I won't do it."

But her anger was weak and soon died in speculation. To be a stockholder, to be independent—weren't they living on the income from Mama's stocks? To all Mama's family, to Uncle Horace and his stuffy tribe, stocks were sacred things only a fraction less holy than gilt-edge bonds.

"I'll keep it to myself," Taffy told herself; "then when I'm rich as everything I'll go to New York and buy a fur coat and ostrich plumes and have four suits all made by an expensive tailor."

And a horseless carriage with red wheels and big brass lamps. The things were still experimental jokes though, coughing and snorting around on silly wheels with silly-looking people sitting up in them all tied up in veils and dusters, looking sillier than ever when the contraption came slinking back from somewhere hauled by an amused farmer with a pair of mules.

She tied Chloe at the hitchrack outside the grocery store and straightened her hat, shaking the dust out of her skirts as she got down. Butter on the list! That meant dashing home as fast as Chloe could go before it melted. Shortening, too. Another greasy spot on the floor boards of the buggy for Dobbs to grumble about. She followed the gaunt old grocer about his little shop, gathering up her purchases absently, ignoring a question as to whether she wanted red salmon or pink because she was cautiously watching the street outside to see if Zach Cavitt would come swaggering by. Presently she saw him emerge from the cemetery gate and cross the shady, sandy street. The old shopkeeper saw him too and snorted.

"That one! Never did figure how Cap'n Cavitt raised such a teetotal worthless boy. Ain't hit a lick since he got back from Cuby, or wherever it was he was scallywaggin' around last trip. Waitin' for the boat to come back, I reckon, figurin' to borrow a dollar or two off of Fox. Ain't heard she's aground, likely."

"Aground?" repeated Taffy. "You mean the *Agnes* has sunk?"

"Don't reckon she sunk. Not in that shoal water. Heard she hit a new sand bar down yonder where South Creek comes in. Some boys that come back on a prawn boat awhile back said Fox was waitin' for the tide to work her off. Be midnight before he gets her in, way the tide's runnin' now. Look, you live upriver, 'crost from the Cavitts. Might be you could get word to the old Cap'n. He didn't go aboard today, got a bad spell with his stummick, Fox said. He'll git wild worryin' if the boat don't come back on time. You could holler acrost maybe and ease his mind."

"We don't have a boat and the river's very wide up there," Taffy said.

"Ain't half a mile wide to your place. Sound travels fur on the water, you could make him hear if you holler loud enough."

"I'd better tell Mr. Zachary the boat's aground." Taffy set her parcels down and hurried out. Zach was standing on the path that skirted the water, studying the Matson tobacco factory. "Mr. Cavitt!" called Taffy, hurrying after him, holding up her skirt. "Oh, Mr. Cavitt!"

He turned and sauntered toward her, his hands in his pockets.

"Need another wing on that building," he said abruptly, turning to look back at it. "A lot of glass facing the river and a sign on it twenty feet high."

"The *Agnes J.* is aground," blurted Taffy. "I came to tell you."

His brows drew in sharply. "Where's she aground? Did you hear?"

"Somewhere off South Creek, the grocer said. He says she won't float off on the tide till nearly midnight."

His eyes hardened. "Midnight, eh? Very romantic! And no moon!"

"The grocer thought someone should get word to your father," Taffy continued. "He wanted me to do it, but I can't of course."

"Midnight and no moon, and the Captain not on board." Zach's voice had a bitter edge. "I suppose the channel shifted—or it might be that the man at the wheel was not attending to his business."

"It was a new sand bar, the man said. You'll have to get word to your father, Mr. Cavitt."

He fell into step beside her. "The small boat will be locked—and of course Fox will have the key! I'll have to hire somebody—and I came away without any change. You wouldn't have a spare dollar to loan me, would you, Miss Keeling?"

"I'm sorry, I haven't. I paid all my money for the groceries."

"Then perhaps you'll let me ride back with you? I can hail Dave Fisher and cross up there."

"I suppose I'd be very unfriendly to refuse." Taffy was half uneasy, half thrilled.

"Shall I meet you at our usual corner?"

"No. I'll tell the grocer that I'm going to take you back to get word to your father. That will make it a public and entirely impersonal arrangement so there can't be any gossip about it."

"By all means," he flashed his smile at her, "let's keep it entirely impersonal and public, little Taffy! I'll drop a canny word in the barbershop, too. That shop is the grinding mill of all the scandal that goes abroad in this community. I'll be distressed and consumed with filial anxiety and extremely indebted to you, practically a stranger."

"You needn't leer!" she flared. "You needn't make it sound sly—and nasty!"

He bowed gravely. "I apologize. Had no thought whatever

of being either sly or nasty. I was merely respecting the provincialism of this town and the necessity for protecting you from the sharp tongues that fly in it. Shall you be ready soon?"

"I'm ready now, as soon as I get my bundles. We'll have to hurry on account of the butter."

"Let us not on any account delay the butter. In five minutes, then, and to you, dear Miss Keeling, the deep gratitude of the Cavitts."

"I could slap you!" she stormed. "I should make you walk every step of the way—or swim!"

"Think of the tremendous loss to the stockholders of the Pamlico Tobacco Company if my sodden body were washed ashore under some reeking fish dock." He tipped his ribboned hat and hurried down the street.

Taffy headed Chloe homeward, past the cemetery and out upon the sandy little road, her head high and excitement making her skin tingle and her cheeks burn. What if he tried to make love to her when they reached the wooded, lonely stretch of road? She decided upon a regal, offended pose as more dramatic than tearful betrayal and disappointment. She was certain that Zach Cavitt was more than a little interested, and preened herself a trifle on charming a sophisticated and mildly dangerous man who was made more attractive by the fact that he was married to a woman with daggers in her eyes.

But, though she tilted her chin at an alluring angle and held the reins in a graceful pose of elegance and adeptness, it became more and more apparent as they rode along that Zach Cavitt was aware of her now only as someone convenient and obliging. He sat scowling moodily ahead as silent as the plodding mare, twisting his mouth now and then as though he chewed on a bitter morsel. Taffy sensed what he was thinking and resented it with blithe unreason and a savage jab of jealousy. He wasn't there at all. He was out on the Sound, on that stupid old boat piled up uselessly like so much lumber on a sand bar with twilight coming on. He was there, watching that Tulia—and Fox Cavitt!

Tulia was no doubt having a wonderful time. She wasn't the sort to be frightened, Taffy was certain, and neither was she a woman to let an opportunity slip. Taffy had seen her face at the Matson party, seen the fury in Tulia's eyes when Frances came walking in with Fox Cavitt, and behind the fury there had been something else plain to Taffy's shrewd young mind—a desperation, a touch of panic, and a raw and momentarily unguarded agony.

Zach had implied that Fox had not been attending to his business. Taffy found herself inwardly defending Fox Cavitt. A woman like Tulia would be an embarrassment, she could be a nuisance, she could even be a menace. Zach ought to kill her, Taffy decided when they reached the gate of the Neary place.

She said good-by there, regretfully explaining that she could not carry him farther, and though he was politely grateful he was a trifle brusque and he set out immediately, heading across the field with long, grim strides. She did not follow him with her eyes. Temporarily, she knew, she had lost him. Temporarily. He would come back. Something young and arrogant within her made her sure, but she allowed herself a brief indulgence in sly malice.

"Your friend Foxworth has run his boat aground down south somewhere," she told Frances when they were alone. "They'll be stuck there till the tide turns—hours and hours maybe, and the lovely Tulia is with him."

Frances avoided her eyes. "That's a stout boat. Anyway, it doesn't matter. Anyway—it's nothing to me. Certainly he wouldn't be interested in his brother's wife."

"Don't be naïve," drawled Taffy. "Why, even in the Bible—"

She stopped abruptly, seeing her sister's lips tighten, seeing her eyes.

Taffy Keeling could be a brat but essentially she was kind to hurt things. Lame kittens and hungry wistful dogs—or a sister with unhappiness lying deep and dark in her eyes.

9

The first ground swell lifted at ten o'clock.

Fox Cavitt, who had been pacing from one side of the deck to the other, dropping a lead on a line every five minutes and muttering sourly to himself, felt the lift of the swell as it shuddered beneath the *Agnes'* frustrated timbers, and pushed back his cap, mopping his face.

Tulia had perched herself on the high, empty stool behind the useless wheel. She reached up impulsively and pulled the whistle cord, and a slow blast shook the distant marshes and echoed in the woodland along South Creek. Fox came banging up, his face dark and angry in the dim lantern light.

"What the devil did you do that for?" he demanded, as feet pounded behind him and someone yelled from the engine pit.

"But we're moving, aren't we?" she asked with carefully wide-eyed innocence.

"We are not moving. When we're afloat I'll be up there and not you!" he snapped. "Go back down, Barney—hold your pressure. Just a woman playing smart aleck."

There were five passengers on board and they gathered, standing loosely hung together on the slightly slanting deck, their dimly seen figures bulks of exasperated patience.

"I could have got back to Bath sooner in a rowboat!" growled one man.

"I'll lower a boat for you," Fox offered promptly. "I'm not enjoying this myself exactly. Maybe I'll go with you if you decide to row back."

"These bars—" began another passenger who had been tiresomely oratorical all day, explaining to any pinioned listener that he had been serving on a federal jury, giving details and evidence of all the cases he had heard, till the victim escaped. "These bars come and go. High water in the Piedmont and the silt comes down. I've seen this shoreline out here shift five times in twenty years. Used to be a nice piece of property on some bluffs a few miles east of here—been gone years now. Big house, barns, windmill—then the erosion set in—gone now, all gone."

The group murmured, shifted, moved. They had heard it all before. What they wanted to hear now was the thrum of the screw under their feet, the wash of the wave turned back from a marching bow, wind moving against ventilators and the funnel.

"She's turned, Captain," a man shouted. "How long now?"

"Can't tell," Fox answered. "When she floats clear we'll be underway. I'll get you to Sandersonville, anyway."

"Might as well be here as there. What can you do in a burg like that—sit on the wharf all night till you're ready to shove off again?"

"You may have to sit longer than that, till I can get under and have a look at her bottom."

"If she was stove anywhere there'd be water coming in, wouldn't there? You're not working the pumps."

"She's my boat!" Fox cut him off. "I'll refund your fare. Drop lead at the stern, Obie. Drop it straight down."

The others moved away, following the boy with the lead. Tulia slid off the stool and came down the two steps to the deck.

"Don't hate me, Fox," she said softly.

"I don't hate you," he replied crisply, "I hate myself. When the Captain piled her up off Swan Quarter he had old age for an alibi. I haven't any excuse."

"Come and sit up in the bow with me and relax, Fox. You've been charging up and down for hours. We have to stay here till the boat floats off, so why not accept it calmly and make the best of it. It's a nice night and the mosquitoes haven't found us, and there's a little breeze."

"I've got to watch the lead," he said. "I can't risk dragging her screws."

"You've never talked to me, Fox." There was definite pleading in her voice. "I don't even know what kind of person you are."

"Maybe I don't know myself," he countered. "I'm a man

stupid enough to get himself and a dozen other people into a jam, like fouling up this boat, but I'm not stupid enough to get myself into a personal jam, Tulia."

"You flatter my ego," she said archly. "You make me sound dangerous. I'm not, you know, I'm just lonely—horribly lonely. You're lonely too, Fox."

"All right then, I'll enjoy my loneliness—alone." He turned abruptly and stalked back to the stern.

She did not follow. She had been born clever, she had known how to manage men from her birth; her tempestuous father and the succession of men, all older and all at the last susceptible, who had always hung around her mother. All but Zachary. Zachary had been cut from the same ruthless fabric as she, endowed with the same sadistic shrewdness, in his case intensified by maleness to the edge of cruelty. Zach had been stimulated by her recklessness, he had admired her in an indulgent fashion for awhile and watched her capers with a kind of dry, paternal amusement, but in the end he was the dominant one, he was the one who dealt out pain and harsh contempt and sarcasm. That was because love meant so little to Zach. A whim, a brief flurry of passion, immediate satiety followed by scorn and boredom, but nothing went deep, nothing that she could play upon with her skilled maneuvers, her calculated moods of anguish, pretty penitence, or fury.

Cavitts! Men made like mollusks, she thought bitterly, each in his polished shell of arrogance with tentacles that reached out rarely, but could not be touched or they were withdrawn. Past that encysting barrier no tenderness moved undiluted by personal desire or caution. Against the wall of it every feminine weapon broke off short, like a knife flung against a rock. They enjoyed their loneliness—alone. They fed it with imperious self-sufficiency that was the more maddening because no appeal reached it, no storm could shake it, no tenderness soften it.

She thought about Zachary and a cold place within her tightened and turned dry and acrid. They had nothing for each other any more, nothing but a slow hate that had a curious quality of mutual respect. She was no longer even afraid of him. And now she was not afraid of Fox, or of herself, because she knew what she wanted and all the torment had crystallized into a grimness that purposed remorselessly not to be defeated.

Zach might threaten, but his threats only exhilarated her. When Fox avoided her, she did not pursue. She waited. It was a savage, inexorable sort of waiting, it had in it the fierce, intent quiet of the spider, the tenacity of the furry web. It was tireless and endless. She leaned back in the old Captain's favorite chair now, relaxed and serene but as taut within as any pouncing thing.

As though her brooding thoughts had some tangible magnetism, Fox came up presently looking whitely out of the dusk, and leaned against the rail near her.

"She should ease herself off in another hour or two," he said, looking down at the water that came shouldering up now to slap with a hollow sound on the high bow. "Are you hungry? I've still got half a sandwich back yonder."

"No, I'm not hungry." Her tone was gentle, casual; no pitiful, shaken helplessness in it, no appeal. She might even have disliked him, from her studiedly polite drawl. "I'm slightly bored, that's all. Even the waves pall when you've had nothing else to look at all day. Don't bother about me, Fox; I know you're too busy to talk to me."

"Nothing to talk about." He took his cap off, slapped it against the rail, put it back on again. "This settles it. I'm going to have some kind of small stove on board. The Captain will gripe about it. He thinks food draws flies and rats, but at least I'm going to arrange some way to make a cup of coffee."

"Lovely hot coffee!" sighed Tulia. "There'll be cold corn bread saved for us when we get back, and cold fried eggs."

"You can fry a hot egg, can't you?"

"Your mother would think it was sinful to waste a perfectly good, already-cooked egg, no matter how stiff it was or how much grease was caked on it. Zach will be furious, no doubt, and so will your father. As though you could help any of this, Fox." Champion him—but cleverly, cleverly! No maternal quality in it, no pity, not even loyalty. The impartial observer, that was her role.

"The Captain will make speeches about what a fool I am, and I'll probably hear about it as long as he lives. He'll forget that he ripped the bottom out of her two years ago, but he'll remember that he never piled her up on a bar."

"And Zach," said Tulia, carefully casual, "will be certain that you and I have been carrying on some kind of romantic affair out here—with five passengers standing around grumbling and the crew hanging about and a hot sun blazing down till the pitch fries out of the planks."

"You and I?" yelped Fox. "Where did he get any such damfool idea as that?"

"You know Zach's ideas." She shrugged. "They never need a point of origin. They incubate out of the peculiar atmosphere that Zach lives in. Fortunately, after they've seethed around in his brain for awhile, they usually dissolve. Like the idea that he's going to make a fortune out of some scheme or other."

"But good Lord, Tulia—I've never looked at you, scarcely! Not with any idea like that, anyway. Just because you like to ride around on the ferry route on hot days—"

"Exactly," she agreed. "Fantastic, isn't it?"

"It's worse than that. It's crazy. It's a lie! I'll knock his head off. What has he had to say—about us?"

"Oh, nothing really. It's the things that Zach doesn't say that trouble you most. A look he gets in his eyes. And that sidelong, sneering way of saying things—some half-finished sentence full of innuendo, but nothing you can really put your finger on. I'm used to it. I've had four years of it."

"*I'm* not used to it—and I won't put up with it. I'll tell him so, damn' quick! I'm not out to steal any man's wife."

"Oh, Fox, please—no! Please don't say anything. It will only make things worse. He'll know we've discussed it and he'll be more suspicious than he is now. Let me handle Zach. I know how. He knows he can go only so far with me. But—isn't it absurd—you and I? You rarely speak to me, you know. I was beginning to believe you didn't even like me." The merest trace of poignancy now, a faint flutter of a white hand, like vague wings in the dusk.

"I don't dislike you, Tulia." He was on the defensive now and from here on she was sure she knew the right words. Only—

go slowly, Tulia, slowly and cleverly. "But, hell-fire," he flared, "you're a married woman!"

"I know. And you're a gentleman, Fox. You could never harbor the kind of thoughts that Zach has, could you? That's why I feel so safe with you. More safe than with anyone I know—safe and rested. That's why I've liked riding around on this boat. Relaxed and away from everything—and safe. You don't care at all for women, I know. But if you should ever let yourself fall in love, Fox, it would be rather wonderful—for the girl, I mean. Everything would be so new, so unspoiled. I envy that girl a little. You don't mind if I envy her, do you—an old lady like me?"

"You're not old. You let things get you down, Tulia."

"Oh, I feel ages old. I'm older than you, I imagine. I'm twenty-six."

"I'll be twenty-eight in January. Sign of Capricorn. All the Cavitts are born in that sign. The Captain says that's why we act like goats and people think we've got horns and hoofs." He laughed hollowly. "Got to drop the lead again. She seems to have a little buoyancy now. Stop worrying about Zach, Tulia. I can handle him. He's five years older than I am, but I could always handle him."

"Five years older than you and still adrift!" She sighed. "I've had a ghastly life since I married Zach, Fox. No security, always running from something, not quite sure that things were honest, that anything could be believed. A woman suffers when things are like that. It was the same with my father. He was a footless and irresponsible person too. I never had a home in my life. I never lived with anyone I felt really loved me or cared what happened to me."

"I know, Tulia. It's been tough." He touched her shoulder lightly as he passed and the warm impact of his hand tingled through her, making her fingers tighten and her heart beat faster.

She did not stir nor follow. She sat quietly while the tide rose higher under the bow and men ran and shouted, and after a little the rumble of the engines sounded below. Fox was in the wheelhouse now and bells jangled. The *Agnes J.* began moving backward very slowly, then faster as the engine beat increased. The bow swung, the stars burning overhead were first on her right, then on the left, and the wind blowing from the land was warm in Tulia's face.

In an hour or two, depending on the wind and tide, she would be back in that dreary old house on the river, the house she hated. It would smell of old people, of their tired beds and their tired bodies, of calico cushions never shaken or aired, of cats, and coffee boiled too long, of the soured resignation of the old, waiting for death.

Her own room would smell of Zachary, too; of the maleness of him, his everlasting tobacco, the salve he used on his mustache, the polish of his boots. It would smell of suspicion, of the unending tension between them that was sometimes as tangible on the air as the smoke of a burning fuse. She was hungry but she did not want to eat, not in that dining room where the lamp was always turned low to save oil and the screens daubed with kerosene to discourage mosquitoes. There would be a spotty tablecloth on the table and a piece of cotton goods spread over the cold food that would be saved for them; gravy congealing on a platter, butter collapsed limply in a glass dish, the cream pitcher with a scum on top, and gnats hovering over the inevitable dish of stewed peaches or apples.

Even to think of it revolted Tulia Cavitt, and she looked down at the black, curling water slipping in deep furrows under the bow and thought of the coolness down there, the quiet, the peace. No one would miss her if she slipped over the side. There would be consternation, and likely the Cavitts would be outraged and aghast at the sensation; there would be boats with grappling hooks and Zachary going grim-faced in one of them; but in a few days life would settle into a routine again for the men born in Capricorn, the men who should have had horns like goats.

Would Fox remember what she had said tonight—the loneliness, the life she had led—and be a little sorry? She wondered about him and looked back at the wheelhouse where the only light was the faint phosphorescent glow of the compass that outlined his chin vaguely and the peak of his nautical cap. He stood so tall, he had an adequate look though life forebore to touch him intimately; he looked as though he strode through life and trod upon it, unconcerned with the fuming small rages of men, and undismayed by wind or tide. Fox had this curious, metallic strength; he would despise her if she was so weak as to give up and seek an easy way out of the turmoil of living. Zachary would despise her too because he was a Cavitt, but his contempt would have rage in it and bitter hate, as if in dying she made him look like a fool.

Nothing that Zachary thought or could do was important to her now, but Fox was important. She turned her eyes away from the water and saw then that the *Agnes* was headed in toward the lights of the town. Every light wrote on the water with a shaky yellow finger and someone had lighted a gasoline torch on the end of the wharf. The whistle yawped against the woodland, mooing hollowly, and the echo came back in a harsh bark. The passengers were huddled near the end of the gangway, grumbling among themselves as the Negro roustabouts made the lines ready.

Tulia did not move. She could see the little crowd on the landing and Zachary was not there. She could always pick out Zachary, standing inches taller than most men, standing always a little apart with his feet braced so that he leaned back a little on his heels, his head tilted arrogantly. Even in that frightening crowd in Cuba when they had met trouble, she had been able to pick out Zachary. He had dominated that mob by the sheer force of his insolence, and he was convinced that he would always dominate.

Fox came walking down the deck then, alone. He had a lantern on his arm and a sheaf of manifests under his elbow.

"You there, Tulia?" he called through the dark. "Come along ashore. You'll have to wait for me while I see about accommodations or transportation for these people."

She rose and followed him without a word. He held the lantern low so that she would not stumble over ropes and the rough planking of the dock. When he had negotiated for a fishing boat to take three passengers upriver to Washington, he moved out among the bystanders, speaking to a few, answering their good-natured sallies with a twitch of a thumb, a slow grin, a lift of eyebrows.

"What were you trying to do, Fox," bantered Wylie Matson; "take her across lots?"

"Your harbor-dredging proposition is a little way behind," Fox answered. "South Creek hasn't found out yet that it's against the law to dump real estate in the channel."

"Sure you were in the channel? Sure you weren't watching the little birdies flying around?"

Fox tensed for an instant and Tulia jerked at his sleeve. "Come along, I'm hungry," she announced in an impatient tone audible to all the loungers. "The next time I take a boat ride with you to pass the time, I'll walk."

They went down the damp, slippery steps to the low landing where the small boat was moored. The tide was so high that the water was almost over the planks and the boat lifted and nudged her bow on wood with every ripple. Fox unlocked the padlock, snapped it on the chain again and tossed the chain aboard. He swung the boat in and waited while Tulia climbed down and settled herself in her usual seat toward the stern. The little engine in the cockpit burned kerosene and the boy whom Fox hired to light the burner ahead of time had done his job early, so there was plenty of steam and the little craft shot out swiftly into the dark river, blowing a blast of hot mist from the escape pipe in the side.

The steam blew back into Tulia's face and she covered her head with her arms and gasped till they were head-on into the wind, and the scalding vapor drifted out to the stern.

"Burn you?" asked Fox from the tiller seat. "Got a little too hot."

"I'm all right," she said shortly, pushing back her damp hair and wiping her face.

"I had to turn her," defended Fox. "I didn't know she was going to pop off like that."

"There are so many things you don't know, Fox," Tulia said a trifle sadly; "so many, many things."

He did not answer and she did not speak again till they were inside the dimly lighted hall of the Cavitt house and Zachary came striding from the sitting room, his face harsh in the raw lamplight. Then she said coldly, "I'm worn out and starved and Fox is no comfort whatever, so if you have any remarks to make, Zach, save them till morning. If you have any consideration for me at all, let me go to bed, and I'd like a hot cup of tea in my room—and if anyone thinks it's a frolic to be stuck on a hot sand bar for hours on a blistering day, they certainly need to have their brains examined. Now, let me alone—will you?"

She was aware of Zach's mother babbling away in the background, saying that the Captain had been in a stew for hours, and what happened to the propellers, and did the planks spring—and all right, she'd make a cup of tea but she'd have to make up the fire first.

It was Zach's mother who brought the tea and, for a wonder, two slices of fresh bread and butter with it and a little dish of wild plum conserve. For once Tulia was glad to see her mother-in-law. She had jerked off her long dress and the hot, binding stays, and pulled all the pins out of her hair. She smiled wanly at Mrs. Cavitt.

"You're awfully good to me," she said. "I'm simply dead. It was pretty awful out there in the heat."

"My goodness," chirped the old lady, "you look like a little girl with your hair down. I said to Zachary—I said, now don't you pick at her. Wasn't none of it her fault nor the boy's neither. It could happen to anybody, even the Captain. Many a time that channel's silted up sudden and there was one spring I remember when the Captain had to keep a boy hanging over the rail with a lead all the time. Come up a bad rain upcountry and you never know what's going to come down the creeks or the river. You drink this now and get to bed. You can sleep as late as you want to in the morning. I told Zach for him to sleep in the spare room. The bed's mighty near as good as this and you can get your rest."

Tulia was too weary and indifferent to wonder why Mrs. Cavitt had become her champion so unexpectedly. But enlightenment came with sharp suddenness when Zach came upstairs and opened the door. He strode in, threw his coat over a chair, and sat down to unlace his shoes.

"You may as well know now," he said without preamble. "We're getting out of here tomorrow morning."

"Leaving?" Tulia sat up. "But—how can we leave? Where can we go without money?"

"We're going into town. I'll make some arrangement. I thought you wanted to get away from this house? You've raised the devil about it ever since we've been here."

"Of course I want to go. I've never been happy being dependent—tolerated! You know it has been like that, Zach. We upset their routine, we disarranged their lives; they like their quiet rut and we brought disruption into it." She swung her feet out of bed suddenly and frowned at him. "You've had trouble! You've had a row with your father. That's why your mother was so friendly all at once—she knew we were leaving."

Zachary folded his necktie carefully, laid it with his stick pin neatly on top, on the old bureau.

"I offered him a reasonable and profitable proposition," he said a bit haughtily. "He not only refused to consider it but he flew into a senile rage and started bellowing and stamping around, dragging up the past, abusing me and calling names. I listened as long as I cared to, then I told him that I'd had enough, that tomorrow I was getting out of his house."

"You could have been kinder, Zach." With a perversity that she hardly understood herself, she arrayed herself against him. "He's an old man. You tried to borrow money, didn't you? After telling me that very likely that old boat was all he had."

His face darkened and he glared at her. "Who are you to talk about being kind to them? You haven't given them a decent word since you came into this house. Time and again I've felt like slapping your jaw for you when you aired that cute sarcasm of yours over their food. Now you don't want to leave! Very obvious why you don't want to go. Plain for anybody to see, anybody but Fox. He'll never see it—he'll never give you a tumble, my dear; you're wasting your wiles and it's time we left before you make a pathetic spectacle of yourself."

She did not fly into fury and this puzzled her a little. She had no feeling at all. She was watching his contorted face with the casual amusement she might have felt for the antics of a comedian.

"The same old routine," she drawled with frigid scorn. "You kick the ground out from under yourself and then you find some weak way to put the blame on me. You can be sure of one thing though; if they throw us into the street, you're not going to sell my ring."

"Did I mention selling the damn' ring? I told you I'd make some sort of arrangement. I'm staying in this town. That's important to me now. So you can still ride around on the ferry, if that's important to you."

"I'll ride the ferry when I please, though it isn't important to me at all." She lay back on her pillow, her eyelids closed against him.

"I'll sleep in the other room. Orders from on high," he stated icily, jerking his nightshirt from the hook on the back of the door. "Pack your things the first thing in the morning. We'll have to go when Fox takes the small boat down."

"I don't know that I'll go when the boat goes down," she said. "If I have to leave I'll leave when it pleases me to be ready."

"We're leaving early in the morning," he repeated at the door. "You heard me."

"I'm sick of hearing you." She turned away and threw an arm over her head. "Leave when you like. I'll leave when I like. Just one thing, Zachary Cavitt. If I follow you now, I'm following you for the last time."

"I've heard that before," he snapped, slamming the door.

When he had gone she lay sick and shuddering. This was a pattern she knew well, but now there was something decadent and intolerable about it. What dismayed her was remembering that only a little while ago she would have been thrilled at the thought of getting away from this old house. Now—oh, Fox, Fox, can't you see that I can't bear it very much longer? That I've been torn on the horns of Capricorn till I'm bleeding inside and sick for want of loving?

She cried long into her pillow. She had not cried in years, no matter how ghastly things became, no matter how deeply she ached inside. She had always had a fine scorn for women who let men break them, who let life maul them and destroy their defenses. Now it shamed her that she had weakened so abjectly that a Cavitt could move her to tears.

10

"I am not in love. I am not!" Frances told herself over and over.

She snatched her gaze firmly away from the windows that looked out on the river and the old Cavitt house; she caught herself wandering out to the bluff at dusk, when the little Cavitt boat was due to come snorting up from the port, and turned herself about with grim determination; but though her body withdrew, her heart went on straining with the queer, aching hunger that she could not conquer or assuage.

She told herself that Fox Cavitt cared nothing for women, that he had talked to her because she was lonely and because he was an aloof and solitary sort of person too. Then a traitor softness reminded her that he had told her things about himself, perhaps never voiced to anyone before; his restlessness, the things he wanted to do. He had said, "I knew you were like me." How could he know, unless he had been thinking about her before?

Wylie Matson and his young brother Rennie appeared on Sunday, very spruce and natty in new summer suits and slick straw hats with gay ribbons. They drove up in a shining buggy with a horse reined cruelly high, and though Lydia was a trifle stiff and unfriendly at first, she thawed slowly under Wylie's blandishments, his extravagant compliments on the improvements she had wrought in the old house, even on her frilled dimity dress—which was old enough, heaven knew, as Lydia remarked later, and even darned under the arms!

For a wonder Taffy was polite and even a trifle effusive with Rennie Matson, and Frances wondered at that. She evaded Wylie's importunities to go for a Sunday drive, and was surprised when her mother said later, "You weren't very gracious, Francie. After all, he was only trying to be neighborly."

"Neighborly, my eye!" snorted Taffy. "I know that lad. He pinches!"

"I thought you didn't care for the Matsons, Mama," Frances remarked.

"Well, they have improved themselves, I have to admit. And I'm a reasonable woman, Francie. I've no objections to your having a beau if he conducts himself like a gentleman."

"He's not my beau. I don't like men who breathe down my neck and use Sen-sen."

"She doesn't like men, *finis*," drawled Taffy, "except now and then one who's dark and mysterious and haunts the cemetery."

"If ever I do become interested in a man it won't be one who belongs to some other woman!" Frances flashed back, with spirit.

Lydia stared, her soft lips working in bewilderment. "I don't know what you're talking about," she worried. "What is this about the cemetery? I suppose we ought to go there sometime." She wavered off again on one of her vague tangents that often spelled relief from family tension. "I hope my papa's tombstone hasn't toppled over. That ground is awfully sandy."

"France has seen it," volunteered Taffy, looking stubbornly away into her mirror. "Has it toppled, Francie?"

"No, it hasn't. It's still there—with Grandmother's inscription on it," Frances replied deliberately. "I'm glad you're not a vindictive person like your mother, Mama."

"If you mean by that have I forgiven the Cavitts, Francie, I'll state plainly that I have not and I never shall!" Lydia's round face set in a mold of grimness that made her look like an affronted baby. "They ruined my mother's life and mine too, you might say. My mother wasn't vindictive, she was just an injured woman."

"Revenge is mine!" said Taffy in a voice of mock tragedy. "I suppose the idea of vengeance goes on and on to the third and fourth generation?"

But Lydia was worrying at another idea. She assimilated ideas slowly, was a trifle frightened by her thoughts at times, and gnawed at them with the small, white teeth of her mind as a kitten might worry a scrap of bone.

"What ever were you doing in the cemetery, Francie?" she asked. "It was always such a gloomy old place. I don't believe I could bear to go there, even now."

"She was viewing the graves of her ancestors," put in Taffy blandly. "Somebody should pay respect to the departed Nearys, don't you think? I'll tell you, Mama—tomorrow you cut a big bunch of posies from your bushes and I'll drive in and carry your respects to your forebears. People will think it odd if we don't appreciate the dead Nearys."

Frances gave her a straight, hard look, but she kept silent and went out alone presently into the yard where a moon, high and intimate and swollen, laid a wash of warm silver over the shadowy trees and the lazy shimmer of the river. Abruptly she walked that way, disdaining her inhibitions, letting her feet have their way till she found herself on the shaky little landing under the bank. There she stopped, fighting an urge to turn and run, for a long sailboat with a naked mast lay a little way offshore and there was a soft dipping of a paddle as the boat swung quietly toward the Neary dock.

She felt the gentle bump of the bow against the wood, and the plop of a flung rope; then a white figure emerged above the edge of the planks and Fox Cavitt's voice said, low and unexcited, "Come on down here. That's a very special moon."

"Thank you—I must go back—" Frances stammered, hating the nervous lack of assurance in her that was making her hands tremble and undoubtedly sending shameful floods of color over her face and neck.

"Still hiding," he said levelly. "You don't need to hide from me, you know. We speak the same language. And I keep my hands off women."

"I wasn't thinking of—anything like that!" She bridled a little, but without volition found herself moving nearer to the boat.

"Don't think at all—not on a night like this. Ever see the moon walk on the water? Watch the tide now. See her footprints there, like a dainty lady walking in silver shoes?" He had her hand. He drew her to the edge of the crumbling planks and held her, his hands on her shoulders. Then he drew back, and thrust his hands into his pockets quickly. "There'll be phosphorus on the water later," he went on hastily. "It burns on the edges of the waves and even on my boat. Then the mullet leap and every one will be painted with silver."

"A silver world," mused Frances, breathing deeply to still the silly beating of her heart.

"And stupid people stay under roofs and miss it all," he said, "except a few wise and lonely souls like you and me."

"Did it damage your boat when it went aground?" Frances strove for the commonplace and made herself remember Tulia.

"No damage to the boat. There was some family wreckage. Zach and Tulia moved out this morning. Zach rented a room at the minister's house."

"You must miss them," remarked Frances with studied casualness.

"The only difference I'll notice is that Zach will probably show up on the wharf to borrow money instead of waiting till I get home," he said dryly.

"But you'll surely miss Tulia?" Some perverseness within her insisted on twisting the barb that hurt in her heart.

His answer startled and confused her. "Why?" he asked.

"But—she's so beautiful and—why am I discussing your family with you?" she broke off harshly. "You must excuse my very bad manners, Mr. Cavitt."

"I began the discussion," he reminded her, "and I won't miss Tulia. She is unhappy and unhappy people irritate me."

"But you're not happy yourself. You told me—about chemistry and electricity and the things you wanted to do," she argued. "You said you wanted to scuttle the *Agnes* and sink her in a deep hole in the Sound."

"Wonder how she'd look, going down?" he interrupted. "Can't you see her—her old stack wobbling and breaking off short and water pouring in at the ports and her tail in the air, silly as a gannet's, with her propellers sticking out like feathers!" He gave a chuckle. "I'm not unhappy, Frances. I was just letting myself dream boyish dreams. How did you like Wylie's new three-dollar hat? He bought it especially to wear courting you, you know."

"He isn't courting me. Do you always change the subject so abruptly? Anyway, I must be going in now."

"And abandon this lady moon? But of course—I'm a Cavitt and the Cavitts have horns. Do you know what's going to happen tomorrow night? About ten o'clock that moon will be out again, bigger and brighter than ever, and you're going to come out of that house up there, bold as brass and a whole lot prettier, and sail down this river with me."

"Oh, thank you—but I couldn't really. I—really I must go in now."

He reached for her hand again and she did not draw away. "Two people in this confounded country who understand each other," he remarked, "you and I. Not a girl on earth I'd take out in that boat—not one, except you. They go to sleep early, your family. Every night I see the lights go out."

"I'd be deceiving my mother. I couldn't—I couldn't possibly—"

"Listen." He let her hand fall, put a foot up on a sagging bollard, and rested an elbow on his knee. "There are some things that ought to die. Old hates and stupid family fights ought to die. Should my father's foolishness and your grandfather's stubbornness be visited upon us—things that were ended years before we were born? You've been taught to despise the Cavitts, but can you look at that moon and tell me there was ever any sense in it?"

"It's not I," she declared unhappily; "but we owe something to our parents. And anyway, I don't know you so very well—"

Moving swiftly, he picked up her hand and kissed it gently on the palm. "No," he agreed, "you don't know me very well. But you're going to, Frances—you're going to know me very well indeed."

Without another word or gesture he flipped the tethering rope back on the bow of the sailboat, swung himself down noiselessly, and pushed the craft out into the current. It was gone almost instantly, a slow, slender white shape against the dark shine of the river. Frances stood where he had left her, her hand burning as she held it open to the moon. Then quickly she put her own lips against the warm place on her palm, and her blood went singing through her body so that she felt light and beautiful and beloved and entirely mistress of her soul as she ran lightly up the slope.

Lydia was still up, rocking on the creaking porch, her dimity flounces a pale blur in the dusk.

"I was just about to come to look for you," she grumbled. "Where in the world have you been? You've got no business roaming out in the dark, Francie. I've told you times enough—"

"The moon walks on the river, Mama." Frances heard the odd stimulation in her own voice and hoped Mama wouldn't interpret it. "She walks like a lady with silver shoes."

"And mosquitoes walk right along behind her," stated Lydia grimly, pushing the chair back and heading for the door. "You'll get a sore throat out in that damp, if nothing worse happens to you. You're just like your papa, he was always saying that trees looked like old men bent over with rheumatism, and that our rose of Sharon bush was a young girl with pink flowers in her hair, and nonsense like that."

"Did he?" asked Frances eagerly. "I wish I'd known Papa better. I wish every day that I'd talked to him more. I missed a lot, didn't I?"

"He couldn't talk without coughing. It was no kindness to try to talk to him. I tried to keep as quiet as I could." Lydia snapped the inside locks on the door firmly. "If having a young man come to call makes you so moony, I'm going to worry about you, Francie."

"A young man? You mean Wylie? He'd never make me moony in a million years! All he evokes in me," Frances announced with spirit, "is something distressingly approaching nausea. So you needn't lie awake and worry, Mama. Go on up. I'll put out the lamp."

She could not keep her eyes away from the clock the next night. She caught Taffy watching her once, and Taffy's eyebrows went up mockingly and her lips drew into a sly, one-sided smile.

"Surely you don't expect him back tonight?" she said, with elaborate casualness.

"Expect who?" Lydia wanted to know.

"Oh, no one. I was just teasing Francie, she looked so lovelorn out of her eyes."

"Francie, the Matsons may have improved their opportunities and tried to make something of themselves, but after all—"

"Oh, Mama, for heavens' sake! If ever I look lovelorn over Wylie Matson, please drown me like a sick kitten!"

"Anybody knows I could never drown a kitten. I can't even kill a chicken. Your papa always said I was too tenderhearted to kill a fly. But I can set traps for mice." Lydia bit off a thread and the stream of her conversation with the same snap of the teeth. "They make everything smell so dreadfully," she babbled on presently when the clock had ticked off four more minutes. "Poor little things—they look innocent enough. I caught one alive once and it had such soft brown eyes—"

"I think I'll go to bed," stated Taffy, picking up the fashion magazine she had been holding carefully so that Mama would not see that *Snappy Stories* was concealed inside it. "Moons pall on me when viewed in maidenly solitude. Now, if some gallant in a nice white boat with a sail would come drifting down the stream—"

"Not at this time of night," snapped her mother. "It's after ten. Francie, see if I locked the kitchen door, will you, please? I never can remember."

He would be gone, she was certain, as she slipped the latch of the kitchen door cautiously and tiptoed across the slivery planks of the porch in her bare feet, sitting down in a dark spot to put on her shoes. She had heard the clock strike eleven before gentle susurrations from the front bedroom told her that her mother was asleep. She skirted the silent barn carefully. Dobbs had returned at noon, blear-eyed and sullen, as he always appeared on Mondays; she hoped he had made a night of it and would sleep like the dead.

The sailboat was still there, a small sail set at the bow catching the air that moved with the current and bowing out delicately like a reaching wing. The moon washed over it and silhouetted the white figure in the stern, and phosphorus, coldly bright and shimmering, ran like weird fire over the ripples and up the blade of an oar that was swinging the boat in toward the dock.

Fox Cavitt leaped up to the planks and reached for her hand

without a word. Frances had a moment of uneasy hesitance as she stepped down into the swaying boat. What if Taffy watched and told? But Taffy would know that she was jeopardizing her own sly reticences if she broke the odd, unspoken pact between herself and her sister. Frances hated the thought of the hold she had over Taffy; there was a kind of ugliness in it that held implications that repelled her. It was dishonest and as vulgar as the conniving of kitchenmaids; it violated the code of a lady and made even this moonlight adventure cheap.

She said abruptly, "I've changed my mind. I can't do this, Fox." She was standing up, steadying herself against his arm while he held to the bollard to overcome the rocking of the boat. "I can't do it," she repeated a trifle hoarsely.

Without a word he helped her back to the landing. Then he took his hands away and put them into his pockets.

"I see what you mean," he said after a little. "I should have known that you couldn't do a sneaky thing. I should have had enough sense."

"When you can come to my door—openly, by daylight even—" She was having trouble with her voice because the cramp in her throat was an anguish. "Oh—this is all so stupid!" she cried out suddenly. "What have we ever done—you and I?"

"What we did was to be born in the wrong houses," he answered. "We chose the wrong people to use for parents. When can I walk up to your front door, Frances? I'm not afraid to walk up there and knock, you know. You're the one who's afraid. You're afraid the door would be slammed in my face— you know mighty well that would happen. Tell me what to do to end this foolishness and I'll do it."

"I don't know what to tell you," she said sadly. "Mama hasn't forgiven the Cavitts. Only last night she said that she never would forgive you. She argues that the Cavitts ruined her mother's life and her own, too. I'll try to think of something—"

"I suppose you know that I love you?" he said bluntly. "Maybe you won't believe that. I've had a hard time believing it myself. But—it was too big for me, Francie. It's torn down everything I've built up. I wasn't going to let anyone in; I was going to hold on to my own remoteness and keep people out.

I was cocksure about it and arrogant, too. Then you came and knocked down my fine wall, and I'm feeling sort of humble now—waiting for you to walk through the gap you made. That is, if you want to?"

She could be honest now, at least. She could meet this pridefully because there was honor in it and truth and sincerity.

"I—think I love you too, Fox," she said simply. "I must love you or I wouldn't have come here tonight. But I don't want it to be all wrong! It has to be right—it has to be!" She put out her hands to him in a groping gesture, but he would not touch her. "We have to show my mother—some way—that it's decent and noble and good," she argued. "I'll try, Fox— I will try."

He bent swiftly and kissed her lightly on the brow.

"We'll both try," he said softly. Then with a quick spring he was gone, and the boat was only a white wraith rimmed with fire, drifting swiftly across the river. . . .

The night had dragged itself through a length of hours, inching painfully over the notched wheels of time, when Taffy came stealing into Frances' room.

"She'll hear you crying," Taffy whispered, dropping on the bed. "I could hear you. I knew this was going to happen. Why don't you run away, France? She'll make the best of it when she knows she can't do anything about it. She always does. Look how she changed her mind about the Matsons. Golly, you work fast, France. You've even got me dizzy!"

"Go away," begged Frances, burying her face in the pillow. "Please leave me alone, Taffy."

"All right." Taffy got up reluctantly. "But I take back everything I ever said about you, France. This is wonderful! It's better than anything in a book. But look out for that Tulia. She has sharp claws and there's a frenzy in her eye."

"You read too much trash," Frances whispered sternly. "Go back to bed. I suppose you sneaked and listened?"

"You were very lofty and full of high purposes and noble impulses," Taffy giggled. "It won't get you a thing, of course. I still say you ought to run away."

She closed the door quietly behind her, and when the light began to gray on the walls, Frances slept at last. But the hollow, gnawing pain struck at her again when she awoke, with the sun high and hot on the counterpane. The horns of Capricorn were cruel and sharp.

11

Crofford Matson had come up the hard way, as he insisted upon telling anyone who would listen.

This constant reiteration, this enlarging upon his past, irritated his daughter Bliss, who was learning elegance at a school for young ladies in Virginia, and distressed his wife, who had shared his upward struggle but had no wish to be reminded of it.

"Nobody wants to hear about the time when you had only one pair of pants, Pa," argued Bliss. "You don't have to keep talking about it all the time."

"Yes, I do," he said wisely, tilting the huge mustache cup he always drank from and smacking his lips as he drained it. "I have to keep talking about it to remind myself that if you come from something you can go back to it, and fast, too. That is, if I listened to all the fancy schemes and things you think up to waste money on."

"You've done well, Mr. Matson," agreed his wife nervously. "We all give you credit for it."

"Nobody gives me credit," he fretted. "I build a big brick house. Now what? Bliss wishes we'd bought some old ruin of a place and fixed it up with old stuff that anybody with sense throws away."

"All I said," defended Bliss with a pout, "was that it would be nice to have some old four-poster beds and maybe a sampler that some ancestress made framed in the hall, and not so much varnish on everything."

"Old ratty junk! I buy the best dining-room furniture they've got in Norfolk and she wishes we had some old junk! I don't see any varnish—Oh, upstairs maybe, but all this down here is stained and waxed, the very newest thing. You wanted flowers on your wall, didn't you? Well, you've got flowers. The biggest darned flowers I could find anywhere and a brass bed with knobs on it bigger than any spittoon in Gus Nordach's saloon."

"Oh, Pa, such conversation at the table! You could be a big manufacturer, you know you could. You could be bigger than James B. Duke, if you'd just get your small ideas out of your head."

"So you were snooping around listening, were you, Miss? I saw that portiere waving. Well, I tell you all and I tell you now that I came up the hard way by putting a little bit on top of the little bit I had and holding on to it. And when I got it, it was mine. It didn't belong to some banker or stockholder, and nobody with a legal paper in his hand and a sneer on his face can come around and set me out in the road and take the roof from over your heads. So if you put Zach Cavitt up to coming here with all his big ideas and his bluff and brass, you made a darn' poor steer."

"I didn't put him up to coming. I don't even know Zach Cavitt very well. He's years older and he's married and I don't like his wife, the way she tries to take all the young men away from girls when she's years older!" Bliss was almost in tears. "Anyway, it was Rennie who thought you ought to consider Zach Cavitt's idea."

"How much money has Rennie got to invest in ideas?" demanded Croff, glaring at his younger son. "I pay him wages and by Tuesday he's broke and drawing on his next week's pay."

"That's because you pay him Negro wages, Pa," Wylie put in quietly. "Ren ought to have a job that requires a little intelligence."

Renwick gulped his coffee, his face red and troubled, and said nothing. His Adam's apple worked painfully up and down in his thin neck, and his eyes were anxious and unhappy.

"Ren's got to know how to do any job in the shop, just as I know how to do it," insisted Matson. "I know how stemming and chopping and mixing ought to be done because I can do those things. I can shape a lump faster than that darned machine, and I can weigh tobacco in my hand and hit the weight as accurate as any pair of scales ever made. That's why I own the place. It's the fellow who stands around with his hands clean and a pencil over his ear that goes out of business."

"Practically everybody," Wylie remarked, "will be smoking cigarettes inside of five years."

"Pimps and young squirts that hang around saloons, that's who'll be smoking those things! No money in it. I work for the workingman who's got cash in his pocket every Saturday night. Take the cigar business—you've got to have Havana wrappers and labels and bands on 'em and Cubans to roll 'em; but what I make, the farmer buys, and the man who likes a good pipe at night—and there are a blamed sight more farmers and workingmen than there are gentlemen or pimps!" Croff pushed his cup back, brushed the supper crumbs from his rounded vest, and shoved back the heavy leather-padded chair. "My fault," he admitted, brushing at a tomato seed that had attached itself to his lapel. "I gave you all too many big ideas. Now you want to forget your raising. You don't want to remember when Mama and I sat up nights grinding snuff in her old coffee mill."

"Why," fumed Bliss, "should anybody want to remember things like that? Anyway, Pa, ladies don't like cigars. They smell up the curtains."

"Don't look at me. I don't make 'em. Don't want any truck with 'em."

"They don't like nasty cuspidors or smelly old pipes either. You'll see."

"Huh! Maybe I ought to turn my shop into a perfume factory. Maybe I ought to set up looms and weave fancy lace and ribbons and stuff to sew on shimmies? Show me a man that lets a woman tell him what he can smoke or chew and I'll show you a poor stick that gets led around by the nose. What have ladies got to do with the tobacco business? You tell me that?"

"Only this—that ladies boss the men," remarked Wylie, with a grin. "Zach Cavitt is right about one thing, Pa. Duke wouldn't be going into the cigarette business if there wasn't going to be money in it."

"I'm not James Duke," roared his father. "I'm Croff Matson, who manages to make a pretty decent living for a lot of people who don't appreciate it one bit. Look at you. You went to college. Did I go to college? No, I never got past the third grade. I had to quit school and scramble to get something to eat. Mighty little of that, a heap of times, too. When I was your age I was working in a warehouse, nailing up hogsheads and grading, with black gum up my arms this far! What has Zach Cavitt ever done except run through every cent he could chisel out of the old Captain? Everybody knows he had to sneak out of Cuba; and he marries a fancy wife who struts around town dressed up like a strumpet—and you think I ought to listen to his pipe dreams! Hah!" He jerked a black pipe from his pocket, dragged out a yellow twist of leaf and whittled off a scrap, packing it into the bowl with a grimy thumb. "Good old Golden Twist," he gloated, "good enough for me. Good enough for anybody."

"All right, Pa, you win," said Wylie wearily. "But I still say there's a proper moment to expand any business and if the time isn't now, then why has Duke ordered all those Bonsack cigarette machines?"

"Exactly! Machines!" snorted Croff. "And Zach Cavitt comes along with a scheme to compete with machines with a handmade product. Advertising, too. Worst waste of money there is."

"It sells Bull Durham and Battle Ax. All along the railroad you can see those big signs. People don't think or consider much, they believe what they see. They see the big signs and when they go to buy it clicks in their mind—what they saw on that sign. It's human nature." Renwick spoke for the first time.

"It's human nature to gamble, too. Maybe I'm not human," Matson laughed harshly. "Anyway I'm not human enough to gamble away what I've made and what I've laid up to take care of your mother's old age, just to get into the fancy cigarette business. Look at what you see in the papers. Women, everywhere, coming out against 'em! Preachers in the pulpit, even. No—I've said my say and this is the end of it."

He tramped out, leaving a trail of acrid smoke behind him. Mrs. Matson fanned at it futilely with a napkin, then began picking up the dishes, sighing audibly. "I don't know why you children want to get him all riled up," she complained. "After all, you should be glad he's done so well."

"Ma, look!" Renwick had a kind of desperation in his voice. "Pa isn't big enough to fight J. B. Duke. Look what's happening. Little concerns like ours are going out of business, all over this state and in Virginia too. You can't compete with a big outfit like American in the same lines. You've got to specialize and create a demand for a high-priced, special product. Tulia Cavitt says that in Paris even the women smoke Turkish cigarettes."

"If you'd rather listen to a woman that never did anybody any good in this world than to your own father—" his mother wailed. "Look at the Cavitts. They bring bad luck to everybody. Specially that Zach. You let your father alone."

"All right, I'm just telling you, Ma," Renwick was plaintive, "that he'd better get me out of those vats and spray his flavoring on the tobacco on belts or someway, or somebody is going to come along and squawk that our place is filthy, and then where will our market be?"

"I don't know. I don't know anything about it, but I say your father has been right all along, and got along without going into debt, and I'm not going to sign any papers to give some bank a hold over us and you can make up your mind to it!" Her face set in a mask, almost knife-edged in its severity.

Bliss got up languidly and began to carry out the dishes. She had been fascinated by Zach Cavitt. He talked so well, like somebody in court or Congress or something; he was so handsome and easy and assured.

Pa had certainly sounded silly, yelling like that, not even willing to listen to Zach's proposition that they convert the Matson factory into a high-class establishment and put up billboards and buy space in New York papers and pack cigarettes in stylish little gold boxes with no cheap pictures of actresses or prize fighters inside.

Bliss knew that she wasn't very bright and that business talk went over her head usually, just as it did over Ma's; but she had understood Zach's arguments about catering to people who liked paying more for something ordinary people couldn't afford to buy. That made sense to her mind. Hadn't Pa sent her to that Virginia school for that very reason? It cost more and nobody learned very much there, but rich men sent their daughters just because it did cost more, applying Zach Cavitt's argument that sixty per cent of Americans bought the things they chose simply by judging cost alone.

Some of the girls at that school had been definitely snippy, and Bliss had had it in her mind to beg not to be sent back there, but now she put that idea aside. Pa wanted her there because he wanted to feel rich—but why didn't he want to manufacture something exclusive and continue to feel rich?

It all came of his dread of banks and legal papers, and Bliss knew that this stemmed from her father's basic ignorance and the stubbornness that had its root in a deep-laid feeling of inferiority. That, and the fact that the Cavitts had been important people when Croff Matson was nobody at all, just a barefoot boy with black gum on his arms from working in tobacco.

The way to handle Pa, she decided, was to sell him the idea that he was the smartest and most successful tobacco man in the Carolina tidewater. Ren and Wylie would have to shut up and help instead of making Pa bristle and fume with their arguments. Being female, Bliss had been born with the certainty in her mind that a man could be flattered into anything. If she could bring her father around, Zach Cavitt would be indebted to her, and he'd have to be grateful. Of course there would be more inducement to help him if he weren't married to that cold-eyed Tulia, but everybody knew that Tulia was sick of Zach anyway and would like to make up to Fox if Fox could be induced to notice her.

Bliss slipped from the dining room and found Renwick sitting gloomily on the front doorstep, his chin clutched in his palm, staring out into the summer darkness. She dropped down beside him and tucked her hand into the curve of his arm.

"Don't mope, Rennie. I think I can manage Pa if you'll help instead of making him mad all the time."

"He makes me mad all the time," grumbled Ren. "Look— you get sent to school, Wylie gets a good education and an office with his name on the door, but what do I get? I get stuck in the factory when I'm seventeen years old, and look!" He waved his outraged, blackened hands under her nose.

"Well, you flunked. You quit school of your own accord because you knew you'd never graduate. That wasn't Pa's fault, he was awfully disappointed in you. He did the next best thing he could for you. Somebody in the family had to inherit the business and be trained to take over when he gets too old."

"That may be, but why can't he treat me fair? Wylie gets the buggy any time he wants it. When I'd like to go any place, Pa has a thousand objections."

"Well, who was it tore up a good buggy and cut the horses' legs on barbed wire?" retorted his sister. "Pa thinks you don't know enough to handle a horse."

"Was it my fault that that fellow from Norfolk came tearing along in that goldarned gasoline buggy and scared the team half to death? Pa couldn't have held them either. Pa would have been thrown out and killed, like as not. I had sense enough to jump clear when the buggy went into that bridge railing. They ought not to allow those stinking things on the roads anyway. Zach Cavitt says that in France, where they've got a lot of them, they have to pull off the road and stop if they see a horse coming. It's the law."

"You've got your boat. You can go almost anywhere you want in that boat."

"Call that a boat? Sure, it's got a bottom in it and it moves if you row hard enough, but when the tide's going out it takes hours to get up the river."

"You're still crazy about that little redhead out at the Neary place! Oh, I saw you—following her around at our party. Rennie, she's younger even than I am. She's just a brat and you're twenty years old."

"She's almost eighteen. She's no child. She's cute as a button, too."

"She's too free with men. Ma thought so too. Rennie, will you help me make Pa think he's the smartest man in the world? If you will, I'll coax him to let you have the buggy to go courting."

"Why bother trying to sell Pa that stuff? He already thinks he's the smartest man in the world. He brags about it. You ought to hear him when we go out to buy tobacco, or when somebody comes into the place to sell him something. But with the little people, the Negroes and the white trash that come in out of the swamps looking for work or wanting to sell him deertongue and stuff, he's right the other way. You'd think he was their grandpa. He keeps little dabs of snuff and broken hunks of plug around to give them, and he always lets the weight go in their favor. He's good, I guess," Renwick admitted with a sigh. "He's honest and everybody trusts him, but he just isn't—"

"Progressive," supplied Bliss, with a faint tinge of superiority.

"Well, he did buy that Pease machine, but not till he'd saved up the whole price of it so he could take his discount, and he never did buy all that went with it—belts and things that eliminate the handwork."

"The same way he had electricity put in the house. *One* light—and he never wants to turn that one on. Says it ruins people's eyes, so we've got to have that old gas thing and remember to pump it up and keep new mantels and it smells and it's hot—and no bathroom or running water!"

"I sure get tired of lugging in water for Ma, after I've worked all day," complained Rennie. "Wylie can't do it—he's a big businessman. But he's got to shave every day, and then again at night, like as not—two big pitchers of hot water, and then if I want some, the fire's out and the kettle empty."

"That Keeling girl—the tall, chilly one!" sniffed Bliss. "He's crazy about her. I heard him begging Ma to go out there with him to make a call. Ma never went calling in all her life. She has those expensive visiting cards and there's never been even one taken out of the box. Wylie knows she's scared to death of people like the Nearys. She says they used to high-hat everybody in the county when she was young."

"She'll end up going. Wylie can talk Ma into anything. That Frances wouldn't go buggy riding with him Sunday, so he had to do his courting in the parlor with the old lady sitting right outside the door. But Taffy's different. She's a friendly kid. We sat out on the dock for a long time. She wants me to teach her how to handle a boat."

"Well, what are you grumbling about then? She already knows how to manage a horse. She drives into town almost

every day. I see her when she stops over there by the cemetery. She stops there to talk to Zach Cavitt."

Rennie flushed and tightened his stained knuckles. "She's
got a right to talk to somebody, hasn't she?"

"He's married."

"Huh, you'd like a chance at him yourself! I saw you, when
he was here tonight, cutting your eyes around and swishing
your skirt."

"I wasn't interested in him. I was interested in his ideas.
Did you ever smoke cigarettes, Rennie?"

"Gosh, no! Pa would paste me one if he saw me smoking
one of those coffin nails. He said he'd give me a good pipe
when I was twenty-one, but if I ever tried cigarettes he'd think
I was a degenerate or something."

"They were cute though, and that little gold box was so
pretty I was wishing he'd give it to me."

"It was just pasteboard covered with gold paper."

"Well, I didn't say it was solid gold, did I? Rennie, you've
got a materialistic mind, just like Pa. You never see beauty in
anything."

"I've never had any chance to see any. You don't see much
beauty in that stinking, dusty shop."

"You could at least look at the Sound. Let's walk down to
the wharf right now. There's not a thing to do and Ma has a
fit if I walk down the street alone after dark."

"What do you want to go down there for? My legs are tired,
standing on my feet and bending over those benches all day."

"You can stretch your legs and rest them," argued Bliss.
"We'll walk slowly. There's going to be a moon after a little."

"You just want to walk by the minister's house," growled
Rennie as they strolled past the cemetery wall and down the
single-brick path that skirted the sandy, open town square.
"You've got that Cavitt fellow on your mind. Why don't you
get a regular beau and give your family some peace?"

"Where would I get a beau, pray tell? All the boys in this
town are countrified as everything, and Pa *would* send me to a
girl's school where we're only allowed to see men for an hour
on Sunday and then with a snoopy chaperone sitting around.

And no letters except by permission from your parents! Rennie, look! Wouldn't you think that Tulia Cavitt would close the blinds—sitting there with scarcely anything on, brushing her hair? You'd think she'd have some respect at least for the minister, when he was decent enough to take them in. Everybody knows they hadn't anywhere else to go."

"She's got pretty hair," approved Rennie, looking over his sister's shoulder at Tulia, intaglioed in a circle of lamplight before a mirror.

"She doesn't have to show it off in such a brassy way! Just that wrapper—and it not even buttoned to the top."

"Women!" muttered Rennie. "You all hate each other like poison."

"I'm sure I'd never disturb myself to hate a woman like Tulia Cavitt," remarked Bliss loftily, hurrying a little.

She urged Rennie on down the short block toward the water front, keeping her head high and her eyelids drooped a bit arrogantly to combat the gnawing feeling of uncertainty that tormented her whenever she saw Tulia. Tulia had a trick of making Bliss feel naïve and too young and bouncingly awkward in her display of charms and graces. "I do have charms and graces!" Bliss told herself fiercely, adding up in her mind her hair that shimmered and curled over the brush and showed a sheen of silver over the gilt; her chin that she knew was delicately rounded—almost too rounded; her cheeks that kept a wild-rose color and not too much of it to look healthy.

If only she didn't have that disgustingly *pretty* look! The look that went with flowers on hats, and ribbons and lace and fluffy things. Tulia could brush her hair back severely over her ears and writhe her body into a sleek, tight frock with no trimming on it anywhere, and put not so much as a flick of rice powder on her olive-tinted clean skin, and men's eyes would follow her every move. But when Bliss tried slicking her own hair back it bulged out in curls and vagrant tresses, no matter how much pomade she put on it or how hard she wielded the brush; and when she pulled her dress tight over her hips she still looked soft in all the wrong places, even though her corset was laced and boned up rigidly.

She got what comfort she could out of the thought that

maybe Zachary liked softness and prettiness. She was pretty sure that he did not greatly appreciate Tulia.

In the back of her mind was the half-crystallized hope that they'd meet him somewhere down here by the water front, and then she and Rennie would reassure him, promising to do what they could to change their father's mind. She could make Rennie do anything, she was certain. But when they had walked all the way around the square, meeting no one except the barber hurrying home to rest his aching feet, and a Negro dock hand off the *Agnes J.*, talking to himself as he shuffled along with a small green watermelon, she agreed finally to go home.

The minister's window was dark now, when they passed. Bliss let her mind go boldly into that room, then winced away from the thought of the intimacy that the darkened window implied. Suddenly she hated the town and everyone in it. Her father had already gone to bed when they entered the house, and his heavy breathing was audible in the quiet rooms. Mrs. Matson sat in the dining room with a kerosene lamp close to her shoulder, doing her endless crocheting. She looked up, and her ball of thread dropped and rolled across the floor.

"Don't lock the door," she said. "Wylie went out to Keelings'. There was a telegram telephoned to Bart's store for them, and Bart had lumbago and his horse wasn't shod in front, so Wylie volunteered to take the telegram out to Keelings'. It was important, I reckon—some of their folks in Washington are dead."

12

"Now we'll be rich!" exulted Taffy, whirling her skirts in a gleeful pirouette. "Now we can have everything we want."

Lydia sat smoothing and smoothing the yellow telegram over her knee. Down the slope Wylie Matson's buggy wheels rumbled over the little bridge.

Daniel Neary's wife was dead. She had died suddenly, the message said. The telegram was signed by a Washington law firm and politely requested to know if Lydia and her family would attend the funeral services and to please advise immediately so that arrangements could be completed. Lydia's round face was still stiff and her eyes dazed, and she kept moving her mouth vaguely though she had said nothing save one gasping, "Oh—oh, mercy!" when Frances read the wire aloud.

"We won't be rich," Frances said. "This means that Mama will inherit Uncle Daniel's share of the brass foundry, but Uncle Horace still owns a third interest and of course he'll go on operating the plant. Mama will have enough to be secure and comfortable all her life, though, I hope."

Lydia folded the paper, scrawled with Bart's wavering penciled lines, pressing it very small.

"I never liked her," she whispered hoarsely. "It makes me feel guilty that I never liked her—and now she's dead!"

"Oh, good grief! You talk as though you'd killed her, Mama! She was an old lady, older than Uncle Daniel, you said, and she was rich as everything herself and mean besides," fumed Taffy.

"Don't talk like that, Taffy." Tears ran down Lydia's face now, the easy, meaningless tears that were so swiftly outpoured and so promptly stanched when any emotion swayed her. "It's wicked to talk like that about the poor woman when she's dead."

"Why is it wicked? She was mean, you said so yourself. She

123

was mean to your mother and you go on hating the Cavitts on account of your mother, Mama, and then sit here crying about Uncle Daniel's horrible wife!"

"I don't hate the Cavitts. I just don't want anything to do with them ever, as long as I live. If I had to see a Cavitt or talk to one of them I would hate them, and hate is a wicked thing." Lydia mopped her eyes with a fold of her skirt. "And I don't hate Daniel's wife, even though he was the only boy that lived and my mother doted on him and then for years she never laid eyes on him all on account of that woman—"

"Oh, Mama, hush! Don't tear yourself all to pieces. I know death is a shock," Frances put her arm around the small, trembling body, "death to anyone. But after all, she wasn't at all decent to you when Uncle Daniel died."

"She treated us as though we were beggars," put in Taffy. "She was furious about the will, of course, and she flounced out of the room almost before he finished reading and she practically threw us out of the house, you know that, Mama."

"Why, Taffy, she did no such thing!"

"Well, the man did come up to carry our bags down in about ten minutes—and the cab was there to take us to the station and the train not due for two hours! I call that being politely shown the door," persisted Taffy. "All that time we had to sit in the depot I was telling myself that when she died I was going to gloat—so now I'm gloating. I'm gloating so gorgeously that I can hardly keep my feet on the floor!" She dropped into a chair and thrust her legs out in front of her. "What a pity the money is all tied up in that old foundry! But you could sell out your shares, Mama, and if you made some shrewd investments you could build it up into millions maybe. I could manage with a nice little steam yacht and maybe a horseless carriage with red wire wheels and big brass lamps and one of those bulb horns to toot and scare Chloe to death."

"Oh, I couldn't!" protested Lydia, frightened. "Uncle Horace would never let me sell any stock. But there will be more money every month, twice as much more as I've been getting. Why, my goodness, it will be almost three hundred dollars a month!"

"Uncle Horace is another old meanie," declared Taffy. "Mama, with your stock you'll have control of the foundry.

Why couldn't you fire Uncle Horace and get somebody young to run the plant? Or you could sell it outright and start a new enterprise—something modern and profitable." Cigarettes! the sudden thought came to her. Somebody was going to make millions out of cigarettes. Zach Cavitt said so.

Frances stood by silently thoughtful. She had heard little of what had been said—not since her mother had stated with spirit that she wanted nothing to do with the Cavitts, not to see them or speak to them so long as she lived! It was all hopeless, she was convinced. She stood sunk in a kind of aching apathy till a name caught her ear.

"You could even get square with the Cavitts, Mama," Taffy was babbling on. "You could buy a new boat and let me run it—and I'd challenge Fox Cavitt to race—and this time it would be the Cavitts old tub that would blow up!"

"Mama," Frances broke in abruptly, "would never do anything that would hurt anyone; especially not Uncle Horace. Grandpa Taft trained Uncle Horace to carry on the brass business and make money for the stockholders. One thing you are going to do though, Mama, you're going to some town where there are good shops and you're going to have a whole brand new outfit of clothes."

"Why, Francie, my clothes are good enough. Where would I go to wear a lot of clothes? I'm happy just to have a home—and stay in it. But you girls can have new dresses—and maybe we can get a new range for the kitchen, one with a tank on the back so we can have plenty of hot water. And maybe a new pump!"

Taffy made an exasperated gesture with flat palms outspread. "She inherits a fortune and all she wants is a pump! Mama, we've got to send an answer to that telegram. Do you want to go to the funeral—or don't you?"

"I think she should go," Frances said, "and then to Baltimore too. There'll be papers to sign and you should have your own lawyer, Mama; somebody to protect your interests and take care of everything for you."

Lydia looked frightened. "Uncle Horace will take care of everything," she protested, "and I just couldn't go to the funeral, Francie. She wouldn't want me there. And you could go to Baltimore and look after all the business just like you did before. Write out a reply to these lawyers, so we can send it in the morning. Just tell them that it will be impossible for me to attend the funeral and that we'll consult with them about the business later. You'll know what to say."

"Write it, France, and I'll get up early and take it into town. Why don't we all go to Baltimore?" Taffy wanted to know. "Mama ought to learn something about her own business. Suppose old Uncle Horace dropped dead. He is Mama's uncle —he must be almost eighty."

"No—no, Francie can go. I'll send Uncle Horace a letter. I'll tell him Francie is coming up to attend to everything."

"And I stay here, no doubt?" sniffed Taffy.

"Why, you wouldn't want me to stay here alone, Taffy? It shouldn't take Francie but a few days to get everything settled. You could stay with Miss Baker, Francie. She's still in the same room in our old house. You couldn't stay with Uncle Horace— being a widower and living in a hotel—"

"Let's all go to bed," sighed Frances.

Nothing would be changed, she thought heavily. There would be more money and that would make things easier, but the money would only make her mother more anxious and more fussily arbitrary and incompetently executive. Taffy would wheedle and coax and maneuver ways to get things for herself, but it would all be futile and as void of direction as Chloe's patient jogging about the hardbeaten barnyard.

"It's because I have no strength in me," she decided, lying in the dark, an arm curled under her head so that she could glimpse through the window a brief far shimmer of the river under the moon. No strength, no fury, no faith. Fox had said that he loved her, but she would not let herself believe it. She wanted to believe that she herself was in love, but doubt was a cold weight on her heart, there was no thrill, no happiness, only a kind of heaviness of resignation. If love had come to her it had come left-handedly, reluctantly, frustrated and all wrong. The honesty that went so deep in her hated the furtiveness it wore, even in her thoughts. The bargaining, the warnings, the conniving that cloaked her attitude with Taffy repelled her. And ahead was nothing.

Vacillating as Lydia was, Frances was certain that her mother would never change her attitude toward the Cavitts. As for running away, as Taffy had suggested, Frances knew her own softheartedness too well to consider even that remote possibility. She had never been able to deal a blow. Was it going to be like that forever—always accepting, deploring, faintly resenting, but never a defiance, never an attack, never so far even a strong conviction?

Spineless. She despised herself. A doormat! Like Papa.

Even her mother had had spirit enough to marry John Keeling against the wishes of the Tafts and the Nearys.

"But I don't know Fox," she mourned silently, pressing her finger tips over her eyeballs to shut out the haunting shine of the river. "I don't really know him at all."

All day she carried the vague shame of being too vulnerable, of being fascinated, as empty-headed women were, by a dark, aloof face, a mocking quirk at the corner of a guarded mouth, by mystery. In vain she had assured herself that this was not true, that she had seen beyond the cool mask Fox Cavitt wore, seen the loneliness there, the solitary, guarded rigidity that he was apparently helpless to defeat, the dreams and desires he had been curiously eager to share with her. Still she knew so little of him, what he believed or disbelieved, what he thought, liked, or hated. All she knew was that he had declared himself in love with her, and that he had struggled against the idea of being in love.

Perhaps he was lying over there now, in that house across the river, relieved because she had had the good sense or the lack of boldness to make the most of the moon, wondering why he had been so rash as to let her breach his wall of remoteness, puzzled as she was puzzled at her own recklessness.

"When I see him again, I'll know," she told herself at last.

Now she would go to Baltimore, and Uncle Horace would frown and figure and worry, and issue a thousand warnings and a multitude of dubious predictions. Ultimately they would be a little better off, but life would merely go on after that, made up of mornings and noons and nights differentiated only by wind and weather, by coffee or tea for dinner, hot bread or cold.

She could perhaps get a job. Women did work now, though men of the old school like Uncle Horace were dismayed by such social upheavals. Women taught school, like Miss Baker, enduring chalky-smelling rooms full of horrible, squirming moppets; or they worked in stores, wearing black sateen aprons and cuffs pinned on over the starched sleeves of their shirt-waists. They trimmed hats, though to be a milliner was to risk being considered slightly fast and having to go out with travel-ing men. And there was still Cliff Houchins. She had had two cards from him, views of Johns Hopkins with a window marked with a cross and the label: *Dissecting Room. Ha-Ha!* She had shuddered at that crudity and torn the card impatiently in two, as she shuddered at the insistent amiability of Wylie Matson and the intent that lay so openly in his eyes.

"What do I want out of life?" she tormented herself.

Far away, down the deep of the Sound, a freight boat mooed hollowly. In the tree beyond her window a little owl sent a shivering cry to the indifferent moon.

13

Taffy drove very slowly past the minister's house in the misty light of early morning.

The blind of the lower front room was still drawn. The minister's wife, in a ruffled wrapper, was sweeping the fallen hackberry leaves in a little heap in the back yard; but the house looked slumberous and still. In that lower room Tulia Cavitt was undoubtedly getting her beauty sleep, and Taffy twisted her mouth in a gamin's grimace and thought that no amount of beauty was going to do Tulia much good.

Tulia wanted Fox, as all the gossips whispered, and Taffy knew now that Fox was falling in love with Frances. Hadn't she herself crouched at the top of the bluff last Monday night and seen Fox kiss Francie on the forehead? If that wasn't love it was outrage, but Taffy was satisfied that all was noble and stiff with honor and that somehow she had to help Francie out of the stupid muddle of the old Neary-Cavitt feud and through the dogged mazes of their mother's honest obstinacy. As for Zach—Taffy clicked her small white teeth. She thought she knew what to do about Zach Cavitt. Probably he had heard already that the Keelings had inherited money. News traveled as swiftly and insidiously as the fogs from the Sound in this isolated little place.

At the wharf the *Agnes J.* was getting up steam for the ferry run and a billow of black smoke from her funnel wormed upward and writhed warmly over the town, over the silvered roof of the old church and the foggy dimness of the cemetery. Fox Cavitt was on the wharf checking over some piled boxes of Matson's Golden Twist; Taffy drove the mare up to the gnawed hitchrack near the water front and called to him.

He came toward her, his eyes still on the papers in his hands, and nodded with curt politeness.

"Good morning," he said. "You're out early."

"Business," Taffy said. "I have a telegram to send when the store opens. My sister will be going out with you tomorrow to take the train for Baltimore. Wait for her, will you, please?"

"We shove off at half past seven," he remarked briskly. "We run on schedule, so tell her to be on time."

Taffy frowned, appraising him. There was no change in his face whatever, not a flicker of an eyelid; not a muscle stirred about his straight-set mouth. She might have informed him that a cow would be coming aboard his boat tomorrow morning. Taffy felt a swift flare of anger. Was he having fun with Francie, because she was new, because she was innocent and naïve? That stoniness could be a pose he put on, liking to make himself enigmatic, liking to have girls speculating about him, whispering that he was difficult and unattainable.

She tossed her head. "I'm so glad Francie is going to Baltimore," she said blithely. "She has wonderful friends there and there's a young doctor she's practically engaged to. He's connected with Johns Hopkins, and he's quite mad about Francie. He was quite heartbroken when we came away."

Fox Cavitt merely nodded. Taffy felt rage press upward in her throat till she wanted to scream maledictions at him. The wooden thing! No more feeling than a graven image! Or had his mouth drawn in a little, his lips moved a bit sensitively over his teeth? She gave Chloe a furious slap with the reins and whirled the buggy about till the wheel screeched on the cramp iron.

"All right for you, Mr. Fox Cavitt!" she snapped, when she had crossed the square. "I'll have no foolishness out of you where my sister is concerned!"

Maybe Mama was right after all. Perhaps it was true that the Cavitts were poisonous people and brought bad luck wherever they went. She was debating this possibility when the mare stopped with a jolt, and Taffy's hat slid over one ear.

Fury crackled on her tongue as Zach Cavitt stepped up between the wheels.

"I might have known!" she snapped. "I'm going to sell this miserable beast for cat meat!"

He said suavely, "I have just heard of a bereavement in your family. Someone quite dear to you, was it?"

"Not dear at all," answered Taffy crisply. "Everybody hears everything in this town. Will you get away, please? I'm on business."

"Business is what I'd like to discuss with you." He ignored her rudeness. "I've learned that that old mill out there on the marsh belongs to you. Innocently, I've been trespassing on your property by storing my tobacco there. Will you talk to your sister and arrange a lease for us—for our company, I mean?"

"What company?" demanded Taffy.

"The company in which you are to be a stockholder. The mill is by way of being a ruin, of course, but it can be restored and it's accessible by water if we build a landing. We could settle it between ourselves, but I understand you are not of age yet?"

"I will be. In September."

"September is still two months off. Please discuss this with your sister." He turned away. "Incidentally," he flung back over his shoulder, "I had no luck with Croff Matson. I'm starting out on an entirely new plan. I'll see you again, little Taffy."

Taffy gave the dashboard a savage kick and whacked at Chloe's fat rump with the whip. *Little Taffy!*

"Humiliate me, will you?" she berated the mare. "Stopping every time you see that conceited scoundrel!"

So he had stored his tobacco in the old mill, and the mill belonged to the Keeling sisters, and arrogantly he was certain that all he had to do was suggest some arrangement and instantly it would be in effect. At least, decided Taffy, if he had been cherishing the illusion that she was halfway in love with him or fascinated by him, he'd soon know better. *Little Taffy!* As though she were ten years old and brainless besides! Taffy's mouth was a Neary mouth, definitely grim, as she tied Chloe in front of the store and went up the three worn wooden steps to the door.

Old Bart looked up from dragging out a wire basket of worn-looking string beans.

"You get your tellygram all right?" he asked. "I would have driv' over there myself but I knew Wylie'd be tickled to have an excuse to go. Wylie sure takes his courtin' serious. Gets a shave at the barbershop every day; hair tonic, too. You want I should 'phone you an answer to that wire?"

"I have the telegram written here," said Taffy with dignity. "I'm to pay all the charges and whatever the cost of delivery may be."

"No charge for delivery—anyway Wylie ain't sent me no bill," Bart cackled. "Be fifty cents each way for the 'phone." He went to the instrument on the wall and cranked it vigorously, yelling into the transmitter, "Hello—hel-lo! Get me Bath, Gert—get me the tellygraph feller up there.... Yonder goes Zach Cavitt," he remarked, looking out the window over his shoulder. "Goin' down to promote a loan from Fox, I reckon. Never did see a feller with so much brass. Been tryin' to horn in on Croff Matson's business, they tell. Hit the wrong man that time. Croff ain't got much education but he sure can add two and two. Cigarettes—that's what Zach's got on his mind. Them things I won't even sell in my store. Hello—hel-lo! This here the tellygraph feller? Want you should send a message to Washington. Yeah—I'll send the money up there. Send it by the ferry tomorrow. Hold on a minute. Gimme that paper, Miss Keeling."

"Let me," said Taffy impulsively. "I've never talked on a telephone."

She approached the instrument gingerly and was surprised at the clearness of the voice over the wire. Carefully she repeated the message Frances had written, then looked uncertainly at Bart.

"What do I do now?" she asked.

"Ask him how much the charge is, and hang up that there. Then you leave the money with me and I'll have Fox Cavitt take it up there, next trip."

The *Agnes* was blowing a melancholy blast on her whistle when Taffy untied the mare. Chloe had pawed a deep hole under the hitchrack and stood in it, her forequarters pitched forward and her head drooping. The mare jerked her ears nervously as the whistle moaned again, cracking back from woods and walls; then the engines of the *Agnes* began to bumble and the boil of dirty water washed up and splashed against the bank. As the boat backed out Taffy saw that Zach

Cavitt was standing on the deck, just opposite the wheelhouse. He waved his hat at her jauntily, and Taffy shrugged and turned deliberately away.

Then a woman screamed behind her, and Taffy jumped, startled, as Tulia Cavitt came flying down the path, clutching a loose gown around her body, her feet bare and her hair blowing.

"Stop that boat!" she was screaming. "Come back here, Fox! Stop that boat!"

The *Agnes* was turned now, bow-on into deep water, and her propellers carved a twisting signature of farewell on the blue surface of the Sound, while smoke wandered ashore and lay lazily under the trees.

"You're too late," Taffy remarked as Tulia stopped, straining forward tensely, every inch of her slim body taut with fury. Even in dishevelment there was a wild beauty about Tulia, even with her eyes blazing and her mouth stiff and white with rage.

"He took my ring!" she cried. "He took my diamond. Now he's gone."

"Definitely he's gone," Taffy agreed. "If you mean your husband, I saw him go on board myself."

"The dog! The low, sneaking hound!" stormed Tulia. "He stole it off the washstand while I was getting some hot water. My diamond that my father gave me. I told him I'd never give it up. Oh, he tried, over and over, to get it away from me! It was the very last thing I had that was mine. Now he'll sell it and waste the money on some wild scheme or other." She began to sob harshly and Taffy was briefly sorry for her.

"The police could get it back," she suggested. "That is if you want to call the police."

"I'll do it!" Tulia twisted her wrapper around her with a jerk. "I'll telephone. I'll have him arrested when he goes ashore, the tricky crook! Oh—you don't know what it is to be married to a worthless scalawag! Here I am—left without a penny, nothing to eat—no way to get away—"

"You'd better get in my buggy and let me take you back to get some clothes on," advised Taffy coolly. "You're attracting considerable attention as it is."

"Thank you." Tulia looked around in confusion, pushing her flying hair from her dead-white cheeks. "I suppose so. I lost my head when I saw my ring was gone—I didn't even stop to button my slippers. I lost them somewhere back by the cemetery."

"The rig's over here." Taffy steered her, with a monitory hand on her elbow. Tulia was shaking all over now, her hands were like ice, her eyes vague and bewildered. She got numbly into the buggy, sagged forward on the seat, then began to plait up her long hair with swift, nervous motions of her fingers.

"You're very good to trouble about me," she said as Taffy got in beside her. "No doubt now the village will have a lovely sensation to enjoy through a dull day! They're convinced that I'm a hussy now—running through the market place all undressed. That I've had a thousand-dollar ring stolen won't weigh a penny's worth in my favor."

"If you go to the store and telephone the police, you'll really stir up a hornet's nest," remarked Taffy, "but I don't blame you for hating to lose a ring like that. It must have been a tremendous diamond."

"It was an unusual stone. My father lived in France and invested all his money in fine gems. When he gave me that ring he told me that as long as I owned it I would be secure, no matter what happened. I've fought to keep it this long, I'm not going to give it up merely to keep the Cavitts from being talked about."

"I doubt if the Cavitts mind being talked about," observed Taffy. "They appear to me to be people who are never affected by anything."

"Oh, there are my slippers," Tulia cried abruptly. "That man's just picking them up. Oh, mister—those belong to me." She thanked the startled elderly man who came shuffling out to the buggy with the abandoned shoes in his hands, stuffed her toes into them, and buttoned the straps. "Cinderella," she said. "Except that there's no prince. It would be no use at all to telephone any police," she went on, as the mare stopped at the minister's gate, "no use at all. I know Zach Cavitt. He has talked himself out of messes with the police everywhere we've gone. He can talk himself out of anything. So far he's been able to talk me out of killing him! You think I'm demented or depraved, I suppose? Sometimes I wonder if I'm in my right mind myself. Oh heaven, here comes Mrs. Drake, poor dear meddlesome soul! She'll think I'm out of my mind too."

The minister's wife came panting out, dropping her broom as she trotted up to the buggy.

"Good gracious, Tulia, I was so frightened!" she panted. "I thought surely the boat must have blown up or that something dreadful had happened to Zach."

"The dreadful thing happened to me, Mrs. Drake," Tulia replied as she got down from the buggy. "Zach ran off with my diamond."

"Oh, but of course he'll take good care of it," comforted the plump little woman. "Probably the stone was loose or something. Good morning, Miss Keeling. I'm Mrs. Drake. So good of you to bring Tulia home. Do come in, both of you, and have a cup of coffee with Father and me. Father's trimming his beard and I haven't been able to get him down to breakfast. He's the vainest man about that beard you ever saw. I tell him it's a mortal sin the way he pets it."

"Thank you very much, but I must go home. My mother will worry." Taffy clucked at Chloe and drove on around the rectangle of the cemetery wall. A mile down the homeward road, she tensed with a sudden inspiration and urged Chloe faster with the whip. Now was her chance to see that old mill, the building Zach Cavitt had pre-empted so casually without bothering to find out to whom it belonged. She had no idea how far it was beyond the Neary gates, but it could not be far if it stood on Neary land. Chloe protested at passing the gate, jerking her head and shying, but Taffy used the whip and got her into the narrowing road, though the mare settled into a sullen, shambling walk that no goading could accelerate.

She was surprised when she came upon water abruptly. She had not guessed that the river turned north and made a sharp bend a little way above the Cavitt place. The old mill stood on a grassy little rise with marshland all around, and a slow creek ran past it, twisting lazily off to the river. The mill was a low stone building with a mossy sagging roof, and in front of it under a huge willow tree stood a vast iron kettle half lost in a tangle of nettles.

The road ended there sharply, and an overgrown path ran to the mill, tall grass and reeds bending in and almost hiding the narrow trodden track. Taffy tied the mare to a sapling and took the path, holding up her long skirt and stepping gingerly in dread of snakes. Then she stopped suddenly, her heart pounding, and turned to run as an old Negro man got up from under the willow tree and came shambling toward her. He halted, calling gently.

"Don't be skeered, li'l Missy. Tobe ain't goin' to hurt nobody. I'se jest a-waitin' here for Mister Zach. Mister Zach, he allow he comin' back today."

He came closer, a bent old creature with watery maroon eyes and limping feet shod in broken shoes.

"Don't come near me," warned Taffy. "If you want to talk to me, stop right there."

"Yes'm," he agreed, peering at her from beneath a pair of shaggy white brows. "You's Miss Liddy's gal, ain't you? I can see you favors the Nearys. You ain't seed Mister Zach Cavitt, has you? He 'lowed to come today and pay me for my 'bacca."

"Mr. Cavitt went away this morning on the ferry," Taffy told him. "This is the old Neary mill, isn't it?"

"Yes'm, this yere's the old Cap'n's mill. Ain't grindin' none now, though. Ain't done no grindin' for many a year. Used to grind a heap of 'lasses, come a time. Made him some rum, too, the Cap'n did. Ain't makin' no rum now neither. I dunno," he sighed and rubbed his bald, fringed head, "I dunno how come Mister Zach to do me this-a-way. He tole me to come here today and he'd fetch me a little piece of money, sho'."

"Money? What for?" asked Taffy shrewdly.

"For my 'bacca, what I brung down here on my barge, Missy."

"You own the tobacco?"

"No'm, I don't rightly own it. I pole the barge down the river. Sukey, she own some and ole Mister Barclay, he own three dem hogsheads. I tooken it down here figurin' Mister Croff Matson, he might buy it offen us. They ain't payin' nothin' for 'bacca up the country. Them big 'bacca men, over

Durham ways, they done beat the price down till it ain't pay us to neither grow it nor pick it. Mister Croff been payin' six cents a pound, but when I meet up with Mister Zach, he say Mister Croff he won't pay but five cents, but Mister Zach, he give me six cents if I wait a day or two. I done waited a week now, Missy."

"How many pounds have you got in there? Is it good tobacco?" Taffy asked.

"Now, that there's the bes' 'bacca ever you see, Missy. And I got most a thousand pounds."

"And you'll sell it all for sixty dollars?"

"Missy, I poled that 'bacca more'n twenty miles down river and done hauled it a long ways up yonder wid my mule afore ever I loaded it. I got to have a li'l piece of money for me, and some for Sukey and Mister Barclay. I reckoned Mister Zach would sho' keep his word. Ole Cap'n Cavitt, he kep' his word, white or black it didn't make no never mind. Did the old Cap'n say 'Boy, you come and I pay you,' you could count that money same as judgment day."

"If I can get sixty dollars will you sell the tobacco to me?"

"Missy, you git me even fifty dollars and you bought yourse'f a bargeload of 'bacca. But you ain't got no use for 'bacca, li'l white lady like you."

"I have a use for money," Taffy said firmly. "Anyway, that tobacco is stored on our property. We could charge you a fee for storing it, and if it isn't moved out right away you're trespassing and we could call the law about that."

The old man looked troubled. "Missy, I done just what Mister Zach tole me to do. You gotta blame Mister Zach, not ole Tobe."

"I'll settle with Mister Zach. Will you wait here till dinnertime, Tobe?"

"Yes'm, reckon I gotta wait. Can't git that barge back up river till the tide turns toward midnight. Reckon, does you come back you could fetch me a cold corn pone? I ain't et since yistiddy and my innards sho' is growling."

"On second thought," said Taffy impulsively, "you come with me. You can talk to my mother. She's old Captain Neary's daughter and she knows all you people. You sit back there in the buggy and I'll try to turn around without tipping over."

With the old man squatting like a dark Buddha in the rear of the vehicle, she maneuvered Chloe around and headed back for the Neary gate. Her mind was clicking busily, adding up figures, building with them a pattern of revenge for the insult of that "little Taffy." She would show Mister Zach Cavitt. She would demonstrate that she was no child to be dismissed indulgently, but a businesswoman worthy of consideration, and she would hold out for a substantial interest and partial control in any company that was planned to occupy the Neary mill. All she needed was fifty dollars and a stout padlock. Mama had much more than fifty dollars in the tin box in Grandfather Neary's desk. And they could always sell the tobacco to the Matsons if Zach Cavitt failed to return.

Lydia stared with incredulous consternation when Taffy drove up to the back door with a flourish and the old Negro climbed stiffly down.

"Taffy—what in the world? Whatever are you thinking of, picking up a strange colored man? Why—it's Tobe Gibson, isn't it?"

"Yes'm, Miss Lyddy." Old Tobe bowed and picked at his vanished forelock. "Dis yere old Tobe. You' lookin' fine and young and handsome, Miss Lyddy."

Lydia flushed, pleased. "You go along, Tobe, you haven't seen me since I was a little girl. I'm an old woman now."

"Law, you ain't old, Miss Lyddy. You sho' do look like your maw, too. You jes' the image of Miss 'Melia."

"He's hungry, Mama," Taffy said. "He's been over at that old mill all night, with nothing to eat."

"My goodness, you come along with me, Tobe, and I'll fix you up a snack. What were you doing at the mill? I thought that place had fallen down long ago."

"No'm, it ain't. I was over yonder, waitin' to sell my 'bacca."

"He'll sell it cheap, Mama, a thousand pounds of it," Taffy pressed her advantage quickly, "and I want to buy it if you'll lend me the money."

Lydia's face changed quickly. "Tobacco?" she repeated. "Our family never had anything to do with tobacco. What do you want to buy tobacco for?"

"To make money with," persisted Taffy. "I just want a loan, Mama. I'll pay you back in September—I'll sell something, some land or something. I can make money on Tobe's tobacco, I know I can."

"I don't want anything to do with tobacco," argued Lydia, "and you're too young to know anything about making money. Come along, Tobe. I think I can find some cold bacon and biscuit for you."

Frances, who had come out on the porch, looked at Taffy sharply.

"What in the world goes on, Taffy?" she questioned.

Taffy whirled on her. "Did you know that we owned a mill? Well, we do! Just now it's full of prime bright-leaf tobacco that belongs to old Tobe, yonder, and he'll sell it for much less than it's worth. I want to borrow enough money from Mama to buy it, and make a profit. You help persuade her, Francie."

"I never heard of anything so utterly fantastic! Tobacco! How do you know you could sell it again, even if Mama was crazy enough to let you buy it?"

"I might not sell it—not in its present crude form," Taffy said smoothly. "I might arrange to have it manufactured into some product or other. After all, I can twist Rennie Matson around my thumb."

Frances' brows drew down and her mouth straightened. "I suppose Zachary Cavitt is mixed up in this somehow?" she said sternly. "Wylie Matson said he had some sort of project going. Taffy, how could you? When we're so new here—on trial, you might say, and you know how Mama feels about the Cavitts."

"It's because I hate Zach Cavitt that I want to buy this tobacco!" stormed Taffy. "Because he patronizes me—he thinks I'm some child—" her voice thickened to a croak and angry tears brimmed in her eyes. "I'm like the Nearys," she went on furiously, fighting her emotion, "I'm practical. I can make money for us—I know I can! What do I care what they say in this stupid town?"

Lydia came back then and dropped into a chair with a sigh. "Taffy, this poor old colored man says you practically promised to buy that dreadful tobacco," she worried. "How could you be so impulsive? After all—fifty dollars!"

"I'll pay it back, Mama. I'll give you a note."

"You aren't legally competent to sign a note," Frances reminded her. "In the eyes of the law you're still a child."

Taffy aimed a savage kick at a post. "The next person who calls me a child is my enemy for life," she raged. "I'm mature enough to know a bargain when I see one. Look at the fortunes people are making out of tobacco! Look at Duke!"

"People have made fortunes out of whisky, too," Lydia remarked, "and gambling and other forms of sin."

"I'm not going to smoke this tobacco. I'm going to sell it. At a handsome profit. Twenty per cent, at least. Even Uncle Horace would agree that twenty per cent was a good profit," argued Taffy desperately.

Old Tobe came shuffling back, brushing crumbs from his vest. "Sho' do thank you, Miss Lyddy," he said. "Sho' do 'preciate the grub you gimme. You want I should fetch you another load of that 'bacca downriver, Miss Lyddy?"

"Tobe, that has to be last year's tobacco," Frances said. "The crop isn't gathered yet this summer."

"Yes'm, got age on it. Makes it more better. Green tobacco ain't no good for nothin'. Got to age it in the wood for a spell."

Frances saw an atavistic cupidity gathering in her mother's small blue eyes, saw the drawing in of her round mouth. The Nearys and the Tafts, the girl was thinking drearily, might have scruples, might have hates and resentments, but none could ever assume importance vast enough to obscure the lure of profit.

"Oh, go ahead and give Taffy the fifty dollars, Mama," she cried. "You will anyway!"

"But she promised this poor old man—" began Lydia half apologetically. "If you're quite sure there won't be a loss, Taffy—"

"The Matsons would pay me sixty dollars," stated Taffy coolly.

"Mr. Zach Cavitt 'lowed he'd give me sixty dollars—but he ain't never kep' his bargain," old Tobe said.

Frances held her breath, watching her mother, but Taffy was ready.

"Very characteristic of the Cavitts, to fail at a bargain." She pushed up her chin, avoiding Frances' eyes. "The tobacco is on Neary property. We do not contemplate any interference by the Cavitts, do we, Mama?"

"I'm going back there with you," announced Lydia firmly. "I want to see that mill myself. And I want a lock on the door! I suppose there is a door still, Tobe?"

"Yes'm, Miss Lyddy, good stout door the ole Cap'n done built."

"I'll find a padlock." Taffy sprang down the steps swiftly. "I saw one in the barn—with a key."

Frances watched them drive away, the old man's broken shoes dangling limply at the rear of the buggy. Something was afoot, she was certain, and she was resigned to the fact that she would never get the truth out of Taffy. Tomorrow she herself would leave for Baltimore. Tomorrow she would see Fox again. She tried to be happy about it, to bring back the magic of night, of the moon printing silvery paths upon the river, but the peace of assurance would not come. The Cavitts, as Taffy had said, were unpredictable.

"We'll both try," he had promised, but immediately he had gone and there had been no word or sign from him since.

What if he looked at her tomorrow with that boldness men had for women who gave too easily? What if he made her feel cheap? What if Tulia chose to spend the day riding the Sound on the old ferry?

"You," Frances spoke sternly to her worried reflection in the kitchen mirror, "need some steel in your spine, you flabby thing!"

She would wear her good white linen suit and the big hat that made her eyes mysterious. She would be cool and aloof and enigmatic herself. She tore down her hair and practiced sleeking it back over her ears in Tulia's fashion, but the effect was wan and she tossed it back again, letting it fluff and curl softly on her forehead.

"Definitely," she sighed aloud, "I'm not the haughty type. But I won't look just good and trusting and stupid—and young! I won't!"

Earrings—unmarried women who dared to wear them were

often considered fast. A virginal swish of talcum powder applied with a piece of chamois was all she dared. Rigidly decent women like her Taft cousins adjured even that pallid allure as touching on vulgarity. A glassy sort of untouchability, long gloves, and a high-boned collar would be her only armor.

14

Tulia Cavitt was already on board the *Agnes J.* when Frances arrived at the wharf early next morning.

Fox was there, checking his cargo, and he gave Frances a casual smile, took her light bag and let her walk ahead of him up the gangway and down the deck to the cabin. Tulia stood near the bow, hatted and gloved, wearing a light wool suit in spite of the July heat, her starched shirtwaist boned high under her chin. She ignored Frances elaborately and Frances noted that Tulia's attitude was one of taut impatience, that she was tapping the deck with her toe and leaning a little forward, frowning, as though she was irked by the slowness of their departure.

"I'll put this here." Fox set the suitcase down under a bench in the cabin. "You can come outside if you like."

"Thank you." Frances kept her tone impersonal, kept her voice cool and her eyes guarded. She did not go outside but found a seat and kept her hands in her lap, clasping them firmly together so that they would not tremble and betray her nervousness. Fox turned away with a little salute and almost immediately she heard the bells jangling, the plop of ropes on the deck and the screech of the plank being hauled aboard. Then the engines throbbed and there was a wash and roll of water outside as the boat backed out and began slowly to turn.

Fox would be up in the wheelhouse now, perched on the high stool, his cap on the back of his head. Was Tulia there beside him, letting her eyes drift full of intimate meanings and demands as Frances had seen them do at the Matson party? She could find out by walking out there casually, but her pride would not let her stir. If Fox Cavitt were regarding her merely as one of his conquests he should never have the satisfaction to his vanity of any sign of betrayal from her. On the other hand, if he were sincere, as she would not let herself hope, she would not embarrass him with any suggestion of intimacy.

The sun grew hot on the glass of the windows as the boat turned, and Frances moved to a shaded corner and took off her gloves. She saw that they were nearing the fish dock. The engines slowed and the wash of the turning bow brought a breath of cool air and with it the salty reek of the marshes and a smell of fish. Then the throbbing below stopped and a hot odor of oil drifted up through the planks. Frances was debating whether to submerge her pride and go outside into the fresher air when the door opened slowly and old Captain Cavitt came shuffling in, peering at her from under the bill of his nautical cap.

"What you hiding in here for?" he shouted.

Frances remembered to raise her voice. "I'm not hiding. I'm a passenger."

"Passengers don't have to stay in here." He dropped into the seat beside her and strangely Frances felt none of the uneasy repulsion she had known when first she saw this old man. "Not unless they're sick or mad or something. Never set in this place before in my life. Except once when a rope broke and hit me in the stomach. Never did like cabins. Don't like to be shut up any place, not even in a house. Where you traveling this trip?"

"To Baltimore." She discovered that by speaking directly at him, slowly and distinctly, she could penetrate the wall of his deafness without shouting.

"Brass business," he remarked, moving his shrunken yellow hands over his mouth. There was a kind of loneliness about him now that stirred a feeling of pity in Frances' mind. His eyes, sunk under beetling brows, held a slow flicker that had the color of fury in it, as though he defied with anger the rheumy quenching of age. "I heard Dan Neary's wife was dead. That fixes your mother up pretty nice—pretty nice! Oh, I hear a lot of things. Ain't as deaf as I let on sometimes. Old Hod Taft is still kicking, I reckon?"

Frances could not restrain a smile at hearing staid and prosy Uncle Horace dismissed with such light disrespect; Uncle Horace whose mind worked with glacial slowness, who thought only in facts and figures, and those grimly and with deliberation.

"Ought to have kicked off long ago, that old scudder," drawled the Captain. "Don't you trust him too far nor let him dicker you out of what belongs to your mother. You keep your eyes open and add up all the figures yourself. You look like a smart gal. You watch out where your mother puts that money, too. You keep her clear away from slickers that wait around to sucker a widow out of what she's got, with a smooth tongue and a cute proposition."

"I will," Frances agreed, though not too optimistically, remembering that greedy look that altered her mother's face at times and the ease with which Taffy had influenced Lydia to buy Tobe Gibson's tobacco.

"I've got a boy like that," the old man went on, rubbing his chin and keeping his eyes shrewdly upon her. "Talk a dead man out of his epitaph, Zach would—but no Neary would ever listen to a Cavitt."

Frances stirred anxiously, wondering what the old man knew, what his remark implied; but the boat was in motion again and she could not make him hear above the sound of the engines.

"She works hard, hating the Cavitts, Lyddy does," he rambled on. "I reckon she wouldn't like my boy Fox sculling his boat up to her landing, neither, did she know about it, would she?" He chuckled. "Oh, I ain't blind if I am old. I can still see in the dark, good as ever I could."

Frances could feel the hateful red washing up over her face and throat and she glanced apprehensively at the windows, remembering Tulia out there with the daggers in her eyes. Then a bit of the steel she had determined to achieve crept into her blood and bones and she stiffened her chin in a challenge to her own silly diffidence and gave the old Captain a wan smile and a resigned shake of the head that reminded him of the hopelessness of her situation. Cannily he read her mood and laid his hand on hers, and where before his touch had made her flinch now there was a gentle sort of comfort in it.

"I'm not dead yet," he said, nodding his head up and down.

"I don't aim to die till I fix up the wrong of this Neary business somehow. An old hate has got no right to live on and be a blight on young people. Take my boy Fox—he's smart and steady and he's got too much conscience, if a man can have too much. Got a hurt in him somehow, down yonder in Cuby, and though I ain't never been able to find out what happened down there I know it gnaws at him—makes him quiet and standoffish, but there ain't any wickedness in Fox. You're a right pretty gal, when you let your face light up some, and you're smart too—I can see. I liked you first time I laid eyes on you, though you did shrink off from me like I was a poison adder or some other evil thing. I like pride and I like blood, but proud blood-foolishness never did anybody any good and it ought to die. I'm going to do something about it."

Frances drew a long breath, eager with hope. "When I can walk up to your front door," Fox had said. Her lips quivered past her control, and Captain Cavitt gave her fingers a fatherly squeeze.

"You quit being afraid of me and hating me," he advised. "Just because I was a headstrong, tough-natured young feller don't mean that I've got to go on acting the fool all my life! Your Grandpa Neary wasn't too sanctified, either. He could outcuss and outdrink a lot of younger fellers, but it's the man that dies that gets a halo hung on him and everything wrong he ever did gets forgotten while they make a martyr out of him. You just go along and keep quiet, and I'll fix things up about this old feud somehow."

They sat in companionable silence for a long interval then. The sun grew hotter on the flat roof and the glass windows and Captain Cavitt got up and lumbered about, flinging windows open to let the fresh sea air drift in.

"Ain't a fit place for anybody—a cabin," he grumbled. "*She's* out there though. Gets me crawly when she looks at me with those long eyes of hers." He flung open the door and below a bell clanged. "Pullin' in," he announced. "You got to get off here and take a hack if you figure on travelin' the railroad."

Frances was assembling her possessions hastily when Fox came to the door.

"Your landing, Frances," he said, picking up her bag.

Frances said, "Thank you," and turned a shoulder so that he could not read in her face the swift tremulous plunge of her heart at his voice.

He waited for her to move ahead of him down the deck, then looked back at the old Captain who came blustering out, yelling orders to the deck hands.

"Don't mind my father," Fox said, "he likes you."

"Oh, I don't. He was very friendly." Frances ached to turn her head, to search his face for reassurance, to touch his hand—anything that she could take with her to fill the empty days ahead and kill the uncertainty that tortured her, but he had made no move or gesture. She walked to the gangplank, but the tide was high and the *Agnes* rode far up above the level of the landing so the plank sloped downward steeply. Fox Cavitt put his hand under her elbow and gave her a little lift.

"Take it slowly," he said, "and hang on to me."

The plank swayed sickeningly for a second as their weight came upon it, but Frances was unaware of it. She was holding to Fox's arm, and because she could not help it she smiled up into his face, and briefly he smiled back; then with a quick, odd change his eyes were masked again, he was merely the skipper of a boat being polite to a passenger. Then Frances saw that Tulia stood behind them, still on the deck. Tulia's face was a frigid, hostile mask.

"Such beautiful gallantry, Fox!" Tulia remarked acidly. "Don't forget that I'm on board and going ashore."

"Be there in a minute." Fox did not turn his head. He bent and released Frances' long skirt when it caught and hung on a timber, then handed her luggage to a Negro boy who shambled up. "You'll be gone for a while?" he asked.

"Only a week, I hope," Frances answered.

"You won't be lonely, likely," he countered. "Your young doctor will see to that."

He wheeled and ran up the sloping plank again and Frances stood still for a stunned instant, forgetting to breathe. Her young doctor! But she hadn't any young doctor! Oh—of course, Cliff Houchins—but who had told Fox Cavitt about Cliff? Taffy, of course! With a flash of anger she knew that only Taffy could have done it. The meddlesome, sly, mischief-making little schemer! She tensed with indignation and half turned to dash back and deny that Cliff Houchins meant anything to her—anything at all. Then she saw Tulia coming down the gangway with Fox holding her arm, and the heat of her anger froze to a bitter chill and she walked off, following the colored boy, and did not even look back.

The hack, the long, sad, covered vehicle that conveyed ferry passengers across country to the railroad station, stood under some trees, the horses' heads sagging, the driver waiting with his foot on the hub of a wheel. Frances climbed in, took the front seat nearest the driver's, instructed the boy to put her bag beside her, handed him a dime and settled herself, though she was still shaking inside and her mouth was full of a coppery-tasting hot water.

As though things were not difficult enough, she was thinking, with her mother nursing the ancient grudge and Tulia lingering like a white-faced bird of prey, without Taffy creating suspicion where no reasonable ground existed! That Taffy had had a shrewd motive and an adolescent idea that she would make her sister more interesting by making her appear less attainable, did not occur to Frances. This was Taffy's revenge, she was sure, for Frances' poorly concealed suspicion of Zach Cavitt. Now, she told herself, she knew there was something underhanded going on concerning the old mill, and Mama had been inveigled into it. And she had to be away for a week!

She was so upset and angry that she paid little attention to Tulia, who took the seat behind her, scolded the boy for not setting her bag upright, and snapped, "Five cents is all you're going to get! It's more than you've earned, really."

This, thought Frances, was the worst irony of all, to have Tulia Cavitt for a traveling companion. They would sit up all night in a cindery day coach, and probably ride most of tomorrow with only brief stops for the dreary refreshment railroad lunchrooms offered. And at the end would be Uncle Horace, rigid with disapproval of everything and undoubtedly primed already to frustrate any plans of his niece Lydia, whom he had always considered flighty and entirely brainless; and along with him, gabby, eager Miss Baker.

It was instantly apparent that Tulia had no intention of leaving her alone to suffer in peace. Tulia's cool voice reached her ear above the yelling of the driver, who was parrying humorous insults with a few bystanders.

"I understand you are going to Baltimore, Miss Keeling?"

"Yes, I am," Frances answered grudgingly, keeping her eyes straight ahead. Something Uncle Horace had once said came into her mind, that democracy was the right of every man to be let alone. Tulia Cavitt's mind, however, was definitely imperious. She was the type of woman, Frances suspected, who would respect nobody's privacy unless it suited her purpose.

The conversation was interrupted, however, by the driver, who climbed to his seat, grunting; set a tin lunch bucket down with a bump that jarred a warm smell of fried meat and onions from beneath the lid; then turned and glared at them with small, watery, bloodshot eyes.

"This all the load I get?" he demanded. "Got to drive all that road and wear my nags out for two women?"

"We pay our fare," answered Tulia coldly.

"Well, gimme fifty cents then! It's worth more, but I can't charge no more or I'll lose my license." He pushed a dirty hand over the back of his seat and waved it in front of Frances' eyes. "Dunno why I bother with this piddlin' job, noway! Just my luck to meet one of them goldarned gasoline buggies up yonder on that narrow causeway."

Frances laid two quarters in his palm and drew back a little from contact with his sweaty sleeve.

"You, too, lady." He reached over her shoulder flexing his fingers at Tulia. "Four bits is the fare and that's robbery in any man's reckoning. If I meet one of them blasted automobiles today he's got to back up, if it's four miles! Last one busted down and I set in the sun two solid hours while the feller tried to fix it, then had to haul him out of there back'ards with my team! Ought to law them things off the public roads. Lady—look here, I can't change no ten-dollar gold piece! All I want is four bits. Just one half dollar is all I want from you."

"I haven't anything else," argued Tulia.

"Well, you'll have to pay me, end of the line then!" He

squirmed back into his seat with a disgusted snort. "Why don't you get you some change when you get aboard this hack? Everybody knows what the fare is."

"I offered you the fare. It's no concern of mine if you can't change money," Tulia said crisply.

"Whyn't you ask Cap'n Cavitt for a half dollar? You got that tenner from him, didn't you? Old Captain never will have anything but gold money. Got it hid all over his house, they say. Pirate money, like as not, some of it."

"You are very offensive and impertinent," snapped Tulia. "I'll pay you at the end of the line, but in the meantime attend to your driving and spare us your personal remarks."

"If you don't like my remarks, lady, get off and walk!" he barked, as he gathered up the reins. "This here is my rig and I'll drive to suit myself and say what I please. Sit in the middle, lady." He changed his tone addressing Frances. "You won't get so much dust on your dress in the middle of the seat."

Frances shifted a little, as the horses lunged into the collars and the hack started with a jerk, but the move brought her nearer to Tulia and she felt an uncomfortable tingle of warmth on the back of her neck, feeling Tulia's eyes upon her. She reached and gathered up the stray hairs that curled above her collar and tucked them in, tightening the hairpins, but the dismal sense of being somehow disheveled persisted, perhaps because her mind was in disorder and she could almost feel Tulia's level eyes boring there, turning up the little aching unhappinesses and the ragged doubts as a wolf dog might disinter bones.

The road ran between marshes, a narrow and twisting track, with here and there a shaded stretch under great, gloomy cypress trees and sandy spaces where the wheels sank deep and the horses strained as the driver laid on the whip. The sun was very hot now and the steamy air from the lowland turned Frances' hair damp, so that it clung to her cheeks and her forehead under her straw hat. But when the wheels dropped into a deep rut and the vehicle careened wildly, she got a glimpse of Tulia Cavitt, sitting bolt erect and looking cool and unruffled in the too-warm suit, her face unflushed and dry and pale.

They had gone several slow miles when Tulia spoke again.

"We may as well talk," she suggested. "After all, we have a wretched day to get through somehow."

"I enjoy being quiet," Frances returned, keeping her eyes straight ahead.

"We do have a few things to say to each other, though," Tulia persisted. "You're frightfully young, aren't you?"

"Not so young. I'm twenty."

"Really? I should have said about seventeen. You've been pretty well kept under, haven't you? So many mothers hate to have their daughters grow up."

"I'd prefer not to discuss my mother, if you don't mind." Frances was rather pleased at the tone of hauteur she was able to achieve.

"Actually I was discussing you," persisted Tulia. "You interest me. There's so much about you that doesn't show on the surface at all. What I mean to say is that you have that sweet and naïve look of utter innocence, so disarming that you startle people with your real capabilities. One sees through that younger sister of yours instantly, she wears her entire character in her face, as you might say; but you dissemble cleverly."

"At least," said Frances icily, "I have been reared to believe that a lady does not deal in personalities."

"Oh, I'm not a lady." Tulia laughed a little. "Hadn't you heard? I'm a shameless baggage, and I make no pretensions of delicacy whatever. I just get what I want. Did you know that I'm on my way to New York, just now, to wheedle enough money out of my mother so that I can divorce my husband?"

"Even if I knew, I would not be interested," Frances retorted. "Your domestic affairs have no concern for me whatever."

Tulia laughed again, so liltingly that the driver turned and looked back, his brows puckered.

"Perhaps they do," she remarked. "It could be that they concern you a great deal, Miss Keeling."

Frances looked at the driver. "May I sit up there with you?" she asked abruptly.

He jerked the team to a standstill. "Sure kin," he agreed. "I was fixin' to stop and water my horses, next creek we ford, anyway, and then I was goin' to eat me a snack. But you can move up now if you want to."

"Thank you." Frances got down between the wheels and climbed back up to the front seat.

The man was unpleasantly redolent of sweat and chewing tobacco, but even those earthy odors were preferable to the delicate French scent that Tulia wore, and the poisonous aura of contempt that she seemed to exude from her very pores.

The team stopped of their own accord when they came to a clear little stream, and the man climbed out on the wagon pole and let their heads down, balancing there while they drank. Then he drove into the shade of a gum tree, halted again, and let the horses graze while he sat on the grass and ate his lunch. He came back to the hack with a yellow biscuit in his fingers, a piece of fried fat meat inside it. The print of his grimy thumb was plain on the pale crust, but when he held it up and said affably, "Better eat you a bite. Be an hour yet against we get anywhere there's any grub," Frances thanked him and did her best to dispose of the dreary offering.

As she had feared, the train was late. The little wooden depot was hot and dirty, smelling of the cuspidors that stood everywhere. Tulia brushed at a bench with a gloved finger, scowled at the smudge on her glove and went outside, where she paced up and down the plank platform, her high heels eloquent of irritation. Frances waited inside, wondering why she had been so impractical as to wear a white suit. Already the bottom of the skirt was drabbled with dust and she felt messy and tired and dismally resigned to the wearisome journey ahead. She could endure it if only Tulia would leave her alone.

It was quickly obvious, however, once the train was underway, that Tulia had no intention of leaving her alone. As soon as she had disposed her baggage under her own seat, she walked deliberately down the length of the car and seated herself opposite Frances.

"Now we'll go on with our conversation," she said calmly, "and don't be rude. Only very young people are rude. We should be able to discuss our situation sensibly."

"Do we have a situation?" asked Frances. "You could be

assuming too much, don't you think? After all, I hardly know you, Mrs. Cavitt."

"You do have something in you." Tulia gave her an analytical survey. "You give the impression of being about as exciting as tapioca, but there's more than appears on your pretty surface. You're a danger—and while I refuse to fear dangers, I do respect them."

"We've been differently trained," Frances said as coldly. "I was taught that personalities were rudeness. I don't care to analyze you and I am sure you have no right to pick me to pieces."

"Oh, I wasn't trained at all," declared Tulia. "I always go directly to whatever is in my mind. You're a danger to me because you have a young notion that you're in love with Fox Cavitt. I suppose you even have a vague sort of hope that Fox is going to fall in love with you. He won't, you know."

Frances struggled with a wild angry impulse to slap the cool, colorless face opposite her and then march away, but that would be surrender, and she had determined that she was done with surrendering. Papa had given up without a fight, she remembered—she was never again going to be told that she was like her father who had been gentle and good and made no protest, struck no retaliating blow when life trampled him.

"You're quite sure of yourself, aren't you?" she said when she could trust herself to speak. "You make your own judgments and believe them to be infallible, yet you've made a wreck of your marriage and now you want to end it."

"I didn't wreck it," defended Tulia. "I admit I was stupid to get into the mess in the first place. I was alone and I was afraid. I'll never be afraid again, and I'll never fall headlong into love again. Every move I make from now on will be deliberate and considered. I see through people. It's a kind of instinct with me. I know Fox Cavitt inside out. I know why he hides inside himself, and I know the frustration he lives with and that left alone he'll never do anything about it. He'll go on being dutiful and conscientious, when it's death to every capability he has and every aspiration. That's why you'd be poison for Fox. Because you're dutiful and conscientious, too—and good. A good woman would be a chain around his neck. There's power in Fox; there could be genius in him, even, but it will be strangled on Pamlico. There's genius in Zachary, too, but it's warped and subtle and dishonest. Yet rascally as he is, Zach gets more out of life than his brother."

"But you say you're going to divorce him," Frances prompted, hurt and furious and yet somehow fascinated by this strange, half-savage woman with the burning wildness lying deep under the evident torment in her eyes.

"We're too much alike," Tulia said. "I can do nothing for Zach—nothing except drive him to doing desperate, rash things to prove to me that he's stronger than I am. He is all Cavitt, and two generations ago the Cavitts were adventurers and swashbuckling, hell-raising scoundrels, if you can believe the old Captain's boastings. Personally, I discount about half of it, but whatever they had, Zach has too much of it—and Fox not half enough. That's his mother in him. She sprang from a psalm-singing tribe up in the hills somewhere, and that is a pressure in Fox that has to be released."

Frances looked out the window. The train was struggling through ragged foothills now, eroded land hot and dry, with dusty scrub oaks and sedge grass sloping up to outline starveling little farms and gullied coves where cabins sent thin feathers of suppertime smoke upward from leaning chimneys. An odd strength and a kind of exultation stiffened her now, easing the feeling of loss that had haunted her all day. Why was Tulia flinging these thinly veiled threats and challenges at her unless she was afraid? And if she was afraid and unsure, as her passionate anger betrayed, what did she know or suspect that made her afraid?

"What you're trying to tell me—with considerable indirection and very poor taste—is that if you can divorce the man you are married to, you intend to have his brother," she said carefully, keeping her voice even and low. "And you're warning me to keep hands off and let you have your way. Are you so sure you'll get your way—with Fox?"

Tulia leaned forward. Her teeth clicked a little and her lips drew apart so that the pink of her lower gum showed. Her eyes grew long and narrowed, giving her a feline look, unlovely but somehow pathetic. She looked like a cat, but like a starved and tortured cat.

"I'm going to have Fox Cavitt," she said slowly and crisply, "and no pretty, sweetmouthed little ignoramus from the country—nobody like you is going to stop me! Is that quite clear?"

"Quite clear," Frances agreed, holding herself in check because suddenly she wanted to laugh aloud, she wanted to sing, she was not unhappy any more or tormented by gnawing doubt. Tulia was afraid, and that meant that Tulia had ground for her fear. Tulia was not sure of Fox, however imperiously she might state her case, however sharply she might bluster and hurl defiances. "And now," said Frances sweetly, "could we call this conversation ended? People are looking at us rather curiously. Your eyes do blaze rather weirdly when you're excited, Mrs. Cavitt."

Tulia got slowly to her feet. "You think you can get the best of me with that smooth ladylike manner of yours, don't you?" she snapped. "You'd like me to scream at you like a fishwife, so that you could crush me with a few polite words. The trouble with women like you is that you stifle men to death! There's no air in you! You're dead as tombs—pretty pink marble tombs. If you'd fly at me and tear my hair out I might have some respect for you, I might even fear you; but as it is I merely despise you and pity you for being so damned dead!"

Frances got up too. She did not know that her eyes could flame. She had never known before the fierce urge to strike out savagely and shriek terrible things at the top of her voice. The surging in her frightened her, made her catch her breath and grip the back of the seat with rigid fingers. Her throat strained, but she controlled the wildness that fought to press past her lips.

"Get away from me!" she said in a quiet, deadly tone. "Get away from me—and stay away, Tulia Cavitt!"

Tulia moved off haughtily down the aisle, her head very high. Frances dropped into her seat again, and as the wave of rage receded she began to quiver inside and her hands shook so in her lap that she gripped them together till her fingers ached. But for all her agitation, a warm triumph thrilled her.

She was through with being humble. She was done with being like Papa. No one was ever going to call her sweet and mealymouthed again, for now she knew what fighting was like. It was exhilarating and intoxicating. It was feeling yourself adequate and tall and splendid with fury. A man could have too much conscience, the old Captain had said, and that went for a woman too.

She turned and looked back through the sooty car. Tulia's head was just visible against the red plush. Her cheek was turned toward the cushion and the burning, tigerish eyes were closed. She looked tired and a bit pitiful. She looked even a little dowdy. Frances smoothed her own skirt over her knees. Tomorrow in Baltimore she would buy herself a smart, stylish dress. Tomorrow she would deal with Uncle Horace coolly and implacably. There was Neary blood in her and the Nearys had not been saints, according to the Captain; they did not accept meekly, bending to the rod, giving back soft answers and tremulously dreading conflict.

She was a Neary and the Nearys knew how to fight.

15

Frances' stimulated mood persisted through the week in Baltimore. Suddenly she had discovered that it was weak and silly to stand in awe of people, who were after all only vulnerable human beings. It was as though the encounter with Tulia Cavitt had cleared her perception, so that now she could see voluble Miss Baker as the tired, half-frightened spinster that she was, terrified of the insecurity of old age and starved for the affection and approval that life had denied her.

Uncle Horace was definitely less formidable, too. Accustomed to bullying John Keeling and scaring his niece Lydia to death, he was baffled and enraged by Frances' newly acquired ability to be firmly cool and sweetly implacable. He floundered and blustered, puzzled at being faced down and having his avuncular authority questioned by a young woman with a purposeful will of her own.

"Add up the figures yourself," Captain Cavitt had counseled, and Frances' insistence on being fully enlightened approached insult in old Horace Taft's mind.

"It's these women's rights females!" he stormed. "It's that Stanton woman and her tribe, getting pieces printed in the papers and making fools out of sensible women. Next thing we know a man can't even call his soul his own."

"The thing that men refuse to admit, Uncle Horace," Frances argued politely, "is that women have any souls that they might wish to call *their* own—or that they can be competent to handle their own money and make their own investments and control them."

"What Lydia knows about investments I could write on the back of a postage stamp," he growled. "She ought to have plenty saved. I've sent her over three hundred dollars since June. She ought not to have to take a cent out of this business till next year anyway."

"She's entitled to take her share out of it," Frances insisted. "Would you like me to look over the books, Uncle Horace, or would it be better if I engaged a lawyer to look after Mama's interests?"

He swelled, his pink jowls turning purple. "What do you want to waste money on lawyers for? I've got the books right here and they're kept up to the minute. What I'm trying to do is protect Lydia from her own foolishness—spending money like water—"

"We had to make some repairs on the old house, you know," Frances reminded him. "After all, it is Mama's money. She has had a lean life for a good many years and if she wants to enjoy a few follies now, I think that's her right. Mama is careful with money. The only unwise thing she has done, in my opinion, was to invest a small sum in some tobacco; but she believes she can make a profit out of that."

"Tobacco?" he exploded. "I knew it! I knew she'd run wild and lose what little sense she had, once she got on her own. Of all the insane investments anybody can make in these times tobacco is the worst. Know what's happening to tobacco companies all over the country? Going busted, that's what's happening to them. Trust wipes 'em out—one after another. Look at Hargraves. They couldn't buck it, so now they're making sashes and doors. Look at Lorillard. He's fighting for his life, too. Fighting the tobacco trust, which is an evil that's trying to strangle all free business in the Southeast—all over the country for that matter. If the trust can't buy out an independent concern, they undersell 'em, underbuy 'em, and put 'em out of business. They're after Reynolds now, and they'll get him too, in the end. Anybody who puts one penny into tobacco stock of any kind is a fool."

"She bought only a little—and there's a very prosperous tobacco factory right there in the town, so she'll have no difficulty in selling."

"Prosperous, is it? Well, it won't be for long! Only so long as the trust lets them alone. You tell your mother to get rid of that tobacco as fast as she can, and if I hear of her fooling with the stuff any more I'll be tempted to have her declared incompetent! Throwing away good money that my father built up, over fifty years, and that I've worked all my life to hang on to!"

"My father helped a little, Uncle Horace," Frances said calmly but firmly. "He put in the life that he had—all of it—into this business."

The old man's snort was eloquent. "Keeling was paid for every day's work he did in this place," he stated grimly.

"Let's not argue and lose our tempers, Uncle Horace. All I want is an accounting of the business to date, and whatever is due to Mama now, partly in cash and the rest to be deposited to her account every month."

"Don't expect that there's going to be a big profit every month," he said. "There's taxes to come out and machinery has to be replaced and the costs on the plating room run high. Time was when a man thought a dollar a day was good wages for anybody, but now they've got to have these newfangled electric lights in their houses and upright pianos for their daughters, and even washing machines! When I was a boy a clean pair of overalls and a hickory shirt every Sunday was enough for any working man, but the country's going to the dogs now with McKinley and Mark Hanna running things. Taking over the Philippine Islands and Hawaii—and all that cannibal country! What does this nation want with a mess of heathen like that? Getting men killed over there to civilize those savages and we pay the bills!"

After three days of arguments and complaints on Uncle Horace's part, Frances had her way finally. A neat roll of bills was tucked inside a pair of cotton stockings in her bag, and a bankbook and checkbook, cautiously wrapped around with a strong rubber band, established the account which Uncle Horace was to replenish every month from the profits of the brass business. Moved by a rash impulse and egged on by Miss Baker, Frances took two twenty-dollar bills from the stocking hoard and bought herself a new gray silk suit and a wide leghorn hat piled with puffs of pale blue and corn-colored maline. The suit had a natty bolero jacket with sleeves ending in wide ruffles of lace below her elbows, and a skirt cut daringly three inches from the ground.

It was the first time she had ever bought clothes without

consulting Mama and listening patiently to exasperating arguments as to whether the goods was durable or suitable to be made over later for Taffy, and she felt reckless and headstrong, and then a trifle anxious later. But she was grateful when she met Cliff Houchins for the poise and self-confidence given her by being well-dressed for once.

She had forgotten that Cliff was so thin and that he stooped. She had thought of him so seldom lately that his eager greeting embarrassed her and the evident approval in his brown myopic eyes moved her to look about her quickly. Though she knew that Tulia Cavitt had gone on to New York she had an uneasy feeling that all the close-set, oblivious houses on the street were regarding her with Tulia's cold eyes, and that somehow Tulia would relay back to the *Agnes* word that here was Frances Keeling, all dressed up, walking a sun-scorched block in Baltimore with young Dr. Houchins.

Cliff said, "Gee whiz, you look great! Have you come home to stay, Francie?"

"No—no, I'm just here on business, Cliff. I'm going back tomorrow, I think. How are you? Is your mother well?"

"Oh, you know Mother." He shrugged his bony shoulders wearily. "She's never really well. She worries too much. I have to work at night a lot now—we do dissecting at night and some lab stuff, too—and she gets lonely. I wish you had time to go out with me to see her, Francie." He shifted a heavy load of books and freed a hand so that he could take her arm.

"I wish I could, Cliff." Frances moved a little away from his too-warm fingers, wondering if his eyes had always held that hungry, doglike look; wondering why she had never noticed before how utterly spiritless and trampled he appeared. "But I've made plans for every minute."

"Mother's so anxious for me to get through my med," he went on, skipping a little to keep step with her. "She thinks I'm going to be a famous specialist and find something to cure her. She'll read all these books with me tonight."

And tomorrow she'll have all the diseases and forge new chains with them to keep you bound hand and foot, Frances was thinking. Audibly she murmured something vague and polite, feeling sorry for Cliff but a trifle smug over her own newly achieved assurance and independence.

At a corner drugstore Cliff said abruptly, "Let's go in here and have a lemonade or something for old times' sake, Francie." Without waiting for an answer he maneuvered her through the open door and found a table under a languidly turning fan.

"Nice," he approved the overhead breeze that made the trimming on her hat flutter. "They're getting these in a lot of places now. We're living in a wonderful age, aren't we? I've been trying to persuade Mother to have a telephone, but she says a telephone is an intrusion. Anyone can ring them and she couldn't bring herself to talk on one unless she was properly dressed. Are things very modern down in Carolina?

"No, we aren't modern at all, but we're quite comfortable," Frances said, thinking that Cliff was lucky that his mother distrusted telephones.

She would be calling him out of his classes every hour of the day, thinking she had a new pain, checking on every move that he made. Poor Cliff! His shirt was not very clean and his shoes definitely needed half-soling. Yet Fox had been jealous of Cliff. There had been a dry withdrawal in his voice when he spoke of her "young doctor."

Now that Tulia was out of the picture Frances could guess what Taffy had intended doing when she told Fox about Cliff. Taffy had tried to make Frances appear more desirable, and in her present expansive mood Frances forgave her little sister. She even found herself basking a little in the knowledge that Cliff's eyes were humbly worshipful, though a kind of awful patience of frustration did dull his frail ardor.

It was the hat, she decided, glimpsing it again in a mirror. It startled her to see how much the hat changed her. That came of being assured, of knowing that she looked nice. Tomorrow she would buy new hats for Mama and Taffy. That made-over affair that Taffy had tied on so jauntily gave Frances a guilty twinge now, and as for Mama, heaven only knew when that dreary thing she packed away in tissue paper had been new! Mama would probably hoard a new hat forever without wearing it, but at least she should have something with more flair than the weedy old straw with the sad black posies on it.

It was so exhilarating to realize that now they could have new things. Uncle Horace would grumble, but he would be meticulously honest and the plant would be run as profitably as possible. Except for beds and birdcages and the shiny things she had seen on the Cavitt boat, Frances had little idea what was done with brass, but she had seen a substantial account with a locomotive works on the books at the plant and the figures had been amazing. It would be so wonderful to be really rich! Then perhaps Mama could be persuaded to send Taffy off to school, so that she could be with young people of her own age and forget adult follies like growing too fascinated with married men.

Lost in her pleasant musings, Frances finished her drink absently, caught a few words Cliff was saying, and came back to awareness with a jolt.

"You'll always be the only girl for me, Francie," he declared, looking at her with eyes that Taffy would have defined as distinctly moony. "It's going to be a long wait, I know—it takes a doctor years to get started, and so many new drugs are being discovered all the time it keeps a man studying just to keep up. And of course there's Mother—"

"Oh, Cliff," Frances protested, interrupting briskly, "you mustn't think about me that way at all! You've got such a hard job ahead of you, and you have to keep your mind single and just—devoted to what you plan to do. Someday you'll be a famous specialist and own a big hospital, maybe, but in the meantime you should put girls out of your mind entirely. You'll feel frustrated and impatient if you don't, and that will tear down your nervous energy and make it hard for you to concentrate."

"That's what my mother says," he admitted sadly. "But I do miss you a lot, Francie. You've been a kind of a dream that I had to hold to, when things got tough—"

"Well, keep the dream if it makes life happier for you, Cliff, but don't let it be a burden to you. And you ought to see some other girls, sometimes, you know. You've never had much fun. You might see somebody who'd make a much better dream-pattern than I do."

"You mean—you don't dream about me, Francie? Is there somebody else?" he asked anxiously.

"There is one man," she admitted, managing a half-truth because Cliff seemed so much in need of reassurance, "but he's not attractive to me at all. He's a lawyer and his father manufactures tobacco, but Wylie doesn't appeal to me though he'd very much like to, I think. I must not be ready, Cliff. I can't make up my mind to anything yet. Now I really must run." She got up and picked up her purse. "I know you have work to do, too. It's been nice seeing you again."

He laid a dime on the table and swung up the heavy burden of books. "I'm just going home to study materia medica. Francie, if I write to you will you answer? If you'd write maybe it would keep us from drifting so far apart."

"Of course I'll answer, but there's really mighty little to write about down there, Cliff. I wouldn't be a very exciting correspondent." She held out her hand. "I'd better say good-by now. Don't let life get you down, Cliff."

"I'll try not to, Francie," he gulped a little, clinging to her fingers, "but I'm not going to try to forget you or even get interested in any other girl, so there's no use asking me."

She got away finally, feeling heavy in spirit as though she had hurt a child. But for Cliff things were so hopeless! His mother would never give him up, her fierce possessiveness would be a blight on his life for years, and it was doubtful if Cliff would ever be strong enough or ruthless enough to live his own life. She recalled the old Captain's words, that a man could have too much conscience, but she remembered too that he had said that about Fox.

Could a parent be disappointed in a too-dutiful child? Did they secretly admire the bold and unfilial ones who refused to let sentiment control or destroy their individualities?

She suspected that this was true in her own family. Her mother did admire Taffy and defer to her, even while she was deploring Taffy's rebelliousness and her headstrong way. I've been too meek, she decided, and determined not to offer any apologies for buying the new suit or the pretty hat.

Her heart beat faster with every mile that the crawling train and the decrepit old hack jolted and bumped nearer to Pamlico. The hack driver had several passengers this time so his mood was expansive, he greeted her effusively and saw to it that she had a good seat away from the dust of the wheels.

"So Cavitt's wife never come back?" he remarked. "Heard down the shore that she'd left Zach for good. Good riddance both ways, I reckon. High-tempered and too free with her tongue, that woman is. You look mighty dressed up today. Cheeks as pink as roses, too. Catch you a beau up north, did you?"

"Not new." Frances gave him a smile, because though the August heat was oppressive, the sun a savage glare in a white-hot sky and the marshes suffocating with steamy miasma, the world was beautiful and blue and gold for her, the blackbirds balancing drowsily on the drying reeds, jaunty in the red cravats and tilted tails they sported. "Not new—just an old one made-over, you might say. But I'm glad to get home."

"Fetched Zach Cavitt back yesterday," he went on, shouting at the horses in the sandy ruts. "Says he's got a scheme cooked up to make a million dollars. Always was a big talker, Zach was. Done a lot of promotin' up north, I reckon. Up to now his talk's been mostly wind. Could make a ten-strike though, sometime. He's got the brains to do it. Cavitts is all smart. Too smart."

That dimmed the day a little, knowing that Zach had come back. Why she distrusted him, Frances could not have explained even to herself, but the uneasiness was there and she determined to begin immediately putting pressure on Mama to send Taffy away in the fall.

"Fox is late," the driver said as they reached the ferry landing late in the afternoon. "That old boat ain't what she used to be. Sooner or later they'll build roads and bridges down in this tidewater country and likely the railroad will come in and then fellers like the Cavitts will be out of business. If them gasoline wagons ever get so they'll run reliable we'd all have to worry, but I don't figure on that yet. Just a plaything for young fellers to fool with, that's all they are."

It was hot under the canopy of the hack, so Frances got down and walked out to the landing where a faint stir of air moved off the flat shining water of the Sound. The tide was slack and there was little motion, a few lazy waves lifting languidly and then settling back with a heavy slap as though even the Sound itself was somnolent and exhausted with the heat.

The heavy hat made her hair damp on her forehead and she pushed back the sticky ringlets and got out the new little powder case she had in her purse. It had a round mirror and a lamb's wool puff, and the powder in it smelled of lilacs and felt deliciously light and dainty when she patted it on her nose. Some of the cases she had seen in the shops had had little cakes of pink rouge in them, but she had not dared to buy one of those. Mama was dubious even of powder, and women who put color on their faces were counted as beyond the pale of respectability.

A gray smudge of smoke against the pale glare of the southern sky grew slowly darker and the ferry passengers moved down to the wharf—hatless, sweating men with soaked shirts sticking to their shoulders and a tired, drab woman in a limp cotton dress. Frances put on her gloves and straightened her hat, ruefully regarding a smudge of soot that had settled on her sleeve and spoiled the crispness of her lace ruffles.

Today she wanted to be pretty more than she had ever wanted anything in the world. Make him look at me! she sent a little prayer skyward; make him look at me and really see me!

She saw the old Captain standing near the gangway as the boat swung in and impulsively she waved at him, then flushed with embarrassment when it was obvious that he did not even see her, being intent on shouting orders to the boys who manned the mooring lines.

When the ropes were taut and the plank fell with a shuddering thump, Fox jumped down from the high wheelhouse and pounded to the wharf, the inevitable board under his elbow.

"Get going, boys," he ordered, standing by to collect the fares. "We're late already."

Purposely Frances stood last in line. She handed him her silver dollar without a word, and he took it absently, then lifted his eyes and a quick change came over his face, sharp excitement first and then the careful guarded look returning.

"Gee whiz!" he exclaimed. "I didn't know you! Have a good time in Baltimore."

"Slightly dull," Frances said. "It was all business, and business can be very stupid in hot weather."

"Wasn't the doctor glad to see you?" he asked directly.

Frances considered coyness briefly, then discarded the thought. Tulia went after what she wanted with deadly directness. Tulia did not quibble or employ subtleties. She took a leaf from Tulia's book.

"He was very glad," she said, "but I find I've outgrown many of my young ideas."

He lifted an eyebrow briefly and his mouth twitched in one of his rare smiles. Then the line was etched again between his brows.

"But the bar is still up on the front door, I suppose?"

Frances' head went up a little. "There have been strong men who have broken down bars," she said.

He slowly shook his head. "A man might have the strength of ten, Frances, but it would do him no good if his name happened to be Cavitt. Not on your side of the river. Better get aboard. We're an hour late and the Captain's fit to be tied."

She walked past him without another word and went to the bow of the boat, holding tightly to her bag. The Captain was there, and when the lines were flung aboard he turned and saw her and his mustache jerked in a wide grin.

"So you got back?" He shuffled over the deck, dragged out a chair for her, and waited till she had settled her skirts before he dropped into his accustomed seat. "Did you put old Hod Taft on the griddle?"

She nodded and smiled at him, patting her bag. "In here." She framed the words without raising her voice.

"Good gal!" He took a black plug of tobacco from his pocket, then looked uncertainly at her, debated in his mind, and put it back again.

"Well, she didn't come back," he went on. "Loaned her a hundred dollars. Best money I ever spent, could be. Zach come back though. Ain't seen him but once or twice. Listen—I'm an old man and I can talk free and say what I think, but I can't talk to Lyddy Neary. You tell your mother to keep that young sister of yours to home closer. Zach Cavitt is my boy, but I don't hold with a lot of things he does. Don't hold with any of it much."

Sharp unease tightened in Frances' chest. The breeze came strongly over the bow of the moving boat now, but it did not cool the burning flush on her face. Alarm must have darkened her eyes for the old man made a quieting gesture with his right hand.

"Didn't figure to scare you," he said quickly, "but I see a lot of things I ain't supposed to see. And that little redhead of yours is easy to see a long ways off. Likes to go traipsing around all by herself. Don't you scare your mother, but you kind of contrive to keep that kid at home more."

He did not speak again until they had passed the fish dock and the *Agnes* was making in to the home landing. Then he came close and put a hand on Frances' shoulder.

"Some of these times I'm coming over to your place," he said. "I've got it all worked out in my mind. Got to do it before long, too, for I ain't going to be navigating these waters forever. You're a smart gal. If I do come, reckon you can keep Lyddy from throwing scalding water on me till I've said my say?"

She had to smile in spite of her anxiety, and when he tightened his dry fingers on her shoulder, she reached impulsively and patted the back of his hand. Then he was gone, shuffling to the rail, bellowing at the scuttling deck hands.

Fox helped Frances down the gangplank. His hands were warm and intimate on her arm, he maneuvered her gently over the rough planks, and there was something in his eyes as he looked down at her that made her heart pound and her fingers tremble.

"I'll be out on the river tonight," he whispered as he saw Taffy coming on the run.

Suddenly Frances felt a sick sort of heaviness. She didn't want it that way. Love had to be splendid or it was worthless and cheap. Hiding, slipping out in the darkness, secrecy and unease, made love a snide thing that had no dignity about it.

"It's no use, Fox," she said evenly, aching all over, "no use at all."

His answer was flat. "That's for you to say, Francie."

She made no reply because Taffy was there then, squealing with excitement.

"Look at you!" she shrilled. "Aren't you elegant? What's in the bandbox? Did you bring back loads of money?"

"I brought you a new hat," Frances said dully, aware that Fox that turned away without a backward look. "I bought one for Mama too. Taffy, is that paint on your face?"

"Crepe paper!" Taffy dabbed unperturbed at her brightly reddened cheeks. "Let me see the hat, quick. I can't wait a minute."

"No, it's all packed in tissue paper and anyway Mama's is on top. Why didn't Mama come with you? You shouldn't run around alone so much, Taffy."

"Oh, good gracious, don't you start preaching! Slide your bag under the seat. You didn't bring me any fancy new suit, I suppose? Whenever Mama comes with me she won't let Chloe go off a walk and she frets all the time for fear the harness is going to break or a wheel come off or something else silly. I suppose you know that Tulia Cavitt has gone for good—we hope?" she added as she picked up the reins.

"We? Who do you mean by *we*?" Frances asked sharply.

"Oh, everybody," Taffy evaded. "You should be glad, I should think. Ren Matson says that old Captain Cavitt paid her to leave, but Bliss says that's ridiculous, that the old man would never let go a nickel. What's the matter?"

"Nothing is the matter. Captain Cavitt did give her the money to go back to her mother. He told me so."

"You mean you've been fraternizing with the enemy? Is he horrible? He looks as though he'd enjoy biting your arm off. As though he should wear horns."

"He isn't like that at all. He's just a tired old man who'd like to live in peace with his neighbors. And he doesn't wear the Cavitt horns, Taffy. Have you been seeing Zach Cavitt again?"

Taffy's eyes hardened. "Naturally, I had to see him. We've got the tobacco he wants for the cigarette business he's planning to start. It's locked up in our old mill and Mama gave me the key, and I'm holding out till I get what I want out of it. I'll make some money for us if you'll keep quiet and not let Mama know I'm seeing Zach. She wouldn't mind taking money away from him, of course—not Mama—but if I spoke ten words to him she'd think I was damned forever."

"You should be in school, a girl like you," Frances said sternly. "I'm going to talk to Mama about it before the term begins in September."

Taffy gave the mare a quick flick with the whip. "I'm not going to any silly school! Bliss goes, and she loathes it. She says it's nothing but a nice, prim, elegantly managed jail. She's trying to coax her father to let her stay home this year. Do you know, she's stupid enough to think that Zach Cavitt admires her—a fluffy mess, with no more brains than a bowlful of bread pudding! You keep out of my affairs, France—or I'll tell a few things that I know. Is that clear?"

"It seems quite clear to me that you're trying to ruin yourself in this town," Frances answered coldly.

Taffy tossed her head. "I'll risk it," she declared blithely. "Anyway, if Tulia gets a divorce they can't make nasty jibes about his being a married man, and if things get too thick I suppose I could marry him, though I don't think I'd care especially for that—he's too old and too smart. I think I'd prefer a nice, dumb husband who'd think I was the most beautiful thing in the world and do everything I wanted him to do. Do I shock you, Sister dear? I think not. I think you have a few rebellious ideas of your own, otherwise you wouldn't have bought that very fetching hat."

16

Fox Cavitt shoved his sailboat into its berth at the Cavitt dock with a resenting bump of the stern against the planks. He snubbed the mooring line around a bollard and tramped up the ragged path to the house, his shoulders slumped. He had been on the river for two hours, alone. There was no moon, but the water lay, a darkened silver roadway, gently quiet, with only soft ripplings and whisperings to show that it was still pursuing an even way south to the sea, unperturbed by human angers and frustrations.

She had not come. The pale lights in the old Neary house had reached their thin fingers through the trees for a time and then gone out one by one, a little light in the gable dying last of all. Fox had slipped his boat in at the Neary dock and waited while that last light flickered out and the soft, hot dark of late summer massed its bulk, devouring all the shapes and shadows. He had waited almost an hour after that before he gave up and paddled the boat back to the landing across the river. The house on the opposite shore was submerged in blackness now, but Fox could see it sharply in his mind, roof and old walls, locked doors, and windows that looked coldly across the current like icy eyes, hating the Cavitts.

His mind envisioned it and a beam of hot anger was directed at it, blasting the narrow prejudices that baffled him; the smugness, the stupidity of any woman who could cherish dead hatreds, letting them grow and spread their poisons to blight the lives of other people. It struck too at his own weakness, the stiff pride that would not let him batter down the barrier.

Those brash and violent gentlemen from whom he was descended, he knew, would not have waited meekly, smoldering in the dark, glaring impotently at barrier walls that shut away the girl they desired. The old dead-and-gone Cavitts, whose ships had mastered these waterways in times past, would have gone striding up the bluff in their high boots and swinging watch coats to kick the door in and snatch out of an atmosphere of stubborn antipathy whatever they wished for, reckoning Lydia Keeling's petty antagonism too puerile a thing to be considered by red-blooded men.

The old girl was only dramatizing a grievance anyway, Fox was certain. He had assayed her on that day when he had relieved the lame horse, seen the smallness of her mouth and the prim way she tightened it, noted the air of childish arrogance she put on like a garment too large for her limited personality.

She was a woman to whom nothing had happened, nothing but the hoarded and savored tradition of a family feud, and she could not surrender the one dramatic bit that made her important and injured in her own eyes. As though it mattered to Francie and Taffy that two half-drunk bragging and strutting boatmen had fought each other for supremacy thirty years ago, and in their absurd battlings precipitated a marine disaster! It mattered to Lydia because it was all she had, the only exciting thing that had colored her drab existence—that and the present gloating satisfaction of sitting there in that old house like a molting little she-eagle defying the Cavitts to raid her nest.

He had, Fox told himself, brought small credit to his swashbuckling forebears by sitting there in a boat for hours, too stiff-necked to yield. That was the Cavitt arrogance in him that he had kept tamped down in a shell of aloofness, partly because he had despised his brother's high-headed showing-off and chiefly because till now nobody worth bothering about had made an attempt to breach the wall. He had gloried in being called remote and walking by his lone, and now he knew that that was as theatrical an absurdity as Lydia Keeling's fierce maintenance of a kind of spite fence around herself and her daughters.

The picture amused him. Himself and little spunky Lydia, each reared back behind their bristling barricades of self-sufficiency, the only difference between them being that Lydia enjoyed her lurking and made it insolent enough to satisfy some uncertainty within herself, while he was all at once lost and unsure and a trifle puzzled as to why such solitariness had been food for his hurting ego for so long.

He knew the beginning of it, his dislike for his father's bellowing arrogance, his distaste for Zach's smart-aleck ways when they were growing up. He had been shy and his shyness had had the interpretation of difference put upon it in school. He had accepted this separation and he realized now that he had liked it, had even been a little vain of it. He was Fox Cavitt and Fox Cavitt was different. He had little to say. He went his way and no girl made any impression on him. Fox played a good game and could wrestle, but he hated being touched, and applause of any kind left him unmoved.

There had been times when he had made an effort to thrust himself outside his self-made wall. There had been the war with Spain. He had despised the idea of war because it clothed itself in a braying, strutting brassiness labeled patriotism, which to his mind was merely political deviousness disguised thinly in the folds of the flag. But he had made himself enlist because he wanted to belong and wrestle himself free from the reputation of being aloof that had followed him to Chapel Hill, and not because he cared a hang what happened to the Cubans.

The arrogance of Spain had been a sort of challenge after that, and the bold simplicity of the Roughrider, Roosevelt. For the first time in his life he had felt free until a hot, stinking afternoon on a sun-scorched hill when a little Spaniard, not more than nineteen years old, had glared at him suddenly from behind a prickly clump of manzanita. Fox could see yet the awful fright in that boy's dark eyes, could feel the hot kick of the rifle in his hands. In that swift, bloody instant the wall had closed in around him again, made more rigid now by his own detestation of himself and his fury at the stupidity of war. So he had come home, to see in the mirror when he shaved a bitter line growing deeper between his brows, and to know that cynicism was crackling in his blood again.

The old ferryboat, the dogged routine of living that was inevitable when his father grew old, had not mattered much. The Captain's senility, his pathetic clinging to what he knew, was something to be lived with and patiently and indulgently endured. His mother's stodgy docility had never touched him at all. She merely was; he accepted her and petted her as he might have humored a faithful little animal, and it never occurred to him to consider whether or not he loved her. She was there with her little niggling habits of domesticity, she was habit just as the *Agnes J.* had too quickly become habit. So the dull pattern had moved on until the night at Matson's when he had torn it to pieces by abruptly and amazingly falling in love.

Now everything that had gone before seemed futile and overemphasized, just as Lydia Keeling's ancient grudge seemed exaggerated in his mind and took on the quality of cruelty and silliness. He had not meant to fall in love. He was still uncertain whether the feeling he had was important enough to be worthy of any woman, but the idea of being frustrated when his whole intent was rigid with honor moved him to rage and he walked into his father's house grim-jawed and furious. When he saw Zach standing at the foot of the stairs, a lamp in his hand, this irritation mounted into his throat and tightened every muscle.

"What the devil are you doing here?" he demanded. "I thought you shook the dust of this place off your feet."

Zach quirked one sardonic eyebrow. "Don't explode, Lochinvar. The she-dragon had the door bolted, didn't she? Was she sitting on the doorstep with a shotgun? I imagine the mosquitoes were bad out on the river too, weren't they?"

"Shut up!" snapped Fox. "Leave my personal affairs alone. I suppose that you're broke again and that the poor old minister's wife got tired of bedding you down for your charming company?"

"On the contrary, she was distressed when I left."

"Does the Captain know you've come back?"

"I've been welcomed again into the fold—not too cordially, it's true, but at least they fed me. As for my financial status, your unkind aspersions insult me. I'm in funds, so if you had in your mind to offer me a dollar, you can save yourself that anguish. I'm not asking any favors whatever."

"You stole Tulia's ring. We heard about that. The Captain gave her money to induce her not to go to the sheriff about it, but her own family may have other ideas," Fox said.

Zach set the lamp down on a stand and opened an un-calloused palm. The big diamond shone there like a head-light.

"More calumny, more falsification," he sighed, with mock resignation. "I did not steal her ring. I merely borrowed it. I wore it and the air of prosperity it lent me worked nicely in the right places. I knew a few gamblers up east who were ready to gamble with me on what I think is a sure thing. When I find out where Tulia is I'll return the ring, now that it's served my purpose. I might even send her a few simoleons to assuage her ire. Nothing like the appearance of being flush when you approach the boys who wangled a little money out of selling beef to the army. But would Tulia listen to an argument like that? You know the answer."

"Settle with Tulia any way you please, that's your affair; but what you do in this town is the concern of anybody named Cavitt. If you've got some scheme figured out to fleece any of the people who'd trust you because you're the Captain's son, that's my affair," Fox said coldly.

"None of our trusting neighbors will be invited to come in on any proposition of mine," Zach declared. "I like to work with a free hand. Meantime, I hope my presence won't distress you too much. I shall leave early and return late—though not so late as you, apparently."

"One more thing," Fox said as Zach picked up the lamp again, "you've been hanging around that little Keeling girl. Put an end to it. That kid is young and innocent and green—"

Zach's interrupting laughter barked ironically. "Young—I agree, and she's innocent as far as I'm concerned, but as for being green—that little redhead is sharper than a shark's tooth and just now she's got me tied hand and foot till I can figure a way to get around her and get her pretty little nose out of my business, or else get in another bargeload of good cured tobacco. You needn't worry about that youngster, she can take care of herself. Old Tobe stored the tobacco in that old Neary mill. Now the kid has got the place locked up and she's holding out to skin the hide off of me."

"Her mother would see you burn in hell before she'd let you set foot inside that old mill."

"Her mother was ready enough to grab the tobacco when she thought she could make a profit off of it. Washington's phiz may be on one side of a dollar, but Zach Cavitt's name could be all over the other side and Sister Keeling would still reach for it. The kid's shrewd. She wants a hunk of this cigarette business I'm planning on starting, and I have to handle her carefully or begin all over."

"You actually think you can make a go of a cigarette business? How can you compete with the mechanized industry that Duke and Reynolds are developing over in the Piedmont? Personally, I think you're crazy."

"I'm competing with nobody except a few foreign concerns who come into the market, and I've got an edge on them on account of the import tax. Fine tailoring didn't pass out of production when they put cheap ready-made suits on the market. I'm designing a product that will attract the same customers. I've already booked a lot of tentative orders. By using a front man and handling the business on the outside myself, I think I can get the use of that old mill and the wharf, and so long as the old lady collects the rent she isn't going to examine too closely into the origin of the cash."

"You've been seen meeting that kid on the road, Zach. Even the Captain is worried about it," Fox persisted.

Zach shrugged. "You know how those little kids are—get the idea you're crazy about them and hang around waiting for a kind word. I won't be seeing her any more after I get going. The younger Matsons are interested and I've ordered a second-hand cutting machine on trial. If the business doesn't show a good profit in two or three months the owner can always repossess it and I won't lose a thing. I've got some superfine cigarette paper coming in and some packaging material. You'll be handling that in a day or two. The only thing that worries me is that oldest Keeling girl."

"Leave her out of it," Fox snapped.

"I can't leave her out—not if she persuades her mother to sell that prime cured tobacco on the market, or into refusing to let us use the mill building. There's nobody here who'd buy the tobacco, however, except Matson, and he's having his troubles right now. The trust is after him, and young Ren has already agreed to come along with me. I offered him twenty dollars a week—the old man's paying him eight-fifty and charging him three dollars a week for board. He's an expert weigher—he can pick up a pinch of tobacco in his fingers and gauge the weight to a fraction of a gram, but old Croff keeps him on dirty jobs with no chance to get ahead."

"The whole thing sounds dirty to me," said Fox scornfully. "You inveigle Ren Matson away from his father and scheme to use that little ignorant seventeen-year-old girl. I suppose you've promised her something that you've no idea of giving her?"

"Ha!" Zach laughed. "I'm not using Taffy—she's as shrewd and hard as a hatful of glass marbles. Right now she's got the whip hand. Unless I'm blind and deaf she means to keep it. I'm likely to be pushed out of the whole proposition unless I can figure some way to get around her. You needn't worry about Taffy Keeling. She can take care of herself."

Fox was not mollified. "Why the devil didn't you stay away from here?" he fumed sorrowfully. "Why did you have to come back here to foul your home nest? You know what people think about cigarettes! Every preacher preaches against them, all the women's clubs and missionary societies are against them, decent dealers won't even handle them in their stores. Even the big newspapers are running editorials blasting cigarette smoking. You'd be less degraded in the eyes of people who've known you all your life if you opened a saloon and sold whisky."

Zach mounted four steps of the stairs, then turned to grin back over his shoulder.

"I'd like to make you a small bet," he said, "say about a dollar or two—a small enough sum so you could lose it without too much agony. I'd like to bet that within ten years every man you meet will have a pack of cigarettes in his shirt pocket—and that even women will be smoking them! I could even go further and bet that you'll be smoking them," he added, his mouth one-sided with malicious mirth.

He went on up the stairs, and Fox flung his hat at a peg, making a small wan lamp flutter and smoke on the hall table.

He had no wish to sleep, though every muscle was weary. Irritation crackled along his nerves like slow fire creeping through marsh grass, his finger tips stung with it and there was a bitter taste on his tongue. He thrust the screen open and went out on the porch, striding to the rail and standing there, hands stiff in his pockets, staring moodily across the river.

The stir of a shape in the darkness at the far end of the porch startled him; then he heard the familiar rusty rasp as the old Captain cleared his throat and spat over the railing.

"Come sit down here," ordered the old man.

Fox crossed the dark space and half sat on the rail, arms crossed, tight fingers clutching his elbows. To make his father hear he would need to shout so that it could be heard across the river, so he made no effort to speak, but sat waiting while the Captain hawked loudly again, then blew his nose with a violent trumpeting.

"Been sitting here a good long spell," he said. "Saw you out there in the boat. Didn't have any company, did you?" His bony fingers prodded his son's thigh, and a chuckle burbled hoarsely in his throat. "Nearys! Stubbornest tribe ever lived on these waters. But you got to remember that nothin' much ever happened to Lyddy. She got married to John Keeling, and he was a good, decent feller but meek as bilge water and built shallow up from the keel. Sink him in a washin' tub, that feller! Used to buy brass from him and old Hod Taft. Taft had Keeling whipped down till he didn't dare spit without looking three ways first."

He gave Fox a playful poke again; then as his voice went on again a new note came into it, a soberness, a dignity that Fox had not heard there in many years. It was as though the Captain were standing tall again, braid on his sleeves and brass on his cap, the imperious firmness of command in his face. It was as though a derelict, rank with barnacles and rotting seaweed, suddenly lifted itself to the wind and spread proud white sails.

"I've made up my mind," he said. "I'm not going to live much longer, Fox. I've logged my course and from here on the chart shows blind. No channel marks to tell where I'm bound and no knowing where the banks and shoals may lie. I never was a timid sailor and strange waters don't daunt me, but I've got to think a little about the port I'm likely to head into and I figure I'll be better off there when I go ashore if I've got a proper manifest to show that I did ship some cargo that was worth stowing aboard. Up to now I ain't too proud of what I've been shipping, Fox."

Fox had never heard his father in such a grave vein before. Always the old man had carried a figurative chip on his shoulder, a challenge to wind, weather, tide, and circumstance. To be a Cavitt was to be undaunted, to live in a continuous mood of defiance, to walk arrogantly and the devil take the hindmost. Fox reached a hand and laid it on the Captain's dry wrist and the old man turned his fingers upward and tightened them, rubbing them over the hard bones of his son's hand, then relaxing the pressure into a kind of caress, as though what he felt under the hard flesh satisfied him.

"What I'm trying to say and sort of foundering in my own wake, more or less, is that a man ought to have something to show for his living when he tosses the last line ashore, Fox," he went on. "One thing I've got to do is straighten out this Neary business. 'Long as all of 'em were gone from here and that house sitting over there, rottening down, I held on to the feeling that I'd licked somebody in a fair fight and made 'em cut and run, but it don't sound sensible now, and it's got to where it ain't my personal affair any more. I can't fetch back the *Mary Conner* nor bring Lyddy Neary's father back to life, but it might be that I could fix things so as you'd have smooth sailing with that girl. I like that girl. She's got something behind them big eyes. Anyway, I'm going to have a try at it."

Fox nodded, letting approval warm his finger ends so that the old man sensed his attitude and his grip relaxed and he sighed with satisfaction. Then quickly his mood changed again and he jerked upright and jabbed a hand into a pocket, hunting his tobacco.

"Zach come back. I reckon you know," he said.

Fox nodded again and the darkness hid his scowl, but some emanation of it was communicated to his father.

"I don't like it any more than you do," declared the Captain. "He's got some kind of sherackety working and somebody is going to get skinned. Then the Cavitts will all be devils, showing their horns again. I can't stop him till I know what he's up to, and I wish to the Lord I could hear. You don't know what it's like to be shut up the way I am, like I was nailed down in the hold and all the hatches battened!"

Fox spoke for the first time. "I know," he said distinctly, so the Captain caught it the first time and did not counter with his usual "Yeh? Heh?"—the time-gaining device of the deaf that Tulia had found so infuriating.

He did know about being nailed up in a box, Fox was thinking, except that he, himself, had built his inhibiting enclosure and had liked the cold privacy he stored there till the wall had yielded and the touch of light and warmth that sifted through the breach had brought with it strange, heady fragrances and songs that he had never troubled to hear before, so that by comparison his aloofness showed itself for the stark, smug bit of postulation that it was.

The Captain got to his feet and groped for the rail, steadying himself with one hand.

"I'm going over there," he announced. "If she throws me out, she can't do it till I've said my say and one thing—" he gave a dry, senile cackle, then spat again, "—one thing sure, she may demean me and call me out of my name, but I won't hear a word she says! But that little dark-eyed one—I could hear her. I can hear her easy and plain—easy and plain!"

"When you go, I'll go with you," Fox offered.

"No. No—you wasn't even thought about when I dared Neary into that race, 'way back yonder. Thing that keeps me awake nights now is—Fox, I knew danged well that that rusty old boiler of Neary's was likely to blow up. I knew he was risking too much head of steam. That makes it murder—mighty near. That's the thought I've been livin' with a long time now. I've got to tell Lyddy that. I've got to cleanse my soul, Fox—if I don't, I'll rot in hell for ten million years!"

17

Taffy Keeling hitched Chloe to the gnawed sapling beside the path and walked with deliberate slowness toward the old mill. The two men who had sat hunkered down in the shade of a willow tree got to their feet, and Zach Cavitt balanced his cigar on the edge of the old syrup kettle and took off his hat with an obsequiousness just enough overdone to make Taffy prickle with fury.

"The mistress of our fate approaches," he intoned dramatically, turning to grin at Ren Matson.

Taffy gave him a scornful look. "Sorry—I don't feel amused," she remarked. "Ren, Bliss told me you were going to walk out on your father. Surely you aren't going to do that?"

"Why not, if he can better himself?" asked Zach. "Ren says he'll enjoy a chance to get his hands clean once more."

"You talk, Ren. And you keep still, Zach Cavitt! If you're going to act the fool, Ren, I think I'm going straight back to town and sell every bit of that tobacco in there to your father."

"Which of course you have every right to do," Zach agreed before Ren could find words to push past his embarrassed dumbness. "Except that Mr. Matson very likely won't be able to buy the tobacco, unless you'd agree to let him have it for about one cent a pound. Perhaps not at that price. He has had some bad luck in the past few days, as Renwick will tell you."

"It's the darned trust, Taffy," stammered Ren, struggling to hold his voice level so it would not rise to a yelp as it did when he was excited. "Last week a fellow came in and talked to Pa about buying him out. Pa thought it was just somebody working with Mr. Cavitt here on the cigarette proposition and Pa mighty near threw this man out of the shop. Now it turns out that this man was from the trust and they offered Pa a good fair price, but it only made him madder. Now

180

they've gone around to all the jobbers and bought up all the Golden Twist anybody had on hand and they're selling it to retailers for about sixty per cent under Pa's price."

"But that's not fair!" protested Taffy.

"Sure, it's fair, if they want to lose their money that way. They mean to put Pa out of business if he won't sell, and the only thing he can think to do is to get him another brand of tobacco and try some more under another name—and he can't bring himself to do that. He's been making Golden Twist ever since 1889, and selling it all over Carolina and southern Virginia—even up in Maryland some—and now he hears they are giving away plugs of it with a sackful of groceries."

"And he can't sell direct to the retailer, of course," prompted Zach amiably.

"A little firm can't do that," Rennie gulped painfully. "You got to have salesmen out with buckboards and teams. And take one country merchant—he'll buy a gross of plug and that won't buy oats for the team scarcely. It could be that I'd need another job bad, Taffy."

"Then if things are so bad, why doesn't your father go in with Mr. Cavitt and make cigarettes? If he has to make a change in his business anyway?"

"Because," said Rennie, "he's just naturally hardheaded and he just naturally hates cigarettes and he just naturally ain't going to do it!"

Taffy wore gloves. She smoothed them now over the backs of her hands and lifted her arms daintily to set the new, stylish hat straight on her runaway hair.

"I'm ready to listen to your proposition, Mr. Cavitt," she said, a trifle loftily, "but you'd better hurry because I'm supposed to be sent to the post office and my mother is getting curious over my delayed absences."

"What I want to talk is a cash lease," Zach said. "I'll pay you the money you invested in the tobacco and a reasonable rent for the mill. Renwick here will present the proposition to your mother, since I'm quite sure she wouldn't care to discuss business with me."

"You promised me a share in this business," Taffy reminded him. "Are you going back on your promise? If you are—well, good day, gentlemen. Sorry I'm not interested in any other proposition."

"I suppose you know that you are not of legal age to carry on any transaction whatever, Taffy?" Zach suggested.

"Oh, yes, I know," she retorted; "and in that case you've got no other recourse except to go and talk to Mama yourself, Mr. Cavitt. She'd never listen to Rennie here at all. Mama would think Rennie was just a boy my age, and she'd insist on going to his father before she'd make any deal at all. She's almost always at home, so you could call at any time." She turned her back and was walking away when Rennie yelled at her.

"Taffy Keeling, you come back here!"

She turned slowly, said "Yes?" in a voice studiedly acid, carefully sweet.

"You come back here and say what you want," Rennie ordered. "What do you want to act so childish for?"

"Mr. Cavitt knows what I want," stated Taffy coolly. "I want at least forty-nine per cent of the stock in his business. After all, we do own the tobacco—and the mill and the wharf and water front and everything."

"The small amount of tobacco stored in that building is unimportant, Taffy," Zach Cavitt said. "We shall need many more thousands of pounds once we get into production. I admit that we can use the building and we are prepared to pay for it."

"So you're going back on your word?" Taffy was angry. "My mother will do whatever I tell her to do and I think I shall throw the key to that mill into the river before I'll ever advise her to lease it to anybody!"

Rennie Matson shrugged impatiently. "I guess we might as well go and talk to Pa again, Mr. Cavitt. He's got the hands and the plant and the machines—might be he'd be willing to listen now."

"You just said he wouldn't listen," Taffy reminded him. "Personally, it doesn't matter to me at all. That tobacco in there will be worth more next year than it is now, because it will be aged more. So now, if you'll politely take yourselves off our property, I'd like to close the gate."

Zach laughed aloud. "Taffy, if I didn't know you so well I'd swear you were fifty years old and tough as whit-leather."

"I doubt if you know me at all," she returned, her voice shaking a trifle. "The Nearys were always practical people. So were my grandmother's family, the Tafts. Fortunately, I inherited from both sides."

"Especially," remarked Zach, "from the merry old blockade-runners and the pirates."

"There were no pirates hanged on my family tree. I will at least be decent enough to give you both a lift back to town if Ren will help me shut the gate."

The two looked at each other. "She's not fooling." Zach lifted an eyebrow.

"I reckon she ain't," sighed Rennie. "Listen, Taffy, even if we wanted to take you in, you know doggone well you're too young. And if we did give you so much stock, there wouldn't be enough left to split up right so Zach would control the business."

"I'm not arguing," Taffy said coolly, "I'm just reminding you that my mother has odd feelings about people named Cavitt. Once I'm out of it you haven't a Chinaman's chance to get this building and you know it. Will you hurry please, Rennie? I do have to get to town. I'm late already."

They helped her shut the gate—the gate that Lydia had sent Dobbs to repair. Then Rennie untied the mare.

"I suppose you know that you're a little highbinder, Taffy," Zach remarked as he got into the buggy. "You worked a trick to get hold of my tobacco and now you're holding us up on the mill."

"There was no trick about it. You left a poor old colored man holding the bag, and we came to his rescue. Both of you will have to get out at the cemetery corner. My sister insists that I'm getting myself talked about by being seen with dissolute characters."

Zach's laughter set the crows to honking excitedly in the marshy woods. "Taffy, if I weren't already married," he said, "I'd marry you just to see what would happen next."

"You exaggerate your desirability, Mr. Cavitt," she cut back smoothly. "When I marry it will be a man whose honor is impeccable."

"Plenty of time." Zach ripped a match on the sole of his shoe and lit a black cigar. "You're still only seventeen, little Taffy."

She set Chloe back on her haunches with a savage tug.

"I hate that name!" she blazed. "Maybe I am seventeen but I'm clever enough to know my rights, and I've beat you at your own game. Get up, Chloe!"

"When I call you 'little Taffy,' " Zach observed, "it's a term of admiration and affection, my dear child. Even though it's often obvious that you aren't affectionate and at times you are far from admirable. Hereafter I promise to greet you formally, as a person of years and an adversary worthy of any man's respect. Does that mollify you, dear madam?"

"Here's the cemetery," snapped Taffy. "Get out, both of you!" From habit Chloe had stopped at the usual corner.

Zach Cavitt said, "Good-by, Taffy. Sorry we couldn't reach an agreement."

She did not answer nor turn her head as he walked away. Ren Matson said peevishly, "Why can't I ride as far as the post office? I walked all the way out there and it's hot. I'm not married. I won't cause any scandal riding with you."

"Oh, all right," she agreed without enthusiasm.

Rennie said presently, "I don't see why my pa has to be so bullheaded. I think Zach Cavitt's smart and Pa ought to see that now the trust is after him they'll never let up till they put him out of business."

"What will stop them from putting Zach Cavitt out of business?"

"Well, if you think they're likely to put him out of business, why are you so dead set to get into it?"

"For reasons you would never understand, Ren Matson. Never in the world."

"I think it's just because you like to be boss, Taffy Keeling. A kid like you!"

She disdained to answer this. Why should she tell Ren Matson anything? He was only a gangly boy with soft yellow down on his cheeks and thin shoulders already stooped a little, who was never certain whether his voice was going to be falsetto or baritone. How could she tell Rennie that she had to be implacable because the person to whom she must be most ruthless was herself? She could imagine Rennie's consternation and the malicious delight of the village gossips if she should announce, abruptly, "I have to hate Zach Cavitt and fight him and frustrate him because I'm so much in love with him that even to look at him is torture and to see that hateful, fatherly look of amusement on his face when he looks at me tears me into little pieces!"

Little Taffy! She ground her teeth fiercely, then sobered and let heaviness descend upon her as she stopped the mare at the post office.

"Well, at least you won't have to tell your father you aren't going to work for him any more," Taffy remarked, "now that the Pamlico Tobacco Company has blown up."

"You haven't got Zach Cavitt licked, Taffy." Ren was grim. "He can make cigarettes in a barn. He can get more tobacco. And I'm still going in with him. That is, unless Pa gets some sense and lets Zach come in with us."

"I'm betting you'll never have the courage to quit," Taffy said. "I'm betting you'll just run away."

Rennie looked down the sandy path skirting the riverbank to the red brick of the Matson factory, his hands twisting on each other as though they felt already the sticky nauseous flavoring vats. His Adam's apple fluttered and his voice broke edgily.

"I'll be twenty-one years old this winter," he flared. "Then you'll see!"

They looked at each other for a moment and a raw, young misery deepened between their eyes. Suddenly they were very young together and the pressure of this cramping, painful youthfulness was so heavy upon them that there were no words adequate to define or dispel it. They were young, in an adult world that made light of their torments and desires, laughed at their frustrations and their little forays into maturity. The wretchedness of being young cramped them so rigidly that neither had the spirit to resent it when Wylie Matson came out of the post office and said cheerfully, "Hello, you kids."

Renwick grunted a listless greeting, but Taffy was instantly alert.

"I want to talk to you, Wylie. I want some legal advice," she said. "Can I go up to your office?"

"Well, I was just going home to dinner and to take Pa his mail, but Ren can tote it to him." Wylie looked quizzically at her as he helped tie up the mare. "What is this? Personal or business?"

"It's business—and you can wipe that sly expression off your face, Wylie Matson."

"Well, you can't blame a man for surmising. Especially as I've been listening to that kid brother of mine talk in his sleep all summer."

"Aw, I do not!" Renwick flung back, brick-red and unhappy as he trudged away.

"Up here." Wylie motioned Taffy up the splintery stairs that climbed steeply up the side of Bart's grocery store. They went up to a naked landing, entered a door into a grimy hall leading to a long room with a worn desk in the middle and some sagging shelves piled with law books. "Now—" he dragged up a dusty chair for Taffy and seated himself on a backless stool, "what's troubling you, Miss Keeling?"

"I want some legal advice, Wylie, and I'm employing you and I'll expect to pay your fee," she said primly. "I want to know how old I have to be before I can act independently."

Wylie grinned. "If you want to get married, Taffy, you have to have your mother's written consent until you're eighteen years old."

"Good heavens, I don't want any such silly advice as that. I've no idea of getting married. I want to know about contracts and things."

"You can't sign a contract or convey property or make any obligations involving your potential estate or the property of another person without your guardian's consent until you're twenty-one, Taffy."

Taffy tapped angrily with a toe. "I never did think much of this women's rights business, but now I think I'm converted," she exclaimed. "You mean I've got to be an infant, practically, for three more years?"

"That's the law. It protects you as well as other people. You can't be taken advantage of, sued, or defrauded because of your youth and inexperience. Look, Taffy, you've got Zach Cavitt on your mind, haven't you? Oh, I know you were to meet them out at the mill today. I got it out of Ren this morning. Well, as your attorney I'm advising you just as I advised my youthful brother, to stay out of that business."

"How can I stay out of it when I've never been in it?" snapped Taffy, confusing her language because she was prickling all over with anger. "After making me a definite promise, Zach Cavitt won't let me in! That's why I wanted a lawyer. I wanted to know how I could make him keep his agreement to give me a certain amount of stock."

"For what, Taffy?" asked Wylie gravely. "A promise like that implies value received—or hadn't you thought of that?"

Taffy looked a trifle dashed. "Well, what he really wanted me to do was persuade Mama to let his company use our old mill."

"Which she'd refuse to do, undoubtedly, having no love for the Cavitts. Had it occurred to you that you might incur some very embarrassing liabilities by owning stock in any business over which Zach Cavitt has control? Suppose he went broke owing a lot of money? Being a stockholder you'd be responsible for your proportion of the indebtedness, unless Zach filed for a limited charter, which he'd never do. He's gone broke on a lot of projects in several places, Taffy. Now he's wangled financing from some source, but he's going up against powerful interests on a shoestring. Are you sure that's all you want from Zach—to compel him to give you a share in this proposition?"

Her cheeks flamed, and Wiley, seeing them, looked a little sick. Damn Zach Cavitt, his devastating insolence, his worldly airs, his handsome face, and his unscrupulous nature!

"Certainly it's all I want!" she replied frigidly.

"Zach's still a married man, Taffy. I doubt if Tulia will go through with the divorce. She's already written me to delay drawing up the papers. She found she couldn't sue in New York, so she'll have to file in this county—and very likely her mother refused to put up the money."

In spite of her control, Taffy's mouth drew straight and colorless against the pallor of her face. Her eyes held a kind of lost look of anguish, but her voice was high and edged and icy.

"All that is nothing to me, I'm sure," she said coldly.

"Well, I'm glad of that." Wylie let his breath out so that his body seemed to expand. "You'll forgive me, but young girls have always been fascinated by Zach Cavitt. There's my little sister Bliss. She's been mad at Pa for weeks because he won't take Zach into his business."

Taffy cried, "Bliss?" angrily; then as she saw awareness and something approaching pity sober Wylie's eyes, she sagged forward and began suddenly, chokingly, to cry. She buried her face in her arms and her hat slid down and all the nasturtium-colored wildness of her hair tumbled loosely about her neck and shoulders.

Wylie said, "Taffy—" and made a move to comfort her, but she fought him off with her hands.

"Go on and despise me!" she cried shrilly. "I do care! I do care!" Then when the spasm of weeping had subsided a little, she raised a stricken face. "Oh, Wylie—don't tell anybody what a little fool I am!"

He patted her awkwardly, brought water from a tin bucket in the corner, where a gourd dipper floated and gnats drowned themselves unmourned. She wiped off her hot face and tucked up her hair, throaty sobs still making her body tremble.

"I'm your attorney, remember, Taffy?" He tried to laugh. "Whatever is said between us in this office I regard with professional discretion and secrecy."

She set her hat straight with a determined jabbing of pins, set her face in order with the same young grimness.

"You needn't tell me any more," she said coldly. "You were going to remind me that I'm young and that I'll get over it."

"Has he tried to make love to you, Taffy?" Wylie asked sharply.

She looked startled. "Zach Cavitt? No—no, never! It isn't— I think I hate him, Wylie. I must hate him for I want to do anything I can to hurt him. Is that being in love? It can't be, can it?"

"It could be, Taffy," he replied gravely. "Being in love can be sweet—or it can be mighty bitter!" He walked to the dusty window, looked down into the sleepy little square, his hands in his pockets. "You can't win, you know," he went on, "not with a fellow like Zach. Tulia couldn't win. She won't divorce him, but if she ever had any part of Zach it's gone now. Zach hasn't anything to give anybody—only himself. There are people like that. Don't beat your brains out against that wall."

She got up, smoothing her gloves over and over. "I'll go home now," she said with metallic flatness. "I've been hours. Mama will be watching the gate and France will have something more to look worried and reproachful about."

"All right. Run home, Taffy. And don't stop anywhere."

She looked at him sharply, wondering what he knew, what anyone knew. But she would not stop. Not at the cemetery corner, not by the gum tree. She would not even move her eyes, searching for a quirked up, teasing eyebrow, a disarming smile under a jaunty mustache. She would not listen ever again for that low voice calling her "little Taffy." She was old now, old and wise and sore and wounded, and she began to cry thinly, almost before she entered her mother's door.

"I'm sick. I think I must be bilious. I was so dizzy I could hardly see the road! I'm going to bed."

Lydia brought the camphor bottle and wrung cloths from cold water.

"Calomel's what you need," she announced. "It could be a touch of the sun. Brother Daniel got a stroke once fishing in an open boat, and he had terrible headaches as long as he lived at home."

Later Frances came quietly into the room and closed the door.

"I'd better tell you," she said tonelessly, "that Dobbs found Chloe's hitch rein over by the mill, still fastened to a tree. Mama had sent him over to put a padlock on the gate—anyway that's what she said. I don't know if she had any other thought than that or not, but anyway I kept her from seeing that strap and told Dobbs not to tell her about it. Taffy—you haven't—"

"No!" cried Taffy, lifting herself with the angry fling of a catapult. "I went there on business. They want to lease the mill. I told them Mama would never agree to it. So if you have any low suspicions in your mind—"

"Oh, Taffy, don't be stupid! You know I'm only thinking of you. He's older and—"

"And married! Put that in. She's not getting the divorce. Maybe that will ease your mind! If you want the Cavitts you can have them, France—horns and all!"

18

There had been a late rain and little lead-colored fountains were leaping gaily up from the flattened surface of the river when Fox Cavitt paddled his boat across the current. Above his head the mast lifted bare, little trickles of rain sliding down its varnished roundness, and on limp lines beads gathered and hung, growing rounder and heavier till they fell with soft drippings on the wet duckboards under his feet. A warm, heavy cloud of mist crept along the shore line, and under it black summer ducks paddled busily, tilting their silly tails and leaving little flat ripples as they dived.

Fox dipped his paddle, first on one side of the boat, then on the other; and the ducks skittered out of the way, turning up yellow eyes in protest at being disturbed, then went on with their exploring of the shallows. The willows on the bank under the bluff hung very low, every branch appearing to reach for something hidden under the dull silver of the river. The old barnacled piles of the Neary dock were reflected crookedly in the dull light from the sky and the dull quiet of the water, and thin puddles lay on the warped planks. Fox flipped a chain over a post, pulled himself up to the landing, abstractedly wiping the mossy stain of the wet wood from the palm of his hand.

The path up the low bluff was already a small, running rivulet of rain. He avoided its slippery steepness, walked through the ragged, soggy grass, scrubbing his shoes clean as he climbed. The day was already growing very dim. September was a few days away, the short days were beginning. Ten days had passed since he had seen Frances. Ten routine days of doing the same thing over and over, of eating a hurried breakfast, by lamplight now, with his mother fussing and padding from kitchen stove to dining table in her purple felt slippers, bringing hot coffee and grits, eggs with grease dripping from their brown, curling edges, and big, flat biscuits always a trifle too yellow with soda. The house always smelled of driftwood smoke in the mornings and of the liniment with which his mother rubbed her rheumatic knee before she put on her thick cotton stockings. It smelled of the starch in her aprons and the calico cushions where the cats slept, and lately of the stuff Zach put on his hair and mustache.

The mornings were thick with smells, Fox often thought with a touch of irritation. The hot, kerosene smell of the engine on the little boat, the sweetish tobacco smell of Croff Matson's factory that lay always on the morning fog over the town, the coal and oil stink that was the breath of the old *Agnes J.*, the fish-and-brine reek of the marshes. That was why he liked the evenings and the clean quiet of his sailboat. But for ten evenings now he had stayed away from the river. He had lain on his bed with gnats and candle moths whirling around the lamp, reading the books he was always ordering down from New York, books and magazines that dealt with the new in science and engineering, reading a paragraph over many times before he tossed the book away, abruptly aware that his mind was far from the printed page.

Two or three times he had sat with the old Captain on the dark porch, listening to the old man's maunderings, his stories of old days on the Sound, stories heard too many times already. On each of these nights the Captain had struggled up from his deep chair to shuffle to the porch rail and look out across the river where the lights in the Neary house blinked through the trees.

"I'm going over there," the old man declared over and over. "One of these days I'm going over and straighten out this Neary business."

Then abruptly on this eleventh day, when the light began to die out of the sky and the slow mourning of the rain against the salt-pitted panes of the windows filled the house with such drowsy dullness that the Captain nodded at the supper table and even the cats slept, bellies flat, claws distended, Fox felt himself come alive with a curious, electric kind of fury, as though the youth in him, pressed down and made toneless and inelastic by the awful sameness of life in this old house, had undergone a shocking chemical change.

Good God, he was young, he was decent, he was a man! Was he going to go on like this, dead before he had lived, accepting the trampling iron of dogged days, of duty, of frustration because he was too cowardly to kick down an impeding wall?

Even if he failed, he told himself grimly as he scrambled up the muddy bluff to the Neary place, he should at least have proved to himself and to her that he was a man! All the way across the river he had thrust his paddle deep, snatching the boat along against the ebbing tide, keeping his anger against himself alive, feeling his muscles crackling with it and the stinging taste of it on his tongue. Slow, slow—a whole summer gone to waste because he had been more dead than alive, old before his time! Only the old accepted frustration meekly, only age brought the deadening of patience. He ran his damp hands over his temples as though he dreaded to feel the hair thinning there, and a kind of sick shame made his fingers uncertain and his mouth twitch, knowing as he did that this gesture of his was inevitably bound to wear the aspect of the anticlimactic, the studied, the delayed.

Undoubtedly already Francie was resigned to the conviction that he was a do-nothing, that the self-pride of the Cavitts was too stiff in him to risk a challenge. She might even laugh. Her eyes might hold the slow scorn that would destroy him even if her lips did not say what he knew he deserved to hear: "Well, really? At last?"

He knew that part of the uncertainty that had tormented him was his own doubt of himself, the cramping pressure of unbelief, the consternation that had dizzied him when he had realized that this thing that had changed and shifted all his personal values and viewpoints was love. It could not occur to him, indifferent to other contacts as he had held himself for years, that an incredulous and stunned feeling of unworthiness was the beginning of the alchemy that love worked in every lover. He had said, "I suppose you know that I love you?" and then he had been aghast for days at his own brash impertinence. Then when she had said, wearily he knew now, "It's no use, Fox, it's no use at all," he had accepted this dismissal as he had accepted every thwarting of his own desires since the old *Agnes* went aground at Swan Quarter and her wheel and compass and binnacle became the galley oars to which his ambition was chained. Old—old before his time!

Pushing through the wet, high grass he found himself stalking grimly, fanning his desperate anger by tightening his muscles and setting his jaw. Then as he came close to the house, he stopped and tried to relax the steely fierceness he could feel stiffening his face. He rubbed his cheeks and made his mouth ease into a wooden smile, he shook his body loose and made himself move slowly and calmly up the bricked path to the door.

The fanlight above the panels showed a thin glow that by its wavering he knew for candle flame, but the door was closed fast though the night was warm. He beat upon it firmly with a knotted fist.

He heard movement inside presently, and the door opened a little way. Frances stood there, snatching off an apron that she tossed quickly behind the door. She held the door cautiously against him till he moved into the thin rectangle of light, and then she opened it wider and put both hands up to her throat, twisting them together nervously.

"I'm here," he announced levelly. "Take down the bars, Francie, they won't keep me out any more."

She said, "Oh!" uncertainly, looking behind her, and then in a little rush, "Mama's in the kitchen—we were just getting supper."

"Not the proper time to make a call." He took off his cap, shook the moisture from it, walked past her into the hall. "Nice," he approved it, the candles in their sconces, the mildewed old mirror above a marble console, the shabby chairs set primly against the wall.

Frances closed the door and picked up her apron, holding it behind her. Her eyes were very dark and her face was pale and rigid, but quickened with a flicker of something passing, a kind of glory, a pain being assuaged. Then color washed over it, her eyes shone but her lips trembled.

"I—I'd better call Mama," she said. Then impulsively she

put out her hands to him. "Oh, Fox—do you think you did right to come? But—I'm glad! I'm glad!"

"I should have come long ago, Francie," he answered gently, all the bristling tension suddenly gone out of him, only tenderness left and with it a steady assurance. "I've been too slow—much too slow."

"But you couldn't help—how things are," she protested. "I don't know—Mama may not be friendly, Fox. I don't know—"

"It doesn't matter." He was easy now, head high with the cool self-confidence of the Cavitts. "It doesn't matter—just so I know that you care, Francie."

Her hands quivered on his. Her eyes misted a little.

"Oh—I do, Fox! I'm so glad you came—I'll tell Mama."

She hurried away, turning to smile back at him, unaware that he stood smiling back a trifle foolishly with the abandoned apron left in his hands. He moved to the chair by the wall and seated himself on it a bit gingerly, shifting to another one further along when the old walnut frame creaked alarmingly under his weight. The candles held their frail banners of fire erect, little tails of smoke waving now and then as currents of air moved, and then fluttering in agitation as a door closed somewhere in the house behind him.

Damp, fresh air blew against Fox's face, boards squeaked, and Taffy Keeling came charging in from the back, stopping short as she saw him. Her bright hair was beaded with the mist, even her eyelids were shining with moisture, and she wiped the back of a hand across her forehead and blew outward with a loud gasp of mock surprise.

"My word!" she exclaimed. "The house is haunted!"

Fox said, "Hello, Taffy. Your heels are muddy."

She looked down, jerking up the drabbled hem of her skirt. "I'm chore-boy," she announced. "Dobbs is on another drunk. I had to feed Chloe. She's our horse. Does France know you've invaded the place?"

"She went to call your mother." Fox was on his feet, still holding the apron. He hung it, a bit awkwardly, on the back of the chair.

"France must have been excited," remarked Taffy dryly. "What is this? A showdown or something? Cavitts under the sacred roof! Mama will come running with the roach powder. Come along in the parlor, for goodness' sake. I'll light a lamp. Wait a minute till I get my shoes clean—I'll outrage the ancestral carpets." She seized the apron and scrubbed her damp soles, shook out the hem of her skirt and tossed the apron into a corner. "Come along," she ordered.

The parlor was hot, and sweet with roses wilting in a glass bowl on the old secretary. Taffy jerked back a plush curtain, threw open a window, motioned Fox to a seat on the blue sofa.

"Great-grandpa did his courting on that," she observed, "so Great-grandma brought it along with her when she moved in, to remind him of all his brags and promises. Don't let Mama scare you, Fox. Stand up and yell right back at her. She bluffs but she backs down when she sees it's no use. Give me that silly cap!" She took the nautical affair from his fingers, turned it in her own. "What does C.L. stand for?" She studied the brass that decorated it.

"Cavitt Lines. That's the way our charter reads. My father was going to have a whole fleet of carriers on the Sound, but they were never built."

"I want a boat." Taffy perched herself on the edge of a big tapestried chair. "Are they going to build them with gasoline engines, Fox? Ren Matson says they have some already on Chesapeake. They'd be fearfully dangerous, wouldn't they? I mean they'd blow up all the time."

"Automobiles don't blow up. They're getting internal-combustion engines pretty well perfected now—that will be the next big development in transportation."

"What use is it to develop automobiles, when the roads are so dreadful? They get stuck in mudholes and on every sandy stretch now."

"They'll build hard roads. Cobbles perhaps, or brick. Even macadam would be practical—crushed up rock with oil to keep down the dust. Sooner or later you'll see the horse go, Taffy, just as the ox team went, just as the railroad put the stagecoach out of business."

"Poor Chloe! I'll miss her when I have my gasoline buggy with brass headlights and fringe on the top." Taffy was quiet for a moment. Speaking of Chloe made her think of Zach

Cavitt. She had not seen Zach since their stormy parting after the scene at the mill. The Pamlico Tobacco Company was getting underway in the loft and the cellar of Bart's store, Ren Matson had told her. They had had to put the Pease cutting machine in the cellar because it was too heavy for the old beams of the building. Zach had gone upriver to buy tobacco and had already lured three hand workers out of the Matson factory. But Renwick's arms and hands were still blackened from his father's flavoring vats.

"Your Chloe is mighty near as old as I am," Fox said. "She won't live to see her era come to a dismal end."

Chloe and the Captain, he was thinking. They were symbols of what had been, what must pass. Steam on the waterways, slow horsepower on the inland roads; sooner or later they would go the way of sail, of the covered wagon, the pony express. And he, Fox Cavitt, wanted a part in it.

He got to his feet abruptly, hearing quick footsteps in the hall. Frances came first, her eyes anxious, her face noncommittal; behind her, moving a little like a sullen tow, walked Lydia Neary Keeling, her chin set so that a small, sagging roll of flesh lay on her neat collar, her arms clasped one on the other over her plump stomach, her short fat fingers cut in deep ridges by the gold of her rings.

Fox bowed politely, his dark face grave. "Mrs. Keeling? I am Foxworth Cavitt."

Lydia did not sit down, though Frances tried to urge her into a chair. Her knuckles tightened a little upon each other, her small blue eyes were opaque and chill.

She said, "You wanted to see me?"

"I do." Fox stood respectfully and Frances' heart scudded, seeing how handsome he was, how sure of himself, his body very tall in the low room, dwarfing all the fussy little feminine affairs like tidies on the chairs and the garland of crepe-paper oranges hung over the corner of a picture frame. He belonged on the bow of a ship, and a wind seemed to blow about him till Frances was breathless with it, her throat fluttering.

She said faintly, "Please, Mama—"

"Everybody sit down and stop glaring," ordered Taffy bluntly. "Surely we are all sensible people!"

But Lydia would not sit down. She was having her hour, this was a scene she had rehearsed many times in her mind, lying awake at night, aware of that house across the river. This was her hour in the presence of her enemy, and she would not forego any small part of the drama and triumph of it.

"Of course we are sensible people, Taffy," she said with a little upward jerk of her chin, because Fox Cavitt's tallness gave him the advantage in presence. "Mr. Cavitt, being a sensible person, must be aware that no one of his name or family could possibly be received as a friend in this house."

"That's not fair, Mama," cried Frances. "Fox had nothing to do with your father's accident—he wasn't even born then and neither was I."

"My own father," Fox said quietly, "is deeply regretful of all that happened a long time ago, Mrs. Keeling. He would like to come and tell you so. He's very old now and feeble. He would like peace of mind before he dies."

"Bascom Cavitt killed my father," Lydia went on remorselessly. "I doubt, if our positions were reversed, Mr. Cavitt, that you would harbor any kindly feeling toward my family. You can have no possible errand in this house except to bring back unpleasant memories which I feel sure you have no wish to do. We will bid you good evening, sir."

"My errand in this house is to tell you that I love your daughter, Mrs. Keeling," Fox said.

"No daughter of mine would be interested in hearing that declaration, Mr. Cavitt." Lydia was enjoying herself. Her eyes glittered, she twisted her hands as though she washed them clean of contamination. "Henrietta, will you show Mr. Cavitt to the door?"

"I will not!" Taffy cried angrily. "Mama, how can you be so horrible—so rude? How can you possibly do this to Francie—break her heart?"

"I know what is best for both of you." Lydia turned grim. "Frances has known all along what my feeling is concerning the Cavitt family. I regret that you have made this scene possible, Mr. Cavitt. I shall be obliged if you do not come here again."

Fox looked at Frances with a slow smile. "You were right,

Francie," he said, "it was no use. But anyway I did what I could."

Anger made Frances' voice icy. "It's not your fault, Fox. It's not my fault either. It's the fault of a stupid, stubborn older generation who made a mess of their own lives and now they want to ruin ours."

"That," said Lydia brusquely, "is a very disrespectful way to speak of your own mother, Frances."

Taffy stamped her foot. "Who started it? Who said ugly things first? I'd run away, France! Take her with you, Fox! You'll never get a fair hearing in this house no matter how honorable your intentions are."

But Fox shook his head. "Not that way, Taffy," he said. "We do it the right way or not at all."

Frances moved ahead of him to the door. "I'm sorry," she said hoarsely, as she opened it. "You couldn't have done any more, Fox."

"Wait—wait—here's your hat." Taffy came running and handed him the white cap. He took it abstractedly as though he had never seen it before, turning it in his hands.

Frances followed him out to the porch. Lydia's sharp call of "Frances!" was cut in half by Taffy's vicious slam of the front door.

Fox held out his hands in the dark. "There's still the river, Francie," he said.

She shook her head. "No—no, I can't, Fox. I can't make it sneaky! It has to be fine—it has to! Some way. I'll talk to Mama. Maybe she'll change—she has to change—it's not your fault—" She began to cry, her face turned up, the tears running down over her cheeks, her lips.

He took her quickly in his arms, kissed her wet mouth, her forehead. "I'll do something—I'll send the Captain. Maybe she'll listen to him," he whispered.

"She must listen—he's so old—she can't be cruel to him, Fox—" She put her hands up and touched his face gently. There was a tension of the hard muscles under her fingers, his jaw was set rigidly, his teeth clicked.

"Hate!" he muttered. "The stupidest damn thing in this stupid world!"

He dropped his arms abruptly, jammed the cap on his head, and plunged off into the rainy dark. Frances stood still for a minute. The rain dripped sadly off the eaves, a leaf drifted down and whirled in wetly at her feet. Summer was dying. Suddenly her heart was full of the sorrow of little deaths, of the leaves dying, of the grass. The tears of the rain seemed part of her own wretchedness; she held out her hands to them and watched the light die out of the sky, thin and yellow-gray in the west. Across the river one thin light burned, but there was no sound from the river.

She went back to the house reluctantly. Taffy was still sitting bolt upright on a chair in the hall, her eyes angry, her foot beating restlessly on the rug.

"I hate her!" she stormed. "I'm sorry I was born into the Neary family! France, you're a fool not to run away."

"No," Frances said wearily, "never that way, Taffy."

"Mama married against her family's wishes herself—I've heard her say so a dozen times. She was never sorry and the family came around right away."

"Maybe Papa was sorry, Taffy. Had you thought of that? He was never anything else after that but a meek servant of the Tafts and the Nearys."

Taffy looked sober. "Funny," she remarked, "I never thought of Papa as having feelings about anything. He was always just Papa who took what Uncle Horace gave him and ate what Mama put before him, and if he ever protested against anything in his life I missed it. But France, don't you see—you could get to be like Papa!"

"I know. Mama's already told me I was like Papa. I don't know what to do, Taffy. I just know I can't hide and be sneaky and underhanded in this. I can't make it cheap—that Fox and I are in love."

"Don't be sneaky. Be bold! Tell Mama plainly that if you can't see the man you love in your own home you'll see him somewhere else. You know Mama—she puts on a stiff front to bolster up her own ego, but she always backs down when she knows she's beaten—like the Matson's party."

"I don't believe she will back down where the Cavitts are

concerned, Taffy. It goes back too far, it goes too deep. It's all Mama has, really. Her one little importance. She'd never give it up."

"I'd try, anyway. Personally, I don't see how Mama could resist Fox. He was the handsomest thing, standing there. He made Mama look so kind of—petty or something."

Frances rose with a sigh. "We'd better go and finish up supper. Let's not talk about it, Taffy—please."

"Mama will talk."

"Then answer politely in monosyllables. She's probably offended by the things you said, but at least we can watch our tongues from here on."

"I'll be an iceberg. I can be offended, too, and I'm going to let Mama know that she's in the doghouse so far as I'm concerned. One thing, France—we do own this house!"

"Yes, but Mama controls the money, remember that. Unless you want to get a job teaching school or something."

"Me?" Taffy struck an attitude. "Teaching drooly little brats? Thank you. I'll sell hats or go on the stage with a tent show or anything else outrageous, but nothing so ghastly dull and respectable as teaching school for me!" She moved toward the kitchen, and turned back with a toss of her head. "I can always go and roll cigarettes for the Pamlico Tobacco Company!"

"Taffy—you haven't been seeing him again?"

"Do I snoop and interfere in your affairs, Miss? I took a stand for you, didn't I? Just remember that. And that what I do is my own affair!"

Fox Cavitt stayed out on the river for hours, letting his boat drift idly, the soft, misty rain wetting his face and hair unheeded. Anger warmed him, made more bitter by the shamed feeling of helplessness that gripped him, the sickening feeling that in some fashion he had not proved himself a man. But he had been a gentleman, he consoled himself—though gentility had definite disadvantages pitted against such obstinacy as had possessed Lydia Keeling.

He tried to decide how his father would have handled the

situation, what could have been said or done to break down Lydia's stubborn antagonism. He even made up stern speeches of defiance in his mind, then shrugged that idea away, knowing that threats would have been futile and that Frances would never have supported him in any rash challenge to maternal authority. He suspected, too, that he would have loved and admired her less had she turned against her mother as Taffy had done.

Why must they be such decent people, cramped and frustrated by duty, when being decent and dutiful won nothing at all? Zach—Fox knew well what Zach would have done. Zach would have laughed at the thought of offering himself as a submissive target for Lydia's hoarded resentments. Zach would have taken the rash and reckless way, snatching what he wanted, running off with it with back-flung scornful laughter, deaf to repercussions and indifferent to consequences.

The rain fell harder and Fox paddled his boat back toward the Cavitt side of the river. Then through the dusky mist he saw another boat being rowed upstream, saw that it was heading in toward the Cavitt landing. There was enough light in the sky so that he made out a huddled figure in the stern behind the oarsman. Fox held his paddle in the air, letting his boat glide slowly till the smaller boat had moved in alongside the landing. The rower climbed up to the planks and made a rope fast, and by the stoop of his body and the slant of his cap Fox knew that this was Ren Matson's boat and that young Ren was mooring it. Zach had come home, undoubtedly.

But the person in the stern made no move till Ren bent down and reached his hands for assistance. Fox heard a soft, feminine voice protesting.

"Oh, I'll fall! I never can get up there! Why didn't you bring a lantern? Oh, I'm soaked! Everything I have on is ruined!"

Tulia! Fox felt a sick clutching at his stomach, shipped his paddle, lay back against his bare mast and held the rudder lines steady, letting the current and the outgoing tide take his craft quickly and silently down the river.

Tulia! He had no wish to see her, her intent, seeking,

demanding eyes, nor her hands with their little enclosing gestures that claimed and held him in some self-contrived mesh of her own ruthless desires. The tide was friendly, it swept him swiftly out of the sound of her voice. He slept in the cabin of the *Agnes* that night.

19

Lydia was enjoying herself. She was being abused and misunderstood; she was resented, but she was in command. Frances moved about the house quietly, answering when she was spoken to, answering Lydia's searching questions with a vague, "Yes, Mama," "No, Mama." Lydia grew peevish and shrill.

"Can't you say anything but 'No, Mama'?" she mimicked acidly. "I asked you if you'd been seeing this man in town?"

"No, Mama." Frances did not raise her voice. "Only at the Matson's party, but everybody in town was there."

"Then how on earth—you're hiding something from me, Miss! No man walks into a house as bold as brass, like he did last night, unless he's had some encouragement. Not when he knows good and well—or ought to know at least—that he's about as welcome as the plague! I should never have agreed to come down here at all, I should never have let you talk me into it. Cavitts! I wouldn't trust one of that name as far as I could throw him!"

"Yes, Mama. Is that all?"

"All? It might as well be all, for all I can get out of you! If you're waiting for me to change my mind you've got a long time to wait, I can tell you that much!"

Lydia grew a little drunk on her heady assumption of final authority. She realized that she had been managed, gently but firmly, for a long time and that she was sick and tired of it. She was tired of having Frances tell her what to wear, and mother and take care of her— "as though I was a half-witted stepchild!" she fumed inwardly. It occurred to her in a rising tide of resentment that she had never in her life really been allowed to make a final decision.

There had been her mother, querulous and always with a tearful grievance; and Grandfather Taft and Uncle Horace who liked raising objections and obstacles because it gave them a feeling of power. She had not even been permitted to manage her own marriage. John Keeling had done that, and though Lydia had enjoyed the brief flurry of indignation that ensued in her family and the petty importance that it gave her in having lived through a successful defiance, the family had decided everything for her after that—Uncle Horace renting the house, and her mother rummaging furniture out of family attics and advice and counsel from the thwarted and repressed recesses of her gloomy soul.

Routine had engulfed her then. The fussy rearing of two babies, the endless struggle with inadequate funds, the contriving and making-do, the resignation that pressed down upon her when it became certain that she was never going to control any aspect of her life; that fate and misfortune were always one jump ahead of her with nothing left in their trail but dreary acceptance.

Daniel's death had been the stroke that meant liberty for her, and she had let a whole summer go by without making one independent move! She had money now, she was in command, and Taffy's sauciness was a little too much and Frances' attitude of terribly resigned patience an irritation that called for action to dispel it.

"I'm going to town—by myself," she announced abruptly at noon, "and don't either of you tell me that I can't drive that fat old horse, because I was driving horses before either of you was born! Taffy, see if Dobbs is sober enough to stand up and if he is, tell him to get the harness on and I want that buggy dusted and wiped off. And if anybody tells me what dress to wear they'll get a piece of my mind!"

Taffy gave Frances a sidelong glance. "Maybe she's going in to have Wylie change her will," she whispered as Lydia marched off up the stairs, setting her little heels down firmly.

When she came down again, hatted and veiled, her small round mouth jerked into a grim line, Taffy was standing meekly at Chloe's head. Lydia disdained so much as to notice Taffy's air of mock servility or the silly way she jerked her forelock and said, "Yes, ma'am," as she handed up the reins.

Then as Chloe ambled slowly off down the lane, Taffy had a

moment of panic. What if Chloe saw Zach Cavitt somewhere along the street and stopped dead still, as she was always determined to do? Well, if Mama was going to act high and mighty she was due for some shocks and there was nothing to be done about it.

Lydia herself had only a dim idea of what she meant to do in town. She knew only that she had to make some definite move, and cease being managed and petted and maneuvered—yes, and fooled! How she had been fooled angered and bewildered her. That Cavitt man—standing up there in her own parlor, as suave and arrogant as though he owned the place! "My errand is to tell you that I love your daughter." Lydia prickled all over with fury thinking of it. Francie! Her quiet child, the daughter she had depended upon, trusted—trusted with business, with money, with everything.

It came clear suddenly, so sharply that Lydia gave an involuntary jerk on the reins and Chloe looked around uncertainly.

"Get up!" Lydia snapped, whacking with the whip with no result except a twitching of Chloe's plump rump, an exasperated jerk of her ear. "That boat!" It was plain now. Those trips to Baltimore. That horrid old boat, the very boat that had brought death to her own father.

She had been obliged to ride that boat herself, on her first visit, and again when she had come down by train, because there was no other transportation to the town; but she had sat bolt upright in the cabin and refused to look about her, or even to think. Obviously Frances had had no such inhibitions.

Lydia was approaching the cemetery corner now, and for some unaccountable reason the mare slowed her pace and seemed to be waiting for an order. When she stopped completely, Lydia frowned and chirped at Chloe, then noting that the cemetery gate was directly before her, she got down on an impulse and tied the mare to a leaning old iron hitching post.

Not in thirty years had she entered the walled, sandy enclosure where hackberry leaves scattered their limp yellow coins on the paths and the ancient marbles sagged in the comfortable postures of great age, clothed in gray-green lichens till most of the inscriptions were lost. There was deep quiet in the shadowed aisles under the trees, and Lydia felt abashed, as though she had intruded upon a guarded home where the inhabitants slept in silent aloofness. She walked on tiptoe between rows of flat tombs overgrown with swarming myrtle and periwinkle, past mildewed and eroded statues of angels and lambs, till she came to the Neary plot.

Honeysuckle had run riot there, making a thick green mat through which a few gnarled camelia bushes struggled to survive; and a single magnolia tree lifted, thrusting to a great height to reach the sun and air but discarding its dry, curved leaves like open palms, a rattling litter over the tombs of the proud and almost forgotten Nearys. Lydia stood looking down at the stone that covered what had been salvaged of her father's shattered body. The scarlet seeds from the magnolia tree made a little jeweled pattern over the bitter lines that her mother had had chiseled on that tomb. Lydia bent and brushed them away, licking her lips and swallowing in a kind of satiety of hate, straightening her shoulders, feeling justified. If she had had any doubts as to the ethics of her stand, they were removed as she studied her mother's last stab at the despised Cavitts. *Slain,* the carving read—and to be slain was to be murdered, just as definitely as though Bascom Cavitt had unsheathed a knife or fired a pistol at Captain Neary's heart!

Lydia walked very erectly as she marched out of the cemetery. She was right, and the proof of her rightness lay there under the honeysuckle. But she had to do something, make some action to prove to herself that she was adequate, that her thinking was clear and proper, that she was a person and not merely the mother of two rebellious daughters. She drove Chloe down to the square, and the sign on the roof of the Matson factory met her gaze.

"I'll sell that tobacco!" she said aloud. "I'll sell it at a profit and show Uncle Horace and Frances and Taffy that I can manage my own business!"

She said good afternoon briefly to Bart, as she tied the mare to his hitchrack, then picked her way down the trodden path along the river to Croff Matson's brick building. A sweetish, strong odor rushed out at her before she reached the door, and she put her handkerchief to her nose and kept it there to indicate that she was a lady and that to a lady the smell of this sort of masculine corruption could not be anything but distasteful.

The door stood open and the dark interior beyond it seemed curiously still. Lydia had no idea what she had expected, but certainly not the sight of Crofford Matson sitting on a packing case, slumped forward with his folded arms resting on his knees. Beyond him loomed a silent machine and rows of high tables, and the floor was deep in an odorous litter.

Lydia took a step inside the dusky room, stopped hesitantly. Croff Matson lifted his head and stared at her, frowning.

"You—are you busy, Mr. Matson?" she asked.

Slowly he lumbered to his feet. His face, swollen a little and strange, was flushed with a look of such anger that Lydia drew back and rested her gloved hand on the doorframe. His graying, sandy hair bristled, his blackened fists were clenched at his sides.

"Busy?" The word was a bellow rather than an echo. "Busy? No, I ain't busy! Look at them there!" He gestured with a huge, dark hand at the piled cases. "Look at 'em!"

Lydia followed the gesturing hand with bewildered eyes. Every case was stenciled with the same words that were blazoned on the roof for all the river traffic to see. *Matson's Golden Twist.* She nodded dazedly, murmured something polite, then cleared her throat sharply.

"I am Mrs. Keeling," she announced. "I have a thousand pounds of prime tobacco, aged in wood, stored in an old mill on my property. I should like to sell it to you, Mr. Matson, if you are in the market for tobacco."

His eyes seemed to bulge above the purpling of his cheeks, his throat swelled for a roar, then subsided in a sort of convulsion. He reached a hand to her.

"Come here!" he ordered in a strangled sort of voice.

Because there was something a little terrifying in his eyes, something that had the blackness of despair in it, Lydia drew back, fending against him with flapping hands.

"Come here," he repeated, "want to show you something.

I ain't going to hurt you. Just want to show you. Hold up your skirt—dusty in here."

Numbly, because there was a kind of anguished entreaty in his eyes, Lydia followed him. No one else was in the shop. The reek of heavy sweetness was everywhere. Lydia touched a table, found it sticky and withdrew her hand quickly. At the back of the shop Croff Matson flung open a wooden door.

"Look yonder!" he ordered.

Lydia looked, seeing nothing but rows of great tuns piled one upon another.

"Know what's in them hogsheads?" he demanded. "Tobacco! Best bright-leaf tobacco can be bought anywheres! Nineteen tons of it. Most two thousand dollars' worth of prime tobacco!"

"Then you don't need to purchase any more tobacco?" Lydia faltered.

"Need it? I don't need this here! I don't need nothing but a rope around my neck!" He slammed the wooden door and snubbed a hook over its iron catch. His voice changed to a kind of sick croak. "Look at them boxes." He jerked a thumb upward and then down to take in a stack of nailed and labeled cases piled against the wall. "Matson's Golden Twist," he said. "Been makin' it since 1889—twelve years! Couldn't hardly keep it long enough for the plugs to season out good. Sold it all over five states. Made money enough to send my boy and girl to college. Money enough to keep the old lady and me comfortable all our lives—I thought. No more washtubs for her, I thought. Now—" He sank down again on the box and his head went down into his horny palms.

Lydia waited. "Is there trouble?" she asked in a faint voice when the silence had stretched past enduring. She had never seen a grown man cry before. It was pretty awful, she thought, standing there trembling.

Croff Matson jerked his breath in roughly, blew his nose with a fierce trumpeting.

"Them boxes yonder—they come back this morning," he said. "Fox Cavitt sure hated unloadin' 'em on me, he sure hated doin' that. Refused! Jobbers won't touch Golden Twist no more. Scared to. Trust hammered the price down till the retailers don't want it either. Trust has got 'em scared. Even if I could sell to retailers, they'd be scared to buy my plugs."

"But that should be against the law!" Lydia essayed a feeble breath of comfort.

"It is against the law," declared Matson, abruptly becoming aware that he was sitting in the presence of a lady, and stumbling to his feet. "Sherman law, passed eleven years ago. Antitrust law. Aimed against any monopoly that tries to control trade and prices and ruin competition."

"Then you could have them arrested," chirped Lydia cheerfully.

He laughed hoarsely. "Me, Mis' Keeling? A little feller like me, no money back of me, nothin' back of me but twelve years of hard, slavin' work? They's a hundred little fellers like me in this state and Virginia, and all of us put together ain't strong enough to lick the trust. I've been watchin' 'em—goin' down, one after another, sellin' out to the trust, turning their plants into shops to make strawberry boxes or screen doors or such stuff. Change your brand, my boy Wylie says. What good would that do? Take a lot of farmers and workingmen around—they're used to Golden Twist. Along comes a brand—just as good, says the man sells it, and 'Look, you get a premium along with this. Save coupons and get a cake of soap!' Premiums eat up all your profit. Does McKinley care what happens to a little feller like me? You make a guess about that. Does the government give a dang about me? No. They got men workin' tryin' to bust up Standard Oil, but if the tobacco trust ruins a whole small industry in the South—well, the South never votes Republican anyhow. What the hell? Excuse me, Mis' Keeling! I get kind of worked up about this business."

"I'm sure you are justified," stated Lydia primly. "And of course you don't want to buy my tobacco."

"If I can't figure a way out of this mess I'll have tobacco to sell myself," said Matson sadly. "My boys argue for me to make cigarettes, but I'd be up against the same thing again— Bonsack machines and mass production. Sorry, Mis' Keeling, but I can't help you out."

Lydia murmured a vague sympathy for his misfortunes and said good-by. She walked back down the path, feeling sorry for Croff Matson but nursing, too, a small smug satisfaction in her own security. There would always be a market for brass so long as they made engines and pins and bird cages and such things, and Uncle Horace was undeniably astute, if slightly difficult. She was outside Bart's store where the mare was tied when she saw a small painted sign being nailed on one of the corner posts by a shirt-sleeved young man who balanced himself expertly on a stepladder. The sign, glistening with red and gilt, read PAMLICO TOBACCO COMPANY.

She waited till the young man descended and stood surveying his handiwork. He was tall and dark, with a jaunty mustache, and he bore a faint resemblance to somebody Lydia knew, but she was certain that she had never seen him before. She approached him hesitantly.

"Young man," she questioned, "are you connected with that tobacco company?"

He turned and bowed. There was a quirk to his eyebrow that Lydia deplored as slightly roguish for a person of his age, but his manner was definitely deferential.

"Yes, madam, I am," he said. "In fact, at present I *am* the Pamlico Tobacco Company."

"Then would you be interested in buying a thousand pounds of prime bright-leaf tobacco?" Lydia persisted.

He removed his straw hat and looked meditatively at the sky.

"You have tobacco for sale, madam? I might be interested. Could I see some samples of your pack?"

"I am Mrs. John Keeling," Lydia said with dignity. "This tobacco is packed in an old building on my property up the river, and it's nailed up tight in big barrels. But it's extra-fine tobacco."

"Ah, yes." He rubbed his chin and the eyebrow flickered more violently. "The old Neary property, I presume? That means that the tobacco would have to be barged down or hauled overland, which would be an expense. How much did you say you had?"

"I paid for a thousand pounds," Lydia replied, standing small and stern, her plump hands gracefully gripping her leather purse. "I'll sell it to you for seven cents a pound."

He gave her a deprecating smile. "You haven't read the

market reports lately, Mrs. Keeling? The American Tobacco Company is paying five cents a pound for prime tobacco."

"That tobacco is a long way off," argued Lydia. "Mine is handy. You can't run a tobacco company without tobacco, can you?"

"I have acquired quite a substantial stock of the filthy weed already, Mrs. Keeling, and I understand that Mr. Matson has a stock which he may decide to turn into cash. He has encountered—ah—difficulties."

"Won't you run into the same difficulties? What's to stop the trust from putting you out of business?"

"I shall manufacture an exclusive product, Mrs. Keeling. Expensive, handmade cigarettes designed for exclusive people who will be willing to pay my price. Would you care to see some of my samples?"

Lydia shook her head violently. "I am opposed to cigarettes, sir. My Ladies' Guild in Baltimore had articles in all the papers last winter warning people against the use of those dangerous things. I suppose yours will be wrapped in lung-destroying paper and contain some kind of narcotic drug?"

He laughed indulgently. "On the contrary, dear lady, they will be wrapped in the most wholesome Japanese rice paper imported at great expense, and will contain nothing but the finest Carolina tobacco. Suppose I offer you six cents a pound for your tobacco, you to pay the expense of delivery either by water or overland."

"How much would delivery cost me?" Lydia wanted to know.

"Oh, not more than a couple of dollars, I should say. The tobacco will be weighed on delivery—in your presence of course, if you wish."

Lydia considered swiftly. She was handicapped by not being able to count on her fingers, arithmetic being her weak point, but she knew that she would at least show a small profit. And she would prove to herself and Uncle Horace, not to speak of Frances and Taffy, that she had sense enough to transact business.

"When do you want it delivered?" she asked.

"I'll send young Renwick Matson to arrange the matter with you, Mrs. Keeling. He's working for me now, since his father has temporarily suspended production. I have orders on file for a large quantity of our product, both from Washington and New York. You wouldn't care to buy a small block of stock in a promising concern, would you? I can almost guarantee you a return of ten per cent."

Lydia pursed her lips. "My money is all invested at present," she said cautiously, unaware that the faint glitter of cupidity that made Frances slightly ill was already showing in her small eyes. "But if I have any funds available later, I might discuss the matter with you."

"Thank you, and good afternoon, Mrs. Keeling. May I untie your animal for you?"

He was certainly a most amazing young man, and quite charming, Lydia decided. But why on earth did he blow in the mare's ear and say "Down the road, Chloe?" Lydia had always refused to call the mare Chloe. The name had a faintly immoral, swampy sound in her mind.

She tried not to appear too triumphant when she walked into the house, but the light was still in her eye and a smug complacency about her mouth.

"Such a nice young gentleman," she babbled, oblivious of the startled looks that flashed between her daughters. "A complete stranger, of course, but I know he'll succeed, he has such a gracious manner and he looks so competent. Poor Croff Matson! Of course he has no background whatever, and that accounts for his failure to profit in his business. He should sell out to this man of the Pamlico Tobacco Company, in my opinion. At least I'm making a profit and I intend to conduct my own business affairs from now on. I must have inherited my shrewdness from Grandpa Taft—certainly poor Mama hadn't a vestige of it!"

In the kitchen Taffy clutched Frances, giggling with malicious delight. "Don't tell her—don't dare breathe a word!" she whispered. "She tosses Fox Cavitt out the door and then gets fascinated by Zach. Don't spoil it, whatever you do."

"But she'll find out sooner or later that Zach Cavitt is the Pamlico Tobacco Company," Frances protested.

"Maybe she won't. We'll warn Wylie and Ren not to cheep."

"She'll be furious at us for not telling her."

"We'll put on the most innocent airs and say 'Good gracious, Mama, don't you find out who you're doing business with?' Anyway, it would spoil it all for her now. She's made a few dollars and she thinks she's the world's most astute business-woman. Let her have her little fling, Francie. Afterward she'll be open to reason, I hope."

"I hope so," Frances said heavily, "but I'm not optimistic, Taffy."

"You're spineless!" snapped Taffy. "If I were in love with a man and knew he cared about me, I'd see him if I had to swim the river! Why don't you go visit Bliss Matson on Sunday? I'll contrive to get word to Fox and you could have the whole day together?"

Frances' eyes held a look of desperate unhappiness that was also a trifle grim. "No," she said, "I won't sneak. If I should go, I'd tell Mama I was going to see Fox and who knows but what she'd make some kind of scene at the Matsons' and embarrass us all."

"She'd adore doing that," Taffy agreed. "At least you're old enough to marry without her consent, Francie."

"I don't want it that way, either. I know you think I'm silly, Taffy, to wait for a miracle which probably will never happen, but I just can't bring myself to do this any other way."

"Thank the Lord I have no conscience," gloated Taffy. "You honorable people make such a lot of misery for your-selves—and after it is all over I'll be willing to bet that Mama comes around and probably makes herself believe that she promoted the whole thing! There was an awful row when she married Papa, but her people were reconciled in no time at all. You're silly, France! You're right about that. After all, it's your life."

"Something's bound to happen, Taffy. I keep praying." Frances wandered to the window and looked out across the river. She could not tell Taffy of the new trouble that worried her. Tulia was back.

Watching very early that morning, as she did so often to see Fox set out down the river in the puffing small boat, she had seen Tulia on the landing, seen her studying the little boat, even climbing down into it, then wandering back to the house again. The small boat was still moored at the dock, and Fox had not appeared, but the sailboat was gone.

Tulia was back, and Tulia had no conscience and laughed at honor—Tulia, who wanted Fox and had sworn to have him.

20

The old Captain could not sleep any more.

Sounds of night were lost to him, sounds that he had loved. The breathless hurry of the river when the tide came in, the mockingbirds singing to the summer moon their hysterical ecstasy in nesting time, the high clamor of geese in autumn, the mournful wail of the loon. Now he heard only the beating of his own heart, tired and uncertain, rasping continually against his eardrums like the dry whispering of minutes that were numbered.

On the other side of the bed his wife breathed heavily, but only the rhythmic lift and fall of the sheet over her breast told him that she slept. But footfalls did come to him, a vibration through his old house that had no need for sound, and he had learned to wait for those vibrations and to identify them. He had known when Zach returned, and Tulia's quick steps through the empty hall late at night had roused him to profane muttering. What was she doing in the house again, when she had declared herself gone for good? But for two nights now Fox had not come back.

He was sleeping on the boat, Zach had told him, and the old Captain had been as infuriated by that information as his wife had been worried. What was Fox eating? she fretted. Why didn't he come home for a clean shirt? Something was definitely wrong.

"Didn't you see him? How'd you get here if you didn't ride the ferry?" she demanded of Tulia.

Tulia, who had maintained a frigid attitude ever since her sudden return, stated that she had come in from the port town on a small fishing craft run by two Portuguese and a Negro boy.

"Fine way to travel!" snorted the Captain's wife.

Zach was as unperturbed as ever. He had hired Ren Matson to fetch him out from town, as had Tulia. He was moving back to town immediately, he announced; Tulia could go with him or stay on the river, as she pleased.

"I thought I gave you a hundred dollars, gold, to get you a divorce," the old Captain bellowed at her.

For answer she had laid five yellow bills on his plate, with a shrug of disdain. "There's your money," she said scornfully.

"I gave you good hard gold, not this Yankee paper stuff," he protested. "Whyn't you get a divorce? What'd you come back here for?"

Zach's eyebrows had done pyrotechnics at that, his mocking mouth twisting wryly. "She had no other place to go," he said dryly, so low that his father lifted a peevish complaint.

"What'd he say? Why don't you talk so I can hear you? What's going on here anyway?"

His wife shrilled at him, trying to enlighten him. She called him Mister Cavitt and argued that of course Zach's wife could stay if she had no other place to go and what did Zach want to go off to town for when he had a good bed upstairs and hadn't she killed a chicken just that morning and got dressing made up and potatoes peeled and divorce was a disgrace anyway and she was thankful not to have one in her family even if Zach and Tulia didn't get along too good. Married people just had to get used to each other's ways anyhow and goodness knew that she had had enough to put up with from Mister Cavitt, chewing tobacco and tracking in black mud from the river all over everything! But the Captain was unappeased.

"You fire up that little boat," he ordered Zach on the second morning. "I aim to go down yonder and see what's going on."

Zach flipped his heavy silver watch from his pocket. "Too late," he shouted. "Fox has already taken the *Agnes* out by this time."

"Fire it up anyway," demanded his father. "I got a right to see what you're up to down there. You can go down with me, and I know enough to fetch a twenty-four foot boat upriver."

Tulia refused to accompany them. She went upstairs to the "spare" room, which she had pre-empted, and sat by the window, looking out across the morning shine of the river, looking with bent brows and mouth twisted in cold anger at the old house across the river. She was stiff with fury at her mother's husband, who had sent her packing back to Zach, agreeing to repay Captain Cavitt's money but to do nothing further for Tulia. Her mother, a lightheaded woman who adored her second husband, had supported his decision and Tulia had been helpless to oppose them.

Some way, she knew, she had to goad Zach into paying for the divorce, and agreeing to it, and there was no time to lose. That girl over there, with her mealymouth and prim Miss-Nancy ways—Fox must be saved from her. Tulia ground her teeth, remembering the scene on the train. She had come off rather badly in that encounter, but at least the Keeling girl knew where she stood and what she could expect. As for Fox, Tulia ran her hands lightly downward over the voluptuous curves of her body and twisted her mouth into a small smile.

Men were men and in each of them was a touch of the beast, and she thought she knew how to handle Fox, stiff with honor and all frozen up as he appeared to be. All she needed was time, and opportunity.

She saw the little boat chug out into the river with Zach at the tiller and the old Captain huddled like a gnome in the bow, and she sent a wave of bitter hate leaping after them. Zach with his stupid schemes that were bound to collapse, bringing trouble to other people but never to Zach—oh, never to Zach! Zach always wriggled free, leaving the people who had helped him outraged, defrauded, and helpless. Somewhere he had gotten hold of some money, by chicanery of course. His suit was new and he had that smooth, insolent assurance that money always gave him. She would tell him tonight that he could pay for her divorce and provide her with separate quarters away from his father's house. She would not be indebted to that horrible old man, not even for good will. If only that little boat would blow up out there on the river and drown both of them!

She should have gone back to the minister's house, where she had left her trunk and most of her possessions, but she had feared that Zach might be there and that the good old people in that house would feel that they had to intervene with prayers and counsel and entreaty to patch up the ruin of a marriage. But at least she had her diamond back! Before he had spoken a word to her last night Zach had marched up and laid the ring in her hand, with that superior, maddening smile. She would not condescend to question him, but the ring should never be off her finger again unless dire emergency overtook her. She turned it in her hand and breathed on the stone and gloated over it, warming herself with the feeling of security that it gave her.

Captain Cavitt waited all day, sitting hunched on a box on the wharf, staring out over the Sound, waiting for the familiar plume of smoke to feather against the southern sky. When the *Agnes J.* was tied up at last, the old man trudged over the gangway before Fox could leap ashore, and squared himself on the deck.

"What goes on?" he demanded. "What you hidin' for? You come along home with me. I fetched down the boat. We can tow that sailboat upriver."

Fox led him into the cabin, closed the door against the curious ears of the loiterers on the landing. "Where is she?" he asked.

The Captain gestured with a thumb, waxed profane, and called his daughter-in-law a rough, water-front name.

"What you scared of her for?" he roared. "Ain't you got the guts to keep her claws off of you? Anyhow, she's married to Zach."

"I know," Fox answered. "It will save trouble if I stay away awhile."

"Scared of a hussy like that!" fumed the old man. "Why didn't she stay up yonder where she belonged? Zach don't want her—you don't want her. But your mother's tenderhearted, she wouldn't turn a wet dog away from her door. I'll give Zach his orders to move her out of the house. You come along home."

"Tomorrow maybe," Fox said. He was not afraid of Tulia, but there was no way to penetrate the wall of the old Captain's deafness with the elusive words he could hardly frame clearly in his own mind. They shaped themselves to something so deep and beautiful and delicate that he could not bring himself to expose it to Tulia, to the feverish, eager intimacy she would save for him. He raised his voice carefully, hating this barrier of senility that shut him away from the hungry affection that lay raw and unhappy in the Captain's faded eyes, wishing he could make his father understand the sensitive shrinking that made him wince from carrying the thought of Francie into the murky atmosphere of contemptuous sexuality that was Tulia's. "I love a girl—a nice girl, Captain," he enunciated distinctly. "I want to keep it that way."

Intuitively the old man nodded and his eyes answered. "She makes everything dirty," he remarked, "that woman of Zach's. It's that gal of Lyddy's, I reckon? I took a fancy to her myself." He sighed. "I've done you a lot of wrong, Fox. This old boat! . . ." He laid a hand against the paneling of the cabin and the hand shook, moving gently, caressing the dried-out wood. "I always was a salt-water man," he said after a little. "A man gets old, he sees things clear."

He shuffled out and across the deck, stepping over a taut line, reaching his hand to touch the rasping fiber of the rope, looking up at the sulky mouth of the blackened stack breathing out the tired smoke of banked fires. He went to the door of the wheelhouse and half lifted himself up to the worn place behind the smooth shining of the wheel, then shook his head and moved away. Fox was clearing the deck, locking doors, doing the routine end-of-run tasks. The Captain turned and yelled at him.

"I can take that boat back alone. I ain't so old I can't handle a little old fresh-water boat, but I never had no time for sail."

Fox nodded, and the Captain yelled again. "I'll come back for you tomorrow. You come home then, you hear?"

Fox did not argue, he helped the Captain make the small boat ready, saw to the water and oil, cast off for him. He even refrained from giving any advice. The little engine coughed, yapped rhythmically, and the boat answered her rudder dutifully. The Captain gripped the tiller hard and it was good under his hand, good to make even a stinking little boat like this obey him. He felt suddenly clearheaded again and the pounding ache that had been beating in the back of his head for days and nights eased a little. He did not blame Fox; he dreaded going back into his own house again, with Tulia there narrowing her eyes about like a lurking cat. Zach was staying in town, he had carried in all his gear and said something about putting a cot in Bart's loft, where he was setting up shop. The Captain had missed most of it, but he knew there would be no Cavitt sons upriver tonight.

Distances are deceiving across water, and before the sun set he could make out the old Neary house, bulking on the bluff under the great trees. Impulsively he swung the boat in toward the north bank. Now was as good a time as any—now when there was no one to protest or muster arguments. He owed Fox something. He owed him the right to love a girl and not have his love fouled by old dead hates. The Neary landing thrust out, spidery-thin, making a sprawling thousand-legged shadow on the sundown copper and rose of the river. He steered for it, stopping the hissing little engine, letting the boat drift slowly in.

He had to make three grunting grabs before he had a grip on a pile, standing slimy and barnacled out of the low tide. To heave the heavy mooring line took all his breath and left him holding to the rough edge of the planks, dizzy and sick, but when the pain of the effort passed he dragged himself up slowly, inching his body up to the landing, lying there flat for a minute or two, his forehead pressed to the sandy planking, his cap lying where it had fallen. Then he sat up, smacked back his thin hair and set the cap at a nautical angle. He got to his knees and crawled to a bollard, pulling himself erect by it, hugging it for a little till the giddiness passed again.

Fierce anger at his own weakness burned him. What sin could any man commit, he thought in fury, to earn this punishment of being old? What was the use of hell when there was torment enough in watching a body go to pieces under you while the spirit that dwelt in it was as avidly alive as ever? Could be that this was all the hell there was, this misery of jerking breath and spinning brain, of weakness of wrist and back and bone? Captain Neary had been lucky, he decided, bemused, as he staggered away from the supporting pillar. Neary had missed seeing himself die by inches, anyway.

The path up the bluff loomed high, though the rim was only a matter of ten feet above low water. He took it, a labored step at a time, setting his foot forward and somehow inching his body up to it. The earth was damp from the rains and slid under him, and he had to hang to the willow brush and tough grass that covered the bank; but he made it to the top and dropped down there on a leaning old bench where he remembered John Neary's wife and child sitting every night, long ago, waiting for John to come home in his dinghy off the *Mary Conner*.

His head was hurting again and time seemed to run together, so that the days and years that had moved over this river were a little lost, and he caught himself looking off down the stream waiting for that dinghy to appear, with an old Negro man rowing and John Neary in the stern—yelling jeers, like as not, to his rival across the river. But nothing moved over the current except a lonely tern, wheeling and dipping and uttering little mewing cries. Captain Cavitt wiped his face with his hand and then looked at his palm with a frown, for the hand dripped with icy sweat and something bothered his throat so that he had trouble swallowing.

He'd better get on up to that house while his legs would still hold him. He felt his knife in his pocket and cut himself a stick from a stout bush, whittling and trimming the leaves and branches away, fitting it to his hand. Night birds were already fretting and quarreling in a knotty, wind-twisted tree overhead, and the light was dying on the river. He turned himself about and made out the house, with a small hot wink of light already shining at one window. Slowly he made his way along the path. Never had he set foot on this side of the river before, and he looked about him curiously. An overgrown lawn that had been cut raggedly with a scythe was bordered with bushes badly in need of pruning. Some kind of a flower bed was ringed with a circle of whitewashed stones. Kind of pretty, he approved it. Posies in it, pink and purple and white. A late-flying butterfly hovered above the blooms.

Approaching the door of the house, the Captain surveyed his clothing. He'd snagged the knee of his pants climbing up to the dock, and bits of bark and sand clung to his sleeves. He brushed himself off as best he could, worked with an anxious thumbnail at a spot on his shirt bosom, ran his fingers over his mustache. Not much to look at, he admitted, but then he hadn't come courting. He wanted only to fix things right for Fox. Fox was a good boy. A boy who was good to his old father ought to have things made easier for him, and the way to do it was to put an end to the feud that had lain like a poisonous fog for so long over this stretch of the river. He stumbled a little on the doorsteps, pulled himself up with difficulty, and knocked hard on the door.

It was a long time before he felt the vibrancy of footsteps approaching inside, and then the door opened and the little red-headed girl stood there, holding a lamp in her hand.

"Oh!" she gasped, making a round mouth and backing away a little. Then she recovered herself and drew back the door and said, "Oh, will you come in?"

The Captain did not hear a word of it, but he followed her gesture and stepped into the hall, holding his cap tight in both hands.

"I'm Bascom Cavitt," he announced loudly, his voice cracking against the walls as deaf men's voices do. "I want to see your mother."

"Oh, yes—" Taffy set the lamp down, the chimney jingling in her excited fingers, and motioned him to a chair. "Sit down please. I'll call her."

"Can't hear a word you say," shouted the Captain. "Your mother at home?"

She nodded rapidly, motioned him into a chair, then flew down the hall. In the dining room she grabbed her sister's shoulders.

"It's Captain Cavitt—the old Captain. He wants to see Mama. Whatever will we do?"

"He said he was coming." Frances brightened a little. "I'll call Mama."

"Suppose she says awful things to him—the way she talked to Fox? I'm scared!" Taffy shivered. "He's terribly old, France —and he's kind of dirty and mixed up and pitiful!"

"She shan't say dreadful things to him—that poor old man!" stated Frances firmly. "Anyway," she added, "he's frightfully deaf. He won't hear a word she says."

"But if she looks at him like that—"

"I'll call her. She's upstairs." Frances ran up the flight lightly.

Lydia was in her own room, pinning the breadths of a wool skirt together on a little sewing table set across her knees. She looked up, her tight mouth bristling with pins, her round, silver-framed glasses making her face look pinched and smaller. The lenses caught the lamplight and gave her an owlish appearance as she looked up.

"Mama, Captain Cavitt's downstairs. He wants to see you," Frances said gravely. "Mama—please listen to the poor old fellow. And Mama—it says to forgive your enemy seventy times seven!"

Lydia took the pins out one by one from between her lips and put them into a cushion in orderly fashion. She smoothed her collar and squared her shoulders a little.

"I have nothing to say to Bascom Cavitt," she said in a voice thin-edged as a knife.

"You can't, Mama!" pleaded Frances. "You can't be that way. It's—it's not Christian!"

"Christianity has nothing to do with Bascom Cavitt," snapped her mother. "Bascom Cavitt wouldn't know the meaning of the word. It's another piece of Cavitt effrontery, coming here to my house!"

Frances' face turned white and set. "I'm sorry if I'm disrespectful, Mama," she said coldly, "but this is my house. My house and Taffy's. Captain Cavitt thinks this silly row has gone on long enough, and I agree with him. Brush your hair and come down and hear what he has to say."

"I never—" gasped Lydia, flushing fiery red. "How can you speak to me like that, Frances Keeling—your own mother? That man is no better than a murderer and I have nothing to say to murderers. If this is your house, you can get him out of it the best way you can, but you shan't subject me to the insult of his presence here!"

"All right, Mama," Frances drew herself up tall, "if you can't find forgiveness in your heart and refuse to live in peace with your neighbors I'll—I'll run away, Mama—I will! I'll walk to town and marry Foxworth Cavitt—and I'll live with him in a tent or under a tree—or anywhere but in this house full of hate!" She had grown a little shrill and her hands shook, but she stood her ground.

Lydia got to her feet, pushing the little table aside.

"I won't be intimidated by silly scenes, Frances," she said frigidly. "Go down and talk to the man yourself, if you feel that you must mingle with people of that stripe. As for running away—you can't frighten me with hysterical talk like that."

"I'm not hysterical, Mama. I never was more calmly determined about anything in my life. If the Captain is generous enough to make the first move—"

"He can make the last move, too. He can take himself back across the river! If you had seen your grandfather brought in—mangled and horrible—if you had seen that, Frances, you wouldn't make silly threats and say ugly things to your own mother. I won't stir a step and you're not marrying anyone by the name of Cavitt—not if I can help it." And Lydia sat down again and picked up her scissors. "I've got nothing more to say," she finished, with a click of finality, her round chin set in a granite mold above her rigid bosom.

Frances felt stunned. This was not Mama, not her too emotional, uncertain Mama with her wavering little fits of domination that always before had yielded into tearful, complaining, worried acceptance—but acceptance. This was the granddaughter of Grandpa Taft, the niece of stern Uncle Horace, with all their uncompromising stubbornness suddenly cropping out, bolstered by security, by the Taft money, by the small sense of power that money brought.

"I don't know you any more, Mama," she said soberly. "You were never hard or cruel before—and it is cruel to ignore that poor old man when he humbles himself enough to come to you."

"It wasn't cruel of him to make me fatherless, of course?" Lydia cried acidly. "To drive me from my home and make my life a nightmare of belonging nowhere, having nothing that was my own? Now he'd like to make it all up with a few mumbling words. You can go and listen and be deluded into believing that the Cavitts are decent people, if you're so weak-minded."

"Perhaps it's because I'm strong-minded that I'm going," Frances retorted. "I shan't apologize for your rudeness, Mama. You wouldn't want that, I'm sure."

"Just because you've got a silly, schoolgirl crush on that dark-faced man with the white teeth!" shrilled her mother. "Just because he looks romantic and wicked—he should look wicked! He's a Cavitt."

Frances went out without another word. She went downstairs slowly, wondering what she could say, how she could make the old Captain understand, but when she stood in the hall door she saw quickly that no words were necessary. The old man got to his feet, stumbling a little, fumbling with his cap. He nodded slowly before he spoke and then his voice was low and hoarse and came in little gusts, as though there were little breath behind it.

"She wouldn't talk, would she? No, Lyddy wouldn't talk to me. You can just tell her what I came to say. Tell her I've been sorry every day of my life for thirty years, for what I done to her and Miss 'Melia. You tell her I'd make it up to her if I could—and that all I came here for was to ask for peace."

Taffy was frankly crying. She looked at Frances with brimming eyes that held both fury and grief.

"I think it's beastly!" she cried.

The Captain was moving slowly, gropingly, to the door. He was a big man but now he looked small and shrunken and lost, with his head bent and his feet shuffling on the floor as though he had no strength to lift them. With a hand on the doorknob he turned and smiled, and Frances felt a straining ache surge up into her throat; she tensed to go rushing with words of comfort, knowing it was useless, knowing it would be unheard, that the episode was ended.

"Just tell Lyddy I came in peace," he said again.

Then he seemed to go plunging out through the door into the early dark, and Frances cried abruptly, "Taffy—help me!"

But he was down before they could reach him. His big body seemed to collapse all at once, and he fell forward on his face. Together they tried to lift and turn him, but a single breath bubbled past his lips and then he was still.

"He's dead!" choked Taffy in a terrible voice. "He's dead—and my mother killed him!"

21

Taffy was a virago, Taffy was a fury. When Lydia came running downstairs in answer to Frances' one sharp scream, Taffy turned on her with a white and awful face.

"Don't touch him! Don't you come near him! He's dead! He came in peace because he was sorry and you wouldn't listen! Now he's dead and you shan't touch him—but I hope you're satisfied, Lydia Keeling! I hope your vengeful little soul has got its fill of vengeance!"

"Taffy, don't!" protested Frances, seeing the stark, shaking contortion of her mother's face, the terror in her eyes. "Don't talk like that!"

"She did it. She killed him!" insisted Taffy.

"He was an old man. The effort was too much for him. Nobody killed him. But what shall we do?"

"Get Dobbs," ordered Lydia, beginning to blubber a little, nervously twisting a fold of her skirt in her hands. "He had no business coming here—no business at all!"

But Dobbs would not touch a dead man. He fled, whimpering, terrified, into the mow of the barn and would not be coaxed down.

"We can never lift him alone. Get a sheet, Taffy," Frances ordered. "We'll have to go for help. I'll get the lantern. We'll have to drive Chloe."

"You shan't drive to town in the dark," argued Lydia. "It's not safe. Call across the river and tell them to come and get him."

"There's no boat over there. There's no way for anyone to come," Frances said. "The Captain's boat is down at our landing, but we could never get it started and it's too heavy to row." She would not tell what she knew, that Fox was not at the house across the river, that he had not come home tonight or last night—that Tulia was there.

227

"You can't go off and leave me alone with him," whimpered Lydia, "and you can't go alone either of you—"

"He can't hurt you now, Mama," Frances said firmly. "Go inside and lock the door. The poor old Captain can never hurt you any more."

Taffy was already running toward the barn with the lighted lantern. Jerking with angry sobs, she struggled with the heavy harness, backed the astonished mare out into the shafts, snapped buckles with furious clickings.

"Get in!" she ordered, when Frances came out. "There's a wrench there under the seat. Hold it, and if anybody stops us or tries to grab the bridle, hit him on the head."

"You shouldn't have talked to Mama like that," worried Frances, forgetting her own fiery anger, the bitter things she had said, in a backwash of compassion that included the poor old man lying there under the sheet and Lydia, frightened and aghast.

"I'm a Neary," Taffy replied brutally. "Get down the road, Chloe. Thank goodness it's early. There will be people around in town. We'll get Wylie Matson."

"We'll fetch Fox," stated Frances. "He didn't come home. He must still be on that boat."

"*She's* over there."

Tulia was there and Fox had not come home. Frances got what comfort she could from that.

"We'll need more than one man. He's frightfully heavy."

"I wonder what will happen now—to the old *Agnes,* I mean—to Fox," said Taffy.

"Fox still has his mother to think about," Frances reminded her.

"You're terribly unlucky. They always have mothers to think about," Taffy remarked.

There were still lights burning in windows of the town as they rounded the corner by the cemetery. Taffy gave a quick glance at the minister's house, wondering if Zach was there. They would have to tell Zach too.

"Something's happened—look at the people!" she exclaimed as they drove into the square. "They can't have heard about the Captain yet."

A knot of men were gathered about the entrance of Bart's store. Two or three women stood on the outskirts, bareheaded, some with aprons still on, as though they had run out of their kitchens, drawn by some excitement. Chloe trotted up to the hitchrail and stopped of her own accord and Frances saw Fox then, standing a little apart, his hands in his pockets. Her throat began to hurt again, and she said hoarsely, "You tell him, Taffy."

Fox came over to the buggy quickly, said, "Well, hello! What brings you girls to town? Did you get the news already?"

Taffy gulped, plunged, "It's your father, Fox. He's dead. At our house."

Fox stiffened, paled, his brows drew down. "Dead? At your house?"

"It was a stroke, I think." Frances got her voice back then. "He came over in the boat to talk to Mama, and just as he was leaving he fell—on our porch. We can't lift him, Fox. We came for help."

"I'll go back with you." He pushed back his cap and they saw that his hand shook. "I'll get Zach and Wylie to help me. You say the boat is on your side of the river?"

"It's at our landing. Fox—I'm so sorry—"

He reached and took Frances' hand gently, then shrugged a little, his face set. "He was old, Francie. I should have gone home with him. He begged me to go. If he came to your house, he was doing that for me, too."

"I know." She could not tell him that it had all been no use, that the Captain had sought peace with his last breath and that he had failed.

"I'll get Zach," he said again. "Wait here."

The group in front of the store dissolved, milled about, as he returned to it. One after another they saw men gripping his hand. Wylie Matson and his brother Ren walked over to the buggy.

"We'll go back with you, Frances," Wylie said. "Fox has gone to find Zach. Can we all ride in this buggy?"

"Ren can sit up here—he's thin." Taffy was executive again. "The rest of you can stand up in the back and hold on. What happened over there. Wylie? Why is everybody so excited?"

"The president was shot today. In Buffalo."

"President McKinley? Is he dead?"

"He's still alive. He was visiting that fair they have up there and some little anarchist shot him when he went to shake his hand."

"Will he die, do they think?"

"They don't know yet. He was shot in the stomach, Bart heard. It looks bad," Wylie said.

"If he dies, Theodore Roosevelt will be president," Renwick remarked, "and Roosevelt hates the trusts. Maybe the little tobacco men like Pa will get justice then."

"That's mean, Rennie, to hope the poor president dies," Taffy remarked.

"Well, if he's going to die anyway, it's lucky for us that we've got Roosevelt," insisted Ren. "Pa's all busted up and mighty near run crazy. He got to drinking today and that worries Ma—he hasn't taken a drink in years."

"So much trouble everywhere," Frances sighed. "Fox has found Zach. They're coming."

Zach Cavitt came up to the buggy. "Bart's hitching up," he said, "I'll ride out with him. Jerry Sims is telephoning Bath for the undertaker. You go ahead with the girls, Fox. We'll be there almost as soon as you are."

"Does my mother know?" Fox asked, as Taffy turned the buggy with a scream of the tire on the cramp iron. He was kneeling in the back, his arms along the back of the seat close to Frances' shoulder.

"No, she doesn't know. We couldn't call across the river and we were afraid to try and move the boat, it's so heavy."

"We need a bridge," Wylie remarked. "This water-locked country can never develop till we have a bridge."

Fox moved his hand and it brushed Frances' neck and made a warm glow move over her body. "I'm sorry it had to happen to you, Francie," he said gently. "The poor old fellow thought that if he talked to your mother it might help."

"That's what hurts, Fox," she said. "He was so gentle—and so humble. Drive faster, Taffy. Mama's there all alone. Dobbs is no protection—he's so terrified of death."

"She won't go any faster," complained Taffy. "She's still in love with Zach Cavitt." She was grateful for the darkness that hid the hot flush she knew was creeping over her own face. Wylie was there behind her, Wylie had heard her pitiful confession. She felt him stir a little, and then with a quick fatherly gesture he patted her head. Was Wylie thinking that she was as silly as Chloe, or was he offering comfort that she would be cured because she had more brains than a mare?

Lydia had hidden herself upstairs, with her door locked, when they arrived at the house. She refused to come out, and Frances could hear her sniffling through the panels; her voice was shrill with outrage and self-pity.

"Just get them all away from here as fast as you can," she ordered. "I can't see anybody. You and Taffy stay in the house and lock the doors."

"I'm sorry to disobey you, Mama," Frances answered, "but I'm going to help if I can."

"Don't you let them carry off my sheet," Lydia called after her as she hurried away.

Fox was bending over his father when Frances went back to the porch. He was smoothing the old man's hair, pressing the dead, dry eyelids down, talking to the silent figure in a low tone that stirred the girl with a poignant pain.

"You did what you could, Captain," he was saying. "I'll keep the old boat running. I'll keep her shipshape for you as long as she holds together."

Zach took command briskly. He and Bart improvised a stretcher from two poles and a tarpaulin from the boat, and slowly the solemn procession moved down the river bluff. Ren Matson went ahead with the lantern. Frances and Taffy followed to the landing and stood gripping each other's hands while Captain Cavitt was lowered to the deck of the boat. Taffy sobbed jerkily, and burst into a flood of tears when Fox came back and without a word took Frances in his arms and kissed her gently on the brow. Wylie Matson stood by and Taffy saw Wylie's face set and stiffen a little, but all he said was, "I'll go with you, Fox. Bart has to drive his rig back to town."

Taffy would not move from the landing till the barking little boat had crossed the river and they saw the door of the Cavitt house flung open and heard, across the stream, the thin, anguished keening of a woman. Frances tugged at her hand.

"We must go back, Taffy. Just don't talk, please."

"No—wait. The boat's going out again—"

"They're going down to fetch the undertaker, probably. They are heading downstream. Come along, Taffy."

Taffy moved woodenly. She was a little sick. She had thought herself cured, and she wasn't. He hadn't looked at her, he had not spoken. And Tulia was over there.

"I hate her! I hate her!" Taffy flared suddenly, grinding her teeth.

"Taffy, please," pleaded Frances, "she is your mother."

"I'm not talking about Mama," screamed Taffy. "Oh, go away—go away and leave me alone! I don't care! I don't care what you think about me. Can you help how *you* feel? He kissed you! So you're smug and I'm a hussy—but I don't care! I could kill her—I could kill her with my bare hands!"

Impulsively Frances put her arms around her little sister. "You poor little kid," she murmured. "Go ahead and cry, Taffy. I know how it hurts."

"How can you know? You never loved somebody who looked through you—laughed behind your back, maybe—oh, I know! I'm young. I'll get over it. I've disgraced you all by falling in love with a married man. I know he's a rascal. Even if Tulia does divorce him, he doesn't want me. He'll want somebody with loads of money—I'm just an amusing episode—I flatter his ego. He jerks that eyebrow and smiles that ironic, amused smile and I could beat his face to pulp, but it doesn't change the way I feel."

"I know." Frances held to her arm as they walked back to the house through the soft darkness. Her own body was glowing with the wild scudding of her blood, her heart beat to the time of a kind of song. "I'm not blaming you, Taffy. Don't let it spoil your life. Someone will come along, after awhile, and then you'll laugh at this and wonder how you could have been so naïve."

"Someone thrilling and handsome like Ren Matson, no doubt," remarked Taffy with bitterness.

A stiff and hostile politeness endured between Lydia Keeling and her daughters for days. Frances was dreamy, she was continually stealing away to the window to watch the house across the river. She saw the small boat go down every morning and return again at dusk. Even though the old mariner lay dead under his mossy roof, the *Agnes J.* must make her round of the ferry landings. She saw Fox walk wearily up the path from the landing in the twilight, and once she saw Tulia come down to meet him, but so calm was Frances, so sure of her love, that she felt no dismay; instead she was a little sorry for Tulia.

Lydia would not have the mare harnessed nor allow Taffy to go to town on Saturday, and on Sunday morning when the dark coffin was carried down to the water by six black-clad men and loaded aboard a river tug for the journey to the church and the cemetery, she looked once briefly and then snatched the curtains down over the windows and locked the front door.

"You girls hate me now," she said acidly, "but there'll come a time when you'll see how right I am about the Cavitts!"

"No, we don't hate you," Taffy answered, "we're just sorry for you, Mama. Maybe people judged the Cavitts before, but now they are judging you. To be unforgiving is to be mighty lonely."

Ren Matson came up the river late in the afternoon bringing his sister Bliss with him. Taffy and Bliss wandered about the yard, with Ren scuffling unhappily after them, his pimply chin prisoned by a high, stiff collar. Ostentatiously he pulled from his pocket a small, gilt-paper-covered box, extracted a cigarette from it, and lit it.

"You'd better not let Pa see you smoking those things," Bliss warned.

"Pa will be making them pretty soon—or else he'll be out of business," Ren gloomily prophesied.

From Bliss, Taffy got all the details of the Cavitt funeral.

"You should have seen that Tulia! She had her hair in the biggest pompadour you ever saw—she must have had it combed over a pillow or something—with a huge black bow at her neck behind and another one under her chin. She had on a black silk dress and it was cut tight as anything over her—hips, you know—and up in front too. And all the while they were burying the poor old Captain she held on to Fox Cavitt's arm like grim death and gave him such sickening, pitying looks! It was disgusting."

"But Zach was there, wasn't he?" Taffy braced herself to ask.

"Oh, yes, he was there. He took care of his mother. But every now and then he'd look at his wife and you know how his lips kind of twist up at the corner, as though he was making fun of something—well, he'd look like that at Tulia and she'd glare at him as though she wanted to cut his throat. I think Zack Cavitt is the handsomest," Bliss babbled on. "I hope he'll go into business with Pa. Wylie's trying to work it out so Pa won't lose everything he's worked for all his life."

"Is Tulia going to get her divorce?" Taffy ventured to inquire.

"Oh, I wouldn't know. You can't get a thing out of Wylie. He says it's a professional secret and we've got no business asking, but some of these days when he's gone to court I'm going to sneak up to his office and see if he's drawn up divorce papers. I know where he hides the key."

Yes, thought Taffy with bitterness, and you know, too, that Zach Cavitt will be up there, in that back loft watching cigarettes being rolled and packed. She saw through Bliss completely.

"You'd marry Zach Cavitt in a minute if he was free, wouldn't you?" Taffy snapped.

Bliss fluttered all her pink flounces. "Oh, my goodness, he'd never look at poor little me! He's much too clever. But if he were in business with Pa, it would be a fine arrangement, wouldn't it? We'd keep all the money in the family. And Zach's going to be rich, I just know it. Why, he showed me—"

Taffy could not bear any more. "Mama's calling me!" She broke away.

"We'd better be going anyway." Bliss followed her, panting slightly because her stays were tight since she had gotten so dismayingly plump. "Mama has a fit if I'm out on the river at night."

It was in mid-September that the Pamlico Tobacco Company moved into the brick factory that for so long had been sacred to Matson's Golden Twist. The big sign came down, and poor Mrs. Matson hid her head in her pillow and wept.

So much had happened meantime. William McKinley, president of the United States, had died. Theodore Roosevelt, who hated all trusts, was now president. But this ray of hope for the little men who made their money in tobacco had come too late for Crofford Matson.

They had found him one rainy morning, in the dim, empty dusk of his factory. He had hanged himself to a rafter and had been dead for a long time.

22

Lydia Keeling had never before admitted herself to be in a position completely on the defensive. Always in crises she had been the aggrieved one, the person to be protected, the helpless and brave little woman other people were sorry for. Now she existed in an atmosphere of chilly remoteness made more infuriating because there was really nothing tangible she could complain about.

Bascom Cavitt had done her another grievous wrong by dying dramatically and thereby ennobling himself in the public mind. Everyone in the community knew, very promptly, that he had made his last sad attempt on a mission of peace, and that he had been repulsed. That she was being condemned as a heartless and unchristian character Lydia could not put out of her mind, had Taffy given her any opportunity to forget it. So, turned inward upon herself and tormented by emotions she could not properly arrange or control, Lydia transferred her old hatred to Bascom's son Foxworth and immediately suffered a fresh fury because the effort was abortive. Fox's attitude of calm patience was magnified into insult in her mind. If he resented her, there was no sign of it, and to be ignored can produce the most unbearable strain of all.

She kept a fiercely maternal eye on Frances, almost eagerly hoping for a definite clash, for the cleansing storm of a quarrel that would give her the chance to reassert her authority and establish her power again in her own mind, but Frances displayed a new and baffling strength and calm that made her somehow untouchable.

"If I mean to see Fox, Mama, I shall tell you," she said, "but I shall see him if I like."

Lydia tried everything. She lashed out in petty tantrums, she made sporadic thrusts and slightly hysterical attempts at self-justification, but every move broke off short against the barrier her daughters had built against her. Taffy was as aloof and hostile as a blade, but Taffy's sarcastic forays were more tolerable than the forgiving air that Frances displayed. To be forgiven was to be despised a little, to Lydia's thinking, and the constraint to do something drastic, defiant and entirely independent grew within her narrow spirit till it was a tearing unrest.

Bascom Cavitt was in his grave, and the Cavitt house across the river presented a withdrawn and secret face. It seemed to Lydia to loom larger with every dawn, and when Fox Cavitt went down the river in his little boat, without so much as a glance across the stream at the lair of his enemy, Lydia had to struggle against a desire to rush down to the bluff and scream maledictions at him.

Then Crofford Matson died, and Lydia had the small comfort of a triumphant superiority.

"I told you he was no good! He was always a weak character to begin with," she fumed. "Just because he made a little money and built a brick house—just because he had the effrontery to send his children to college—now, look at them! Likely that poor ignorant creature doesn't know where her next meal's coming from! A trashy thing to do—leaving a woman like that!"

"We're going to the funeral, Mama," Frances announced. "Do you want to come along?"

She went along, smugly complacent in her black silk and white gloves. She was a woman of property. She was a Neary and the Nearys had never been upstarts. She sat stiffly upright in the church, but declined to get out of the buggy at the cemetery. The sight of Foxworth Cavitt helping to carry Croff Matson's casket upset her more than a little. He was handsome, the swaggering scalawag, in his black clothes and stiff white collar that set off the dark quietness of his face and eyes.

"Portuguese! Foreigners! Pirates!" sniffed Lydia to herself, as she sat alone outside the wall. The tall young man to whom she had sold her tobacco was there, a pallbearer too. She had an impulse to ask his name, then disdained to yield to curiosity. At least, she decided, he had the manners of a gentleman, and seeing him again gave her inner revolt a direction and purpose it had lacked. She knew now what she would do. She would show her girls, and Uncle Horace too, that she was no weak and silly creature who needed scolding, mothering and condescension!

"I'm going into town on business," she announced on the Monday morning following the funeral.

As usual, there was no comment or objection. Nobody suggested cheerfully, "Mama, you missed one hook on your placket." Lydia felt like screaming something vicious as she marched out to the buggy, her small snub nose shining, her hat skewered to a tight knob of hair on top of her head. She took the reins from Dobbs with what she felt to be an imperious gesture, but the awareness that it was wasted made her jerk at Chloe's head till that obtuse animal twitched her ears and refused to move at faster than a slow walk, answering an irritated flick of the whip only with a disgusted shudder of her fat rump.

A rain had cooled the air but made the marshes steam, and in the wooded stretches gnats whirled in giddy clouds so that the mare snorted and offered the ultimate insult by clamping her tail tight over the reins and keeping it taut there, till finally Lydia was forced to climb out and free the straps before she drove into town.

As she passed the Matson house she noted that all the shades were drawn and wondered what would become of that house now. Little likelihood that Croff had left anything at all. Now his sons would have to support their mother, probably, and Lydia nursed a small inward glow that at least she would never be beholden to anybody.

Let Frances run off and marry that white-toothed rascal, as she had threatened to do! As for Taffy, Lydia wished she had listened to Frances earlier. Taffy should have been sent off to some school but now it was mid-September and too late, even if the money could have been nagged out of Uncle Horace. But she would make plans to send Taffy somewhere at midterm, maybe to that same girls' school at Salem where Croff Matson had sent his daughter. If Croff, whose fortunes had so easily been broken, could afford to educate his children, so could she, Lydia decided, smacking her lips and setting them into a stern line again.

She tied the mare at the square, flirted horse hairs off her skirt, and looked up at the post where the Pamlico Tobacco sign had been nailed, only a little while ago. Now it was gone and she was baffled momentarily, till she discovered the sign nailed to a tree halfway down the sandy river path. She walked that way, and as she neared the Matson factory she saw young Rennie on the roof. He was smearing gray paint over the old Golden Twist sign on the shingles. He scrambled down as she approached, and stood waiting, wiping his palms on his dirty overalls.

"Hello, Mrs. Keeling. You looking for somebody?"

"What are you doing up there?" she inquired.

"Going to paint a new sign. Pamlico Tobacco Company's moving into Pa's old shop. Ma finally agreed to lease the place this morning. She cried and held out awhile, but Wylie persuaded her it was the best thing she could do right now. I'm going to work here. Maybe like it better."

"I wanted to see that young man—the tall one, who runs the Pamlico Company," stated Lydia. "Is he anywhere around?"

Renwick examined a painted thumbnail. "No'm, he ain't right now. He went down on the ferry this morning—got to see about a charter, or something, he said. Wylie went with him. There's a lot of papers to fix up. He's giving Ma a big block of stock. Pa never left no will and Wylie's got to be my guardian till I'm twenty-one. Was you wanting to sell more tobacco, Mrs. Keeling? We ain't buying any right now. Pa laid in a big stock before they busted him and it ought to run this business a right smart time. Sure hate painting out that old sign. Ma says it will kill her to look at this place now, but I reckon she'll get over it. Pa hadn't ought to have give up so easy though, I figure."

"You think this concern will be a success, do you?" Lydia inquired.

Renwick studied his stained hands thoughtfully. "Well, that I can't say, Mrs. Keeling. Only thing I can say is, Pamlico is going to have mighty little competition. There won't be any pictures of Lillian Russell nor Corbett and Fitzsimmons in the packs, but they figure to sell to people that want to pay more for good stuff. Anyway, I hope it pays on Ma's account."

"I had decided," Lydia said, a bit loftily, "that I might buy a small block of stock in the Pamlico Tobacco Company."

"Huh?" The boy looked startled. "You mean you want to invest some money in it? Hadn't you better wait to see how things work out, Mrs. Keeling? That's what Wylie said he was going to do. He said if it worked out that the business did make a profit, he might put some money into it."

This was more opposition, more caution, more unsolicited advice, of which Lydia had had too much already. She bridled a little and set her chin. "Young man," she said reprovingly, "I am a woman accustomed to handling property. I know how to manage my affairs."

"Yeah," said Rennie slowly, "I reckon you do, Mrs. Keeling. How much money do you want to put in?"

Lydia felt her breath tingle in her nostrils. She was a trifle intoxicated by her own recklessness. Mentally she thumbed her nose at Uncle Horace and all his stodgy warnings and objurgations. Wasn't it her own money, anyway? She was sick of being answerable, lectured and repressed.

"I had thought of investing a thousand dollars," she said. "I can pay for the stock at the rate of a hundred dollars a month, but it must bring me at least ten per cent interest. That's what that young man assured me that it should pay."

"Yeah," muttered Rennie again, "Yes'm, Z—, he knows what it ought to pay all right, I reckon. That would be ten dollars a year on every share, wouldn't it?"

"Of course I should demand my dividends regularly," stated Lydia primly, "and also I would want the transaction held in complete confidence. I do not discuss my business with others."

"Yes'm." Rennie's Adam's apple did a few contortions. "I wish Ma was reasonable like you, Mrs. Keeling. She hasn't got any nerve at all. She thinks we're fixing to throw away all Pa made and saved, just putting in this building and the machinery and stuff. She'd rather see a stinky old canning factory or something in here, I guess."

"When that young man comes back, I should like an appointment to talk to him—here," Lydia said. "Naturally you are not authorized to carry on such a transaction."

"No'm, I ain't. I know there's some stock papers printed up in that old table drawer over yonder where Pa kept his order books, but I haven't never looked at 'em much, just know they're green, that's all." He scratched one ankle with the toe of a paint-smeared shoe. "I'll tell—I'll tell the boss you came in, Mrs. Keeling."

"Thank you. And this is to go no further, Rennie, remember that. If you are to be in business you must learn to respect confidences."

"Yes'm, I learnt that already. I reckon Taffy wouldn't like it, you buying into the firm when she didn't get in."

"Taffy? What has she got to do with this firm?"

"Not a thing, Mrs. Keeling. She just wanted in, was all—but Wylie told her she wasn't of age—" Rennie floundered, noting that he had said far too much already.

"She is certainly not of age!" sniffed her mother. "She has no knowledge of business whatever, naturally."

"Yes'm," agreed Rennie gratefully, discerning that the interview was at an end. "Golly gee!" he muttered to himself as he climbed back to the roof a few minutes later. "I'd ought to have told her! She finds out this business is run by a Cavitt, she'll have my hide, I bet." But he had given Taffy a promise, for no good reason that he could discover, and for Taffy's temper he had profound respect. Anyway, that old fight was none of his troubles. He'd have melancholy woes enough when Ma found out the old sign was gone from the roof and that he had been the one to erase it.

He was a little frightened when Lydia appeared again two days later. He had told Zach Cavitt about her visit and Zach had grinned and given him a poke in the ribs.

"Good going, kid," he approved. "I'll have to make you a front man yet." He had put some papers into a manila envelope. "When she comes back, give her these—the green ones. And she signs this white paper, here on this lower line. Tell her how lucky she is to get in on the ground floor, and that the stock is bound to go up when we begin to deliver. Just keep me out of it, that's all, Rennie. I'll stay out of sight if I'm around."

"But she wants specially to talk to you," Rennie argued.

"After she signs, Rennie! We won't risk a nice juicy thousand-dollar investment till it's sealed and delivered." Zach quirked the eyebrow. "Tomorrow," he stated, "we put the hands back to work. The wheels of progress will hum again. Sorry we can't make 'em with the straw tips just yet, but the last batch I tried tasted of glue. Got to devise some kind of machine to attach the paper and let it dry before the tobacco goes in. You study that in your spare moments, son."

Zach was teaching a Negro girl named Hester to weigh tobacco accurately on the little brass scale he had brought back from the county seat, when Lydia came walking down the path. He vanished swiftly into the storage room, closing the door, with a gesture to Rennie ordering him to take over. Rennie gulped and dusted off his hands and tried to look businesslike, though a perturbed cowlick was standing erect on the crown of his yellow head when Lydia appeared at the door.

"Has that young man come back yet?" she asked, ignoring the stares of the four Negro women who worked at the long table.

"Yes'm—I mean no'm," stammered Rennie. "He was here but he had to leave a little while back, but he left the papers for you, Mrs. Keeling. Here—" Rennie jerked them awkwardly out of the drawer, spilling some green sheets into the litter of tobacco stems on the floor and retrieving them anxiously. "There's ten of these here—and you sign this white one on this line—you wait a minute till I shake up this ink."

"What do I sign—and why should I sign anything?" Lydia demanded.

"You agreed to pay by the month, didn't you? Well, that's a kind of paper that says you agree to pay."

"I have a hundred dollars to pay now."

"That's fine, Mrs. Keeling, that's just fine. And you get ten of these certificates and then sign this paper—no'm, not there—down at the bottom." He almost moved her hand, pushing the pen into it, pointing out the dotted line with a smudgy finger.

Lydia held the pen in air, frowning a little. "I do prefer to deal with someone with authority," she protested. "You're sure this is all correct?"

"Oh, yes'm. It's just like Mr. Za—like the boss fixed it. He told me to give you the certificates and a receipt for the money you paid. You sign this paper and then I'll make out a receipt, Mrs. Keeling. You still want to pay in a hundred dollars?"

"I suppose I might as well." She scrawled her name quickly on the white slip, wandering from the line a little because she had forgotten to fetch her glasses and couldn't read a word without them. She took the receipt Rennie penned laboriously on a small printed form, folded it carefully and put it in the envelope with the slick green folded certificates, and stuffed them into her deep, old leather purse, feeling pleasantly furtive and triumphant; and reckless because she had done one thing in her life on impulse, without asking anyone's advice, accepting counsel, or even consulting anybody. "Remember," she called back, as she headed for the door, "remember to re- mind the man at the head of this concern that I shall expect my ten per cent promptly."

"Yes'm," Rennie breathed gratefully as she departed. He folded the little wad of bills between his fingers and waited for the storeroom door to open, as it did almost immediately. "She left a hundred," he told Zach Cavitt. "Four twenties and four fives. And she signed the paper."

"Good boy," applauded Zach. "But you almost let my name slip there one time, Ren. I heard you. You'd have knocked the whole business into a cocked hat."

"Yassuh, sho' would!" cackled Hester. "Does she find out Mist' Zach running this place, she gwine raise a ruction some of these days."

"She won't say a word, Hester," Zach stated with cool con- fidence, "not a word. She'll never let it be known, even inside her own house, that she had dealings with a Cavitt." He peeled off two five-dollar bills from the roll Lydia had left. "Put these away somewhere, Rennie," he ordered. "The next time she comes in to make a payment, hand her this money. Tell her it's her first dividend. After that she'll rob the old family sock to pay for the rest of the stock."

"Yessir." Rennie grinned, a trifle wryly. "But that ain't going to be exactly legal, is it? I mean—paying her back with her own money?"

"It's her money that will earn a part of the profits we make later, isn't it? You and I are running this outfit, Renwick. If we say a thing is legal, it's legal." Zach smiled his one-sided smile.

"I reckon it is, Mister Zach," Rennie agreed. But an odd feeling of unease would not leave him. He wished he could talk to Wylie about it, but he had determined to be loyal to Zach and he meant to work hard, because this business had to make money or what would become of Ma?

Zach Cavitt tucked the remaining ninety dollars inside his wallet and buttoned a pocket flap over it.

Tonight he would hand that money to Tulia, tell her to hire her lawyer and go ahead with her confounded divorce. After that let Fox take care of himself.

23

I'm going down to the river, Mama," Frances said calmly that night, when the dishtowels were hung neatly on the line behind the kitchen stove. "Don't be disturbed. Fox won't set a foot on Neary soil."

Lydia glared. "Well, I could tell you not to make a fool of yourself, but it wouldn't do any good!" she snapped.

"No, it wouldn't do any good. I'm not going to make a fool of myself. I'm merely going to spend a few minutes with a man who loves me."

"So he says! If you're weak-minded enough to believe a Cavitt!"

The autumn moon was low and heavy and languid, leaning against a cloud as though sated, with a round stomach full of liquid silver. Late-nesting mockingbirds sang themselves silly in the trees and there was a heady perfume on the air from the insignificant bloom of the old soap bushes around the leaning smokehouse. The dew was heavy and Frances held her long skirt up and kept to the middle of the path. At the foot of the bluff the river lay washed in moonlight, the slow current a rhythmic stream of gilt, as though a fairy paint pot had been spilled into the water and was being gaily washed to sea.

Frances' heart felt light and strange, as though moth wings fluttered in her breast. Her throat kept filling so that she had to swallow desperately, but she walked out to the end of the landing dock and sat down on the rounded top of a pile, holding her hands tightly together in her lap.

What if he did not come tonight? Watching from the screening trees she had seen the slim-masted sailboat move slowly up and down the river night after night, but it had taken her a long time to get her courage up to the point where she could boldly oppose her mother. Only Taffy's taunt had finally stirred her into action.

"You're a worm!" her sister had said. "If a man cared about me I'd swim that river to see him. But nobody cares whether I'm alive or dead!"

"Rennie Matson does," Frances reminded her teasingly. "Rennie fairly oozes adoration every time he comes on the place."

"The poor little insect! He reminds me of a chicken just beginning to feather out, all legs and neck and squawk. Anyway, he has one of those mothers. I saw how she grabbed at him there in the cemetery. Wylie will slide out and leave Ren holding the bag, you'll see! He'll be the one to listen to his mamma's wails for the next thirty years. Bliss will marry the first man that asks her—or the first man she can corner whether he asks her or not."

Bliss was bitterness in Taffy's mind. Bliss was in town, where she could see Zach Cavitt every day. She had not gone back to school after the funeral. She was staying at home to comfort her Ma, she had stated rather disconsolately, but Taffy had put her own interpretation on that.

Across the river a pale light burned in the second story of the Cavitt house and Frances could see a figure moving back and forth across the light, obviously busy about something. She could make out the sailboat, pale and slim, a wraith of a shape beside the Cavitt dock. Then the front door opened, showing a yellow rectangle of light, and closed again. She stirred a little, and her heart began to race as she caught the soft thud of an oar against a hollow gunwale. She was glad she had worn her white dress. It was a bit too thin for the late September night, but in the brilliance of the moonlight it could be plainly seen.

The long boat approached as silently as something seen in a dream. It slid quietly up to the landing, and Frances said, "Fox?" and then, "Don't come ashore. Hold the boat steady and I'll come down."

He laughed but there was no bitterness in the laugh, only an amused acceptance of the situation. "Forbidden ground," he said as he held up his hands to her. "Should I shove her out beyond gunshot range, Francie?"

"I was only thinking of you, Fox," she said unhappily. "I

can't bear any more insults for you. We've tried and tried to shame Mama out of her attitude, but it just doesn't work."

He dropped down beside her, wrapped the tiller rope around his wrist and let the boat drift out into the current. "We can't change other people," he said, "so we can only build something for ourselves and leave them out. I have a mother too. She's hurt now and frightened, and when Tulia leaves she'll be all alone. Not that Tulia is much company, but at least my mother can talk to her, even though Tulia pretends not to listen."

"She's—going? Tulia, I mean?" Frances tried to keep relief out of her voice, remembering the fierce challenge Tulia had flung at her on that train. Tulia had seen that it was no use, perhaps; she was giving up, taking herself away. Then Frances' heart took a heavy downward plunge again as Fox answered.

"I'm taking her in town tonight, when she finishes packing her stuff. Wylie filed her divorce papers today, so she's moving out—moving in with Mrs. Drake. Zach got hold of some money somewhere and I brought it out to Tulia tonight, so she's leaving. Zach rented a room at Mrs. Matson's—he and Ren are going to try to carry on that cigarette business in the old Matson shop. It looks dubious to me, but they might make a go of it."

Frances heard only part of this. Tulia would be in town, Tulia would be free. Tulia could set Fox free, she had said. "You'd be poison for Fox!" she had raged. "You're so damned dead!"

Frances cried in rash desperation, "She's in love with you, Fox!"

He lifted an oar and turned the bow of the boat away from the reedy shore, where it was drifting. "I'm in love with you, Francie," he answered gently.

"She told me I was all wrong for you—that I'd ruin you, and frustrate your life! She said you were prisoned and stifled and that I was stifled too—that we had consciences and that they would kill us—that I was dead inside already."

"Are you dead inside?" He turned up her chin and studied her eyes in the moonlight. Tears lay there, but they were angry tears. He kissed her softly and the boat gave a little lurch as the tiller swung, so that he had to right it quickly.

"People can be alive inside without having flames shooting out of their eyes," he went on. "That's why Tulia hates us—because we've got something that belongs to us alone, that she can't understand or share. She thinks I'm a fool, of course, to stick on with the old *Agnes*. She thinks the Captain was a rich man, but there was mighty little left for my mother. Until I can build up a little security for her, I have to go on in the same way and Tulia thinks I'm crazy."

"She doesn't hate you, Fox."

"There's a kind of love that's worse than hate, Francie. It's a possessive, cannibal kind of thing that wants to devour and change the thing it loves. Tulia wants to own me and she's got into a kind of frenzy because she knows she never will."

"I thing she's dangerous." Frances sighed. "I'm afraid of her, Fox."

"You needn't be. You needn't be afraid of anything where I'm concerned. I'm not a changeable person. When I decided that I was in love with you, that finished it, so far as my mind goes. Unless you decide that you don't want me to be in love with you."

"I'll never decide that—but it's all so hopeless, somehow."

"It isn't hopeless. Why don't we get married right away, Francie? You'd like my mother, I think. She's a simple sort of person—she's never had much of a life outside that old house, but she'd be good to you. She likes being needed— fussing over people; she even enjoys fussing over Tulia, I think, though Tulia isn't kind to her. Of course we can never put any dependence on Zach. He's always been a rover, he always will be. Nothing interests him very long. He likes excitement and he'll get a little now, trying to buck the tobacco trust, but when he tires of that he'll drift again."

She drew away from him a little and folded her hands in her lap, because the longing to fling herself into his arms and surrender was so chokingly strong.

"There's my mother, Fox. She might forgive me, but I don't believe she would, ever. There's a hard little core in my mother's nature that I'd never suspected. It's made up of obstinacy with a little malice mixed in, I think, but underneath she's hurt too. I don't know what to do!"

"In a month she'd accept the situation, Francie. Listen, why don't I get the license when I go down tomorrow, and we can get married on Sunday? That's my only free day—we'd just take the small boat downriver and let Dr. Drake marry us after church."

"I don't know what to do, Fox! I wanted it to be right for us—I don't even like coming down here to see you this way!"

"You leave it to me, Francie. I'd better take you back now. I want to get Tulia down to town before old Mrs. Drake goes to bed. You leave everything to me." He took the oar and swung the boat back upstream. They had drifted a long way on the current, Frances saw. "I'd better rig a little sail," Fox said. "There's enough wind to take us back. I could have brought the other boat, but it's noisy."

Frances laughed uncertainly. "Mama can't shoot, Fox. I told her I was seeing you. I'm not going to sneak or hide. If I decide to marry you I'll tell her that too. I'm twenty. I can be married without her consent but I don't like it that way. I'd always have a guilty feeling—it would spoil things for us." Tulia had been right about her. She was stifled. She might be a pretty, pink tomb but there was more than a body inside; there was a heart that ached and tore at her.

Fox had genius that would be strangled on Pamlico, Tulia had said. If I married him—if I just let him give up I could destroy him, Frances was thinking. Aloud she said, "You're just going on, Fox? With the old *Agnes*? You're giving up all the things you wanted—engines and chemistry and all the new things that are going to happen?"

He was busy lashing ropes, breaking out a little spread of canvas at the bow. The wind caught it and heeled the boat over slightly, so that Frances shifted away from the too near lap of the bow wave. When he came back, holding to a line, to perch on the high edge of the seat, his whole body had a sober air, as though he had withdrawn again into that aloneness that he was reluctant to share.

"No, I haven't given up," he said slowly. "When you give up

it's time to choose your grave. The world is moving and I'll move with it. I just don't fight things, Francie. I wait—and do the thing that seems next to do—that seems right."

"Duty!" she cried bitterly. "*She* said that. Tulia said that about both of us. That we were all wrong for each other. Maybe we are, Fox! Perhaps you do need to be dragged out from behind your wall and I'm not strong enough or ruthless enough to do it."

"Inside my wall, Francie, there'll never be anyone but you! I let you break through because I wanted you—I needed you. You had the answers that I'd been searching for. They're in your eyes. Look in your mirror when you go home and maybe you'll see them there. Something that was fine and true—that was what I'd been hunting for. A steadfast thing that wouldn't despise what was decent and right, even if it did have the label of conscience upon it. I killed a boy once. It was in battle and I had to kill or be killed, but I swore then never to hurt anything alive again if I could help it. So—" he drew a long breath and leaned on the tiller rope, swinging the boat in toward the Neary shore, " I won't marry you—not till it's right for you. I won't hurt you or put a burden of guilt on you. When you call, Francie, I'll be ready."

"But—suppose things never change? Suppose my mother goes on hating you forever?"

"Everything changes. She'll change or you will. Till then I'll wait."

The boat swung in gently against the Neary landing. Fox moved to leap up to the planks but Frances protested.

"No. Let me go alone. This is Neary ground. It's all sowed with hate and I hate walking on it, even though it's mine; but not you, Fox!"

He lifted her up, held her hands tightly for a minute, then turned without a word. She heard the oar dipped, heard the faint wash of water under the stern as the boat moved outward, but she did not turn nor watch him go. But at the top of the bluff she stopped, and looked long across the river. She saw the Cavitt door open as he went into the house, and then unable to stir from the spot, waited till the light showed again, with people moving against it. Then presently the small boat set up a coughing bark that cracked thinly against the banks, and in the wan light Frances could see it moving, low and shadowy, downriver, its wake an arrow of bright silver under the moon.

She pressed her fingers hard over her eyes for a moment, as though she could shut out the awareness of Tulia, out there in that boat. Then she turned and ran toward the house, not caring how her skirt drabbled, letting her hair blow untidily about her face, unaware that there was a frantic look about her as she plunged in through the hall door, slamming it behind her.

Lydia was sitting primly in the parlor with Taffy. She wore a black dress and a company air, as though this evening were some sort of occasion, and the heavy tightness of her round face made the occasion tragic.

"I hope you enjoyed yourself!" she said, stiffly. "You look dirty and all mixed-up, certainly mighty little like a lady!"

"I'm certainly a lady," Frances cut back as coldly. "I'm dirty because I had to see the man I'm going to marry in a bilgy little boat instead of decently, in my own home! And I'm mixed-up because I don't know whether I'm a dutiful daughter or just a silly fool!"

"So you're going to marry that scummy son of an old river pirate!" Lydia's eyes burned, red-edged, like the hot eyes of a cornered animal. "Thank heaven, that you had two parents! I don't have to torment myself thinking you got your low inclinations from me."

Frances' eyes narrowed. "I certainly have no inclination to abuse the memory of my father, Mama! Blame me if you must do it to appease that vindictive spirit you coddle so fiercely, but let Father rest in peace. He never harmed anybody, and I know that he would never have visited the angers of an older generation upon his children. Yes, I'm going to marry Fox Cavitt, and I think I shall marry him here in my house—decently and honorably. Yes, I think I shall!"

"You won't marry any Cavitt in this house while I'm in it!" screamed Lydia. "I suppose you'll be pleased with that? You'd be happy to turn your own mother out of her old home so you can fill it with water-front trash—foreigners—Portuguese pirates! Very well, if you want it that way I have nothing more to say."

"Oh, Mama, for heavens' sake, don't be so melodramatic!" put in Taffy. "You haven't got the build for it in the first place; you're too short for tragedy and your face gets red. Sit down and stop popping your eyes out and stop pretending you hate all the Cavitts. There's one of them you don't hate, I'm sure."

Lydia gulped a trifle and opened her mouth in bewilderment.

"I don't know what you're talking about! I've certainly never had any association with the Cavitts except what has been forced upon me, here under my own mother's roof! I never intend to associate with them. Just because that horrible old man pushed himself in here when he was already at the point of death and worked himself into such a state that he had a stroke on this doorstep, and Frances so far forgets that she was reared a lady, I am not surrendering one inch of my stand against the Cavitts! As for marrying a Cavitt in this room—where my poor father was laid out for his burial—when you can force an abomination like that upon your own mother—"

"You'll have a stroke yourself, Mama, if you let yourself get so mad," remarked Taffy calmly. "Those pretty green certificates you bought in town this morning—up there in your bureau drawer. Did you happen to read them over after you brought them home?" she pursued sweetly.

"What are you doing, snooping in my bureau drawer?" demanded Lydia. "Haven't I any right to privacy in this house? I don't snoop through your things."

"I was putting away your clean stockings. I didn't know you had secrets from us. Of course you had a right to buy them—and hide them too, if you wanted to. I wasn't questioning your right to do that, I was just wondering if you'd read what was printed and written on the things?"

"I know what I'm doing!" snapped Lydia, but her eyes were a little frightened.

Taffy said, "Come along, France, we have to go and set the bread." She dragged Frances with her into the hall. "Stop shaking all over!" she whispered. "Leave her alone. She'll slip upstairs as soon as she can, without our noticing, and read over those things. Zach Cavitt's signature is on every one in big black letters. Ten shares in the Pamlico Tobacco Company. A thousand dollars of good brass money sunk in that concern, and Mr. Zach Cavitt had better make good or he'll have me at his handsome, curly hair!"

"We should have told her. That was wrong, Taffy, to let her blunder into a thing like that," worried Frances.

"Oh, you and your ethics! It was the slickest thing that ever happened, and you know it. You heard her, telling us what a charming young man he was—the smirking scoundrel! Fox is water-front trash but brother Zach is an elegant gentleman. Let her discover that her judgment of people isn't infallible and the results will be cheap, even if they cost us a thousand dollars."

"I feel sick, Taffy. I can't bear talking to Mama like this! I can't stand it, to have ugly thoughts in my mind and feel like a stranger with my own mother. Fox made me ashamed tonight—he spoke so nicely about his mother. He said she was frightened and wanted to be needed—maybe Mama needs to feel secure too. Maybe she needs more loving and less criticism."

"Don't you weaken now! Mama needs discipline, and to get this childish peeve against the Cavitts out of her mind. By the same reasoning she uses, we ought to hate Grandpa Taft and Uncle Horace and all her relatives. They put our father in that reeking foundry and kept him there, inhaling poisonous fumes, when they knew his lungs were weak. You could say they killed Papa too—and he wasn't demonstrating his brash ego and having fun at it the way Grandfather Neary probably was doing when his old *Mary Conner* busted her boiler. I'll bet that old man was hooting insults over the rail of that boat when she suddenly gave a big whoosh and took him to glory, while poor Papa had to cough his life out in that little back bedroom with his pay check stopped and a thousand worries to make his last days a horror."

"Mama thinks all her family were perfect."

"She doesn't now," stated Taffy brutally. "I told her what I thought of them, tonight. She reminded me that Uncle Daniel left us this place and I told her he probably hated his old wife and that his conscience hurt him because he'd never done anything to help his mother. I had a grand time slinging mud on all the family portraits and I reminded her that at least Fox Cavitt was looking after his mother—which was more than her family had the decency to do. That's why she was so particularly nasty when you came in."

"I can't bear this atmosphere, Taffy. I'm going back right now and tell Mama I'm sorry—but that I'm not going to change my mind about Fox Cavitt."

"Wait a little while. Give her time to discover that she's been taken in by a Cavitt—that charming young man! Neither of us will speak of it, however. We'll be as maddeningly dumb as oysters. We'll be surprised that she didn't investigate and know whom she was dealing with—but I'm betting she'll never peep about it. She'll hide the things or she'll try some way to make Zach give her the money back—and a long way she'll get with that endeavor!"

"Poor little Mama! We're being awfully brutal, Taffy."

"If we can cure her it will be worth it. Like surgery. She has a cancer of hate in her heart, most of it fostered in her own imagination, and it poisons her whole nature. She can be sweet and she will be again when she finds out it's all no use," Taffy declared blithely.

Up in her room, where already the fall air was beginning to be a little chilly, Lydia sat with a lamp very close to her hair and the ten green certificates unfolded in a smooth pile on her lap.

There it was, plain and bold, with an arrogance about the downsweep of the letters that was characteristic of the breed, she thought.

Zachary Cavitt, President.

Fury and a sick dismay shook her, so that she felt cold as ice and dragged a shawl off the foot of the bed to wrap around her shoulders.

The liar! But no, he hadn't lied—not in words at least. The folly had been hers. Why hadn't she demanded, "And who are you, young man?" Why hadn't she asked his name that day at Crofford Matson's burial? Why hadn't she made inquiry of Rennie Matson? Lydia was not a person to accept blame lightly or even to accept it at all, if she could wriggle herself out of it, but there seemed no loophole of escape from this dilemma. Then she remembered some things Rennie Matson had said.

Rigidly she marched downstairs, clutching the stock certificates in her hand. Taffy was beating up a yeast cake in a bowl of lukewarm milk when her mother stalked into the kitchen, white-faced.

"You knew that this fellow was head of that tobacco company!" she cried. "You knew it, and you let me make a spectacle of myself—deliberately!"

"I knew it when you sold that tobacco to Zach, Mama," Taffy admitted, "and you were so pleased at having made a little money on it that I didn't want to spoil your fun by telling you that you'd sold it to a Cavitt. But I didn't know you were going to dash down there and invest money with Zach Cavitt. You were terribly careful not to let us know you planned to do anything so rash as that."

"He knew it! He knew who I was!" Lydia declared. "I know now—the way he grinned, the smooth way he talked, he knew he was taking advantage of me!"

"Maybe he thought he was doing you a favor, Mama, letting you have a share in that business. Maybe you will make a big profit and then you can crow over us and brag about how smart you've been. Or it could be you could sell your stock at a profit and beat Zach Cavitt at his own game," Taffy suggested.

"I'll do it!" Lydia snapped. "I'll get rid of it. I'll make him take it back tomorrow."

She was dressed and ready to go almost as soon as it was light. She nagged Dobbs into getting the mare into the shafts, and wore her grimmest hat and a face to match. It was so early when she drove in to town that the *Agnes J.* was still moored at the wharf with her rusty old stack breathing smoke in a green, acrid cloud.

Rennie Matson was stumbling sleepily down the path to the factory when Lydia hailed him.

"You Rennie! You come here!"

He approached the buggy uneasily, and Lydia thrust the green bundle at him.

"You've got to take this back," she told him. "I want nothing to do with anything that's concerned with a Cavitt. You take this back and sell it to somebody else, but I want a good profit out of the deal, you understand? You knew how I felt about the Cavitts—anyway you should have known, and you should have told me. Now, you give me back that paper I signed and all my money!"

Rennie twisted one foot over the other. He did not take the envelope with the certificates. He said, "I don't know, Mrs. Keeling— you'd better talk to Zach, I guess—he took your money, and that note you signed he sent up to the bank—and I don't know can I take these back or not. You wait here— yonder he's coming right now, down the street."

Lydia felt a queer cramp of dread, as Rennie ran to meet Zach Cavitt. Here was the same handsome young man who had charmed her before, but now he wore a sinister aspect in her eyes, as though horns had sprouted through his black forelock and his smile had turned into a leer. She swallowed desperately and braced herself against the back of the seat.

Zach bowed politely. "You wished to see me, Mrs. Keeling? Is something wrong?"

"Everything is wrong." She got control of her throat again. "I should never have invested in your concern had I known who you were. You knew that. I have been cheated. I want my money back."

"Not cheated, Mrs. Keeling," he protested. "You have value received for all your money. And already—" his smile expanded to a graciousness that made Rennie grin in fatuous sympathy, "your investment has produced a very nice little dividend. I had intended mailing it to you—Renwick, fetch the envelope that I told you to mail to Mrs. Keeling."

Rennie looked briefly startled, then ran quickly to the shop. Lydia sat uneasily, determined not to be taken in again, not to be mollified.

"You can just sell your stock to somebody else," Lydia declared, "and I want that paper back that I signed."

Zach rested a foot on the hub of the wheel and idly patted Chloe's rump, making her wriggle with delight.

"That will take a little time to arrange, Mrs. Keeling, but of course we will do whatever you wish. If you should change your mind, and decide to remain with us, you can let us know."

"I won't. I want nothing to do with any Cavitt business," snapped Lydia.

"As you wish. We regret losing you. Thank you, Renwick. Mrs. Keeling, here is ten dollars. Not a large profit, but at least you know your money has been working for you, and we will arrange to cancel the stock sale as rapidly as it can be managed."

Zach bowed again, as Lydia stuffed the two bills into her purse, her mouth tucked in at the corners. After all, she thought, as she turned the mare around awkwardly, her money had earned it. They had had the use of it for twenty-four hours and she was entitled to some return! Of course, if the whole thousand dollars she had contracted to pay in should earn interest like that—no, she'd have nothing to do with Zach Cavitt! Treating her as though she were a queen—all poppycock, all part of the Cavitt impudence!

"Horns and hoofs!" she sniffed to herself. "Horns and hoofs is what they should wear! Every one of them!"

24

Tulia had not slept at all, and her hair felt heavy and cold on her head, her brow was hot and her face ached as she dabbed powder over a skin too starkly white already. Her eyes were hot as coals and sunken a little, under the proud arch of her eyebrows, and her mouth kept jerking as though she tasted pain, raw and sour on her tongue. The pain had grown through the night till now it was greater than her body, a dark, enveloping fog that shut out the pale light of dawn and made everything in the room swim giddily, as though seen through water. It had begun when Fox Cavitt set her bags down on the Drake porch the night before, when he said with careful casualness, "Sorry everything went wrong for you, Tulia. Well, good-by and good luck!"

She had put out her hands then gropingly, and cried, "Fox?" But he had only called good-by again and tramped away. It was an ending, and Tulia had never been ready to accept endings, unless she herself wielded the severing knife.

With Zach, yes—that ending had been easy. She had taken the money he offered, imperiously, as though it had been long past due; she had listened to him when he said that Wylie Matson would arrange everything and that she was to go down with Fox to the county seat today with Wylie, and that Zach wished her well with her freedom. She had listened absently because none of this was important except being free. She had not minded saying good-by to Zach's mother, though that poor, limited old soul had done her best to make Tulia comfortable, had turned to her eagerly in her own sorrow and waxed definitely boresome in her naïve efforts to patch up the wreck of Zach's marriage. That ending had been a relief, and Tulia had left the dreary old Cavitt house with the firm determination that never again would she set foot in it.

She would have Fox—nothing should shake her determination to make Fox love her, make him see that he needed her, make him see that he was being destroyed by slow degrees here in this miasmic backwater where life had stood still for a generation. They would go far away, where Fox could see his dreams materialize, where his potentialities would not be wasted, where the curse of Capricorn should never touch either of them again. The past was for forgetting in Tulia's book, the future was what she wished to make of it—and she would not accept this ending.

All the way downriver she had kept silent, deciding that the time was not ripe, that Fox was being decent and reticent because she was not yet free—but now in this sick morning she knew that she had risked loss, she had been too cautious, too discreet. Success was for the ruthless, as Zach had so often told her, mockingly, in the old desperate days when they had shared their succession of dramatic catastrophes. Now Zach was riding high again, and she had nothing but a pain in her heart, and a good-by.

She combed her hair carefully, every strand of it aching as she puffed it lightly into a smart pompadour, caught curls at her neck with a jaunty bow, let two gay little locks twine themselves into beau-catchers against her cheeks. She put on her smartest frock, and a wide hat with practically no crown, moored with two jeweled pins. Her long gloves wrinkled fashionably to her elbows and a silk petticoat made an alluring rustling about her ankles. The crisp bills Zach had given her she had pinned cannily inside her corset. In her purse were two silver dollars for her ferry passage. Oh, yes, she would pay her fare! Her pride would not permit her to be under obligations to the Cavitts. The money she had hoarded was her due—much less than her due. The Cavitts owed her far more—payment for this wretchedness that had torn her apart all night.

She declined the breakfast Mrs. Drake tried anxiously to press upon her, and walked through the drowsy town to the wharf. Fox was loading his cargo, and Tulia noted how little there was to go aboard, a few bales of marsh hay, a single case of eggs. She curled her lip a little, feeling a twinge of triumph. Couldn't they see that the old *Agnes* was finished, that to carry on doggedly as Fox was doing was slow disintegration, death from dry rot? Somehow she had to make him see. He nodded to her cheerfully, took the coin she held out without comment. Wylie Matson was already aboard, sitting on a box in the stern smoking a cigar. He gave her a flick of the hand for greeting and Tulia walked directly to the cabin and found a seat there, arranging her skirts daintily around her.

If only Wylie had not come along! But of course she had engaged him to act as her attorney, and undoubtedly he had his eye on a fee. Tulia pressed a hand over her bosom and felt the reassuring crackle and stiffness of the four twenty-dollar bills pinned there. Old Mrs. Cavitt had gone on at dismal length about the state of Croff Matson's affairs, and that he had died leaving everything in a muddle, and nobody knew whether his poor widow had anything to live on or not. But of course, she had rambled on endlessly, Mrs. Matson had her boys! "And I've got my boy too," she always finished fatuously, twisting dry hands with complacency till Tulia had ached to shriek at her. "It was terrible, having to see the Captain go, but I've still got my boy and his boat!"

Tulia glared around the dry, sea-stained walls of the cabin with disgust. A steampipe ran along under the seat and hissed and gobbled, sending out a little warmth against the freshening winds of the Sound. The mildewed life preservers swayed with every bumble of the tired old engine. A jail, she thought bitterly, a creaking, barnacled, lurching prison for the spark that burned in Fox Cavitt's mind—why couldn't he see? How could he be content to be chained with soggy chains, the drag of his mother's possessiveness, the foolishness of mistaken loyalties? How could he be so spiritless as to accept a treadmill routine that went about in a stupid circle, leaving no impress upon the world, just as the old boat circled her dogged route, day after day, while the wake of her passing died in ripples behind her, unconsidered and profitless?

She waited quietly, till they had cleared the fish dock and gained the deep water of the Sound, where a slow ground swell made the timbers groan and the cabin door chatter hysterically against its salt-eroded latch. Then she ventured out, saw that Wylie had perched himself high in the bow, and that Fox was alone on the high stool of the wheelhouse. The door of the little structure was open, and Tulia stepped in, mounting the two worn steps, pulling the door shut behind her. Fox looked down at her, smiled absently and nodded, resting one brown hand on the polished wheel, pushing his cap back with the other.

"Sorry I can't ask you to sit down, Tulia," he said. "No room for easy chairs in here."

Tulia gripped the slanting edge of the open window before her. Her hair blew back and the wind snapped at the brim of her hat so that she had to reach and hold it.

"It's a cell, Fox!" she cried, hating the wind and the smell of salt and bilge that lay on the air. "It's a dungeon—and you're locked in it, forever and ever unless you have the courage to escape."

Fox reached for the cord and signaled for more speed. The *Agnes* gathered herself together like a too-heavy old woman and shuddered to obey.

"You like escapes, don't you, Tulia?" he said evenly.

"I like life," she declared. "I like the world and what it can give to people who have the boldness to take it—who aren't afraid to cut themselves loose from stupid traps and the nooses that life spreads out to frustrate them."

"So you're going to cut loose from your noose. And what are you going to take from life, once you've fought free?" he asked.

She looked up at him, and only a blind man could have missed the poignant torment that lay in her eyes.

"I want love, Fox," she said flatly. "That's all any woman wants to take from life."

The whistle boomed overhead, and a crawling prawn boat replied with a raucous toot. Fox took off his cap and hung it on a peg above the wheel. The wind caught at the dark swirl of his hair and tossed it.

"I thought you were through with love," he countered. "Aren't you on your way to get love legally tossed out of your life?"

"I've never had love." She stood taut, not looking at him. "I've had the dirty shadow of it—passion, possession, a foul thing that dressed itself up in wings and fooled me into giving it harbor. What I had was not love, it was degradation. It cheated me and laughed at me because I was young and frightened and eager for loving. A woman must have love, Fox, or she dies inside—as I've been dying for days—days and nights! Watching you—waiting for a word from you—dying, little bit by little bit!"

Fox frowned and put his cap back on, jerking it straight as though he put on calm judgment with it.

"You know I don't love you, Tulia. I've told you so, times enough."

"You could love me—if you'd look at me—if you'd think, Fox—but you won't think! You're letting them destroy you and I could make life wonderful for you! You could make all your dreams come true, I'd help you—but no one will help you here; they'll only devour your youth and quench the fire that's in you. Oh, Fox—I love you so much!" She gave a little whimper and put her head down on her wrists. "I love you till I'm sick with it—can't you see? Always, ever since we came from Cuba, there's been no one but you, Fox! And you wouldn't see! You wouldn't listen."

"Yes, I did see, Tulia, and I told you all along it was no good. You were another man's wife and I—"

"I'm not another man's wife now. I won't be—I'll be free! We could go away—New York or somewhere where men are doing the big things you want to do! I'd believe in you—I'd make you famous, Fox! My stepfather knows people—he's influential. And all I'd ask is to be loved, Fox! Love me a little—"

Fox looked uneasily about the little cuddy. He could not move away from the wheel; he could lash it down, it was true, but she was between him and the door. Her body was trembling all over now, and presently she lifted her head and showed him a ravaged, piteous face.

"You're killing me!" she whispered fiercely. "You're killing me and it doesn't matter—if only you loved me a little it wouldn't matter! I'd die here gladly. Hold me, Fox! Tell me you do love me, even a little!"

"No," he said grimly, keeping his face turned away. "I

don't love you, Tulia, and I won't lie. I love somebody else."

Her face tightened, her jaw muscles drew down. "That creature!" she snapped. "That pretty, spiritless thing, with nothing to offer—nothing in the world! A female! Something female and sickeningly aware of it. She'd ruin you! What does she have except a body? Nothing! Just a female body. You could as well love a cow—you could—"

"Shut up!" barked Fox, goaded past gallantry. "I've heard enough. I've been patient with you because you were unhappy, I tried to make up to you a little for what Zach has done to you but I don't love you and I want to hear no more about it."

"You could love me—if it weren't for her, for that female thing! A face and a pretty body—phah!" She spat at him savagely and Fox reached across the wheel, past her shoulder, jerking open the door.

"Get out now, Tulia," he said in a low tone. "Get out before you shame yourself and me any further!"

She drew backward slowly, her eyes like dagger points. The wild gleam in them matched the straight slash of her mouth and the angry breath that hissed through her pale lips.

Too late Fox Cavitt saw the gun. It was old. For years it had hung holstered behind the wheelhouse door. He made a wild snatch for it, but Tulia was quicker.

"She shan't have you!" she screamed. "Nobody shall have you—nobody, you hear? Nobody!"

There was a hollow roar and smoke blinded Fox as the wheel swung over blindly and the *Agnes* veered. A bolt of fire struck through his left shoulder as he grappled with the maddened woman, while men came running and yelling. Tulia jerked free and ran screaming down the deck. Fox dragged himself erect, caught the wheel and righted it, clinging to its support while sweat ran down his body and stung his eyes, and cold, sick shudders ran over him. Pain grew to a black blur, behind which he dimly saw Wylie in the door, and Fox sagged against him, retching.

"The wheel! Hold it! She shot me!" he gasped.

Wylie was shouting orders to two frightened deck hands.

"Get him in the cabin! Lay him flat! Then one of you come here and take this wheel. I've got to stop that bleeding."

"Get the gun—she's got a gun," Fox remembered, whispering as they lifted him.

He was aware of silence next, the engines stilled, the drone of a fly among the flapping life preservers overhead. Wylie was bending over him, swabbing anxiously with a towel.

"Got that little artery," Wylie was worrying. "I'll have to stop this, Fox—it will hurt some when I twist this. Hold your breath a minute—"

"Boat's stopped," muttered Fox vaguely, licking dry lips.

"We'll get her going—put her in somewhere the best we can. Got to get you to a doctor. This blood vessel will have to be sewed or tied or something."

"Tulia—" Fox pushed out a frail whisper past the black blur of the pain and shock.

Wylie straightened and cleared his throat. "You might as well know, Fox—she threw herself over the side. She ran past me screaming and jumped over before I could catch her. She never came up—probably caught in the weeds there. Don't move now—this boy is going to hold this tourniquet and loosen it every few minutes while I try to get the boat in. That was a big old slug and it's a nasty wound. What was the matter with her, anyway? Always did think she was a little crazy."

"Let me up—I can steer her in—"

"You lie still or you'll bleed to death. Sit on him, boy, if he doesn't lie still," Wylie ordered.

The black blur thickened again and Fox let it take him.

25

Rennie Matson brought the news, maneuvering the sailboat across the river awkwardly, digging with an oar, standing in the bow and shouting. Taffy ran out to the bluff and yelled back, then came flying.

"Fox has been shot!" she cried, crashing through the door. "Quick—they've just brought him home. Zach brought him in the little boat. Rennie's down there—he's holding the boat—hurry, France!"

Frances felt her knees give under her, she clutched at a chair, her face draining to grayness.

"Shot? I'm going, Mama—don't talk—don't say a word—I'm going! Fox is shot, and I'm going."

Lydia opened and shut her mouth dazedly. "Who shot him?" she demanded, but no one answered. Taffy and Frances were running down the path, Taffy's bright hair tossing behind her. Lydia trotted after them, calling questions, but before she could negotiate the slippery passageway down the bluff the sailboat was already in midcurrent, with Rennie standing in the stern splashing water desperately as he struggled to keep the bow headed toward the opposite shore. The little tender was lying alongside the Cavitt dock, pale smoke still wavering from her stack, and the old house turned a withdrawn and secret face, with only one wan light burning through the early dusk.

Taffy perched on the gunwale of the sailboat, indifferent to the water that was flung in her face as the heavy mast made the boat heel over. Frances huddled, shivering, in the bow, her whole body straining toward the Cavitt shore.

Taffy asked bluntly, "Who shot him?"

"Tulia," answered Rennie. "Tulia shot him. On the ferry."

"Why?" persisted Taffy, "why did she shoot him?"

"I dunno," Rennie said. "She shot Fox and then she jumped overboard. They never did find her."

Frances gave a little moan. "Hurry, Rennie," she begged.

"Is he going to die?" Taffy asked, when they were halfway over.

"Don't reckon so," Rennie answered, "just got hit in the shoulder. Couple more inches, the doctor said, and it would have been too bad. Lookit—I can't talk and paddle this heavy thing—ain't got enough wind."

The darkness was falling swiftly, pressing a gray curtain down over the water. There was no moon and a sullen cloud in the west lay heavy and black above a thin line of sulphur. The tide was low and the Cavitt landing stood high out of the river. Rennie made three tries before he got the bow alongside so that Taffy could scramble up to the planks and catch the line. Her skirt caught and ripped and she exclaimed impatiently and ripped off a length of tattered ruffle, throwing it away. Frances' palms stung with slivers when she got to her knees on the dock and stumbled up.

"You go first, Rennie," she said weakly. "You know the way."

"Never been up here in my life," grumbled Rennie. "Wait a minute—somebody's coming with a lantern."

A low yellow light bobbed down the path, and two pairs of legs flickered in the glimmer of it.

"Mr. Zach," said Rennie; "he's taking the doctor back."

Zach Cavitt said, "Hello, Taffy," as he came down to the dock. "How are you, Miss Keeling?"

"Lend me that lantern a minute till I take the girls up, will you, Mr. Zach? They'll go blundering into the bushes."

"How is he?" asked Frances faintly.

"Weak," replied the doctor. "Don't let him talk—and don't stay long."

Taffy looked about her curiously as they entered the old Cavitt house. "It smells like I always thought it would," she whispered.

"Hush" warned Frances. "We'd better sit down and wait till someone comes."

Rennie had run back to the shore with the lantern, and they were alone in a pine-walled hall dimly lighted by a lamp.

A deer's head and a stuffed fish hung opposite the darkly mounting stairway; there was a hard little settee with leather cushions and on this they sat, stiffly on the edge, Frances' eyes and ears straining upward. There were sounds of footsteps above, and presently a small, plump woman in a gray calico dress and gingham apron appeared at the head of the stairs.

"Who is it?" she asked, peering down.

Frances was up the stairs swiftly. "I'm Frances," she said. "I had to come—I had to know—"

"Yes—yes." Mrs. Cavitt held out a hand, and began to cry, dabbing at her eyes with the corner of her apron. "You come along with me. Why she did such a dreadful thing I'll never know! We treated her like our own daughter in this house—and Fox was always good to her. Zach's all torn up—he feels like it's his fault, somehow—but she wasn't ever satisfied no matter what I tried to do for her. And just last night, tired as he was, Fox took her back to town—In here, miss. They've got the bleeding stopped, but it's a nasty wound. Why the Captain kept that old gun hanging in there, is a question. Was a time when the dock hands got ugly—and one time they threw a lot of tobacco overboard. Captain bought the gun then, but it ought to have been thrown in the Sound long ago. Rusty too!"

The babble of the tired voice led them to an open door. From beyond it streamed a light, and odors drifted out, druggy and strange. Frances paused, but the older woman gave her a gentle push.

"Go along in—but don't let him move nor talk. You're the girl with the dark eyes, aren't you—the one the Captain talked about?"

"My mother was Lydia Neary," Frances said levelly, "but I loved the Captain—and I love Fox."

"He's a good boy. I'll go down. I was just putting supper on when they came. I can't remember did I finish stirring the grits into the boiling water or not, I was so upset." Mrs. Cavitt scrubbed her eyes again. Then her voice lifted cheerfully. "You've got company, Foxworth," she called, "pretty company. Go along in, Miss Frances."

Frances tiptoed across the braided rug to the high bed, with its gay quilt spread across the foot.

"It's Francie, Fox," she said, "but you're not to move or talk, the doctor says."

He lay very flat, one side swathed in bandages. He turned his head a little, and smiled at her. There had always been a kind of vividness about Fox Cavitt, a flash of deep, dark eyes, a flash of white teeth against the clear, glowing tan of his skin, but now he was all pale ivory, like marble; even his hands lying on the sheet were colorless.

"Come here," he whispered.

"Don't talk," repeated Frances, as she obeyed. She touched his forehead, a bit timidly, and it felt cold and moist under her fingers. He lifted his good hand and caught hers, and drew it down to his cheek.

"Kiss me, Francie," he breathed.

She stooped and kissed him full on the lips, and felt their bitten dryness; knew that they had been gnawed in agony.

"You'll be well soon," she said. "Then I'll marry you, Fox—whenever you want me."

"Francie?" Her name was a croak.

"Please, Fox—don't try to talk."

"I have to tell you. She had no reason—no reason at all—"

"I know. It's all right. I'll go now—I'll come every day if I can get across the river."

"If you could row my boat—"

"I will. Taffy will help me. We'll keep the boat on our side of the river till you're well again."

"Kiss me again, Francie."

She went down the dim stairs blindly. Taffy and Mrs. Cavitt were sitting on the little settee, Taffy holding the older woman's hand and patting it. Mrs. Cavitt was sobbing.

"She could have killed him," she was saying chokingly. "She could have killed him—and she meant to do it! All summer long she was after him—oh, we could see, the Captain and me. She hated Zach and she wanted Fox—and she could have killed my boy, and the Captain now scarcely cold in his grave. She was a wicked woman! I was good to her, too. Just yesterday I ironed all her petticoats and crimped every ruffle, and my feet trouble me a lot when I stand very long. When she left she didn't even tell me good-by. I can't mourn she's dead. Anyway, she didn't take my boy with her."

"It was my fault," Frances said. "Fox loved me—and she knew it. She wanted to take him away from this place."

"I heard that enough," agreed the older woman. "She hated everything here. Listen, you come and have a cup of tea with me. I don't know if I can bear to be alone. Zach said he'd come back maybe, but he's got to run the boat till Fox gets well again—he might not come back tonight. Seems like I can't bear this empty house. I've got Fox to do for, but he can't talk—and there's so much stillness! Like death!"

"I'll stay," Frances said impulsively. "I'll stay with you if you'll let me. Taffy can go back with Rennie and tell Mama."

"Would you stay now? That would be a real kindness, and it would be good for Fox too. The Captain always said you were a fine girl, Miss Frances. It troubled him a lot—you and Fox—and things like they are—across the river."

"I know," said Frances.

She followed Fox's mother into the kitchen when Taffy had gone. This will be my home—this is where I will live, she was thinking, looking around the big room with its faint odor of wood smoke, of cats and long-forgotten meals. Mrs. Cavitt followed her eyes.

"We never did fix up this house in a long time," she remarked, stuffing wood into the range. "You see, I married an old man, set in his ways, and he liked things to stay just the same. Now, if this place was painted inside—and I always did wish for a window in that wall, so I could look at the river while I was washing dishes." She came close, and her lips trembled softly, her eyes brimming as she put her hands on Frances' shoulders. "Captain said I'd like you! I never was jealous-natured, not even with—her! I like things pretty too. She hated me because I tried to be saving, but she didn't know how much it cost the Captain to pay Zach out of some of his trouble. Zach was always our heartbreak—but Foxworth made up for everything. You sit down now, and I'll fetch the tea. I made doughnuts this morning too."

"Will the doctor let Fox have some supper?"

"Hot tea and a poached egg, he said. You can carry it up, after we finish. Then I've got to give him that blue pill the doctor left so he'll sleep."

Frances was coming down the stairs with the tray, when the front door opened softly. Fox had eaten little, had smiled at her wanly, patted her fingers, dropped into a quiet sleep. Frances stood still halfway down the flight, staring incredulously at the two figures tiptoeing into the hall. Then she gave a little cry.

"Mama!"

Lydia advanced hesitantly, stood blinking in the light, her lips trembling. Behind her Taffy grinned smugly.

"I made her come. I made Rennie bring her over," she said. "Mama looked so kind of lost and lonesome, sitting there on that dock."

Lydia began to sob hoarsely, held out her hands. "Francie— maybe you didn't want me—maybe I shouldn't have come—"

Frances flew down, dumped the tray abruptly, flung herself into her mother's arms. "Oh, Mama!" she cried. "Oh, Mama!"

Mrs. Cavitt emerged from the kitchen, a puzzled look on her face.

"This is my mother, Mrs. Cavitt." Taffy took command briskly. "She's terribly sorry for your trouble. She came over to help if she can."

"Well, well!" the Captain's widow bustled up beaming. "This is a kindness, I'm sure. This is a right neighborly thing for you to do, Mrs. Keeling. My boy will be happy about it too. Now you just come along with me and have you a good cup of tea. There's nothing like a hot cup of tea when you're kind of upset, I always say. You've got two fine girls, Mrs. Keeling."

"Yes—yes—" Lydia fumbled for her handkerchief, clinging to Frances' hand, "they're good girls. Yes—I would like a cup of tea."

"I'll put some fresh in the pot this minute. You come along with me. Frances, I gave Fox a little bell to ring—you listen, if he needs anything."

When the older women had gone back to the kitchen Taffy

danced a silent, gleeful jig, making an impudent face at the solemnly staring deer's head.

"Dead and buried—one ancient feud!" she exulted. "And I did it. Little Taffy!"

"But how, Taffy—how?"

"Simple," stated Taffy. "She was all melancholy, sitting there in the dark—and I just kissed her. I told her we hated acting the way we've been doing, and that suppose one of us were hurt, wouldn't she be glad to see even Mrs. Cavitt? And that she ought to remember that you loved Fox the way she had loved Papa—and all of a sudden she melted all up, inside, and said she wasn't mean really. So I just shoved her into the boat and made Rennie fetch us over. She was just frozen up. She didn't know how to relent gracefully, and a little tenderness broke down her resistance. Just one thing though, now. I'm going to have my own boat, definitely. With a gasoline engine and everything. Think how it would be with you over here and me stuck on that side!"

"Taffy, have you thought about it? Tulia is gone. Zach will be free now—Taffy, I do hope—"

"That I won't make a fool of myself? Don't worry. I killed that thing. I want to have fun, for years—I might go to school, I don't know. You'll be getting married—Mama will be all alone."

"I'm glad," Frances said. "It was just one of those young things that happen to girls, Taffy. I'm glad it's finished."

Later she led her mother up the stairs. Lydia was uncertain, she pressed her fingers over a shaking mouth, kept blinking back tears.

Fox had wakened. He moved his eyes, smiled, and then looked a bit startled as Lydia approached the bed.

"Fox," Frances said, "here's Mama."

Fox moved his good hand, with a groping, questioning gesture. Lydia lifted the hand, smoothed the bloodless fingers between her palms.

"Hello, Mama," Fox said, and grinned.

"Hello, Son," whispered Lydia Neary.

26

Bliss Matson crept out of her bed, twitched off her night-gown, and jerked on her clothes, her hands icy, her heart pounding.

It was cold for November, and her room was chilly, her breath making a little cloud on the mirror as she twisted up her yellow hair and pinned it in a knot at her neck. The clock downstairs had struck two when first she heard the faint sounds of movement in the room across the hall. For days a secret awareness, a prescience, an unease, had troubled her. Now she was sure. Suspicion was sharpened into certainty.

She got a coat from her closet, pushing aside the pale blue fluff of her bridesmaid's dress. Fox Cavitt was well again, Fox was taking over the *Agnes* tomorrow, in a week Fox and Frances Keeling would be married in the little church.

"We're to be bridesmaids," Taffy had said. "You wear blue and mine will have to be yellow. I look like a pickled beet in blue. I told Fox we simply had to have yellow roses. They'll match your hair and my dress."

Bliss scarcely looked at the dress. Fox was taking over the ferry tomorrow—that was the important thing. And across the hall she heard a bureau drawer close softly, cautiously. Wylie and Renwick were sleeping, down the hall, and her mother was in her own room below at the back of the house. Bliss blew out the lamp, picked up her purse and a knitted scarf and crossed the hall. She tapped softly at a door, pushed it open and stepped in. Zach Cavitt looked up from the suitcase he was packing, spread open on the bed.

"So—you're going?" Bliss whispered.

Zach frowned darkly. "Shut that door!" he hissed.

"They won't hear me. They're all sound asleep. How are you going?" Bliss persisted.

"The boat. I'll run her down the Sound—leave her there.

Tonight is my last chance," he said. A savage sort of desperation lay in his face. "Go back to bed!" he said harshly.

"No." Bliss seated herself on the foot of the bed. "So you have to go?"

"I got word. They'll be down here—those fellows from Washington—with a warrant. A fraud warrant! I'm no criminal! Can I help it if the trust closed the market against us? Can I help it if they bought up our product and gave it away—fine, hand-made cigarettes given away with packs of their dirty machine-made stuff? I made good cigarettes—"

"Not many though. Rennie said—"

"Rennie! That blabber-mouth kid! He's worked against me from the beginning."

"He has not. He was just worried—trying to protect Ma—"

"She won't lose—much. She'll get her building back, probably."

"You made her take stock. She's liable for the debts of the firm. You got rid of all your stock, didn't you, Zach?"

"That's my business," he snapped. "Will you get out of here, Bliss? I don't want Wylie wakened. What the hell do you want, anyway?"

Bliss folded her hands complacently. "I'm going with you," she announced.

"The devil you are! I'm going alone—and fast."

"I'm going with you," she repeated. "I love you, though you aren't worth loving. You've got no conscience and no honor—you've probably ruined my mother and a lot of other people too; people who trusted you. I'm a fool, I know, but I love you. And I'm going—where you go. If you suffer, I'll suffer with you."

"You little fool!" Zach curled his lip back from his teeth. "I don't want you! You've been hanging after me ever since I lost my wife. I'm sick of your fawning and running after me, hanging around the shop—making a spectacle of yourself before the whole town! Get out of my room!"

"If I get out—if I don't go with you," said Bliss coolly, "I shall walk down that hall and wake Wylie. I'll tell him you're running off, with all the money you got from selling stock— leaving Ma and all the others ruined. Oh, Zach, you did pretend to love me! You did! That night in the cemetery when you kissed me—and other times. Let me go with you? You love me now—you're just in trouble and angry and upset. I won't be any trouble. I'll help you."

His eyes narrowed, and a sly twist tightened his lips. "I haven't enough money to take you with me—even if I wanted you, Bliss. And I tell you now that I don't want you."

"I've got money. I've got it here. I've been saving it. Here it is—a hundred dollars. The money for my winter clothes, but you can have it. Please, Zach—you hurt me so, saying those ugly things when you know you do care!" Tears were running down her face. She pulled a wad of bills from her purse and held them out to him.

"How far do you think you can go on a hundred dollars?" he asked brutally. But he took the money.

"I'll be with you. You'll take care of me. Oh, I knew you didn't mean all those dreadful things you said! Kiss me, Zach, and say you didn't mean a word of it!"

"No time! How about your things?" He was brusque, snapping the locks of his bag, twisting into an overcoat.

"I packed this afternoon. I knew—somehow—I knew you were planning to get away."

"You think Wylie knows?"

"Oh, no, I don't think he suspects anything. He's been worried about the tobacco company, but he knew you'd been tied down, running the ferry since Fox got hurt, and he thought you were worried too but that as soon as you were free things would get moving again. Why are you going, Zach? Why don't you stay and try to make the business succeed?"

"Because those fellows up there are after me. I got the news up at the port two days ago. I can't satisfy them now and if legal methods don't work for them, they'll have no scruples about trying—other ways. I know. I worked with them in Cuba."

"I'll get my bag."

"Hurry, and get going. You go ahead and keep quiet. I'll meet you down the street."

"Oh, Zach—we will be happy, won't we?"

"I said, keep quiet. And hurry!

There was no stir or movement as Zach let himself out of the darkened house. He closed the door softly behind him, locked it again and was careful with the noisy latch of the gate.

Ahead a little way he could make out the dim figure of Bliss, her shoulder sagging with the weight of a grip. He made no effort to overtake her, but his hand slipped into his pocket and felt the roll of bills she had given him, and a sudden savage anger against Tulia burned him; not because Tulia had brought opprobrium upon him by her theatrical death, but because she had been stupid enough to take with her a nice bit of money, money he needed now and could use to advantage.

Raw wood smoke was drifting thickly over the sleeping town. Zach sniffed it with satisfaction. The Negro hand he had bribed was on the job, the *Agnes J.'s* gauges would show a head of steam. Zach concentrated the hate that tore him on that old boat, and on Tulia. But for Tulia and the demands of the *Agnes J.* he would have been free to combat the trust, to work out some scheme to defeat the effort to ruin the Pamlico Tobacco Company, to prod Rennie Matson and the help into production. Half the orders he had gotten in the eastern cities had not yet been filled, but now time had run out. There was only one way out for him, to reach the port town and get a fruit boat out of the country. He felt no twinge of compunction about leaving, not his mother, nor the town, nor the duped people who would suffer from his failure.

Bliss Matson was waiting on the wharf, the green riding light of the ferry shining faintly on her dress.

"Wait here," he ordered. "I'll slide the plank down when we've got upsteam."

From the corner of his eyes he saw her sitting forlornly on a waiting bale, pulling her coat around her against the November chill. He flung his bag over the rail, sprang after it and ran along the deck, cutting both mooring ropes with one quick slash of the hatchet he had carefully sharpened that day. At the engine-room door he shouted down into the oily depths, where a lantern swung over the head of the drowsy Negro deck hand.

"Push her!" he yelled. "Reverse like I showed you—then give her all she's got when I signal."

"Yessuh!" The Negro stumbled to the levers. Steam hissed from the boat's side, boiling over the quiet wash of the river. The tide was low. Zach did not like that, but he had had no choice but to get away tonight.

He climbed to the wheelhouse and felt the quick, plunging rhythm of the engine, the power in the worn old pistons that had once made the Captain gloat and triumph. The old tub still had it, thank God!

He heard Bliss screaming on the wharf, but paid no attention as the *Agnes* backed swiftly out into deep water. Let Bliss rouse Wylie, let her shriek the town into action. There wasn't a craft that could overtake him once he got into the channel. Let old Croff Matson's widow worry when the creditors clamped down; let Bart Mitchell rage, and Lydia Keeling; even poor credulous old Parson Drake! Their names were all on the list of stockholders, and what was left of their money was safe in his pocket along with Bliss's naïve contribution. Let the whole rotten, smug little town grind its teeth and curse his name—what did he care? He would never see the place again.

He fought the wheel to bring the heavy boat about and headed her into the channel, signaling desperately for more steam. There was a ground swell, and the timbers strained and creaked. The rudder was cranky, which meant that the tide was about at the slack and would soon turn. A thin rain began to beat in at the open windows of the wheelhouse, stinging his face, but he dared not close the glass; there was little visibility, as it was, and he was not sure enough of the channel to depend on the compass.

As though she knew the urgency of this flight, the old boat surged ahead. The bow wave made a hollow thunderous crash as she plowed into the Sound, and the lift and surge of the uneasy seas grew stronger. Zach took the rain in his face, leaning forward, gripping the wheel as though by his own wild frenzy he could drive the thumping screws along. Then the door opened and the Negro boy poked in a worried face.

"She's running mighty hot, Mister Zach," he protested in a frightened voice.

"Shove her! She can take it!" Zach yelled back.

All through his boyhood he had heard the stories of his father's wild races on the Sound, of the catastrophe of the *Mary Conner* that had brought the hatred of the Nearys upon the Cavitts. He felt a kinship to the old Captain now; it was as though the old man stood beside him, blood throbbing to the obedient throb of the pistons, spirit reaching to split the tumbling seas ahead with the power of her thrust and forward heave.

The Negro came back again. "Mister Zach," he whimpered, "you runnin' mighty clost to the south shore. I can see fish-trap stakes right out yonder!"

"I'm running this boat!" Zach answered, his hair blowing, wet with rain, his eyes fanatic with the thrill of escape. "Keep that steam up! Watch the water, keep the oil pumping."

"Yessuh, Mister Zach—but she makin' too far south—"

Ten minutes later she struck. There was a crash, a shudder, a sound of rending metal, of wildly blowing steam, then the *Agnes* slewed crazily, heeled over slightly to port, and though the engines beat in frantic impotence for a few minutes, she did not stir.

Zach fell backward from the stool with the impact, struck his head against a bulwark, lost his hat and felt his teeth cut through a lip so that blood was salty on his tongue.

He staggered up, tore down the deck that slanted now under his feet. The Negro, gray-faced in what light issued from below, was crawling from the engine pit, retching and squirming.

"She's aground, Mister Zach!" he blubbered, rolling over on the planks. "Lever hit me in the stummick—she's pounding her screws to pieces!"

Zach dropped into the steamy pit, killed the futile convulsions of the engines, and groped back, eyeballs seared and fiery with steam, wild curses fuming from his lips. He kicked at the sprawled body of the Negro, who wriggled **away,** moaning.

"Dat's South Creek yonder." The boy pointed. "You run her on the bar."

Zach strode back to the wheelhouse, lighted a lantern and swung it over the side, surveying the damage. The *Agnes* had plunged high on the sandbar, so that her bow was almost out of the water. Till the steam cleared out of the pit there was no way to discover what wreckage had been wrought with her propellers, whether or not she would float when the tide rose, or if she had been stove in and would settle slowly. The tide—he could not wait for the tide! Five hours would see daylight, men in pursuit, likely, roused by the Matsons—he could not wait.

The single lifeboat hung in davits on the starboard side. Fox had kept it calked and painted, kept the oars shipshape and ready, but in these two months while Fox was laid up with his wound, Zach had not touched the boat. He studied the ropes and pulleys now. They looked in good order.

"Get up from there!" he shouted to the prostrate boy. "Get up and help me get this boat down."

"I'm hurt, Mister Zach," wailed the boy, "I'm hurt bad."

"Get up! Get up before I kill you!"

The Negro dragged himself up to his hands and knees, reeled to his feet and fell again, finally making his way forward hanging to the rail. Zach had already loosed the lashings of the boat, and with the strength of desperation swung it outward. It went down jerkily, the stern striking the water first and shipping water, but Zach was down the rope before it righted, fighting it free, pushing away from the listing *Agnes*.

"Let my bag down on a line!" he shouted to the boy.

The Negro was bawling forlornly. "Mister Zach, you ain't goin' leave me here all alone? What I do when she floats off the bar? You can't go nowheres in that little boat."

"Drop my bag, I tell you!"

A sulphur-tinted hint of dawn was brightening the east when Zach pulled away, heading southward. Light creeping over the waters touched the blades of his oars with silver. There would be creeks and inlets to hide in through the day, toward night the tide would take him seaward again. Somewhere would be a dirty old freighter heading south.

Rio, the Guianas, the Islands—a thousand little towns down that way to offer haven to an adventurer.

Behind him were the women whose lives he had changed a little. He had no particular sorrow for any of them, not even his mother. Not for Tulia, nor silly little Bliss, nor gay Taffy Keeling, though Taffy would have made a good comrade on a flight, reckless and afraid of nothing. Only one female he missed, with a curious, rueful sense of loss.

"Good-by, Chloe," he muttered, as he headed the lifeboat into the narrow channel of South Creek.

27

At dusk a snorting little tug maneuvered the crippled *Agnes J.* into her old berth at the wharf.

All day the town had been stunned, people gathering in the Matson house where Bliss lay, hysterical, her eyes swollen, her face averted in shame and woe, and where Mrs. Matson wore a face of doom; in Bart's store where men muttered maledictions and swore helplessly to get even—with Zach Cavitt, with the tobacco trust that had crushed the Matson's last hope, with somebody—anybody!

Wylie Matson was in a frenzy of business, telephoning lawyers, bankers, the sheriff, drawing up papers to plunge the Pamlico Tobacco Company into bankruptcy and thereby save his neighbors from calamity. Lydia Keeling's note was in the bank at Bath, the white paper she had signed obligating her to pay a thousand dollars for stock that she had never received. Parson Drake's pitiful little nest egg had vanished; Bart Mitchell had mortgaged his store to buy a substantial block of stock when orders for Zach's fancy cigarettes began coming in.

"Everybody but the Cavitts!" muttered a disgruntled tobacco grower who was still unpaid. "The Cavitts ain't hurt none!"

"Leave the Cavitts be!" flared Rennie, who had been defensively on the verge of shameful tears all day. "They're hurt worse than anybody. It wasn't Zach's fault the trust busted us."

"It was his fault he run—and took off the ferry, leaving us all stranded here with no way to get to the sheriff or nobody!"

"Wylie called the sheriff. Wylie'll take care of things."

"Zach never lost a penny in this business. He never put in a penny to lose."

"Zach lost everything a man can lose," said the parson gently; "he has lost being a man. He has lost his mother and his country. He can never come back."

A quiet fell over the crowd that had tramped down to the wharf, when the Keeling buggy drove up and Frances helped Zach's mother down. Taffy had brought her across the river in a borrowed rowboat when the alarm sounded and Fox dashed off in the small boat to look for the missing *Agnes*. Mrs. Cavitt looked little and drained and piteous, and the townspeople watched Lydia Keeling sharply.

"Now that feud will start all over," men whispered among themselves. "Zach discounted Mis' Keeling's note and she didn't get nothing for it."

But there was, oddly, no anger in Lydia's eyes as she walked with Mrs. Cavitt out to the end of the wharf and stood, tensely watching as the little tug struggled in, dragging the wounded *Agnes J.* Mrs. Cavitt's lips quivered, but she stood quietly, Frances holding her hand. When the *Agnes* was finally moored, Fox came ashore, the group parting to make way for him, solemnly, in a silence as somber as death.

Fox went straight to his mother. "No sign of him, Mother," he said. "Eph says he got away before daylight in the lifeboat."

She nodded, crossing her arms on her breast, her throat working.

"He must never come back!" she said quietly and firmly. "Zach must never come back."

Lydia took command briskly. "Fox, you and Francie take your mother upriver in your boat. Fetch her straight to our house. Taffy and I will go along home and make a big pot of coffee."

"What about the *Agnes?*" Frances asked of Fox, as they stood together later on the porch of the old Neary house. "Is she ruined forever?"

Fox looked thoughtfully off into the darkness. "No, Francie. She's lost her propellers and there's a rip in her hold. It will cost money to repair her—money it will take me a long time to earn and pay back. Francie," he laid his hands on her shoulders and drew her close, "it's for you to say."

"What shall I say, Fox?"

"It's for you to say whether I stay—or go. There'll be a living for us, if the *Agnes* gets back into commission. If I rebuild her I'll build her to ferry automobiles, Francie. They're coming fast, and when they come roads will come with them. Bridges sometimes, maybe—but that time is far away. But it means staying here—a little town—giving up dreams, ambitions—living on little. It's for you to say, Francie."

"If you should go, Fox, what happens to the town? Water-bound, isolated, until somebody else builds a boat. The people trusted Zach and he ran away. They trust you too—" Frances drew a long breath, linked her hands behind his head, stood firm. "They trusted the Captain, Fox."

"If I stay, Francie, I'll pay back everything," he said firmly. "Your mother, the parson, everybody who trusted Zach and lost. Wylie may salvage something, he's a smart lawyer. But the rest I'll pay. I'm the last Cavitt—and the Cavitts must pay."

"I'll be a Cavitt too, Fox. I'll help you pay. You wanted me to tell you to stay, didn't you? You would have despised me a little if I told you to give up and go away."

He kissed her swiftly, and straightened his shoulders.

"I'll wire Philadelphia for new parts tomorrow," he said. "I'll have to have her towed downriver and put up on the ways. We'll paint her up and shine her brightwork." His voice sank a little. "I'll have to borrow money, Francie."

"I'll help you, Fox. I'll be of age soon. I could sell some land or something. The Cavitts will pay."

The door crashed open. Taffy's bright head appeared, framed in lamplight.

"Do you two lovebirds want any supper?" she demanded. "The coffee is getting cold."

(1)